Leonardo's Horse

Leonardo's Horse

a novel by

R. M. Berry

Normal

Published by FC2 with support given by the English Department
Unit for Contemporary Literature of Illinois State University,
and the Illinois Arts Council.

Address all inquiries to: FC2, Unit for Contemporary Literature,
Campus Box 4241, Illinois State University, Normal, IL,
61790-4241.

Leonardo's Horse
R. M. Berry

ISBN: 1-57366-031-0 (paperback)

Book Design: David A. Dean, Michele Steinbacher-Kemp
Cover Design: Todd Michael Bushman
Produced and printed in the United States of America

The author gratefully acknowledges the assistance of a State of Florida Individual Artist Grant in the completion of this work.

Portions of this work originally appeared in *The Iowa Review* (vol. 18, no. 1: 1988), *Apalachee Quarterly* (29/30: 1988; 35: 1990), and *An Illuminated History of the Future*, ed. Curtis White (FC2: 1989).

For Sally,
horsewoman.

The new difficulty that comes to light in the modernist situation is that of maintaining one's belief in one's own enterprise, for the past and the present become problematic together.

Stanley Cavell, 1969

THE UNIVERSE

Leonardo da Vinci is dying. From beneath the heap of sheets, blankets, rugs, comforts, skins, quilts, old coats and, to judge from the foul scent, perhaps even the bag used for butcher's offal—these barbarians having no notion of the fit use of anything—from beneath this mass of sundry bedclothes that has made the simple act of breathing a feat, Leonardo has managed to slide his one good hand tangentially to the downward thrust, much the way that in better circumstances two well-shaped gears might transfer work or motion, so that now his fingers dangle from the edge of the bed in the grime stirred up by his servant's—Mathurine's—ox-hide sabots each time she shuffles past on her way out the door. It hardly matters that spring has come and with it warmth and an end to the drizzle that all winter long has rattled Leonardo's teeth and bones. Leonardo, nevertheless, finds himself smothered beneath this witless attempt to encase the soul in vital heat and by sheer bulk keep it on the ground. None of this being, of course, Leonardo's doing. Three damp winters have passed since, already an old man, he crossed the Alps and, stepping for the first time onto French soil, walked apart from the royal escort, removed his velvet slippers and, holding them over the last hectare of Italian dirt his eyes would ever see, slapped the dust from their soles in dismissal of the world he believed in too easily or perhaps never revered enough or at least didn't understand, and so arrived here at last to end his days in this chamber where he realized at once the feeble strand of pale light would never illuminate the darkness into which he'd already begun to leak. The slate roofs, the ragged line of crenelations, the silver film of clouds or, what you really can't see from here, the river that is so idle Leonardo has counted the hairs of his beard in it—all this is darkness, and at each moment it threatens to soak him up like a wine sop and squeeze him out again onto the steaming stones of some Florentine loggia where boys' voices echo through the arches and sweating men in black gowns dispute the spelling of Latin prepositions in the Tuscan heat. It would be wise now, Leonardo thinks, not to know longing, but for no worthwhile reason he finds himself recalling the smell of clammy hands. Surely, if only the light were correctly placed, a man could slap his thigh once and soar from the slopes of Mount Cecero or gaze up at Venezia from the bottom of the sea or square the circle or sniff the vital sprite as it flutters from the ventricle of a pig's heart.

From beside his bed comes a rough sound like sweeping, and Leonardo mistakes it for the slovenly broom of Salai—his nemesis, irredeemable miscreant—on the workshop floor. Spruce chips rattle over the planks. School–children squeal in the piazza. The taste of flesh can be so pungent fools have fattened on it, and Leonardo marvels that the motion of Salai's narrow hips should trace the same careless parabola as the fir trees swaying above the Arno or the eels that glide through provincial streams. Surely the universe is an ingenious invention, and somewhere in its hollow rests a single idea that, if only you knew it, could release you like a flight of pigeons, though Leonardo has forever renounced this light or, at least, learned to live without it. But that was decades ago and in Imola, Fiesole, Pavia, Civitavecchia, Rome and, well, it's *not* the sound of Salai's broom, as Leonardo squints up through one eye at Mathurine's impossibly rotund face peering down from a platter of turnips and beans. The weasel Salai has high-tailed it, God knows where, flown most likely to Milan to squat on a smidgen of ground he thinks will make him the honorable man his wits haven't. So fornicate, fart, and fair riddance! Well, if it's not Salai—this shuffling of Mathurine's feet across the filthy floor—then Leonardo has work to do. With his good left hand he twists his fingers back and upward, using the elaborate pulley mechanism of the wrist and elbow along with the shoulder ball–joint which, though imperfect in isolation, can altogether enable mortals to reverse themselves in the forward movement of their deeds, until he finally touches the sheep's tripe inflated and fastened to the underside of the ticking just where he positioned it two days before. With a little squeeze he makes sure the pressure's firm—no air leaks—and then uses his fingers to number the cords. All taut, all ready. Nothing's lacking now but the moment.

Leonardo smiles. Only the dead anatomist, Marcantonio della Torre, could have appreciated these elaborate preparations. Only someone whose youth had passed through the ordeals of light, the sniffing and poking about in nature's bunghole, stings of the icy real, only an idol–smasher like Marcantonio, and perhaps even he lacked the sprightliness to grasp this last dimostrazione—though Leonardo recalls the heat of the candles, the unbreathable miasma in the Pavian night, and the knife's blue sheen teasing tissue from a cadaver's cheek: So much for beauty, heh? No, the anatomist della Torre probably died too young to grow curious about darkness, to suspect that in the endless night of the dissecting table, confronted with the certainty of sinew and bile, glottis and gum, the hard and the pulpy of creation's engine, that even there it was as much the silence, the black border of approaching day, that held them poised in the stench, not so much amazed as greedy, while layer opened onto layer and took them always deeper into what was probably never there at all. No, della Torre was too much the new man to feel this confusion, and so he'd probably scoff at Leonardo's last clutch for the veil. What's to be said of motion? he'd ask. You can't place it on the table; you can't pare its sections; what are the names of its parts? And afterwards, in the warmth of the Pavian sunlight, sipping goat's milk on the veranda, he'd be too merry, too ready to name what they'd seen, always quick to call Leonardo's silence flagging vigor. It wasn't wit that killed Marcantonio, but something more like embarrassment or fear: Pity the poor child who offers me her heart, he'd said chuckling. I'll carve her up on the altar.

The tripe is blue, the color of the afternoon sky over Lucca when the olive trees are nearly ripe and the grape vines twist up like thumbs. Leonardo worked the color carefully, mixing plant resins and Dutch oils, for he wants the spectacle to amaze Mathurine, not scare her, just like the Ligurian water that fills you with rich thoughts at evening near Rapallo. From where his head lies immersed in this pillow Leonardo can see that the woman has poised the platter of steaming vegetables at the apex of the mountain of bedclothes, and he calculates by sighting upward along the ridge of his nose that it rests nearly ten degrees westward of the heap's axis, so that if he twitches his shoulder in the manipulation of his wrist the red china bowl rattles softly against the goblet, a sound not unlike the chime of finger-cymbals or the faint trundling of a tambour. This threatens a ruinous distraction. The exterior ligament from the hinge of the elbow running dorsally to the pectoralis minor is a potential but not necessary agent in the mobility of the hand and, Leonardo determines, it will be possible given adequate patience to test the tripe's resilience and loosen the pin without troubling glass, china or cutlery—if, that is, the woman has even thought to bring cutlery. He's seen her feeding like a horse, face half concealed by the sides of her bowl. And, of course, all the above must be done dexterously and at the very last moment with dispatch. Mathurine waddles across the floor kicking up clouds of crumbs as she touches a cold andiron, brushes a vague hand against a tapestry, seems only to gaze sadly at a frame out of plumb, her position in Leonardo's household being nearer havoc's ally than its enemy. Her round back, as she hoists her girth onto the window ledge, still seems to conceal a memory of once–straight shoulders, and Leonardo thinks that years ago he might have tried to paint that, a lost figure in the amorphous meat, though the trick would have involved shade less than disegno, an outline so coy it couldn't be believed.

If Mathurine could comment on her situation, gazing as she does at nothing much, she'd say, si le maitre ne mange pas comme un homme, il va mourir comme un lapin—unless Leonardo starts eating meat pretty soon, he's going to kick–off like a bunny—which probably means a sixteenth century French peasant can feel as jaded as any savant. Despite her well–developed curiosity about occultism, kinkiness, freaks and gore, Mathurine figures she's already seen everything her life's going to offer. A wealthy courtier who lives on radishes and leeks is uncouth but not interesting. Ditto for Italians generally, artists, Renaissance engineers, natural philosophers, or any madman who ever tried to build a bronze horse weighing 120,000 pounds. She cooks and cleans for Leonardo da Vinci. So? Of course, if she were to complain to Leonardo about his daily affairs or his diet, about how long he's taking to die, or about the lackluster wickedness around here, Leonardo—whose French amounts to half a dozen tourist phrases— would assume she's commenting on the vast and hideously yellow engine that the ingrate Salai deposited in the courtyard, a phenomenon more disturbing to think on than Mathurine's boredom or the carnage and perversion required to relieve it. Leonardo, as a matter of fact, prefers not to think on Salai's engine—to say nothing of Mathurine whom, in three years, he's managed never to think about at all—and if only his chest were not pinned beneath this mountain of blankets and coverlets and goose feathers and what looks like from here the corner of a very bristly stable mat, he would dismiss the whole business of Salai with a peremptory snort, but when—in an instance of characteristic self–forgetfulness and without due allowance for the difficulty of even normal respiration under all this weight—he tries, all he manages is a feeble wheeze, which tickles his throat and provokes him to cough in earnest, thereby rocking the platter on his knees and threatening to bury his face in a cascade of garlicky beans. One ought not attempt the impossible. Leonardo sighs, droops his fingers in the muck, and with time to kill, decides to have a dream.

Leonardo's dream isn't very interesting. Everybody's accustomed to deathbed visions, especially those of famous men and women, to presentiments of future repute or infamy, moments of profound remorse, a final communication with an estranged lover, but Leonardo's dream concerns updrafts. More particularly, this one concerns the critical moment when any circularly augmenting torrent, by accumulation of superfluous force, undergoes a catastrophe and returns to quiescence. We possess whole libraries to disabuse us of our wonder at such spectacles, and even if we can't make sense of these libraries ourselves, we're confident that someone in California or Chicago can; so little need to find them amusing. However, Leonardo right now is feeling gleeful about what looks to him like a game of comeuppance nature plays in wind and water. Having already discovered the inseparability of aerodynamic push and shove and suspecting that human ambition is just a way of being blown, Leonardo traces with inconceivable enthusiasm the oscillating lunulae of a nubile boy astride a giant sycamore leaf, now zigging down a groundswirl, now zagging roundly upward in a thermal, neither air–toy nor wind's master but a kind of player in the atmospheric catch–as–catch–can: The purpose being just to stay afloat and not look stupid, so it seems. The boy zips down in a power dive, body leaning forward, then with hardly a movement, he shifts his weight, the leaf gives a ripple, they turn skyward and swirl out of sight again. This goes on for the dreaming equivalent of all afternoon. Boy, leaf, sky, earth: Zoooom down a cloud bank, bottom out, scoot up an air flume. Maybe Leonardo expects the repetition to yield a principle. He's probably after something technical, can't say what.

Which is what he was after in 1490 in Pavia—same Pavia but two decades before Marcantonio della Torre ever arrived there—when the not–yet–forty–year–old Leonardo saw nature equivocate. He'd been called in to advise the locals on a building project and, while rummaging the castle's manuscript library, had run into one Fazio Cardano, Lombard mathematician, jurist, celebrated know–it–all and a lunatic. Cardano had pressed on him—it had to do with some argument they were having about distance vision—a copy of an optics text by an Englishman, John Pecham, which Cardano had been glossing at the time, and Leonardo spent all the next day studying it. Leonardo thought he glimpsed a way to connect Pecham's perspective to Pythagorean number theory and scurried over to Cardano's home the next night eager to argue over harmonia, Golden Sections, the even and odd. But Fazio met him at the door half–naked in a scarlet gown, eyelids hopping, fingers a–flutter about his throat, and would hear nothing but that Leonardo dine with him and his guest, the ignoramus blacksmith. An inspired geometer! The last philosopher in Lombardy! Well, Leonardo made an effort but soon grew bored—chitchat about horseshoes with Cardano dancing on the chifforobe—and recalling urgent affairs, he escaped to the moonlit banks of the Ticino. The Platonists were maintaining at the time that the tiny eye could send out beams in an instant and bag distant planets like tigers, and in one of Pecham's illustrations Leonardo saw a way to refute them. He ambled along winking first one eye then the other, shifting his glance from his thumb to distant objects, trying to count the seconds required to fetch a faraway hitching post home or a furlong marker, and not having a whole lot of luck, when an inscrutable movement in the shadows drew his attention. It was a man who spoke no words.

In the distance he looked pretty scurvy, misshapen, and no higher than a nipple, and Leonardo followed him at first out of idleness and then for the twist of his nose, or for the flurry of knees and elbows that against all nature propelled him over the footbridge and past the lunga dimora, but finally followed him just because the moon was round and pandemonium was having its way. He followed him all the way to the brothel called Malnido, a squat fugitive from reason, where the women sprawled upon purple divans like corn–stuffed capons and a tubercular castrati plucked a chitarra and sang through his nose and huge white Persians flicked their tails upon the window sills, and where the man without words threw himself into space like a wind–driven dustball, appearing from beneath a staircase bearing cinnabar and cumin or powdered linens or vinegar–water for a douche, hovering in the air before the smiling concubines, his breath coming in hissing heaves, his pupils bobbing in a sea of phlegmy white. The women called him Jacopo when they were about their business and Il Poggio when they were weary from love, and whenever they lay upon a cushion scratching their fur with black–rimmed nails it was just: Where's the little fart? But Leonardo suspected that in his self–accumulation from under ferns and behind balusters and from within the wrinkles of a rug, this gathering of the human form was letting space speak its name, and Leonardo had wanted to draw that, the silent speech of twitching hip and foot and cheek and thigh. So through the subsequent evenings as his silver–point skimmed over the bone–meal leaves and the pet pheasant flapped noisily at the end of its tether and the cloying gum of female unguents stole across his fidgety skin, Leonardo again and again tried to discover the line of the mute's flight, tried to catch it in tangled strokes, flurries of corrections, in this scratch or the next one. But it was no use. Each time that he seemed on its verge, Leonardo saw the figure attenuate and snap or turn prosy and still, saw himself tumble from near recognition into nothing at all.

And so one morning Leonardo da Vinci roused the mute from the rag box where he coiled like a spring and, calling him teacher, offered him dinari, then scuzi, and finally a Rhenish florin to compose himself upon the roof before Leonardo's eye while the sun rose from the gable to the chimney's edge so this hieroglyph could be deciphered in purest light. But the man without words said no. That is, he said nothing, merely scrambled up the steps onto the flat housetop, cocked his head, slurped the morning air into his nostrils, hissed it out his teeth, sliding his eyes both left and right in a tic Leonardo mistook for annoyance or fear, and spinning upon a foot like a weathercock upon a swivel, flew toward a terra cotta half–wall that divided the building. Over the top of the tiles Leonardo could see the steaming valley of the Po, the lazy curve of a goshawk hanging in the sky, could see no façade or tile or spire, no destination, no place at all and so was astonished when the little fart—with his shoulder lowered and head tucked in—didn't slow, didn't veer, simply smashed his small sack of flesh and bones directly into the wall, lunged forward and bounced off, staggering back, recollected himself roughly, only to fly at the obstacle again, once, twice, refusing to stop, three times. Leonardo waved his arms, bellowed: This wasn't what he had in mind! This was ...was madness! But each time, Jacopo or Poggio—or whatever he was called—remained furiously stupid, impenetrable, persisted in his pointless suffering, until with his sleeve torn and the thin muscle of his shoulder beginning to redden he seemed to draw himself up, gazed sharply into Leonardo's eyes and, flying a last time past the horrified young painter, had aimed his outstretched skull directly at the wall's face, sought out its clay edge as if to lay a final sacrifice there, his flight seeming to refuse the bare fact of stone, and with something less than a shiver, a kind of hitch in his spine that would always lie just the other side of recall's horizon, that would cast its shadow over Leonardo's notes and games, the man without words opened himself to the wall's uncompromising geometry. And vanished.

Sixteen years would pass before Leonardo would know what he'd seen. He'd return to Milan, begin to erect the colossal horse and see it destroyed, flee Lombardy with the charlatan Pacioli, roam Mantua, Venice, find himself one morning with Machiavelli and Cesare Borgia's troops overlooking a decapitated torso in Ceseno's muddy piazza, return to Florence, botch the great canal to the sea, abandon his last chance to become the painter everyone expected, and would end up standing between two merchants' stalls on the Old Bridge one afternoon during the spring runoff where, happening to glance down into the Arno, he'd notice an eddy spin once, twice, three times into a frustrated vortex and then simply vanish! Enter a fissure in the current! Become its own absence! As if all along this pattern had been waiting for someone curious enough, lost enough ...well, not until then would Leonardo realize that Jacopo il Poggio had already possessed the secret of updrafts—the little fart!—and that if only Leonardo had accepted Jacopo's gift, or been able to bear his own bewilderment, that is, if Leonardo had been ready to die, then he might have told Marcantonio della Torre—twenty years later in that same Pavia—why knowledge moves and so have understood his own surprising fate. Statues crumble, walls peel, in the vast accumulation of words and still more words even legends lose their way, and Leonardo wishes he'd said to the young anatomist, della Torre, on their last evening what he wishes four days ago he'd had presence of mind to tell Salai but didn't actually get around to telling anyone until yesterday when he told the aristocratic simpleton, Francesco Melzi, who stood there with that dewy–eyed, beatific look of his and, of course, understood not a word: Only a dullard gets to the end of something. A scandal to Aristotle but then, tuff tutu, he wrote in Greek.

It's partly as a respite from these frustrations that Leonardo's dream delights him. The naked, amber–skinned lad straddles a huge platan leaf as it sails along currents of air, steered by the lightest nip and tug, until whipped into a swirl of clouds, it tucks up under itself and, with the boy hugging sky and vapor, puffs right out again like cream squeezed from an eclair. Lying here beneath this crushing mound of smelly bedding Leonardo finds physics' inversion of effort and success a remarkable game, something a clever man might play, the gleeful flip–flop of nature and destiny, and so begins to giggle softly down in his throat setting his nose to wheezing and his gullet to gurgling, a sound enough like the death–rattle to bring Mathurine clambering up from the kitchen, her hips rising and falling like the rocker–arm of a waterwheel, the half–formed question on her lips: Is it now? Of course, what she says is more like: Let this be the last time I ever have to climb these God-forsaken stairs! Or actually: Mon Dieu, s'il vous plait, kill him—Leonardo having reassured her just three days ago that she'd receive a certain black velvet house cloak upon his passing, a tactical blunder if ever there was one, inasmuch as Mathurine's job is to postpone that passing as long as possible. But then, Leonardo's never been especially savvy in his dealings with persons not spectacularly wicked or covetous on the grand scale.

Leonardo hears what she says, but having long ago decided that everyone in this country is trying to speak Italian and doing it badly, he concludes that she's announcing Salai's return for the garishly yellow contraption in the courtyard, another of her fabrications or flat–footed solecisms or, at any rate, a simple indication of the boundless ineptitude with which she manages Leonardo's affairs. No, he explains to her, Salai can't have returned because Salai is in hell, where he's obliged to suffer hideous torment for having rendered the past unintelligible, or if not in hell then in Italy, but either way he won't arrive here except with a good deal of clatter, and when he does, he's not to be allowed to fling himself tastelessly upon Leonardo's chest declaring that he always worshipped nature or anything as low–life as that. Leonardo feels pleased with this statement but can't understand why Mathurine has slipped off her house dress and started zig–zagging toward earth on a giant sycamore leaf. Her face is turned rapturously toward him with the wan eyes, curls, opalescent cheeks of a Florentine ephebos, and Leonardo demands that she dismount from his dream at once and remind Melzi about the eighty–seven books on astronomy that Leonardo intended to write next spring and Marcantonio della Torre about the aortic valve that traces the very outline of this giant sycamore leaf's descent or—if she can't manage straightforward tasks—then at least have the decency to sweep this floor and get undressed in the kitchen. Mathurine, however, isn't about to sweep this or any other floor, leaning as she is about four inches from Leonardo's face and thoroughly aggrieved at what she sees there—a smirk, possibly annoyance and, without a doubt, breathing—and as she raises her hands heavenward in protest at one more injustice done her by malign stars and Italians who won't eat horse steak for dinner, she vents her frustration in a muttered litany of the fornications, sexual parts and products of elimination to be stepped in around any Touraine farmyard. But alas! For the rising knuckles of her left hand slam at this moment into the far edge of the platter balanced upon the fulcrum of her master's knees, catapulting the goblet and cutlery over her head, muddling her words in the clatter of breaking glass, and inundating Leonardo in turnips, onions, leeks, garlic, a bay leaf, and half a kilo of white kidney beans. At this point Leonardo wakes, decides the sensation is extraordinary but not death, and gazing up through the glutinous film of boiled carrot drippings, says: No, Salai will be riding a horse.

May 2, 1519 at the Clos-Lucé in Amboise on the Loire, and Leonardo da Vinci is dying. Twenty years from this day King François premier, who has brought Leonardo to France just to talk to him, will declare in front of the goldsmith Benvenuto Cellini that no other mortal ever knew so much, and though François himself probably understood about a tenth of what Leonardo told him, next week when he learns of Leonardo's death, the King will sob. Isabella d'Este, who could boss Correggio and Mantegna like chambermaids and managed Ariosto as deftly as a suitor and who has been trying much of her life to trade anything short of her reputation for a smear of Leonardo's paint, will within two months of this day make one of his forgotten doodles the centerpiece of her studio, and though Florence, Rome, Milan were never sure what to make of Leonardo alive, tomorrow they'll make a legend of him: The most beautiful man Tuscany ever saw; able to bend horseshoes in his bare hands; a singer with an incomparable voice; Cesare Borgia's personal military engineer; the best verse improvisor of the quattrocento; architectural rival of Bramante; true author of Luca Pacioli's great mathematical treatise; an irresistible orator; according to Paolo Giovio, the ultimate authority on matters of beauty; for Raffaello another Plato; in Castiglione's *Courtier*, the first among the great painters; to Lomazzo, a critic of preternatural insight ...and on and on and on. After awhile the hyperboles become cloying. Giorgio Vasari probably speaks for the age when he says that, in order to explain Leonardo, one must speak of God. And yet how puzzling all this seems to anyone standing here in Leonardo's death–chamber, surrounded by grime and gewgaws, in the spring dampness, with the odor of hair, sweat, vegetables, urine, as an illiterate housekeeper complains in an unintelligible tongue and wagons creak past in the street. What's unforgettable here? In Rome on the same day, young Raffaello Santi finishes the splendid papal corridors that bear no mark of Leonardo's passage through them. In Florence Michelangelo's *David* guards the entrance to the Palazzo Vecchio where Leonardo's botched *Battle of Anghiari* awaits obliteration. Before the Castello Sforzesco in Milan the cartwheels of silk merchants roll over clay pebbles that are the only remains of Leonardo's colossal horse, and as the monks chew their bread at Santa Maria delle Grazie, the plaster peels off Christ's nose. As of tomorrow the miracle of Leonardo da Vinci will amount to several thousand jumbled, unnumbered pages of backwards notes, sketches, outlines, jokes, revisions, titles, studies, chimeras, drafts— herein the nine essentials of painting, painting has only five parts, the art of painting can be reduced to thirteen constituents, painters should know the seven elements of which the art consists, painting comprises exactly three—all mixed in with grocery lists, expense accounts and allusions to works that, except in these pages, don't exist.

The puzzle is less Leonardo's life than our involvement with it. Others who achieved more matter less. And though the stories of youthful promise prematurely blighted have an understandable fascination, Leonardo da Vinci lived in reasonably good health to sixty- seven years old. His grip on the imagination seems more like a dream we know better than to believe in, or like a childhood humiliation, something maturity ought to get over but that at moments of half– wakefulness returns with its original horror still intact, rousing us to sit bolt–upright, almost to shout: This time don't do it! Perhaps he was Europe's most talented man; he was certainly among the most curious; he was learned, though probably not as learned as his contemporaries believed; it has been argued that he was Europe's greatest painter and also that his stature has been absurdly overrated; he made no contributions to science; his most famous inventions were borrowed; he hardly read Latin. But the world has never known a failure to match him. No one else ever imagined so extravagantly, planned in such detail, possessed the needed facility, mastered both theory and practice, went so far toward realization, and left so little behind. A dozen paintings, perhaps a baker's dozen, badly preserved or damned in the materials used to make them, often altered or hinting at clumsy collaboration, many of these unfinished, some of doubtful authenticity, most quite small, no disciples worth mentioning, no school or movement, no buildings or sculpture, no engineering projects, no family or children, few close friends—this, plus accounts of lost masterpieces, hints of improbable deeds, unverifiable tales, more beginnings than sanity can account for, and always plans, plans, plans. How to take seriously a sixty–year–old who's still deciding what to do with his life? The barrage of explanations that preserve Leonardo's fame may merely protect us from the statement his life makes. May 3, 1519, Leonardo da Vinci will be dead as dust. What does such a man imagine when he can't imagine tomorrow? At the moment when a life becomes equivalent to its deeds, when everyone has forgotten the reasons for what happened, but no matter, because intentions don't count, when the perpetual worship of light has brought you to a land where each day is the color of raw wool and out your window you can see nothing you remember and behind you stretches a series of missed opportunities that stagger the mind and the fact that you may have once been right amounts to nothing at all—at this moment does the force of so much futility come rushing back and, seeing yourself trying to refine a superior fresco material from walnuts or spending years revising a cartoon that will never know paint or diddling with fantastic wooden birds four centuries too early or seeking to unriddle the entire universe just to persuade a 120,000 pound bronze horse to stand, does such a man shudder, sit bolt–upright, shout: This time don't do it!!?

Well, Leonardo da Vinci is thinking of paper lilies. They have been attached with thread made from a horse's tail to the blue sheep's tripe, and right now as Leonardo edges his hand around Mathurine's sabots and back up under the tick again, he wonders if he has arranged the strings of flowers so that they will not catch upon the posts of the bed and prematurely stop the inflated tripe in its upward trajectory. Actually, this is a vast simplification. Leonardo's last dimostrazione has to do with ultimate things—nature, fidelity, a cave's dark mouth—and it consists not of this single balloon made from a mutton's rubbery innards but of a whole roomful of them, thirty–nine to be precise, and a truckload of paper carnations, irises, roses, who–knows–what–all, that only a Leonardo—whose self–abstraction can be monumental—could have colored and folded and fluffed for an entire night with a single good hand and the inept, sporadic assistance of his baffled servant, Battista de Vilanis, who nodded off somewhere around four in the morning, all this only three days before the afternoon that will be Leonardo's last. To tell the truth, if Marcantonio della Torre were here right now, he'd think Leonardo is a colossal nut. From the blue tripe pinned to the ticking and dangling the lilies like a kite's tail run seventeen cords which each pass over pulley–wheels equipped with primitive wooden rollers—the forerunners, someone will one day

21

claim, of the modern steel bearing—located at the four corners of the bed, thus enabling the cords to pass around angles without sacrificing the greater part of their work–efficiency to friction, and from there up to the canopy and along the molding to the tapestry on the left of the fireplace and the two sets of curtains adjacent to the south window— which is the only one worth looking out of—and to the west one, through which all you can make out is the stone wall across the street and the hill behind. The effect of all this is to connect every surface and corner of the room to a wooden trigger beneath the mattress and beside Leonardo's index finger. It's hopelessly intricate, of course, and even Leonardo suspects his dimostrazione won't come off, not at the right time. Nevertheless, its intricacy hardly flirts with the machinery that drives the universe along, and if it should erupt in a dazzling illumina- tion, a comeuppance, or just a muddle, there may still be much to observe, much to learn. After all, the point's not to know what's ahead or win honor or ape God; the point's to … well, the point involves Salai.

Or that's what Leonardo recollects. Of course, he hasn't always been so blasé about outcomes. If he weren't moribund and scrambled, if he were capable of caring about the future or feeling remorse—which he isn't, being afflicted with a temper for puzzling over conch shells and face warts and for getting angry in a muttering, can–kicking sort of way but not one that's had much practice or, at least, gotten very good at endless, circular, futile self–doubt—if, in short, Leonardo were a modern man, he might recall right now the night in Milan when, hardly even a courtier, merely a painter and jack–leg lutenist with a bag full of drawings of tanks and machine guns and the preposterous claim that he would construct a bronze horse weighing between a hundred thousand and half a million pounds, he had stood in a stairwell of the Castello Sforzesco as the guests strutted across the adjacent ballroom tiles in gold–brocade tunics that could have made an iceberg perspire and, listening to the rattle of tambourines, the blare of sackbuts, an occasional whoop from the gallery and—of all things!—the clatter of horse hoofs across the floor, Leonardo had for the first time realized that he might not rise upon the broad curve of history as he'd always assumed but might find his fate in a masonry crack not four inches from his thumb. It was the poet Bellincioni who revealed this to him, another Florentine and a man who, even thirty years later, Leonardo doesn't know whether to venerate or despise. If Bellincioni had a failing, it was that you couldn't help listening to him, and so being no more vile a flatterer than Leonardo himself or any of the astrologers, jugglers, monkey–trainers, procurers, blood–letters, fops, or transvestite eye- brow pluckers whose only ambition was to lick for the rest of their natural lives the mud from Ludovico Sforza's dancing shoes, no more vile but perhaps more skillful, Bellincioni had managed to convince the sallow–faced Ludovico Sforza that a Florentine poet would be infinitely superior to any Lombard nobleman at an activity infinitely less important than Milanese statecraft but nevertheless indispensable— i.e., Bellincioni could say better than Ludovico whatever Ludovico wanted to say—and so had succeeded in installing himself here on the backstairs of the Castello's ballroom to oversee the theatrical flattery of a duchess whose father, a very touchy king of Spain, was threatening to reclaim her twenty–thousand ducat dowry because her husband, a wildly neurotic child–duke of Milan, couldn't fulfill his obligation 'twixt the sheets.

Even at thirty–eight years old and still waiting with considerable impatience for civilization to fling itself at his feet, Leonardo had not been fool enough to imagine Bellincioni could be trusted, but glancing into the passageway through whose opening he could see four Turkish captains dismount from their horses to declare that they, though benighted pagans, had galloped half a continent to gaze upon the unspeakable beauty of the daughter of Spain—a bit of histrionics that had taxed even Bellincioni's powers of exaggeration—Leonardo was startled to hear Bellincioni chuckle and, turning, to see him indicate a crevice running between two pink stones in the castle wall right where Leonardo stood. Nothing built matters, the poet said. Agility's everything! Leonardo cursed for the ninety–third time the miserable education that had deprived him of a stinging Latin retort and, turning his back on Bellincioni, began to rehearse again the clockwork machinery and series of gears that after four centuries would be termed a power–relay but for Leonardo right then was just a way to get something done, one that would actually succeed—though he didn't know it yet—and win him about as much celebrity as he'd ever possess. For not five meters from where Bellincioni stood was a spectacle more impressive to the eye than anything Bellincioni could offer the ear: Leonardo's universe, the seven planets in their spheres with a heavenly choir and zodiac of gods, all floating in a ceiling–high indigo cosmos that when unveiled would suck the breath from the onlookers' throats. Just a toy, of course, but a really incredible toy. And so Leonardo had wanted to reply that impressive deeds were what truly mattered, that once his ingenious spring and counter–weight mechanism was set in motion, once the planets had begun to glide across the sky and the candle flames trembled through the niches in the night and Jupiter descended from his heavenly perch, that after this, the world's memory would never be the same: Bastard Leonardo, novice of dreams, would be Leonardo da Firenze, master of facts! But lacking both Latin and the bravado to boast to another Florentine who, like himself, had gazed up at Brunelleschi's dome and stood slack–jawed before Ghiberti's doors— all this plus the fact that Leonardo wasn't sure the damn thing would work—Leonardo merely coughed into his fist and, leaning toward the passageway through which he glimpsed the same four Turks flinging up their arms in choreographed obeisance and a clown stuffing bananas in his codpiece and a be–ribboned stallion relieving himself beside a table set with pheasant livers and calf brains, he remarked that walls cracked because the earth was alive. Bellincioni's pinched face twitched into a smile, and laying his finger three times on Leonardo's sternum, he said: No, solidity's a harlot; the trick is to float on air.

It was never a question of belief. And if Leonardo were really capable of lingering upon his own disappointments he might gaze up right now from his mucky pillow, here in this French bedroom so many years and furlongs from that night on the Castello's stairs, and seeing Mathurine staring stupidly back at him as she decides whether to sponge the catastrophe from the master's face or just to gather the dishes and call it lunch, Leonardo might acknowledge that even in Milan, at the far edge of his fourth decade, he'd already felt the uselessness of disagreeing, and if Salai were still here, Leonardo might grant him that, all right, sometimes you just had to finish something, that deferred longing could get as tiresome as a carbuncle under your arm. Not that it would have made a difference. Still, it might've sounded less harsh, if only so that looking out at the yellow monster in the courtyard now Leonardo might feel he'd made an effort, acknowledged his fears, conceded something. He could at least have said it was Bellincioni who first tempted him with the conceit of being blown, that this boy sailing through the air on sycamore leaves now ... well, wasn't this the poet's doing? But Salai's a carp who feeds on shame, and besides, Leonardo doesn't know whether to hate Bellincioni or admire him. What if Leonardo got suckered? It's perfectly possible—and who would have known this better than Bellincioni?—it's possible that protecting yourself from some kinds of doom is the way you fall victim to them. All Leonardo can say for certain is that the crack snaking upwards from the castle stair where he stood that night in Milan, snaking upwards and—within reach of his own arm—opening itself wide enough that a maiden might slide her hand between the pink stones almost up to her wrist, that this crack seemed to run as deep as the fist into which the planet's center was balled and as high as the wide–open palm of God, and as he'd paused to stare into it, he'd heard Bellincioni reciting—as if from tablets held open against the back of his eyes—the crumbling of the rock, the spreading of fissures in the creaking night, the first snap of mortar in the arch, and then the smashing, uproarious schism as the Castello and Italy and all earth collapsed into the hole where nature used to stay.

The Milanese court had been acrawl with more intrigues than

cockroaches: There were at least one too many rulers, two too many wives, more mistresses than could be easily numbered, foreign sodomites in the garrisons, bastards in every yard, pedophiles in the baptistery, conspirators between the bedsheets, and whole empires rising and falling with each pizzle, bosom and savings account, and yet throughout all of this, Leonardo had never doubted that his ingenuity would get him somewhere. It wasn't a confidence he'd struggled for. He would have hardly thought to defend it. It was merely a faith into which he was born, like speech or sight or breathing, but twelve minutes away from his bid for recognition in front of the richest batch of patrons in Europe, he wasn't keen on having it tested, so he tried to ease himself past Bellincioni's hovering arm and toward the passageway at the end of which he could already see the herald angel fluffing his wings in preparation for the announcement Leonardo hysterically prayed would be heard in Florence and Venice and Paris and Rome, that something had appeared on the world's face from which amazement would pour like rivers, something called Leonardo. But Bellincioni's hand pushed him back against the stone: You imagine, he whispered, that to be steadfast is for some reason, you imagine it's essential if power's to come, but don't be stupid! There's no distinction. Raze these walls and what's left of all you've learned?

And Leonardo had wrapped his fingers around Bellincioni's skinny wrist determined to rid himself of the pinched mouth, its luxuriant words, the eyes that glistened like cream, for it was hardly the first time he'd encountered poetry's power to lift you up just to dash you on the ground. But even as he moved to brush this pest from his face, even as he prepared his body to glide into the passageway from which at this very moment the herald was stepping out into the vast ballroom, Leonardo found himself lingering within the silence hollowed out by Bellincioni's voice, feeling with his own right shoulder the crack into which his body was pressing as if to enter a secret there, and suddenly giving way, letting himself collapse against the pink stone, he'd recalled an afternoon on Monte Albano when watching a Tuscan girl run through the piebald shade of a cypress grove he'd first recognized as something unmistakable and deliriously plain the inseparability of color and shape, that as light goes it carries understanding along, and so had understood with a kind of fright why an utterly luminous world would leave humans deaf, stupid, dumb, and as Bellincioni drew his pinched mouth so close that Leonardo smelled the citronella on his gums, Leonardo knew he could reply that Bellincioni was confusing hue and disegno, that accidents crumbled, figures remained, that such a retort, though wholly false, would allow him to escape into the passage where the world might call his name. But when Leonardo opened his mouth, all he said was:

Horses? In the hall?

Bellincioni chuckled. Look down upon yourself from a great height; be as weightless as you seem; know watchfulness as your mother, but when the solid world has vanished, remember—no one ever asks what you knew; they ask did you conquer. And the words they'll use are these: Are you still there?

And then Bellincioni kissed him. Or later it seemed that he'd kissed him. Leonardo was never sure. For at this precise second a mighty rush of air arose from the ballroom like the sucking of the earth when Atlantis slid away, and somehow shoving the poet's face aside or dodging his outstretched arm or sidestepping his body or perhaps simply knocking him down and running right over him, Leonardo had rushed into the passageway in time to see the curtain finish rising on a universe more reliable than any other he'd ever know. The astonished guests at once collapsed into a thunderous beating of tables, benches, cutlery, spoons. The sacbuts blared in a raucous chord. The clown somersaulted into the laps of the squatting Turks. And the horses— who'd grown quite bored by now—began to frolic at the ends of their bridles, twist their necks, stomp and squeal. Trays of soggy fruit and picked bones overturned. A few young girls squealed. A youth caught a hoof in the neck, went down. Blood sprinkled the floor. In the back of the hall there were people running about, loud whoops, food fights, screams. And as the angelic choir began to sing, the planets to revolve across the heavens, the gods to come gracefully down from the sky, with the clamor and bedlam and applause and whinnies growing louder by the minute, Leonardo rested his spine against the doorway, eased himself to the floor and, gazing into the miraculous spectacle of his own future, tried to believe that feeling this good could never be a lie.

". . . that Reagan negotiated with terrorists?"

"Don't be naive."

"But breaking the law? I mean, a U.S. president—"

"King did it. Johnson did it. Kennedy, Nixon . . ."

"And you disapprove."

"C'mon, I disapprove of cancer. I disapprove of San Francisco."

"But you felt . . . you *supported* Reagan—"

"Both times."

"—because all in all, on balance, you, like millions of other concerned, responsible, voting Americans, believed he was right. He cheated, okay, but—"

"Naw. I work for the airlines."

Blip, static, garble.

26

". . . deregulation?"

"Yeah. They all cheat."

"So there's no room—I mean, in politics—no room for ol' fashioned right and wrong, common decency, the ten—"

"Hey, it's a free country. There's room for everything."

I click off the radio and lean back in my seat. It must be 120 degrees in here and, instead of distracting me, the talk–show makes it hotter. I'd like to hear something cool—Bill Evans or Ravel—but not a chance. I'm caught in some kind of traffic snafu, nobody's moving, and can't stop gawking at a thirty–foot woman in a swimsuit—or underwear?—anyway black with laces and seams, on a towel with her spine arched, left knee stuck out, head back, eyes half–closed: a pose that, if you see it on the beach, you call a doctor. I probably desire her, although up so close it's hard to tell. The billboard's for either auto insurance or a restaurant but my gaze keeps rising to the yellow letters at top: "VOTED BEST!" In a box on the seat beside me are the delicious and peculiar sentences I once heard this goddess speak, twelve pounds of secrets she divulged, although now I'm doubtful. Maybe between my box and her there's no link, no story that could contain us. In the utopia where she's everything and nothing, does memory exist? The traffic doesn't budge. So I sweat in the shadow of my icon with a dog panting in my ears, and the preposterous anxiety that, at forty–five years old, I'll be the last earthling to see Disneyworld.

Leonardo da Vinci really is dying, and Mathurine who sees no reason to sponge a cadaver twice has gathered up the broken glassware and saucer shards and is shuffling back toward the kitchen again hoping that the little King will happen by today with the blonde squire who may be a trifle saucy but is always full of news, or even without the squire, just so long as there's someone to talk to. If the magic potion she purchased can't rid her of the Italians, then she'll have to settle for a distraction. Which just then and in a fashion perfectly acceptable to her, if only she weren't starting down the stairs, a beneficent star or the ambitions of Battista de Vilanis or perhaps the nose Francesco Melzi has spent his youth poking into phials of musk actually does provide, with the unexpected cry, *God's thorns and the holy vinegar!*—or its Italian equivalent—and a commotion like Armageddon coming from the hall. Mathurine, food and china step down the stairway just as Melzi rushes up it.

Oh most excellent teacher, exclaims Melzi.

Oh most generous master, exclaims Battista.

Oh shit, says Mathurine.

27

And the lunch goes airborne again.

Melzi keeps his feet. Battista sidesteps danger. But Mathurine hits the floor with a thud. In different circumstances she'd suspect that the veal kidney she gave to Nadira the neighborhood necromancer had provoked demonic retaliation, but inasmuch as a quarrel among superiors ranks just below public flogging on her list of amusing spectacles, she's nearly as beguiled by the yelling as dazzled by the blow. Having acquired this chance to eavesdrop, if she can avoid passing out, she remains prostrate, pretending to be as dazed as she feels.

Battista de Vilanis, meanwhile, paces the length of Leonardo's bed profaning his way through the passion week, crucifixion, and burial in a virtuoso attempt to distract Melzi from what Melzi's absolutely determined to say, specifically, that Battista's been mucking with the portraits again. Melzi, having spent the morning wandering the chateau in search of courtiers not yet bored to tears by him, has returned to the Clos–Lucé with senses alert and encountered just within the foyer the odor of drying paint. Meeting at this very moment Battista de Vilanis who began to steer him toward the kitchen, Melzi— who's no genius but can recognize *this* ploy—took a sharp left toward the studio and, following his nose, found the source of the odor in a sticky contour just to the left of Giocondo's wife where the squiggles become sky. The usual words were exchanged—Battista claiming an apprentice's rights, and Melzi insisting Battista's the butler—followed by the aforementioned scramble up the stairs.

Leonardo's interested in this story. In fact, he intends to give it his full attention very soon, having understood enough to be impressed by Melzi's olfactory organ and to compose a series of questions about the formal training of noses. However, first he must deal with a worry. While swinging around the doorjamb and just before catching Mathurine square in the breast with his elbow, Melzi lifted his right hand and extended his index finger in the gesture to accompany decisive impre- cation from Luccio's *Primer of Declamatory Tropes and Speech Orna- ments*, Venice, 1463. The meeting with Mathurine being unexpected, this gesture was a trifle erratic, and the raised index somehow managed to hook the handle of a teacup resting upon the platter, carrying it away and flipping it inadvertently ceilingward in the ensuing melee. It was the rising trajectory of this teacup that—having interrupted Leonardo's dream—made him worry that the miniature catapult he installed behind the cornice above the westernmost win- dow two afternoons ago might not be propped at the necessary angle to jettison the blue sheep's tripe and string of lilies directly out into the room but might instead, as Leonardo now fears, be arranged for an upward trajectory identical to that of the teacup, that is, a trajectory that's surely to bounce the tripe off the ceiling and send it right back into the cornice again. The more Leonardo considers this possibility, the more certain he becomes of it and the worse he feels. He feels so bad, in fact, that he imagines Salai has returned from Milan and is kicking him in the butt for botching even this last attempt to make something hold still. The kick in his butt is a muscle cramp, of course, but no matter, for Leonardo is about to instruct Battista to climb up on top of the wardrobe, as soon as Mathurine isn't watching, and to stuff a slipper under the back of the catapult, when, opening one eye, he finds Melzi's finger in it.

What's this? Melzi asks.

The aperture of the optic gate, thinks Leonardo.

A stye? Battista offers.

An accident, Mathurine protests, in the universal language of dodging blame.

An indignity! A desecration! Melzi declares.

Battista dips a finger into Leonardo's beard, tastes. Carrot broth with garlic and, mmmmmm, that's a kidney bean.

Mathurine begins to explain the caprices of fortune on the even days of odd months, the hostility of bedroom poltergeists to vegetables, the indecorum of the master's slow demise, her swelling feet, the best saints for foreigners, the heterodox drawings belowstairs, and the necessity of a velvet cloak on winter evenings, in a display of close reasoning that puts medieval casuistry to shame.

Melzi, who understands less French than he lets on, gets pieces of this—mostly nouns—confuses tenses, moods, and idioms, and decides she's announcing Leonardo's demise. The glop on the Maestro's face is regurgitated lunch. The odor is the humiliating corporeal side-effect of the soul's departure. Melzi gazes down at Leonardo's immobile torso, his hand dangling in the grime on the floor, his lidded eyes and horrific scowl. Being the scion of a noble family means doing whatever's required. Melzi flings himself onto the porridge–soaked mound of bedclothes and begins to grieve.

Ooph! thinks Leonardo.

Does he actually eat this stuff? Battista asks.

Not in three days, Leonardo gasps.

Comme un lapin, Mathurine says.

Bring the washbasin, Melzi orders over his blubbering. I'll prepare the body with my own hands!

Mathurine slinks from the room, somewhat disappointed, but relieved to get off easy. Battista wants to slip out with her, but he's not sure how long Melzi's confusion will last, and he doesn't want to leave himself undefended. Also, Leonardo has him by the ankle. Leonardo meanwhile has discovered that there *really is a kidney bean* in the

29

corner of his eye and has postponed dreams of updrafts and the pressing affair of the catapult until he's decided what this sticky vegetable could have to do with Salai. Melzi, of course, is completely out of it.

SCIENCE

Perhaps Marcantonio della Torre wouldn't find these entanglements surprising. During the Pope's jockeying about at Cambrai in 1509 as France blundered across the peninsula and allies swapped sides every afternoon, even Marcantonio had gotten jostled in the roughhouse, and if in his youth he'd expected his learning to protect him, the growing list of traitors to the Venetian state soon made him think again. He may have smirked when a Dalmatian prince carved up a slovenly colleague on the colleague's own workbench, and he probably dismissed the Dominicans' diatribes on autopsy with a flutter of his hand, but the paranoia of empire finally rattled the door of his dissecting theater, and by morning the students had gone and della Torre was fleeing town. Truth required peace, leisure, money, libraries, one competent cook, somewhere to sleep afterwards, a few confederates amply garrulous—in short, little justice but much force—and so by the time Leonardo had arrived in Pavia to watch the young anatomist bend over a cadaver in the rank and smoky light, della Torre was already behaving like a man who'd lost his life. That was in 1511. Leonardo was almost sixty; Marcantonio, not half so old. If the young man seemed to delight in his own fall and seemed to despise Leonardo's reticence as beggarly, then perhaps this was because he'd already dipped his hands too often in the mortal stew to believe in mistakes, but whatever the reason, as Leonardo watched—on that last night—as the anatomist's knife traced a paper–thin seam in the cadaver's cheek, Marcantonio della Torre paused, half–straightened and, glancing past the candles at the darkness, said that flesh was hardly a puzzle, as tiresomely manifest as crosses and naughts, but that fidelity was a phenomenon that made no sense at all. And then he told Leonardo about Guido da Forlì.

It seems that as a boy in Verona della Torre had for some time been under the tutelage of a harmless rogue who, perhaps by virtue of lively conversation, certainly not by that of acuity, had contrived or wheedled or possibly just stumbled his way into the affections of Marcantonio's father, Girolamo, then professor of medicine at Padua. Why the elder della Torre, a man whom Marcantonio best remembered as a baritone voice reading to him aloud from Aristotle's *De generatione* just outside the door of the privy as the five year old child struggled to unclench the terrified fist of his rectum—a practice the father claimed would acquaint the boy with the language of scholarship but which only succeeded in convincing him that nothing mattered much that didn't stink—why his father had chosen such a man to oversee his son's education, the adult Marcantonio never knew. Not that Guido da Forlì was a dullard. He'd mustered some Latin and Greek, could bisect a circle, had read Mondino and Avicenna in translation, wrote a respectable sonnet, for a short time had lectured on mechanics somewhere in Umbria, and in his youth had even been apprenticed for a year to Alberti, an unpleasant experience of which he'd seldom speak, but ten minutes acquaintance sufficed to discover that, though he could reason, recite, quip, declaim, listen, argue, syllogize, explain—all on a thousand different subjects from fifty different sides—the man had nothing to teach. Possessed of every notion, none had taken hold, and Guido had become a universal commentary, full of verve and delight, concluding in a muddle. By the time Marcantonio was nine, the boy had already realized that his daily exegeses of Albertus Magnus were passing through Guido as through an open window. By eleven he was deeply enough immersed in Galen's *De usu partium* to ignore Guido's quibbles and huffy rebukes. At twelve he'd supervised his father's Circassian slave dissecting a rabbit's flank, and it seemed a mercy just to tolerate Guido's presence, padding about the table, waving off the houseflies, airing out the little room. There was no longer any pretense of oversight, no more cataloguing of the boy's progress, not even the weekly schoolbook exercises that for over two years had been Guido's one attempt to convince Marcantonio or Girolamo or perhaps only himself that he was in fact what he was being fed and housed to, at the very least, seem. Now Guido watched. In the evenings at table he would sop his bread, hum, chew, and whenever Marcantonio spoke, Guido would stare at his pupil's lips as if peering into a fantastic wilderness from which mythic birds might fly. When for his father Marcantonio was called upon to elaborate the flux and reflux of blood, the subtilizing of vapors in the diastole, the emanation of the optic sprite from the ventricle of the eye, Guido would sink more deeply into his own face, his lips pursed tightly in what appeared to be a last effort to, if not master, then simply memorize, and every morning when he entered the library where for three hours Marcantonio had already been glossing passages on animal myology and the branching of the veins, the intelligible shape of the world seemed to have fled farther and farther from Guido's wet, startled eyes.

Then one morning Guido did not appear in the library, and when Marcantonio got back home from the apothecary that afternoon, Guido was still nowhere to be seen. Shortly before sundown as the boy

31

watched a scullery maid pare the fat and veins from a pig's goiter, he heard a clamor in the hall and in burst Guido, his face ruddy and sweating, and in his hand a copy of al–Jahiz on animals, bound and translated into Latin with a compendious commentary. He was babbling of places, names—two physicians in Bologna, a manuscript the Montefeltro family owned, the location of a Tuscan bookseller—and shoving the volume into Marcantonio's arms, he cut himself short, lay his hands on the boy's shoulders and, suddenly quite grave, asked only if the day had been well spent. Marcantonio, who was uncertain whether to thank him profusely for the book or just continue working, merely nodded, and Guido said, fine, fine, fine, yes, that's fine, then spun on his heel and was gone. During the months that followed, Marcantonio rarely saw his tutor. Rising early to begin his translations and occasionally retiring in the afternoon to the little schoolroom where he directed a groomsman or butcher's lad to carve up a kitten, Marcantonio would be startled to find lying on the table an entire horse's trunk or freshly severed ox head, once the arm of a small child, twice a man's hand. Daily the library filled with unfamiliar tomes and pamphlets—Galen on the faculties, a German surgeon's tract on amputation, the life of Hippocrates, Averrhoës in vulgar Italian—and at night there'd arrive students to tell of dissections they'd witnessed in Pavia or a Genoese physician eager to speak of choler or, once, an aged surgeon who, serving under Francesco Sforza, had peered into a beating heart and watched the bowels slither from a sobbing youth's side and could describe how the warm brain feels as it trickles through your hands. The adult Marcantonio still remembered it as a time of great enchantment. The days were never long enough for all the world he had to learn. He began taking his meals in the library, awaking before daylight, bending over gore and bones in the candle's radiance, and now and again late in the night as he staggered down a corridor to collapse on his bed, he'd be frightened by a figure who, stepping abruptly from a shadow, would rest his hands on the boy's shoulders to ask if this day too had been well spent, and if so, then that would be fine, fine, yes, very fine indeed.

These were the years when cadavers could not be bought, could hardly even be stolen, when papal disapproval and the hope of resurrection forced even Marcantonio's father to pass months and more with nothing but a traitor's torso or suicide's thigh, and these so far gone in decay that you could hardly bear to touch them. As a matter of fact, no one of decent family did touch them. Barbers or brutes from the charnel house or butchery were paid to do the cutting, often badly supervised, so that Marcantonio's father, Girolamo, could himself claim to have laid his own hand to only one dissection—an experience that convinced him more could be learned from reading Mondino.

Medical education proceeded largely by scholarly paraphrase; autopsy was little more than a ritual of illustration. By age fourteen Marcantonio with his slight acquaintance with the knife and incessant reading was already more deeply immersed in the study of life than many students a decade his senior, and as the boy's precocity became evident to his father, Girolamo began to speak of bringing his son to Padua and told Guido to prepare him. Marcantonio, who had watched the brows of his learned visitors rise when he asked his lucid questions and had committed whole chapters of Galen to memory and who suspected himself of being already prepared for Padua and every other center of so-called learning, if not advanced far beyond them, never dreamed that Guido, whose irrelevance had been virtually conceded even by himself, would be so scatterbrained as to take Girolamo's instructions literally.

But now when Marcantonio arrived in the library each morning, Guido would already be there pacing nervously or rapping his fingers on a table. Without a greeting and before the boy could locate the disquisition on animal spirits he'd been reading the night before, Guido would demand an explanation of the convergence of nerves in the rete mirabile or the transport of phlegm from the heart to the eye, and thinking to be rid of this nuisance quickly, Marcantonio would oblige him, pointing out that Guido's question was itself inept, a jumble of Alcmaeon, the Arabs, peasant husbandry and Plato, and then framing the question correctly so that elucidation could proceed. At such moments Guido would straighten slightly, blink, and then with a nod begin to inscribe on his tablet the boy's every word. But having returned to his book Marcantonio would be startled seconds later by Guido's tablet thrust beneath his nose and his quill tapping on a sentence as the man demanded how such an absurdity could be made sound with Herophilus or Aristotle. And on occasion his objections were incisive, a happy encounter of lore and common sense, but more often they were as bungled as before and Marcantonio would tell him so, enumerating the several sources of confusion and where the true objections lay. Each time Guido's spine would twitch or his eyes would dart toward the window, but then he'd nod and his quill would flutter across the page and presently he'd be on his feet again assailing the boy with new complaints. Entire mornings passed in this fashion, the man sometimes dogging the boy down corridors, following him to the table and bath, and then on into the afternoons, Guido's demands for restatement, amplification, proof, intensifying as Marcantonio belittled his antagonist now without mercy, laughed even into his strangely vacant eyes, sought to flee down garden paths or into the stable, recalled urgent obligations, invented afflictions, until finally almost weeping simply shouted, enough! enough! And so throughout a whole month as the departure was readied, plans made, trunks packed, dates set, always there was Guido waiting in the library, questions ready, or if Marcantonio sought to postpone the torment, then in the boy's bedroom and into the very bed itself, never stymied by the persistent and obvious rejoinder that his mind was utterly unfit for this task, but ceaselessly intent upon the subject to hand, probing, quibbling, wildly guessing, until by evening Marcantonio would have no strength for the knife, no strength for books or conversation, only a crushing need for the refuge of sleep where for a few hours he might escape the witless badgering of this man who in a thousand years could never learn.

And yet, despite the obvious fact that, no matter how exacting the boy's replies, Guido would forever wander the wilderness of his own imagination, Marcantonio always answered. Perhaps it was just a child's habit of respect or a love of display or simply his befuddlement with a tenacity so stupid, but something in Guido's sallies held his attention, and Marcantonio was puzzled to discover a perverse pleasure in this annoyance, in his need to encircle with words every organ, member, tissue, bone so that, their paths traced and retraced, their lines worn clean, the whole human body seemed momentarily to arise out of its profusion, a thing so familiar you could almost feel it resting in your mind. And so late one night after his trunks had been sent with the coachman and his departure set for two days hence and only those books and clothes remaining that he'd carry or wear, Marcantonio awoke in the murky stillness of his chamber to find Guido standing by the bed, a riding cloak on his back and a valise against his thigh. He did not rest his hands upon the boy's shoulders, he did not ease himself down upon the quilt, but standing erect and in a voice that was firm but oddly hollow he began to speak.

It matters little that you don't admire me or that we'll never converse again, he said. My faculties aren't so mean as you insinuate, but I've never regarded myself more than slightly. Perhaps I've lived too much in the midst of things. What matters is that you not make the same mistake, and of this I've labored mightily to be sure. Little remains for other men to teach you. All you lack is wisdom, something terrible, and you'll find it in the schoolroom in the morning. Go there early. Take nothing with you. Two days should be the proper time.

And bidding him farewell, Guido had turned to leave when, suddenly frightened, Marcantonio sat up in bed. And the days? the boy asked.

Guido stopped in the doorway.

Have the days been well spent?

Guido stared at the boy a moment before replying in a quiet voice: It is I, *I* who have been fine.

And Marcantonio passed the remainder of the night uneasily,

noticing for the first time the unaccountable remoteness of the walls of his room. But next morning he arose before daylight, and doing all as he'd been instructed, he entered the schoolroom as the sun broke the sky. He hadn't visited the room in nearly a month, and, at first, everything looked as he'd remembered, the ancient desk, the stool with a broken rung, a map of Asia on the wall. And then he saw heaped upon the table a dark and massive bundle. Rushing over he tore away the drape, and there in the amber light lay a man, his flesh as pallid as a moon, his eyes pellucid and starkly open, his lips parted as if to utter the final, perfect word. Beside him were a knife, two pairs of wooden tweezers, some pins, a crudely-made clamp, chisels, a saw and three stays. Against his thigh lay a copy of Mondino. And gazing down at the wondrously still and glowing shape as daylight embarrassed the room, Marcantonio understood that he was only a child, that he lived in a world where no one could ever teach him what he needed to learn, and staggering back against the desk and fumbling for the stool, Marcantonio had wanted to die.

It was the last night Leonardo would ever know the celebrated anatomist, and looking back years later, he'd find it incredible that Marcantonio had told the story just there, just then. Guido had, of course, taught the man natural philosophy, but what Marcantonio seemed to find bewildering was his need for this teaching, his ache to vanish under the glowing light. Leonardo recalled the young man's eyes staring past the candles. An iridescent fly crawled down his thumb. The Venetian state had been right, there was subversion in the dissecting theater, but it wasn't della Torre who was the traitor. Or at any rate, killing him wouldn't help. Lingering in the fetid air Leonardo felt a clumsy urge to protect the young man but could think of nothing to say.

Finally della Torre spoke: Of course, even to the last he was probably confounded. I mean, how would you distinguish devotion like that from revenge?

Faith has different kinds, Leonardo replied.

But the point is—and here della Torre had laughed—if I'm to live, he has to be wrong. Completely. It was knowledge he feared, that he wanted me to despise. Just think of it, God mocking us, our minds a wretched joke. Even upon this very table, nothing fast, nothing hard, merely a squirming lump of unspeakable . . . what?

And Leonardo glanced down at the cadaver's cheek, about to remark that even a host of particulars couldn't disallow proportion. But recalling the pages of notes covering his own workroom floor, he simply said: Perhaps you haven't understood his lesson.

Undoubtedly, my friend, undoubtedly. But can you disclose this teaching to me? I'm the student. Here, place it in my hand.

Leonardo shrugged. Perhaps he spoke of patience.

Perhaps, but I'm deaf to his words. The knowledge we wait for, don't we call it ignorance? Guido da Forlì died of this waiting.

You've looked deeply into it, Leonardo said. Still, the man hardly threw himself away upon a dullard. There's a difference between a weasel and a hen, though both wait.

But two weasels waiting in the same hen's coop, one will drive the other out. I admire Guido da Forlì—in my way—I owe him much, but really, no one gives a bishop's prick for your high–mindedness.

Youth often speaks in this way, Leonardo said.

Experience often speaks in this way, della Torre said.

Leonardo looked at the man. How much darkness did he need now if he was to see at all? The anatomist's breathing came in quick spasms, and Leonardo knew it would be a mercy to let him recompose himself. Mercy?

I've gazed into death's eyes and seen the vitreous humor dribble out, seen the orb turn as shapeless as a sucked dug, Leonardo said. And still, vision traces lines in a plane. Tell me. You picked up the knife, you carved the man on the table, you had a look inside?

Della Torre smiled: I've stood before the miracle of flesh and trembled, but to tolerate confusion is to tempt death. Believe in what you see, my friend; pray to see better.

Pray for time, Leonardo said.

And the weasel in your hen-coop?

The two men stared at one another across the candle's fume, and then it was past.

Here, bring closer the light, the anatomist said. And bending over the cadaver's face and tracing with his knife a geometer's curve, della Torre teased loose the cheek to expose a ruddy bone. So much for beauty, eh?

The Port-A-Phone's bleeping.

"I really can't deal with human problems. Not today." It's Deirdre, my wife. Her voice sounds pretty tense.

"Did you tell him I'm in the hospital?" I ask.

"He just laughed."

"Okay, admit you lied," I say. "Tell him your boss is on the toilet, act embarrassed, stammer, promise that—swear like you're young and mousy and desperate—that as soon as you hear the flush you'll..."

"We tried that one last week. Same guy. Look, there's no future, can't we just forget him?"

Actually, Deirdre's my not wife. We've lived together nineteen years—pretty continuously—and up until a few years ago we'd spent most of it married, but after our careers turned mysterious and what we'd mistaken for a financial crisis became a new mode of social organization, Deirdre came home from an attorney's office one afternoon and explained that we weren't feasible. Now, she's proprietor, manager and sole employee of DeeDee's Live-in Kitchen Kleen and Katering, in which capacity she's paid a pittance by her principal client, me. When angry calls come in on her boss's home phone, she answers that she only works here, knows nothing, sympathizes with the paint wholesaler or collection agent or exasperated secretary or IRS functionary or credit union officer or whomever, but then sighs, says she's my not wife, that when her contractor returns she'll relay the message, that she has to get back to work now, bye.

"I'll impersonate a lawyer," I say. "You don't think he's a fed, do you?"

"He won't break the connection. Says he's going to stay on the line till you pick up."

"I'm in the car, for Chrissakes, twelve miles away!"

"I told him," Deirdre says. "He thinks it's funny."

"Oh shit."

Just then, somewhere about thirty cars ahead of me, this plume of water shoots three stories into the sky. I glance over at the Toyota parked beside me, give the driver—young woman in goofy glasses and a jacket with huge shoulder pads—one of those "whazzat?" looks. Either she thinks I'm flirting or she's just noticed my car. Anyway, I get the glacier. I start punching radio buttons for a traffic report.

"Sorry you got stuck with him," I tell Deirdre. "There's a wreck or busted hydrant or something up ahead. It could be an hour before—"

"Look, I gotta go. No time, etcetera."

Long silence.

"Are you scared?" I ask.

Deirdre sighs. "I'm sitting here and the nightmares ...well, they're somebody else's. I mean, for people like me, ordinary life's possible. I *know* it is. Can you tell me why I'm doing this?"

"You're beset with narcissistic fantasies of personal power and your parents read Dr. Spock. You despise yourself, lack values, suffer from an amorphous feminine alienation and attended college in sixty-two. You once used an illegal drug. In clinical terms, you're antisocial, bi-polar, anorexic, given to hysteria and weak self-image on the MMPI, fear responsibility, secretly long to be dominated, are incapable of ever becoming a productive member of society, aren't blonde, and display unmistakable signs of Durkheim's diddly-squat donald duck dementia—"

Dial tone.

Throughout his life Leonardo da Vinci would never understand why he always had words left over. If only Marcantonio della Torre had replied that his weasel would gobble Leonardo's hen in no time at all, Leonardo would've replied that truth and virtue couldn't long be at enmity. Or if della Torre had countered that fidelity in a losing cause was stubbornness, Leonardo would've said: I want only time and Guido's patience to snatch truth as it flutters past! And if in a last, desperate attempt della Torre had snickered, time's a luxury and your candle's burning out, Leonardo would've triumphed with: Yes, but one live truth will buy many dead chickens! Or some such. But the fact is that Leonardo was always considering a question from twenty sides while his antagonist was answering it, and the eventuality for which he was never prepared was that his antagonist might ask a new one. Of course, what Leonardo had really wanted to tell della Torre was what he'd learned along with roots and proportions from Luca Pacioli in Milan, specifically, that if a sliver of nothing divides ocean from air and an intangible cause tethers now to then and an impossible point cradles space in its belly—that is, if the world is just plain weirder than anything you've imagined about it, then pray for patience and fancy math or give up on understanding altogether. Or more succinctly,

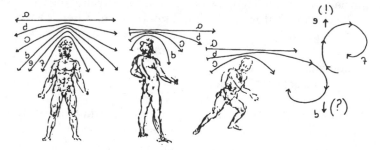

which was roughly what on the Malnido's roof Leonardo had seen but did not see until sixteen years later when on the banks of the Arno he saw it again.

Now, the reason the man without words' vanishing act was such a bother to Leonardo wasn't that disappearing dwarfs were unheard of. Constructing a two-hundred-foot-wide brick dome three hundred feet up in the air with no machine larger than a hammer, wedge, or pulley— now, *that* was unheard of, but Brunelleschi in Florence had managed it, so Leonardo wasn't distraught over miracles. He was distraught

38

because, until he saw Jacopo il Poggio turn down into up, Leonardo imagined he knew enough physics to complete the most ambitious undertaking of his life. This was the summer of 1490, and just six months earlier his clockwork universe had scored a hit at Ludovico Sforza il Moro's Paradiso festival. In the intervening period the petty nobility of nearby Spain, France, and Italy—none of whom were inclined to split hairs where luck or gimmickry was concerned—had made Maestro Leonardo da Vinci into a household word, and this had resulted in practical benefits for the thirty-eight-year-old *ingegnere*— the Italian word felicitously combining genius and engineering. Leonardo began to be featured in diplomatic extravaganzas, to be consulted on anything technical, and, in general, to be treated like a tasty plum. Materials became more plentiful. He ate better. Dangerous people acknowledged him. Most important, however, he was able to resume work on the project that had brought him to Milan in the first place: the great bronze equestrian monument to the founder of the Sforza line. Or as the statue was more often called, *il cavallo*—the horse.

Ludovico Sforza's reasons for the massive statue were the typical mishmash of lofty and crass aspirations that make historians throw up their hands and snort: The renaissance! Among them was the uninspiring fact that any titanic mountain of bronze called Sforza and squatting in front of the Milanese fortress would by its sheer immobility contribute to the stability of his family's reign. You could murder the descendants, but how would you get rid of *it*? No one knows exactly how Leonardo became part of Ludovico's scheme, but sometime around Leonardo's thirtieth year he showed up in Milan proclaiming himself a ballistics expert, architect and master sculptor capable of taking charge of the project. From our knowledge of Leonardo's apprenticeship in Florence and from his notes on casting while in Milan, we can figure that this last was only about ninety-percent untrue. He'd probably garnered some experience of clay modeling, copper work, gilding, and bronze sculpture in Andrea del Verrocchio's workshop, and he'd associated with Antonio Pollaiuolo who'd submitted drawings for the Sforza monument at an earlier time. However, when his contemporaries later recalled Leonardo's career in Florence, they recalled the career of a painter, and we have no records of any sculptural commission to indicate otherwise. The equestrian statue Verrocchio contracted to build during the same period was only about a tenth the size of the one Leonardo was undertaking, and no free-standing sculpture in the pose Leonardo envisioned had ever been achieved. But he was gifted and young. He'd apprenticed in a city where inconceivable feats were the order of the day. And everybody said he was amazing. Leonardo figured he could handle what Milan had in store.

He was wrong. For nearly eight years Leonardo made sporadic forays into the Sforza project, got nowhere. He justified his modest ducal stipend by undertaking trivial tasks around court—emblems, theatrical costumes, bric-a-brac, fancy toys for jaded nobles—and he put together a modest living by collaborating with the local artist, Ambrogio de Predis, who had no skill but much work. Leonardo's one consolation, as he daily grew more intimidated by his task, as he began to glimpse the obstacles to making anything so large, not to mention making it *look like* something—his one consolation was that no one at court paid any attention. Evidently, they hadn't taken his boasts seriously in the first place, or they'd just figured he was another Florentine painter and there was always work for another Florentine painter. He completed the *Madonna of the Rocks* for the friars of the Immaculate Conception, painted a portrait of Ludovico's mistress Cecilia Gallerani, experimented with mechanics, anatomized some birdwings, learned a little Latin—none of which justified talk of godlike abilities but were something. As the eighties drew to a close, Ludovico got interested in the bronze horse again and went looking for Florentine maestri who could actually build it for him. The evidence suggests Leonardo was going to be demoted, possibly sacked. Then came the Paradiso festival.

The result was that during the early months of 1490, while the success of Leonardo's universe was making him the deadliest weapon in Ludovico Sforza's culture arsenal, Leonardo found himself entrusted with an artistic project whose unprecedented vastness and complexity scared him to death. And now the whole court was watching. All that spring he shuttled between his studio and Galleazzo Sanseverino's stables where he drew huge Sicilian and Berber stallions kicking their hoofs into the sky, ears back and nostrils flared, biting, beating the earth, pissing, squealing, rolling in the dust. He bought carcasses of dying or lame nags and cut the flanks open right where the animals dropped. He learned to disregard flies and vile odors, to keep a thumb and index clean enough to draw the flayed muscles without smearing his paper, worked in the cool of night to avoid the worst of the insects, and continually singed his beard in his candle trying to get a closer look. He visited cannon foundries, took notes on the viscosity of molten bronze—after six hours firing, after twelve, on cloudy afternoons, when more tin was added, first with imported then with local brass—built elaborate balancing contraptions to map shifting centers of gravity, and pestered every scholar and maestro and engineer in the Castello. At the end of six months he hadn't found any solutions, but he'd seemed to be making progress. For example, he'd concocted a kind of vocabulary of paired contraries—water v. stone, hair v. machinery, illusion v. bulk, melody v. number, and so forth—and an elementary calculus according to which adjustments in one might compensate for a disproportion in its opposite, as well as a rudimentary system of substitutions whereby whole pairs or constellations of pairs might act on behalf of an element that was weak or missing. It didn't really work, of course, but it made sense in the same way perspective made sense, and that had seemed a great reassurance at the time.

The man without words looked like the next step. In Florence Leonardo had studied painting as a repertory of devices, effects, geometry, illusions. Even at the time, he hadn't felt this was enough—getting lost in a painting was too much like getting lost in a cavern; you could know all the pathways and still never get back out—but the question of what he was acquiring in Verrocchio's workshop, if more than just a knack, hadn't seemed urgent. Taking on the horse, however, made it urgent. Either painting was knowledge, a doorway into nature, or he'd never complete the project. No mere knack was going to raise sixty tons of bronze twenty-three feet in the air, and no illusion of perspective could make it look like a horse from both the castle wall and the far end of the Corso Dante. It wasn't clear to Leonardo exactly how the man without words could help, but watching him move, Leonardo had thought he glimpsed something, a link between two and three dimensions, how a picture took on life. Perhaps if someone were to watch the dwarf long enough, closely enough, thoughtfully enough, he might see how making something appear was like making it move was like making it stand was like …well, making it.

So, when on the Malnido's roof Leonardo had seen the wordless man vanish, he'd nearly decided to take up necromancy. Leonardo hardly inclined to superstition, and though he loved pranks and gadgets immoderately, he had little taste for obfuscation, having floundered about in it long enough. But after so much calculation, observation, study, to wind up bereft of sense …well, it was like decoding the Jabberwocky. You could figure it by mechanics, by Euclid, by the stars or by John Pecham, but even if you figured it according to scullery gossip, the man without words should've been sprawled out bloody on the rooftop with no mystery but why he'd done such a thing. But there was the steaming roof, the hot, blue sky, the green valley of the Po, a goshawk hanging above some willows, silence, and nothing more. Leonardo had rested his elbow on the wall and touched the rough mortar, scraped his nail across a tile, finally slapped the brown brick with his palm, maintaining just enough self-possession not to fling himself down on the gravel, kick his feet, and scream. What was there to deny? The dwarf had simply set his shoulder on a line with death, lowered his head, wiped his nose, hopped once, and with his slippers zipping across the macadam and his tiny fists whipping the air, all this plus the shiver in his spine that Leonardo would for the rest of his life

41

remember but not quite name, the man had launched his skull at the brick's edge and, in less time than the optic sprite needs to fetch an image to the eye, passed through it, over it, into it, beyond it, was—at any rate—gone. A perfectly straightforward affair that made nature crazy.

For nine years Leonardo told no one what he'd seen. Or no one except Fazio Cardano, who'd declared: But far, far stranger is justice! Which was a lot of help. Leonardo tried to forget that there'd ever been a man who spoke with his hands and feet and eyes, kept on working as if genius and persistence could make up for what, on the Malnido's roof, had broken nature in two. And even when the futility of his efforts had to have seemed obvious to him, after Salai had recognized that the bronze horse was just a chimera and spit in Leonardo's face and disappeared, even as the Castello opened its gates and the French marched in and Milan fell into hushed waiting as one courtier after another either gathered his possessions and departed for Florence or Bologna or Montpellier or Rome or, if unlucky, for the dank cells underground, even during this period when, really, nothing could have made much sense to Leonardo anymore—still he told no one. So that when at last he told Fra Luca Pacioli—seated on their dozing mounts beside an almond orchard before sunrise on an unfamiliar highway in a remote part of Lombardy, having ridden out the Vercellina gate and along the southern road for the entire night hoping to put Milan as far behind them as their despair and the horses' strength would allow— Leonardo had given up on ever making anything.

Now, Fra Luca Pacioli was as thoroughgoing a reprobate as Leonardo would ever manage to know, but unlike Bellincioni, there was no danger he'd mislead you. In part this was because, if anyone had trusted the monk, Fra Luca would hardly have known how to act. But more fundamentally it was because—being that rarest of creatures, an undiluted ego-maniac—Pacioli was given to raptures of self-disclosure so earnest they'd knock you over. So, when he explained to Leonardo that perfect circles and right triangles, not to mention dodecahedrons, exponential progressions, and a rudimentary calculus, could be found on any beach, Leonardo had realized, here was a man that facts wouldn't dismay. And he'd set out to learn from him. So they'd strolled and declaimed and quarreled and snickered throughout the pink Castello, and Leonardo had drawn polygons for Pacioli's new treatise, and Pacioli had taught diminution ratios to Leonardo, and together they'd bemoaned Ludovico's fall and slipped out of Milan on the west side to avoid passing the ruins of the horse in the piazza and when— just before dawn on a road that would eventually take them both back to Florence—when Leonardo had finally divulged to Pacioli the madness he'd witnessed nine years before, Pacioli had fallen silent. He eased his head back into his cowl, sat perfectly still, and then Leonardo heard him say: …so what you don't know, study, and while you study, look about you, and whatever you see, try to understand, and what you come to understand you'll one day see is what you didn't know.

All of which advice Leonardo tried to follow, taking up roots and Euclid, tracing a bat's wing and listing sixty-four words for running water, so that when at last he stood on the old bridge in Florence in 1506 and gazed down into the Arno, he was able to see for the first time what he'd seen but hadn't seen when he'd seen it before and to begin to understand what he'd one day see again in his dreams of platan leaves and updrafts, about which Marcantonio della Torre could profitably learn a great deal, or so Leonardo wished he'd been able to say, standing beside della Torre's dissecting table back in Pavia in 1510.

The reason Leonardo didn't say any of this wasn't just that he probably would've begun to stammer and ended up looking like a pompous jerk—although he was certainly conscious of this excellent reason for staying mum. It was that he was far from sure Marcantonio della Torre wasn't right. I mean, it sounded pretty flashy for Pacioli to ramble on about the secret geometry of conch shells or for Platonists to read God's mind in comets or for old Toscanelli back in Florence to reassure the monomaniac Cristoforo Colombo that the earth was round as a pea. Who among them would ever load five boats with thirty days' provisions and sail into nothing? But by the time Leonardo stood in the candlelight of della Torre's apartment, he knew too well what courting disaster felt like, and if your nightmare ever came knocking at the dissecting theater one morning or someone gave away all the bronze you needed for the statue you were about to cast or if that universally predictable human comeuppance overtook you during the sixty–seven years you spent investigating everything to understand something to do one thing correctly …well, you probably wouldn't need to know about updrafts. So when della Torre warned Leonardo to disregard motion's glamour, to study only what would hold its shape even if it died, Leonardo had felt like screaming right into his face: Who are you to be telling this to me?! Which is exactly what he did scream at Salai, who replied: I am your life.

THE LAST DIMOSTRAZIONE

If Leonardo da Vinci weren't presently absorbed in the attempt to bobble a kidney bean out of the corner of his eye and jiggle it far enough down his cheek so that his tongue could snake up over his mustache and snare it, he might recall for the thousandth time in four days how Salai stood there beside the southernmost window, his lips damp, the black curls encircling his eyes, and waited for Leonardo to explain about the horse. If ever Leonardo ached to make himself understood, it was then, and he'd described the spilled light, the riot and swirl, vapor rising, the collapse of nature that sucked your mind away, but Salai just gazed down into the courtyard and said nothing. Not that Leonardo blames him—or not for that anyway. Hadn't his own words sounded empty, even to Leonardo? Still, you have to say something when your enemy stares you in the face, and if spirit fails on the first utterance, then rest your eyes on a distant willow and—puff, splutter—have at it again. And Salai had been patient—Leonardo grants him that much—had floated just below Leonardo's eyes, face turned upwards as if to say: All right; here's your chance; make me understand. Like you could just do that. Like rage and grief hadn't already so warped his heart that up would always lead down and black look white and every light be devoured by its own shadow. Okay, maybe more was possible than Leonardo had imagined, and much he'd imagined was as phantasmagoric as griffins and gnomes. Still, he'd tried! And Leonardo said so, pounded and slashed the air, insisted that what he'd groaned over, dreamed a hundred deaths for, that Horse was no lie, Horse could destroy you. But no amount of eloquence was a match for the facts. And Salai had shaken his head, and Leonardo had shaken his fist, and by morning the yellow engine was there.

Trying to peer across his nose at the kidney bean with one eye as he twitches and flutters the other in a tour de force display of facial myology, Leonardo isn't thinking of Salai just now, but is concentrating his considerable powers of invention on getting this legume to move. Possibly a smidgen of broth or vegetable drippings that—as he tried to memorize the quarter–moon–shaped trajectory of the platan leaf gliding in and out of his dream—dried and hardened, has glued it to his lid. Winking seems to have no effect. Leonardo's right hand's useless, paralyzed three years ago for God–only–knows what iniquity and, even if it weren't, presently buried beneath these coverlets. And his left, which remains as strong as when he used to bend crate–fasteners with it in Verrocchio's shop, still hangs on to Battista's ankle. If only the transverse ligature of his nostril were heftier, it might be possible to summon sufficient animal spirits there and, applying leverage, thrust, and declivity, to dislodge the bean, guide it down the fissure of tears, catch it in his mustache, wriggle it nose–ward and snatch it with his tongue. Unfortunately, Leonardo has cut up enough faces to know that most of the muscles needed for this maneuver are missing. The result: he finds himself in the epistemologist's predicament, having only the eye itself with which to overcome an obstacle to its seeing. In no time at all Leonardo recognizes the potential for self–defeat here. He stops fidgeting, grows still, asks: Exactly what is a kidney bean that it should obscure man's vision? As it turns out, there's more in this question than meets the etc.

Leonardo's difficulty looks like this: According to the old physics, a kidney bean is a creature of considerable longing. It aches for its home within the earth where, being fruit and nurtured by water, it will seek air, imbibe fire, rise, foliate, grow, thus fulfilling its many ends in the several spheres of what the Renaissance called being and modernity calls a mistake. Whether its path is through bowels or vapor makes little difference. Beans want to go down. This is their nature. Resting here beside Leonardo's nostril this bean is, therefore, not really resting at all but is struggling with considerable might to vent its frustration, all in accordance with orderly principles of mechanics, dynamics, balance and flux. In short, it's alive—a condition it shares with Leonardo's dimostrazione. The cinquecento knows six sources of this life—muscles, wind, springs, water, weights, steam—and five ways to manage it—levers, pulleys, winches, wedges, screws. Using four of the former, Leonardo has infused life into the bulging walls of the sheep's tripe under his mattress, into the bowstrings and bent shafts of several tiny catapults strategically placed about his room, and now this life yearns for annihilation as eagerly as any lemming. Its animosity towards obstacles is notorious, its determination well-attested, all it lacks is freedom, which Leonardo will eventually provide by means of a workmanlike arrangement of four of the aforementioned five basic machines appropriately adapted. Simple as a kidney bean. The principles are all there in Aristotle, and you can find wilder contraptions in Valturio's treatise on armaments, which is where Leonardo found his.

So here's the question: Why's the world such an unpredictable place? Part of the answer is that Leonardo still thinks the time of falling is directly proportional to the distance, and he inhabits an age that understands precious little about friction. Despite Pacioli's help, Leonardo will go to his grave applying arithmetical solutions to exponential problems, but this is just the start of his troubles. The earth is spinning. That means that even without wind resistance a kidney bean plummeting as straight as possible toward the center of the planet will inscribe, not a line, but a spiral, and Leonardo can figure this out even before Newton. All of Leonardo's calculations depend on geometric phantoms, and he's aware of this: The midpoint on a line is conveniently insubstantial, but the axis of a balance beam is heavy and, what's worse, tilt the beam and the weight shifts. Then there's the eye. You've only got to hold a piece of straw up close and peer around it to know that sight's a good deal more complicated than the point and pyramid of artists' perspective, and Leonardo's begun to suspect that eyes give to vision much of what they find there. Eyes twinkle; stars don't. What if the light itself were misleading? And if you add to all this the scrumptious detail that the nuisance beside Leonardo's nostril was once sacred fruit to the band of Greeks who divided the universe into proportions in the first place, that Pythagoras himself preferred death at the hands of a mob over irreverent escape through a patch of kidney beans, well, then maybe you see why Leonardo's more impressed by patience these days than by anything he knows. No certainty has ever satisfied him. If this bean won't act like a Renaissance vegetable, maybe that's interesting too.

Leonardo raises his eyebrows, sniffs, wiggles an ear. The bean rocks, doesn't roll, and Melzi sees it. He's been weeping for twenty minutes face–down on what turns out to be a very gamy pig–bristle throw–rug, and even allowing for his fanatical devotion to protocol, he can't be expected to endure the torment any longer. His cheeks are as pitted as a potato field, and though he's separated from Leonardo's corpse by forty–three layers of bedclothes, it's pretty obvious to him that his master's still breathing. Peering over at Leonardo's face, which appears to be wadding itself up like a dishrag right now, Melzi knows the world for a savage place. Daily he searches for allies at court, but he's too callow for good intrigue, and a clumsily conjugated subjunctive will glaze over even the lowliest Frenchman's eyes. The master acts less masterful every hour, and although Melzi knows Leonardo's estate is bequeathed to him, he also knows he's in France and has to get everything back to Italy first. Whenever of late Melzi has brought up the treatise on painting or the book of the human form, Leonardo has turned away, bellowed, Beleaguered eyes!—or similar gibberish—and if what's presently happening on Leonardo's face isn't death, then Melzi will probably find the man in a week perched on top of his dirty linen flapping his arms like a cockatoo. The only display of decency in the last month was when the weasel Salai slunk back to Milan, but when Leonardo locked himself in the studio the very next afternoon— with Battista de Vilanis no less!—and emerged eighteen hours later only to writhe, squeal, and collapse on the porch ...well, the weight of so much futility seems crushing. Melzi's not averse to heroics. This may be his only chance to overcome the insult of being born rich and ordinary. But he wishes the potential for making a fool of oneself were less appalling. He has no idea how he'll bring it all off. Rocking back on his heels and pawing his face, he begins to reconnoitre the situation.

Beside him, Battista de Vilanis gazes forlornly at the door. He has passed the interval of Melzi's grief plotting ways to pry his master's fingers loose and escape down the stairs that Mathurine is sitting in the kitchen inventing reasons not to climb back up. Having labored ten years as a servant of Leonardo da Vinci with his sole worry being how to remain one, Battista has glimpsed in the prospect of Leonardo's death both a crisis and an opportunity. If he can return to Milan after three years exile with the Maestro, having in the meantime hobnobbed with engineers and dons, stockpiled anecdotes, and generally familiarized himself with Leonardo's routines, who's to say he isn't a painter? The journeyman's documents can be finagled, and Battista figures he can get around Melzi somehow. His sole worry is that, although having assisted in Leonardo's workshop, he's never really learned to paint, and so for the past months he's been diligently following the best–known renaissance pedagogy for learning anything, i.e., imitating a master, which in the present case means learning to paint the *St. John* and *Gioconda* by painting right over them. If Leonardo can just keep on dying long enough, Battista's plan is likely to work. As soon as Leonardo dozes off again, Battista means to slip back down to the studio on the pretext of hurrying up Mathurine with Melzi's washbasin. He's not really sure how long his paint on the *Gioconda* is going to remain malleable, since he mixed in a little egg yolk to speed drying.

Melzi is probably gullible enough to let Battista get away with this scheme, but unfortunately for Battista, Melzi's just hit on the same idea for making off with Battista's pigments, so forestalling further disaster until Battista grinds more linseed or gets to an apothecary. In his darkest moments Melzi has never dreamed that Battista might use egg tempera to overpaint oils—lucky for Melzi who needs a good night's sleep as much as the next fellow. The two men exchange glances, smile. Each wonders aloud about the woman's delay, curses the greater portion of French peasantry, protests against the other's disturbance in petty affairs and, in unison, offers himself as a willing inciter of this foreign wench to haste and action. The situation is actually more complicated than this. Melzi can't be certain that Leonardo's facial contortions aren't, in fact, the harbingers of death, and he's determined to be on hand for any final remarks, pathetic gestures, prayers, or whatever will bear repeating. Either he needs to hold his ground here until Leonardo's out of danger or to escape on good enough terms with Battista to be confident of getting called back. Battista knows that, left alone with the master for ten minutes, Melzi can claim to have talked him into anything, and though unsure what's to fear on this count, fears finding out. In short, neither man wants to let the other do anything the other wants to do, but both require the other's cooperation. This calls for diplomacy.

Offers of accommodation having passed, shows of deference follow. Deference becomes polite importunity, importunity self–abnegating insistence, insistence turns into assurances of good–faith. Pretty soon Battista has freely admitted to tampering with Leonardo's paintings, and Melzi has warmly forgiven him. Battista marvels at Melzi's condescension and pleads for a chance to serve him. Melzi confesses to base envy of Battista's prodigious talents, demands a penance. Both men are genuinely moved by their own declarations. Both are genuinely astonished by the other's shame. Neither commits the blunder of looking at Leonardo, whose contortions are persuasive evidence that the mortuary ablutions in question are unnecessary, the sticky garbage on his face having never been a consideration. The affair's becoming lively. Battista's and Melzi's voices are getting loud.

In the kitchen Mathurine hears them. She can't understand Italian but knows that noise means trouble and she's involved. For three years these foreigners have been a scourge and trial. The master is possessed by devils and tallies every copper and pocket silk, and the young ones wiggle their bums, wave their arms at table and screech. They're dealing in black arts, philters, raptures, perpetuum mobile, and she figures them for sodomites every one. Their vapors are pestilent, and twice she's suffered the strangury, more than five times the tercians and quotidiens, has grave fears for her yellow bile, and she's been victim of the flux days without number. If it weren't that her own king had fallen victim to the old one's hex, she'd have fled long before, but the King's a dandy rogue and chortles like a magpie and gives her a pinch on the rump and sometimes money to boot, so she has stayed for the honor of France, and when last week the little spider crawled off and the mad master signed his will and took to bed, she had hopes of outlasting the villainy, but now it's all plainly Lucifer's ruse, and doom comes apace, for her gout and dropsy will never endure a month more. She's divided whether to stay put till mischief seeks her out or haul herself up to meet it halfway. Either way she loses, and the latter alternative has nothing going for it but curiosity, which is, all things considered, a good deal. She heaves her body upright, tosses a greasy towel in the basin, and complaining to saints and seraphim, starts back upstairs.

In the bedroom Melzi is just finishing an elaboration on the topos of noblesse oblige, having demonstrated indisputably his fitness to fetch the washbasin, when, in an inspired maneuver, Battista prostrates himself at Melzi's feet and states what they both know: Every word Battista's uttering is a mere ploy for returning to the Gioconda; fetching the basin's a strategic diversion; even this unbosoming now is calculated; there's not one trustworthy sinew in his churlish heart—choke, kiss, splutter—save yourself from my pathetic villainy, oh beloved master! And that settles it: Melzi's paralyzed by the lie that must be true. This confusion offers a disastrous opening. Leonardo meanwhile has continued smirking and contorting and grimacing until, in incontrovertible demonstration of nature's fidelity, the kidney bean in his eye has popped loose, and he's just snaking his tongue up to snare it when Mathurine—who's witnessed five exorcisms, including the spitting–demon conjured from the draper's nephew last fall—enters the room. She sees Battista weeping on the floor, Leonardo writhing in his bed and, slashing the air in a network of mystic pentagons, she dashes toward the south window, from which she's prepared to plunge just in case the foul thing in the master's face flies forth in bliss and frenzy intent on her virgin soul. At this same instant Battista recognizes his opportunity. He leaps up, shouts, My shame is boundless, oh Master!—and bolts for the door, having made no allowance for the ankle that, remaining all this time in Leonardo's grip, has known neither blood nor feeling for an hour. The foot collapses sending Battista flat on his face and his toe back up under the bed where it strikes the wooden pin—PING!—connecting inflated tripe to paper lilies, cords, pulleys, levers, springs. The sound startles Leonardo. His tongue misses the bean which lodges in his nostril, provoking a thunderous ker–chew propelling the legume directly at Mathurine's forehead amid a shower of blue balloons, yellow lilies, lavender carnations—the catapult in the westernmost cornice having ejected perfectly. Mathurine has dreamed damnation a million times but never expected it to be colorful. Still, she recognizes Satan when he comes at her. She shrieks, dives for the window that opens like all French windows inward, cracking her head on the crossposts and dropping her out–cold on the floor. Battista, who spent the better part of four nights putting these flowers in place and just can't believe he's going to have to do it all over again, figures he might as well pass out too. Leonardo opens both eyes, surveys his glorious handiwork, and exclaims in a jubilant voice: I *knew* it wasn't fear!

I've made a hideous miscalculation. There's a demonstration underway ahead, and because all the radio stations were competing for the longest continuous rock'n'roll, I drove right into it. *Now*, of course, the air waves are resplendent with warnings. The demonstration's part of a series; I know all about it. The participants are mostly men, mostly young, mostly gay, dressed in suits—some of them—or in other respectable, middle–class clothing, and they're lying in the road as though too weak and ill to move. This is not altogether a pretense. The leaders of the protest insist—the newspapers have been delighted to repeat this disturbing detail while surrounding it with participles like "alleged" and "supposed" so that sticking scrupulously to facts they can gratify our basest appetites—they insist that among the demonstrators are a number of individuals who really are dying from the recent plague, and the police, who are removing them from the road, have donned asbestos suits—or that's what they look like on the news—to protect themselves from the vermin. Every night you can see the shiny officers, as ethereal and bulbous as astronauts, arm and arm with the demonstrators in their painted ties and oxfords. The young men are saying to the police, "I'm dying. I'm dying. Why are you doing this to me?" And the police are answering, "I'm not doing anything to you; I'm doing my job. Get outa the street." And the young men are saying, "Aren't you a creature of flesh and blood?" And the police are answering, "When you call a cop, d'you want a dialogue?" And the young men are saying, "Where is your humanity?" And the policemen are answering, "Don't talk stupid."

Why is this crazy?

In my car's backseat is my dog, Metropolis. He's the fattest dog I've ever seen, and more than one well–meaning person has reminded me that for what he eats daily three small children in New Delhi could be rescued from starvation. He's not a friendly dog. He's not attractive or especially affectionate or loyal, although he's okay as unfriendly dogs go. He is brown and middling dirty and weighs almost a hundred pounds and has a bark that sounds like a motorscooter crank–starting on a dry day. He is also minus a left hindleg and one eye. It's ninety–eight degrees on the large flashing bank sign underneath the thirty foot woman to my right, and because my car is nearly four decades old, a bona fide antique and technological disaster that turns the head of everyone we pass and produces astonishing gray clouds of unbreathable miasma, it's not air conditioned in here. As a result, Metropolis pants. He pants softly for a time, then when we lurch about a foot closer to the demonstration he leans forward—timed to make it seem inadvertent, although I'm not fooled—and pants exuberantly onto my Port–A–Phone, onto the large box in the seat beside me, and onto my neck. His breath smells like decaying fish, and his drool mingles with the perspiration that covers everything I touch. I suspect that this makes him happy, that it's as close to animal solidarity as Metropolis ever comes, though I won't presume to speak for him. In a white Mercedes up ahead an elderly woman gets out of her passenger door, starts gesturing in the direction of those morosely waiting behind her as if to explain how they might move out of her way. For no apparent reason, this makes Metropolis growl.

Port-A-Phone.

"If Earth's temperature increased seven degrees, what would debts matter?" It's Deirdre. "Picayune. Less than nothing. A single major oil spill can deprive fifty thousand people of their livelihood and kill twelve million plants and animals—all in a day. Every twenty-nine minutes an expanse of virgin forest the size of Central Park gets decimated. If you or I were dying—"

"We *are* dying."

50

"They know about this phone line," she says.

"They can't know—"

"I picked up to see if he'd gone, and he told me to put your receiver down next to his."

"Can't we sue somebody for telling him that?"

"He says if I put it up close, he'll yell at you."

On the afternoon when Deirdre explained that we should divorce, she spread a number of sheets of computer paper over our kitchen table, cleared her throat, and explained: "It's not necessary to be rich—though that's the simplest solution—but if you're not rich, then you must make sense to people who are. What makes sense is marketing, new cars, statistics, crime, and anything connected with sex. Our problem is that we aren't classifiable. It isn't that we don't love each other, it's that long marriages without IRA's, children, adultery or investments have problems with intelligibility. Like rape and gas shortages, it's the sort of phenomena the present can't know." Then she showed me how the lawyer had showed her how we could become what we were by becoming what we weren't. "The idea is to suffer in the right way, fail in the right way, appear conventionally unlucky but demographically salvageable. None of this is, of course, untrue or illegal. It's just a systematic distortion."

Her solution, the one she and the attorney had worked out, was to create two lives. The first of these would be our life, the one we'd lived for more than a dozen years: two people, married, who read books and made things, ate vegetables, played music, maintained fierce loyalties to losing teams, tried to be civilized and funny. There was, of course, a little more to it, but we didn't go into everything with the lawyer. The second life was for the purpose of protecting the first one. It was complex, consisting of various subdivisions—some destitute, others enterprising—as well as a composite category made from the interrelationships of the whole. The strategy was, evidently, to provide us with maximum adaptability in our defiance of everything big, well–organized and numerical. For example, we'd found a small house to be leased by Deirdre's business containing a tiny apartment I rented for a song all situated on a large piece of property owned by the composite category. Somehow this made us look as desperate to the IRS as we often were, as reliable as loan officers and policemen required us to appear, and surprisingly formidable to creditors and collection agencies. Of some things we had only one—e.g., Metropolis—while of others we had two—a flawless Toyota pickup and a yellow, 1955 Buick Roadmaster that sometimes passed for a valuable collector's item and sometimes for junk. And then there were a few three–things, like the telephone: 1) the number of DeeDee's Kitchen Kleen, 2) her employer's number, 3) the unpublicized number of our first life, the secret one.

51

This last had to be—like other precious things—portable.

"Maybe he's guessing," I say. "Try imitating the answering machine. Has he threatened you? Can we get him for harass—"

"Talks like a member of the family."

"Turn on the Englebert Humperdink tape."

"He liked it." Deirdre sighs. "Just think of the ozone layer. Or did you know the Sahara gets nine miles wider every year? By comparison, this problem's really, really human."

"Look, I know the timing sucks—"

"I gotta go."

"I'd impersonate a psycho, but I'm caught in that damn demonstra—"

"I know."

"How could you know?"

"You're on TV."

My closest friend—variously Arnold, Arno, Army, Aardvark, whom I fondly call Sport—is forty–six years old and getting his MBA. He has a Ph.D. in comparative lit, a bizarre but unpublishable novel about a transvestite rock band in Saigon during the sixties, two fine books of poems, a trunkful of unfilmed screenplays, a dreary French one–act that actually ran to good reviews once in Lyons, the sixteen–track master for an experimental jazz album—minus only the vocals—on which he plays sax and keyboards, a hilarious photo–essay on Montana, and a partially revised dissertation about the evolution of medieval scripts. He also has an eleven year old daughter and a debt in six figures. Arno is witty, hard–working, prolific, and heartbroken. I haven't heard his voice in almost two years, and this is because we've become too painful to bear each other. In his last postcard he told me that if things go as he hopes, he will have completed the MBA just in time to send his daughter to an academy in Massachusetts. If not, he may keep her out awhile. The public schools are, I gather, jungles, and Arno isn't sure he wants her to learn what America teaches anyway. "Are the private ones better?" I once asked. "They're businesses," he explained, meaning that you can get whatever you pay for. He rarely mentions his daughter's mother, may not know what happened to her—one of the funniest and most charming mortals I've ever known who seems to have gotten out of bed one morning, taken two aspirins, and vanished—but I gather she sends money from time to time. He doesn't write much that's personal, mentions a date now and then or makes a tired joke about a subject he's studying—"insurance market-ing demographics" or "sales theory" or "cyclical patterns in hyper-consumerism"—and I've learned that it's a rule of our continuing friendship to edit my own postcards in similar fashion. Once on the phone in a frank moment we divulged our suspicions to each other and haven't spoken since.

In the backseat Metropolis lets out a remarkable noise, one any blues singer would make if he or she could. It sounds like keening but may be gas. I glance into the mirror, meet the mysterious dry buttonhole that was my doggy's eye. For a moment I maintain with Metro's socket that directness which, in the case of seeing creatures, is thought to be the extreme point of intimacy, the holding of a gaze, exchanging stare for stare. This may be as close to nature as I get. Metropolis eats, moves, makes noise, eliminates, and these prosy facts give him a position in my affairs distinct from carpeting and house plants. He represents, in some ultimately befuddling sense, a version of me as matter and motion. I long to feel that we share a world but can't. Today I'm curious about this pit in his face, happy that I don't have to be coy about staring at it. It has a little yellow crust at the edge of the withered skin, a crust that I've noticed is sometimes thicker than others, and if only I could master my urge to vomit at such phenomena, I'd like to know whether the gunk comes from inside the hole or is formed on the lid. I have no idea what this would tell me, but I have difficulty watching the stuff come and go everyday without sometimes wondering about it. This seems understandable enough. I stare at his forehead a long time, but Metro never acknowledges me. Finally his seeing eye passes across the mirror on its way outdoors.

Deirdre received Metropolis instead of her Ph.D. She'd finished four years of a clinical psychology program before realizing that, though compassionate, she didn't like humans, and was trying to salvage something from her labor by looking into interdisciplinary degrees. At the university where she was a grad student and where I had recently ended my career as a young historian, there were, still are, several anthropologists conducting weird but interesting research—a guy studying altruism in higher vertebrates, two women with a huge grant for observing women with huge grants, and an Australian who believes consciousness originated in salamanders—and having partied and chatted with their lab assistants over the years, Deirdre figured that some variety of life-science might be worth looking into.

I don't know what happened. She left one morning to go talk to someone and returned just before lunchtime flush–faced, tight–lipped, with a blood stain on her sleeve and a really gruesome looking beast in the back seat of her Datsun. One of the creature's eyes was gone, but this injury wasn't fresh. There were two small, hairless pink spots on his neck, a horrible odor of something like rubbing alcohol, grey–brown mattes of doggy fur everywhere and, on the rag in which he was wrapped, shit–looking smears that for some reason had no odor at all. He appeared all but technically dead, and I figured we were going through the life–saving motions because lost causes were something

53

people like us sometimes had to go through with. Later I realized that Metropolis had never appeared other than all but technically dead, that his perpetually moribund appearance had in fact no relation whatsoever to his longevity. We took him to a vet. He stayed a month. They removed his hindleg. He ate dog food by truckloads. His shit started to smell. The bill came to $5,938. Some months later Deirdre found in the mailbox a very unofficial–looking, white, unpostmarked package containing various documents that—we have always assumed—constitute every trace of her having ever attended the university.

Something seems to be happening up ahead. I see a number of drivers opening their doors, stepping out, some hiking themselves up by putting one foot on the floorboard and their hands on the top of the open door, craning their necks to see. I have no idea what they're looking at. However, I do make out something, an article of clothing maybe, sailing through the air and, a second later, a stream of water, like a fire hydrant spewing. In a few minutes a half–clothed man comes running through the snarl of cars with an annoyed policewoman in only half–serious pursuit. She's wearing this Darth Vadar outfit minus the cape, and I don't even want to *think* about how hot she is in there. I flick on the radio, start searching for a news report. There's a helicopter overhead, so somebody must be in a position to say what's going on. Between 91.5 and 97.2 I hear a million dollars worth of advertising and the history of rock and roll but nothing I need to know. I buzz Deirdre.

"Jesus Abraham Washington, do you think I've got nothing better to do than watch TV? Hey, you're no hub of the universe. You're not even the main character. A single individual, one white male heterosexual not physically challenged anglo protestant individual!"

"I thought the demonstration—"

"Do demonstrations matter? Demonstrations every minute. Demonstrations in Patagonia. You and me, we must have a hundred demonstrations between us. Live cinema, real blood. D'you know how many gallons of non–degradable pesticide this year alone—"

"Sorry sorry sorry sorry sorry."

"The police got rough, so a demonstrator tried to pee on them. Fear of bodily fluids, etc. So they brought in a fire hose, tried to break up the group, tangle the guys in …I dunno, they were using something looked like fishnets. Then the newscast switched to hand-helds, lots of drama, jiggling, splashes, but I couldn't see for poobah."

"How far behind me do the cars stretch?"

"Way back, and no trouble spotting you, boy. Wheeew! Like a eunuch in a nudist colony."

"That guy still on the line?"

"Beats me. Not my problem. I'm outa here."

Long silence, but I can still hear her breathing.

"I'll stay near the phone," I say. "No matter what happens, you can reach me."

"R—, I don't think I'm going to go through with it," she finally says. Her voice has changed, almost as if she were talking to me. "Really, I've thought, and I don't see any reason why I can't just spend the rest of the day here on this sofa. It's an imperfect world. Maybe the demonstration'll surprise me! Besides, no reason to weep for justice—"

"You *don't* have to go through with it. You really don't."

"Asshole."

I take a deep breath. "Okay, you don't have to go through with it because science will discover a solution. A vigorous economic system, despite temporary imbalances, will correct itself, so you don't have to go through with it. In a mass democracy, the people can be trusted to recognize their interests and find a workable remedy. You don't have to go through with it because the media will provide the really necessary information, and the experts will display penetrating insight into domestic entanglements and the complex problems of foreign cultures. You also don't have to go through with it because hollywood is already examining our deepest beliefs, and television continually invents plots to foreground our most disturbing contradictions. In our arts and culture generally, nothing essential is missing, so relax: you don't have to go through with it. Our schools can certainly be relied upon to confront our citizenry with the hard lessons of the past, so you don't need to do anything for that reason, and the universities will consistently encourage the most provocative ideas. In fact, you might as well spend the day on the sofa because psychologists know how to correct the physiological causes of your aberrant behavior, and social workers can identify the nurturing and supportive conditions necessary for your successful readjustment. Most of all, you can be sure there'll be no need for egomaniacs like you to recall us to ourselves, for our freely elected leaders are in little danger of losing direction or misrepresenting what it means to be us. The future stretches before us as an inviting vista, and we possess ingenuity, wealth and resources without foreseeable end."

"Thanks." She means it.

"If we lived in a world where it mattered, I'd tell you I love you."

"I know." Dial tone.

It hasn't always been this way. Once upon a time I lived an undivided life. I had a career, good prospects, and even if my marriage was no better than others, it was indisputably a marriage. What happened is in this box on the passenger seat, or perhaps I merely recollect my ordeal as something contained there. In my aging mother's front closet between her house—slippers and the Mr. Coffee she pulls out whenever her children visit is another box just like the one here. On

55

a shelf in the office technically still assigned to me at the university I haven't visited in a decade is a third; in the L.L. Bean doggy–bed Metropolis won't use in DeeDee's Kitchen Kleen kitchen is a fourth, and numerous not quite identical ones have been scattered in the sundry nooks of my friends' and relatives' homes. In fact, custodianship of such a box would seem the all but inevitable consequence of knowing me. On the afternoon when the chair of the history department confided in his fatherly way that tenure was a surmountable but inescapable obstacle to my prosperity, I went right out and purchased nine reams of computer paper. I took these home, dumped the paper onto the floor surrounding my printer, made a neat and intricate arrangement of the large cardboard containers, and began to fill them with everything I knew that I knew. They are one foot in three dimensions. Their tops, which are removable, are blue. When three years later I presented one of these boxes to the Dean of Arts and Sciences, he hefted it, hmmm–ed approvingly, lifted his patriarch's shaggy eyebrows and said that the university placed great faith in me. It would wait. Two more years passed, during which time the boxes grew in wisdom and stature. When next the Dean hefted my box, he observed chuckling that it was considerably heavier than when he'd last balanced it on his knee. He raised a single shaggy eyebrow, said that, being a biologist, he understood the exhausting and slow process of obtaining reliable data, respected my commitment as well as—in the quaint idiom of scientists addressing persons in the humanities—my "lofty ideals." The university still placed great faith in me, he went on, though somewhat less faith than formerly. It would wait another year.

I can't say what happened, or I can and will say but my saying will sound peculiar. It's continually threatened with passive voice. My "own" fortune is recounted like a spell that came over me, and yet I certainly authored everything myself. If—as I believe I believe—forces are to blame, then only changed circumstances could reveal the names of these forces to me. At any rate, I became interested in Leonardo da Vinci because the world I mistook for a world was. You didn't have to be a genius to see that, since 1800, Leonardo had functioned in the west as an icon. Whatever an age or movement or class imagined itself to be, however it conceived its aspirations, paradoxes, the obstacles to desire, achievement, hope, it sooner or later incarnated them in Leonardo. Or more accurately, in "Leonardo," for in retrospect every representation separated from its base. Sometimes, as under Mussolini or during the Risorgimento, this quotation, this "Leonardo," amounted to outright propaganda. Other times it seemed merely naive, perverse, or blind. I had no illusion of salvaging the "real" Leonardo from this hodge podge. I just wanted to explain how he'd functioned in an interpretive economy. I became convinced that a minor cultural history of the west,

56

at least since about 1750, could be written as the history of Leonardo's versions, or of "Leonardos". There were systems within systems, of course, circles within circles, but "Leonardo da Vinci" continually shaped the empty center of an all–inclusive sphere. The idea seemed ambitious but focused. It looked half done as soon as clearly conceived. In short, my teachers dubbed it a "perfect dissertation topic," and (wink) "M'boy, there's a book in it!"

Before the Dean ever raised his shaggy brows at me, however, I knew my iconography of "Leonardo da Vinci" was in trouble. For reasons I still can't explain, Leonardo da Vinci wasn't satisfied with being "Leonardo da Vinci." He wanted to be a garage. Everything disposable but odd and interesting and perhaps one day useful to somebody had gotten stored there, and any attempt to bracket the cornucopia, if only to preserve it, seemed self–defeating. The problem wasn't just the volume of facts or historical junk; it was that, by comparison, every "Leonardo"—even mine, even my quotation of a quotation—seemed less seductive than any Leonardo. I'd started out assuming that other ages had done something to him, that they'd projected themselves onto Leonardo as if he were a blank or a mirror or, at most, a textured surface. But now with time running out I found myself thinking that "reality" or "life" or "history" or "nature" or some other phantasm I didn't believe I believed in had done something to him. *I* felt like a projection. *I* was doing the quotation. Being civilization's garage was simply what it meant to be him. It was underway in his notebooks, his drawings, his paintings, the anecdotes by contemporaries, etc. From birth to grave this bastard son of an upwardly mobile petty clerk had struggled with one ambition: to defeat "Leonardo da Vinci," become *this*, escape the story I was writing. Everything I suppressed started to look like his essence. Every interest I exposed was my own. All of which is just a way of admitting that my "Leonardo" had turned into Leonardo again.

I wasn't beaten, but I knew I needed a stronger theoretical frame and at least six months. The frame, I figured, I could devise; the time I'd have to steal. I concocted a dozen queries for books that I feared might be published if anyone were energetic, silly, and opportunistic enough to undertake them: *Why You Already Know Everything You Need To*; *The Greenhouse Effect and Biblical Prophecy*; *Everywoman's Twelve Steps to Sexual Fulfillment in Marriage*; *Professional Writing without Books*; and, my masterwork, *Win!* I then sent spectacular but plausible–sounding descriptions of these and other equally savory projects to forty or so junior editors at our most prestigious publishing houses and, in a few weeks, received nine replies: seven expressing varying degrees of non–committal enthusiasm, one from a woman named Sharp (no joke) who scolded me for my crassness before—out of deference to intellectual freedom—offering a tiny advance, and another that reminisced about our afternoon drinking rum punch in Bangkok. But among the responses was exactly what I needed: one hand–signed letter from a celebrated publisher on white bond paper with an ostentatious letterhead entirely in black ink. Using a borrowed printer, I matched typefaces, drafted a note expressing deep admiration for *The Cultural Iconography of "Leonardo da Vinci"*, offering some helpful criticisms, insightful commentary, discussing its relation to Leonardo studies, to cultural historiography, mentioning prospective audiences, and concluding with an offer to negotiate terms immediately upon completion. I then attached this with rubber cement to the white and black stationery so that the body of the letter was completely covered but the letterhead, address, date, acknowledgment still showed at top and the signature at bottom. For twenty–seven cents plus tax the local copy center made me three perfect copies on stationery-quality bond. I put one in my tenure file, sent another to my department chair, and took the liberty of passing the third along to the Dean himself.

My superiors were overjoyed. I was assured that the ordeal of tenure would conclude triumphantly for me, that my personal and professional happiness was a fait accompli. The university placed complete faith etcetera. Just let the Dean know when the book was in press. Everyone would, of course, wait.

Deirdre and I then hit up parents, siblings, maiden aunts, rich cousins, friends, enemies, loan sharks, taxi–drivers, frightened children, and every credit union in the city for, in all, twenty–three thousand bucks and hightailed it to northern Michigan. I still remember this interlude as among the most romantic of my life. The leave of absence my department allowed me was exactly the time I needed, or believed that I did, and Deirdre, who hadn't yet traded in her doctorate for Metropolis and so was preparing for exams that year, made sure I didn't squander a minute. We put me on a schedule; I wrote and wrote. This many pages by noon, that many more before supper. Deirdre monitored my progress with a green pocket calendar we'd annotated for the project. We had a ritual of tearing out the day at seven–thirty if I'd made my quota, toasting "Leonardo da Vinci"—we wiggled our fingers in the air to mark the quotation—with vodka gimlets, and sitting by the window fantasizing the future till bedtime. Whenever I checked off a chapter, we dressed—linen suit for me, she wore heels—and drove forty miles to a tolerable restaurant where over salmon steaks we discussed nothing but the paintings by unknown artists we would spend our holidays collecting in obscure places and the view we wanted from our retirement cottage in Nova Scotia. When I reached the halfway point we rode away on bikes and went skinny dipping; at two thirds we found a drive–in movie.

But if the truth be told, I didn't enjoy stopping work, even to celebrate, and I suppose this reluctance should have been my first warning. I lived in a perfect fever; I woke each morning, feet already on the floor, walking toward the computer. I ate breakfast and usually lunch at my desk, and more than once Deirdre had to throw the circuit breaker to make me come to dinner. I slept like death; we made whallopping, mattress–bashing love. Years later on the rare occasions when I could persuade Deirdre to recall those days, she always insisted that we were two miles from the nearest water, that our cabin was at the end of a gravel road and bordered a scraggly pasture, but I distinctly remember a pond that turned a remarkable shade of ocher most mornings. She says there was snow and ice. I don't remember snow or ice. What did I think about my *Cultural Iconography of "Leonardo da Vinci"*? What did I think about the institution that had placed its faith in me? What did I think about my family and friends whose money I was spending hand over fist? Oh hell, what did I think? I remember thinking that my initial idea was turning upside down. What I'd naively imagined as something history had done to Leonardo, now looked like something he had done to us, to me. All the power seemed to run against the flow of time. Leonardo's "life"—and I never once kidded myself that I knew what a "life" was—had acquired a future tense. It seemed less a matter of influence than of contamination. I felt unable to make sense of the past, which is to say I could make no sense of the present, which is to say I couldn't tell my story, without making sense of this "life," although I never asked myself what making sense of Leonardo da Vinci's "life"—or, for that matter, "Leonardo da Vinci's 'life'"—could involve. At the same time, I recall a commonplace incident from the same period that belies this innocence. I was working at my computer one morning while Deirdre changed a bulb in the hall when, all at once, I broke out guffawing. I heard the hall light click, heard steps approaching. Without a second's hesitation, without a glimmer of that self–consciousness I customarily misidentify as thinking, I hit the "save" key and exited the screen. Deirdre stopped, asked what was so funny? I stood, smiled, shrugged, and wandered off into the kitchen. I remember feeling a little uneasy, noticing that my mind really was as blank as I pretended about what, only seconds earlier, absorbed my whole attention—as if *I* were what had been erased. And yet I could feel my heart pounding and knew that, as soon as I recalled my computer file, the answer to Deirdre's question would be waiting. How to make sense of lies that occur as naturally as groaning? How to account for those times when, to become what one later is, one becomes a stranger? I kept on working in this state of narcosis. Every deception—they must have been legion—seemed to die with my voice or prior to it. The fact that I never asked myself what I was hiding or why or even what in the

somber tale of history's repressions could've struck me as guffawable—
all this seems to point to one explanation. I was very scared.

None of which recounts what was happening, only what had to
have been happening to account for what, eventually, did. For what
was happening was that I was undeviatingly happy, was twenty–four
glorious hours a day, seven remarkable days every week, for six and a
half months, happy. I produced over five hundred pages of revised text,
not counting drafts or rejected versions. I incessantly admired, enjoyed, and lusted after my wife as men often imagine they'll do but
don't. I felt an unshakable faith in the course of the world. Happy.

If I must count, then I suppose it was near the beginning of the
two–hundred and third day of this idyll when I positioned myself in
front of Deirdre one morning and broke irreparably with everything I'd
ever known I'd ever known. For no clear reason, that morning is the
only experience in my life I remember being undergone by another
person. Perhaps this is because, of all present, the person I up to that
instant was was last to grasp what was happening and so can't serve
as witness. In truth, he may never have grasped what happened at all.
For him probably all that occurred that morning was that he opened his
mouth in his customary bovine joy and oblivion, intent on uttering an
insipid nugget of amiability to his adored wife, when the noise of a
stranger's voice came out of his throat. Instantly the pond and horizon
disappeared into a flash of perfectly white light, he felt an anguish
beyond words, love filled his heart, and he died. I, on the other hand,
was less fortunate. Anyway, I recall the man I was standing in canvas
shorts with muscular but thin knees, beside a banister with one leg
flung over the rail, on the porch of our cottage, and with a really stupid
looking grin—can someone observe the stupid–looking–ness of his own
grin? can he observe it and keep on grinning?—a stupid looking grin on
his face, his heart throbbing, and forehead clammy. The sun was yellow
as a lemon, the sky was the identical blue Leonardo da Vinci woke to
as a boy. That about to be dead man was so happy, happy, and
something else too. Deirdre sat there in a pale green skirt, serene, far
less confident about the course of the world than he was but knowing,
just the same, that the two of them would thrive, that they'd make a
way for others, that however much they talked of fissures and margins,
they'd always remain in the abundant midst and so would take
responsibility for mending, struggling, resisting, criticizing, because
they! they! were among the fortunate few for whom the universe—
pandemonium though it might be—had worked. She looked up, laughed
at him a little, one corner of her mouth smirking just to show that, okay,
even if she loved this klutz to distraction, here was no sappy woman.

"I have an announcement," he said.

Deirdre jumped. She tried not to, tried to remain ethereal, but he saw the jump, and knew everything that for two hundred and two days had gone without saying. It was eight a.m., the first of August, seventeen days till their return. Not since January had he stood so leisurely on the porch at eight a.m., not since announcing his plan to Deirdre the previous December had he spoken in so soft, so measured a tone. They'd stopped counting pages at the three–fourths mark two months before, had continued toasting every night, carried out all the rituals, but without the watchfulness and calculation the rituals were designed to obscure. Neither had acknowledged a change or offered any explanation. I suppose they thought talking would destroy it. They'd continued the routines in that serene and perfect understanding that reckless people call "being of one mind." The pages in the large cardboard box on the floor beside the computer had reached seven inches. These people were tired, but they had accomplished a great feat. A cardinal fluttered in a shrub beside the eaves and, although there was no pond, its surface was ocher and a mallard floated on it.

"Y—yes?" Deirdre's lip trembled.

He took a breath, stepped to her. Other men might not call Deirdre lovely, but at that moment and on a few occasions before and since, he and I have both been entirely convinced that we'd unhesitatingly do for her what ancient warriors were said to have been ready to do for only the loveliest women on the earth. Not that Deirdre cares a damn, but we do, did. He took her by the shoulders. She rose, grabbed his arms.

"Honey…"

My voice caught in his throat. Until that second, he had never even dreamed what I was going to say.

"Honey, I'm writing a novel."

"YOU'RE WHAAAAAAAAAAAAAAA?!"

Leonardo's last dimostrazione is a reasonably straightforward affair. As a youth, his notebooks tell us, he once stood before the mouth of a cave, hesitant to enter but reluctant to depart. Perhaps it was just the swallows dipping above the olive branches, the cool breath of the rock, or maybe the grass edging over his sandals that held him there, amazed at all the secrets the world contained. He would later compose a hymn to the sun, map light, deify vision, study fire and eyes, and would claim that love comes of knowing, that penetration yields to beauty, never masters it, but peering into the cave's black throat, his knees bent and brows shaded in an old man's crouch, Leonardo saw Monte Albano's reds and ochers flicker briefly like shadows on a wall. If he ducked the overhanging rocks, groped his way along the wet stone, slipped on moss and mud, ran his finger on a shard of quartz, sniffed the mold and loam, he never said so, for the moment between darkness and light seems to have figured his memory more than anything he touched with his hands. But if he did enter, then he only discovered as a youth what he would discover so many times as a man, that descent never gets you to the bottom of anything, and so re—emerged into the sunlight more puzzled than before. Perhaps he felt then the smallness of his village. Vinci's rambling walls and lopsided cottages teetered on a spur of Albano's slope like a drunken peddlar, and trudging back to his father's villa, passing the stone house where he no longer heard his mother's voice, Leonardo must've ached to run and stumble, to fling himself forward, to fall. Or perhaps he simply turned his back on the cave, hearing the hornets in the cypresses as distant now, a question, and for the first time knew the earth as somewhere in—between.

Money soon brought his father to Florence, and Ser Piero brought his bastard. It was a city in love with the sky. In nearby Careggi, Marsilio Ficino was just completing his translations of Plato, and by the time Leonardo was installed in Verrochio's workshop, Ficino's disciples had pretty well split the universe up and down. Beauty rose, bodies fell, everything alive was in motion. In the afternoon lavender—and—orange—robed buyers from Constantinople, Salonica, and Chios elbowed one another in the narrow streets, twisting brocade about their fingers and scrutinizing silk vendors with yellow eyes. The scaffolding was coming down from Brunelleschi's cupola at the duomo, going up for Alberti's façade at Santa Maria Novella, and amid the sweat, laughter, and fierce light Leonardo discovered everything his greedy heart could dream. Verrochio taught him perspective, gilding, and the new oils from Belgium, and in the workshop next door he watched Antonio Pollaiuolo lower himself into a tub of clammy plaster to study the contour of his own muscles. At the Studium Generale he could hear Aristotle's last holdout, the Greek Argyropoulos, still preaching the *Physics*, and Brunelleschi's geometry teacher, Old Toscanelli, showed him the Astrolabe, cross—staff, and crystal—sphere. There were wars, plagues, murder, pageantry, friends like Migliorotti with the lovely voice and the charlatan Masini. In Florence you lived beneath a firmament as blue as the mind of God. Leonardo should have thrived there.

For what connected Giotto's tower to Christ's throne, made geometry into a religion, and contrived capital, rhetoric, ancient learning, the pox and hokum into an endless theater of man—was the human eye. Fifty years before Leonardo arrived in Florence Brunelleschi had painted a picture of the baptistery on a panel with a hole in it. If you sat on the front steps of the cathedral, stood the panel up on your knees—painted side away from you—and peeked through the hole, you could see the real baptistery fifty feet in front of you. If you then reached around the panel with your hand and held a mirror up in front of the hole, you saw the same thing—except for the eyeball staring back. For the first time, reality and art had become interchangeable. A generation later Alberti would make Brunelleschi's magic into a method simple enough that twelve–year–olds could calculate the proportions of a horse's head on a mural, and by mid–century Ghiberti had coupled painter's perspective to medieval optics and light mysticism. People were wearing spectacles, Neoplatonists were experiencing rapture in a glance, and Galileo's telescope was in the offing. Sponsored by the hottest studio in Italy's classiest town during the years when the modern world was being made, son of an upwardly mobile father, possessed of dazzling beauty, mythical eloquence, facility in both hands, and the smartest eye the Renaissance could boast, Leonardo joined the Florentine painters' guild in 1472 with success in a bucket. But over the next ten years his important commissions were abandoned unfinished. Patrons became leery of hiring him. He was indicted for sodomy. His stepmother gave birth to a legitimate heir. And when at thirty he struck out for Milan, he called himself a musician, sculptor and military engineer.

Perhaps it was his lack of Latin or his practice of a craft not highly regarded or just that he was too much the tinkerer for the humanists' high minds, perhaps it was wanderlust, politics, money, but having walked on a mountain and looked into a cave, how could he be at home again in water, earth or air? It was as if gazing into the rock the boy had discovered longing and was astonished less at what his eyes revealed than at himself. He could doubt China and his own pancreas more readily than a buckthorn twig, and the visible world of color and shape seemed as inescapable as the clouds descending on Anchiano, but if the landscape was your mother, then you rested on her breast uneasily, orphaned, beneath a sky that left you dizzy, on grounds that shut you out. How could anyone live on the surface of things? And standing on Albano's slope, the boy had known that a cave wanted looking into. For just a moment he'd turned away, faced up into the bright firmament until the heat ate his brain, and then turning back, he'd imagined nature's marvel in a green ball, fading to red then blue and purple, until at last he saw only blackness and knew that his eyes were closed, that the darkness was of his own making, that he'd never seen anything at all. Or so it seems now.

Anyway, perhaps that's why, even though Leonardo couldn't love Milan—or *because* he couldn't love Milan—it was the one place his life made sense. For there was never any hope of feeling at home in the Castello Sforzesco, no depths a painter of scant reputation could peer into, and very little hooplah about the life of the mind. In Milan there was just dominion. Whatever didn't serve it didn't stay. And Leonardo—finding himself unyoung, unfamous, disinherited and unemployed—learned to flatter and grovel with the best of them, designed the altarpieces Ambrogio de Predis had contracted, contrived the carnival stunts Ludovico Sforza dribbled his way, until finally he got a chance to make his ingenuity pay off and so concocted before the gathered nobility of Italy and Spain a clockwork universe of spinning planets and musical gods that simply sucked the onlookers' breath away. Milan, not being inclined to fine discriminations, assumed he was a wizard.

Were they just wrong? By 1493 Leonardo had managed to persuade a clay model of his twenty–three foot tall horse to stand unsquarely on three legs in the Castello's piazza, so becoming about as close to godlike as he would ever be, and was furiously surveying foundries in search of some way to melt the bronze—sixty tons of it now—so he could complete the statue. He'd given up his dream of making the behemoth rear on its hindlegs, and he still didn't know how he'd join the different sections, assuming he could find a furnace hot enough and huge enough to cast them, but the clay model stood there as much a monument to Leonardo's prowess as to the Sforzas'. You could hardly blame him for thinking he was onto something. So when the funds began to dwindle and the French marched on Lombardy, when the horse's bronze got sold for armaments and Salai spit in Leonardo's face and Ludovico disappeared, Leonardo refused to panic. Even if nature seemed impossibly intricate, he was mapping it, replicating God's machinery. All he needed was time. But then one night he awoke to the glint of black curls beside his bed and knew there'd been a miscalculation. By morning fist fights and shouting filled the streets. Louis Douze had taken the Castello, the clay horse was demolished, and Leonardo had to flee town.

In the dark you become your senses—the drooling of water past your ear, the breeze across your toes, the rough soapstone shard that fits into your palm. Silence wakes you, and you suck on each sensation, swill its juice across your tongue. Even if Leonardo's notebooks don't mention it, surely he entered the cave! Ducking under the granite lip, he must've run his fingers along a fissure, slid his foot across the pulpy loam. The rock unexpectedly disappeared overhead, and he groped for a ridge—left? right? upward? back?—until he touched it. The earth apparently yawned there. He could feel the wet air drift past his nose and knew that the hectic vapors from earth's fire were seeking heaven, their natural level, probably imprisoning themselves overhead in a hollow, giving the mountain life. The smell was as dank as rotten beef. It must've struck Leonardo then that he might be standing scarcely an arm's length from a chasm, a depth that, were you to see it in the light, would drive the spirits from your knees and fill your head with morbid

64

humors. He squinted, but all he could see were melting shapes, the emptying of color into a single purpling gray. No one, not his father, not his uncle Francesco, not even the surly brickmaker who'd dragged his mother away—no man could boast of experience here. Perhaps at the chasm's bottom would be a vortex swirling earth and souls together; perhaps the boy was standing only inches from the primordial stew. He reached overhead to steady himself against the ridge, touched nothing. His foot oozed over slick stone. Why did shadows always seem to be going away from you? Suddenly he felt himself falling, knew that the breeze on his face was his own body toppling through air. He saw the stippled gray as fantastic rocks rushing toward him. Where was up? And in a desperate lunge he jerked his shoulders back, shot his elbows outward, and splooshed his buttocks down on the muddy ground. He'd come no more than four steps from the entrance. He could see now that the cave's mouth opened into a small vestibule, that the fissure in the rock spread out above and to one side. The dark lay further in.

And even if he followed it, even if he blundered on into his own ignorance, risked everything, came to an end, what could Leonardo—or anyone—have hoped to find?

Some questions you don't stop to answer. With his satchels full of scribbles and tools, Leonardo traveled from Milan to Mantua, where he sketched Isabella d'Este's profile on a napkin, and then on to besieged Venice, where he designed the paraphernalia needed to sink Sultan Bayazid's bellicose galleons but probably never told anyone. By the time he reached Florence in the spring of 1500, rumors of his prowess had been circulating a decade, and he entered to a celebrity's welcome. He even accepted a couple of commissions, not that his patrons ever received a painting, but by 1502 he'd wandered off again, this time with the army of Cesare Borgia, drawing the occasional tactical map, trading quips with Machiavelli, and marching belligerently on—of all places—Florence. Where he blithely returned a year later, began a portrait of Francesco del Giocondo's chubby wife—or someone else we now call by that name—talked a dying man out of his own cadaver, and abandoned the most prestigious project of his career. Though Leonardo was by this time just over fifty and nowhere near dead, it was obvious he'd never get to the end of anything. The cracked stones he passed beside the Arno interested him more than the canal he was commissioned to dig. An odd sound could divert his attention for hours. Every morning he rose as if daylight weren't anticipated, and he consumed whole afternoons sketching the quarter moons in his toenails. In 1506 he concocted an excuse to return to Milan where he dabbled in architecture, met the anatomical prodigy Marcantonio della Torre, and began countless treatises. He then wasted three years in Rome discovering that not even Bramante, not even a Medici Pope, not all the wisdom of antiquity could recall a chance once it was gone, and when at age sixty–four he somehow crossed the Alps in a grandiose, So there! to everyone who'd ever gnawed a thumb at him, Leonardo's last hope was just to make sense, not of nature now, but of his own plans. Even if he couldn't make a horse, he still thought he could make a book.

But there was no light. How strange to wake up in an unfamiliar bedchamber one spring morning in an incomprehensible country beneath a film of silver–gray clouds only to discover yourself adrift in longing for a sky that never mattered when it floated over every rooftop but now that death looms blacker than a lecher's lie seems like the most precious vision your heart ever knew. On a table in the cellar of the Clos–Lucé he spread out his 6000 pages. He made piles and outlines, conceived titles and divisions: *The Book of the Human Form* by Maestro Leonardo, philosopher and Florentine, formerly of Vinci, in fourteen parts. The drawings were countless. His notes comprised a lifetime. And lunching with earringed bishops and squires from Chambord, he began to speak of his former disappointments as mere preparations, the acts of an impostor. But then perusing drawings of burr–reed and knee joints one night he noticed his lines were turning dull. The flash of light he remembered snatching beside a drainage ditch near Rapallo shone only dimly now, and when, lying in bed, he thought he heard the echo of boys' voices in a Florentine loggia, Leonardo feared madness and set about to memorize every principle that would hold itself firm.

It was then he began to fear that he'd taken a wrong turn, lived his life backwards or upside down. He began rampaging his loose notebook leaves, hoping to find some ratio, parable, or pun that might transfix him. It wasn't order he wanted. Optics was order, math was order, mechanics was order, perspective and hydraulics and painting were order, the entirety of everything was order. What he needed was a place to rest his eyes. Shapes writhed. Pages moved. If the little King, François Premier, bustled down the castle path, Leonardo would leap at the interruption. He warbled, sapdrunk and reckless, spoke beguiling nonsense, maybe even believed his own words. Never had chatter delighted him so, and the King—bouncing like a spaniel—could mouth no platitude so witless that Leonardo couldn't map the stars with it. The blue–cedar boughs surrounding the mansion, the dripping stones and somber moss beneath his feet, the spring water that was cold enough to take your breath away, everything reached out to him now, and embracing His bedazzled Highness warmly, Leonardo would rush back inside to write it all down. But once alone he grew muddled. Outlines merged. Instead of daylight, he found caverns, depths, obscurities further down. For all his experience, Leonardo could make a book no better than he could make a statue or a canal. The miracle was over.

Leonardo da Vinci had flopped. So when Salai finally appeared at Leonardo's southernmost window—black curls glistening, mouth juicy as a plum—and asked Leonardo what Leonardo was laboring so mightily not to ask himself, i.e., How for Chrissakes had this happened?—well, maybe in four lifetimes Leonardo could've answered, but in four days?

It's 1519, and the experimental method hasn't been invented yet. Humans have been using their eyes since long before Aristotle, but to have an experience, you have to do more than just look. You have to come undone. That is, you have to look until you don't have to look anymore, until acting blindly isn't acting, isn't anything, is just so natural that, when you finally come to grief over the obvious, you won't be able to explain how you could have been so stupid. Nothing's ever as convincing as what your life was organized not to know. Anyway, Leonardo, who was one of the world's great contrivers and harped on experience as on an incantation, glimpsed these conditions but confusedly. He dribbled balls on the parquet to study percussion and compared changes in distance against changes in incline of successive shots from a mortar, but if Salai—or whoever it was that Leonardo became Leonardo to ignore—if Salai hadn't insisted that Leonardo's struggles were evasions, Leonardo might never have suspected what every chemistry lab–assistant knows before taking out her second student loan, that the purpose of exacting arrangements isn't transparency; it's speed. There's never enough time to defeat the past. A medieval library on weight and motion—which without Latin you couldn't read anyway and required fifteen years to gloss and three generations to refute—could be forgotten in a single afternoon if you just gathered a crowd of patrons in a belltower and tossed some anvils out a window. The point being not to prove anything, even less to put nature on a leash, but merely to repeat a mistake often enough till you see what you've always seen.

Now, Leonardo da Vinci, though innocent of laboratory methods and half a century before Galileo, would here at the end of his days concoct the world's first social science experiment, then die without noticing he'd done anything weird, without saying a word to anyone or ever writing it down, so depriving us of any inkling of it—all because with time running out he'd realized that, having looked in a cave just once, he'd never seen anything at all, and so couldn't confront Salai's yellow monstrosity in the courtyard until he'd contrived his first experience a second time.

Sorry. This is simply the best I can do.

For on Monte Albano fifty years earlier, Leonardo had backed out. He'd clambered to his feet from the cave's muddy floor where he'd sat feeling foolish and small, had hoisted a knee into the wall's crack, pinched his skin as he dragged his belly over the stone, and poising with the husky taste of fetor in his throat, had realized he was acting crazy. Did he intend to go sticking his nose into every profundity he happened onto? Okay, maybe you couldn't just forget about a cave, but still, you didn't have to explore it alone. There were elders, guides, companions. They could show him what to watch for, what a sound or smell meant, offer wisdom. Only fools descended without a torch. Why for God's sake was he doing this? And amazed at how simple his predicament had suddenly become, the boy was backing away from suicide and what felt at that moment like a sandstone shelf, when the ground disappeared. It may have been a table of porous shale made fragile by several millenia of dripping; perhaps it was a half–rotten spruce trunk left there by underground floods and coated with lime; it was definitely not the gigantic back of a mythic beaked tortoise hungrily awaiting the arrival of befuddled carnage, but for all Leonardo cared, it could have been all three. For without a surface to stand on, without light, planes, colors, lines, what good's lucidity? And Leonardo was falling, reaching out for night's cusp, clawing at a roughness that slithered away, tearing the very sinews that fifty years later in Marcantonio della Torre's closet under the candle's waxy light with flies humming round his ear he'd watch being peeled one by one like threads from a spool, each cord plucked loose and flapping damply on the bench, until with the pink carpus glowing in the flame Leonardo would recognize that the hand was a miracle of intricate, twisting machinery and so, despite the teeming air, would nearly choke when the anatomist snickered: Only the beginning! It was these very sinews that the boy felt rip and burn in his palm as the darkness of the cave whistled past, heard them pop loose, the crunch of cartilage, skin scraping from his wrist as his foot kicked sludge, his face bashed the dark, not sure if toppling had come to get him or if this was just the cutting cold that startled pain into your bones. A flapping sound, high squeals. The sour perfume of rot. His nose struck stone, head bounced backward, knee crashed, teeth jarred. This was dying, he understood, and wanted only for it to be over, was yielding to whatever wind or depth or moisture would take him away when he felt his belly bite rock, knew in a flash the sharp edge of up and down, scratched dirt, yanked his screaming weight toward daylight, groaned, and all at once found himself spilled back onto the cave's muddy floor—God knows how. Safe? Blood streamed from everywhere. His nails were crammed with sand. And dragging himself back out into the shrill sun, he wiped his face on the mountain grass, let his chest collapse in the dust and weeds, and shivering, vowed he'd do any-thing—anything!—never to be that frightened again.

And now with four days left, he needed to know why. Was it light that Leonardo da Vinci loved or darkness? Was it nature he sought, or was nature what he fled? So he'd transformed his bedroom into a hurdy–gurdy, calculated the ratio of tautness to angles using a bowstring, invented a pulley lubricant from armagnac and earwax, and while de Vilanis traipsed through the village purchasing resins, tried to determine just how deluded a person could be without sometime, somewhere, suspecting it. Melzi popped in a dozen times, equal parts exhilarated that Salai was gone and annoyed not to know why, and when he noticed Leonardo's sketch of the bedroom, hoped this new scheme wasn't brain–softening. He offered to help, gnawing his cheek in that manner he fell into when trying to look shrewd, and for about the hundredth time Leonardo wondered if leaving Melzi his notebooks were tossing them into the Loire. Leonardo got rid of the nuisance by sending him off to buy a pound of sienna, and when a few minutes later the woman appeared with leeks boiled in fennel, Leonardo chased her back down the stairs. By the time de Vilanis returned with the compounds, Leonardo had concluded that what the dimostrazione required was a loveliness as sublime as Filippo Lippi's madonnas, a beauty so maddening you'd desert your beloved and take her likeness to bed. For the effect must be overpowering, an attraction wondrous enough to make you dizzy. It mustn't fail of spectacle, but neither should it simply amuse. For if it left the phlegm viscous and the sprites drowsy or stirred them into mere hum–drum life, then the depths of the human heart or liver or spleen or pituitary gland or wherever it was that darkness and light got so whipped up together you could never tell if mating were love or warfare—if the spectacle failed simply to knock you over, then the inner chamber of whichever organ would remain as black as a cavern's cranny and Leonardo would die a lost man.

And so Leonardo had Battista grind azurite until the pestle blistered his palm, mix it with woad and gum of cedar, sprinkle in elixir of gentian and a few grains of lapis lazuli until he'd found the precise shade of blue to transport anyone who saw it back to Florence where the whisk of Salai's broom across the rough cedar floor and the smell of bone meal and drying gesso almost made Leonardo think he was blessed, and then sulfur, arsenic and naphthol for yellow—to startle age, drive out stupor, fling you back into Albano's light, pounding down a dusty hill, just a boy. And so with crimson, pale lavendar, the silver of clattering olive leaves, fuchsia scent of rain. The whole idea being to let a soul betray itself. For how else would you find out who you were? So the woman would be Leonardo's childhood asleep in her flesh—don't examine this too closely, it doesn't make much sense—and Leonardo would watch nature lunge and cower, harmony of estranged longings, and when Salai finally returned to swallow comeuppance, he'd understand too. Or if he didn't return—damp swill of maggot droppings!— then expire benighted among syphilitics and infidels, so there.

Finally around sundown, Leonardo lugged sketches, pestle, Battista, and earwax to the studio, locked them all in, Battista whining. When an hour later Melzi banged on the door—his slippers muddy and skin barked from fleeing three brigands through a slough on his way back from the hovel of Hadjani the alchemist—Leonardo told him to pour the sienna into a small chamois pouch and wedge it tightly between the rightmost picket and jamb of the stable gate. Which Melzi did. It stayed there all evening as Leonardo assembled tiny catapults and crossbows on the studio workbench and persuaded Battista to puff up thirty–nine painted sheep's tripes into blue balloons while Melzi stood with his ear pressed against the studio door trying to figure from all the hammering and grunting what was afoot and chewed his thumb. Mathurine showed up with a platter of steaming vegetables, and when Melzi banged on the door announcing dinner, Leonardo bellowed to go away. She waddled off—Italians!—and Melzi got himself a book in case this turned out to be a siege. Midnight came, went; the chamois pouch of sienna stayed put. Battista stopped complaining about supper and flatly refused to fold rice–paper lilies with his left hand while painting them with his right, even if Leonardo really had folded a hundred and eight with his left hand alone. Singing. About four a.m. the servant nodded off to sleep halfway through a lop–eared tulip, and Melzi—summoning his bravado—knocked on the door to ask was Leonardo ready yet for the pouch of sienna which Melzi estimated would be sufficiently moisturized now from its exposure to the evening air. Melzi offered to fetch the chamois pouch from the stable gate, bake its contents to a proper auburn, pulverize, sift, and emulsify them, if Leonardo would just withdraw the doorbolt and allow.... At which point Leonardo asked: It's still there? And Melzi's feet padded off down the corridor then padded back to report that, yes, he was holding the bag of precious earth even now in his hand and was prepared to.... At which point Leonardo said: Put it back. And while he was at it, would Melzi also make sure the other stable entrances were secure? Having long ago recognized the futility of questions, Melzi did as he was told.

And on and on till well past daybreak, as Leonardo finished assembling the five contraptions for getting the balloons aloft, tied the last of the yellow and crimson and lavendar streamers, and roused de Vilanis to sneak up the stairs and install the machines behind tapestries and cornices before the woman's curiosity got the better of her sloth. Leonardo meanwhile burnished the parts of the trigger–relay he'd carved from a block of ebony Old Toscanelli'd given him and prepared for the encounter that he fully expected to be grimly unpleasant but relished all the same. Salai's error was more than miscalculation. It was treachery, the fruit of infected character, a worm in the soul. And having lived a kind of faith, however incomprehensible, Leonardo was far from sure he should forgive it. Placing the trigger's smooth pieces into his wallet and gingerly straightening his spine, Leonardo decided that Bellincioni was right, that the horse had always been a bottomless hole and that Leonardo's mistake—if it made sense to speak of mistakes—had been to stand firm, never hover, tread air. Or some such. If only Bellincioni hadn't denied his eyes, or if Leonardo had been surer of them, then maybe Bellincioni could've saved him, might have explained to Leonardo about updrafts, thus providing him with the retort he'd need ten years later in Marcantonio della Torre's apartment and so making it unnecessary for Salai to slink shamefacedly back here in the middle of the night. It all seemed so wasteful, so inefficient. But Leonardo never learned anything any other way.

Leonardo opened the studio door and, stepping over the dozing Melzi—who, having collapsed some hours earlier against the molding, awoke now just in time to notice the disconcerting fact that his master wore no hose—marched down the corridor, through the foyer, and out onto the little mansion's stone porch where, squinting his eyes into the glare, he was surprised to find the silver clouds lovelier and less oppressive than he'd recalled. It was spring. The air was growing warm. Within a few hours Leonardo would slip his hand beneath the mattress, pluck the ebony trigger, and see fifty years bite its tail. He was beginning to appreciate now how Salai had strayed into anger, how he had himself—yes, even he—how he'd been partly to blame. Much had been left undone that could have been completed, and—why deny it?—he'd known fear. Whose idea was all this godlike crap anyway? But his struggle, the endless passage through the tortuous dark—well, *that* wasn't cowardice! And so strolling across the stone porch of the Clos–Lucé, feeling the spring sap ooze through his bones, Leonardo still didn't know what he'd tell Salai, but he realized he could at least tell Melzi—whose slippers he heard flapping up the corridor behind him—to run out to the stable and inform the remorseful apostate that although he deserved neither forgiveness nor compassion he could nevertheless sleep in a bed like a man instead of in the straw like a horse—that part seemed especially good; Salai like a horse! har har! And Leonardo was opening his mouth to say it, when he came to the end of the porch. The lawn was that color of blue–green that the first shoots take on whenever the air gets so spongy it turns the day opalescent, and this ache of color stretched from the porch's edge around the shrubs and flower beds, under the canopy of frail sycamore leaves, over a hump, between the path's clammy stones, and right up to the wooden gate that provided the only access to those outbuildings where an exhausted traveler arriving in the middle of the night might hope to collapse on the flea infested grass and find some water and perhaps a little fodder too for the weary horse that remained *the only means of conveying themselves that mortals would ever know*! Between the jamb and gatepost rested the pouch of sienna, exactly where Melzi had left it. How had Leonardo imagined that Salai, who for thirty-nine years had been depraved and vile but never once mistaken, how had Leonardo imagined he'd return? Leonardo da Vinci was going to die alone. And as Melzi stepped forward, pestle in hand, to say that he too believed the brown earth would be richer and more soluble for its night in the air and to compliment Leonardo on the ingenious innovation of allowing the notoriously recalcitrant granules to undergo extended atmospheric maceration, just one more irrefutable indication of the godlike intelligence and learning with which later ages would forever recall..., Melzi saw Leonardo stiffen, lurch backwards as if struck in the chest, and clutching at the wall, hiss: Terror!

"You're whaaat?!"

"I—I'm writing a novel."

"When have you had the time? I mean, a novel's wonderful, R—, terrific, but if you've been working twelve hours a day on your book, I don't understand—"

"No, you see..." Where was the ocher pond? Where was the mallard floating on it? "I'm writing a novel, not the cultural iconog—"

"EEEEEEEEEEEEEE!"

"Stoppit! Stoppit! I can explain."

"I'm very glad you can explain because for an instant I thought you'd plunged us twenty thousand dollars into debt and lost your job."

"I suppose in a manner of speaking—"

"EEEEEEEEEEEEEEEEEEEEEEEEEEEEE!"

"Stoppit! I haven't abandoned the book. It's still the same book or—"

"But it's a novel?"

"Are you going to scream?"

"Do I have something to scream about?"

"Can't we wait a moment to decide?"

"Do you expect me to answer that?"

"I was writing a cultural history—"

"Of," Deirdre wiggled her fingers in the air, "'Leonardo da Vinci.'"

I wiggled my fingers in the air. "Of 'Leonardo da Vinci.' But there was trouble."

"You hadn't framed the problem adequately," Deirdre took over. "So you developed a system of cultural paradigms and a typology of tropes—"

"It didn't work."

"Whaddaya mean it didn't work?"

What did I mean it didn't work? "The book didn't...well, it turned weird. Are you going to scream?"

"I really want to."

"My dissertation was correct. There's a profession, norms, methods, conventions...I'd learned my craft. The argument was situated, theoretically self–aware, dense with primary sources—"

"Why do you sound footnoted?"

"Nobody ever pretended the dissertation was wrong. I just couldn't reread it. I mean, I could *justify* it, but what I wanted to learn wasn't...I dunno, it seemed so predictable! More frames made it worse."

"This is one of those novels that doesn't make anybody any money, isn't it?"

"I haven't finished yet."

"But when it's finished, it won't make us any money?"

"I haven't decided how to market—"

"When you finish your novel and market it, is someone going to pay us forty–thousand dollars?"

"It won't make any money."

"So you've spent, lessee, six months, a couple of weeks, four or five days plus all this morning beheading everyone who stuck a neck out for you, and your explanation is: the book turned weird?"

"Just because I can't give you a reason doesn't mean I'm wrong."

"Lest there be any confusion," Deirdre said, "let me give *my* reasons. I'm compassionate, but not suicidally loyal. Regardless of the futile and self–destructive familial psycho–dramas you're compelled to recycle throughout your adulthood, I prefer marriage for better, for richer, and in health. If we thrive, I'm confident we can thrive together. This promise should lift your dashed spirits. However, R—, I'm far from confident that, if you sink, you don't sink alone."

I was starting to sweat. "Has it ever struck you...I mean we're only interested in Leonardo—"

"Some of 'we' aren't interested in Leonardo."

"—ever struck you that the people who're interested in Leonardo are only interested because we/they read his life backwards, from end to beginning. I'm giving you an explanation. So the angel that Leonardo painted in Verrochio's *Baptism* is interesting, not because the hair's well done—I mean, there can be two opinions about that—but because it was painted by the man who eventually painted waterfalls and *The Last Supper*. But when Leonardo painted the angel, he wasn't the man who painted *The Last Supper*, he was just—"

"Leonardo da Vinci didn't know how famous he would become. Is this the illumination that has wrecked my life?"

"No, Leonardo knew exactly how famous he'd become, by middle age he was already famous. But he *died* a failure."

"So, out of sympathy, you decided to fail—"

"Don't you get it?! Leonardo was a cultural icon only for spectators. For himself, for anyone who cared, he was lost, naked, crazy, embarrassing. I don't know what—"

"But you're novel sets the record straight. It tells what Leonardo *really* was. For himself."

"It tells what Leonardo's becoming—for us! What he probably has to mean if I'm me. Or vice versa. That's what it tries to do."

"Honey, I admit that in my eagerness to see you punished I'm probably not listening to you, and I know that on some distant day I may understand how you feel, might glimpse why you ruined our future when—with so little effort—you could have secured it, but even making very, very wide allowances for my presently sealed mind, I don't think you're saying anything."

"I'm just saying there are things a person might need to do or see or hear, or a group might need to, or a nation might—things that under, y'know, certain pressures...well, you might only find them in fiction."

"Name twelve I can't live without."

I took a deep breath. "Leonardo da Vinci built this horse—"

IN WHICH FRANCESCO MELZI DISCOVERS FICTION

Francesco Melzi is still standing at the foot of Leonardo's bed where amid prone bodies and a profusion of paper lilies we abandoned him two minutes and countless digressions ago. A washbasin rests on the floor beside his slipper. In it floats a kidney bean. He's been sufficiently impressed by the madness he's witnessed—the proliferation of color, the tiny military engines, all the shouts and banging—to recognize the last dimostrazione as Leonardo's doing, but he has no earthly idea what he was supposed to have seen. Worse still, he suspects that whatever it was, it had to do with whatever Battista was privy to during the night Melzi passed against the studio doorjamb scrunched up muddy and wet from trouncing through the marsh northwest of town escaping the brigands who attacked him on his way back from the hovel of Hadjani, the infidel alchemist, who in addition to smelling to high heaven of tumeric and crawling with purple vermin the likes of which Melzi has never before seen in his life, also drove a damn hard bargain—a fine gold earring with the Melzi family imprint on it for a pouch of dirt Leonardo never even used!—still dripping mud and swampwater from this adventure, shivering in the cool night air, listening to the clatter within the studio and waiting resolutely for

74

nothing more glorious than a task. Melzi's always known Leonardo was beyond him, but the degree of his own inconsequence just now assails him like a mosquito. To have been born with neither facility nor prowess is very vile, but it's altogether intolerable to be stuck with an imagination.

Of course, Melzi has been given a task. Fate and Leonardo's last will and testament have selected him to carry the 6,000 plus pages of all the Maestro meant to accomplish—as well as a suitably dignified narration of his demise—back across the Alps to Milan where what currently passes for civilization awaits it. Although the task doesn't require heroics, Melzi expects to fail. King François Premier, who brought Leonardo here in the first place, is no fool. He has already claimed the *Gioconda*, the *St. Anne*, and the really disgraceful *St. John*, and Melzi figures he'll confiscate the manuscripts as soon as the body's cold. Will schmill. And as if this weren't enough, Leonardo's taking so long to die—displaying ever more convincing evidence of senility along with an astonishing repertory of physiological indignities—that Melzi's begun to wonder if the one scene he's going to get to narrate will turn out to be a farce. All in all, his present predicament resembles the sort he's been mired in his whole life, and he longs for newness with the sharpness of a puncture wound. Every step he's ever taken has been slightly awry, and now he suspects this will always be the case, that nothing he learns will make any difference. It's not really his fault, of course, anymore than plague or drought is. Still, they kill you.

Watching the kidney bean wriggle toward the basin's lip, Melzi decides that his disappointments began with the Margrave of Tarvisio, Paolo Zanetta di Cristoforo da Sestri, count of Tyrolo, Bressanone, and God–knows–where–all, widely known as the Sky. About the time he was first becoming acquainted with Leonardo, while still only a boy, Francesco got himself embroiled in an affair of honor with a lord thirty years his senior and no inconsiderable figure. How exactly it happened no one at the time could say, but there had been slights, words, clumsy jostling, two slaps, someone's cup of punch splashed on a doublet and, of course, a lady—Francesco's youthful aunt whose commonplace flirtations he'd misinterpreted much as the Margrave had misinterpreted the skinny, whiskerless fellow standing at her elbow. It would later be rumored—as partial excuse for the unseemly mismatch—that the Sky was in truth a cast–off son of a disgraced doge's younger brother, no margrave, hardly even a count, possibly a merchant, ill–bred, bumptious, left–handed, certainly the pox–infested diddler of all things concave—but no matter, for when startled into overhastily challenging the lady's young escort who, he soon learned, was a *young* escort indeed, the Margrave was still much favored by the Castello demi–monde, widely sought for masques and cicirlanda, and very nearly the latest rage. All agreed that for the fifteen–year–old Francesco it was a marvelous opportunity.

No sooner had the two antagonists spun on their heels than the Melzi cousins, Amalfi, Andrea, Arturo, were proclaiming Francesco's prodigious manhood in the Piazza del Duomo. In her parlor Francesco's mother wrung her hands over the slovenly points of her son's dueling hose and declared to Eleanor da Sanseverino that the condescension had been entirely on the Melzi's part. In the Giardini Pubblici Francesco's youthful aunt was overheard sighing into her handkerchief that, yes, it was fine to be fought over but what a pity no one played the lute. Only Francesco's father seemed sensible of any danger. Throughout the afternoon he fretted in his library, terrified that the Margrave, having contracted a match so far beneath himself, would call upon the French regent to intervene and force a retraction, or worse, would simply disdain to acknowledge Francesco's rights in the affair, would dispatch his man—or ghastly thought! a mere hireling—to declare his scorn for the boy's insolence and refuse him satisfaction. What everyone in the Villa Melzi was celebrating as a coup might result in their family's humiliation! But to his unspeakable relief when the awaited message arrived it was delivered by the Margrave's amanuensis and personal companion, a comely youth widely rumored to be the Margrave's bastard–bloodkin in the maternal line, and joy of joys, rather than renege, the Margrave announced himself eager for the meeting. Never had a family's hopes for its son been confirmed so early! Paolo Zanetta di Cristoforo da Sestri, Margrave of Tarvisio, count of Tyrolo and Bressanone, popularly called the Sky, had recognized Francesco as his rival. Between the boy and glory only gangrene stood in the way.

The appointed morning arrived slowly. The Melzi family were unprepared for so spectacular an undertaking in their son's youth and so had to barter some of Francesco's strategic advantages—choice of weapons, ground, hour, number of passes, etc.—to gain additional time. An entire wardrobe of figured nether socks, brocade jerkins, short–capes, doublets, and clasps had to be ordered for Francesco, for Amalfi his second, for their three attendants, half a dozen witnesses and all those family members who considered themselves personally implicated. Who could have anticipated that a still–growing boy might have to intimidate a middle–aged lord with the cut of his waistcoat or that such an honor would arrive so unexpectedly? As the days passed, negotiations turned subtle. The Margrave insisted on a specific vintage of Spanish sherry to be served between passes; Francesco's mother finagled for the angle of sunlight on her son's fil d'or; both sides had an opinion about the aunt's missal, motto and veil. There were officials to bribe, of course—dueling being strictly illegal—and a host of Melzi younger brothers in ecclesiastical positions set about the tricky busi-

77

ness of indulgences. Kinsmen and well–wishers poured in from outlying towns. Meals became complex, multiple–stage affairs, and every night skirmishes broke out between the retainers of the factions. Milan was a party.

And yet through it all Francesco remained calm. Inside his head a rich humming sound, like viola d'amore strings, vibrated day and night. There was a new ease in his movements, a manliness and joviality, as if the part of family champion had been created for him in a lost moment before the earth was formed. Nature itself carried him along. So this was glory, he thought, the reason he'd been born. Its nearness lifted his spirits, kept his thoughts tranquil amid the hubbub. For the first time in his life he and the world seemed a single thing.

When on the morning of the ninth day Francesco and Amalfi finally saw the sun leak through the aspens outside the Roman gate and so began to lead the nineteen horsemen, seven coaches, innumerable lackeys and noisy coda of tag–along cretins, lepers, amputees and consumptives down the narrow lane of the French regent's mulberry grove, the weather had already turned hot and sultry. The ostrich plumes hung from the men's caps at a noticeably less jaunty angle than when sewn in place, and moisture could be seen on the horses' nostrils. No one spoke. At the end of the lane was a clearing bounded by willows and a shallow pool. The Margrave liked it, his man explained, for its youthful air—a remark Francesco's father suspected of impudence. As the Melzis entered the clearing they could see their rivals waiting across the field, silent as doom in their bright blue cloaks. The mist obscured details, but Francesco assumed his enemy was the horseman riding slightly taller than the rest, plumed, erect, head turned blithely askance. For several minutes he tried to glimpse the man's face—all the while affecting indifference—but each time his eyes passed in the Margrave's vicinity all Francesco saw was the amorphous drapery of a riding cloak. This unnerved him. How could someone on a spirited horse manage always to have his back toward you? The distraction caused by this enigma could be strategic, Francesco realized, and so he tried to concentrate on the nearby chatter instead. Amalfi was complaining that their adversary had used Flemish tailors. Someone had neglected to bring the trumpets, and a serving man was being dispatched to get them. Everyone agreed the Margrave was a splendid foe.

Thinking back on this moment years later, Francesco would suspect that it was then that the first hint of his life's inscrutability had come to him. As everywhere around him figures started leaping to the ground, abusing servants, lifting ladies from coaches and congregating in little wads of gesticulating kinsmen, Francesco realized he didn't know how to dismount. It wasn't a lack of training. He had, in fact, mastered five ways: the hoist, the escalier du cavalier, the leg–over, the rump vault and, of course, toppling, but he knew of no way for a family champion with viola d'amore strings in his head to do it. His former ease had vanished. His legs were planks. Large portions of his body had filled with cold water. Part of the problem seemed to be that everyone else had something to do. And while Francesco could imagine a family champion seething inwardly, or gazing off abstractedly, or pronouncing doom in his grave baritone, or doing almost anything, so long as he was the focus of attention, he really couldn't imagine a champion trying to look inconspicuous or wiping the sweat from his lip or whistling or scratching or doing virtually any of the things that, if truth be told, until nine days ago Francesco did a great portion of the time. It seemed astonishing how inept he'd suddenly become. And all that saved him from a debilitating attack of self-knowledge was the sight of his father, Uncle Baldassare, Amalfi, and four retainers marching authoritatively across the field just as someone clutched his thigh. He looked down into his cousin Arturo's somber face. Don't worry about the hood, Arturo reassured him. We've decided on the stratagem of La Croix. If this fails, there are diversions. All is being managed. The advantage is ours.

Now, if there was anything that seated on his horse like a cigar store Indian, struggling to maintain his poise for the benefit of onlookers who hadn't noticed him since the Roman gate, and trying desperately to come up with a way to sneak over behind the carriages and relieve his screaming bladder ...if there was anything Francesco wasn't worried about just now, it was the hood. Mainly because, until Arturo's remark, Francesco hadn't known there was one. So that was how the Sky kept his cloak turned towards you. His head was draped! This realization brought with it eight seconds of relief followed by the most paralyzing sensation of public nakedness Francesco had ever known. How, for God's sake, had he wound up seated out here in this sizzling, yellow light, unhidden, unbearded, unbejeweled—as prosy as a length of string—while across the clearing lurked his enemy shrouded in Olympian blue? No wonder no one was paying Francesco any mind. Every member of the Melzi contingent was preoccupied with one question: What was the enemy concealing? There might be deceptions here, depths, mistakes. What if Francesco were about to sacrifice his limbs and flawless complexion to a joke? But when Francesco tried to confide these fears to Arturo, he was chided for cowardice. Didn't he trust his kinsmen to know what they were about? Surely, having behaved so well until now he wasn't going to embarrass them with unmanly qualms. Francesco decided to mind his bladder and stay put.

Three hours passed. It was soon apparent that the Margrave's disguise was a more elaborate obstacle than Arturo's jocular tone had let on, and accusations of stalling were beginning to be heard on both sides. Several neutral observers had earlier noted an air of the executioner about the draped head, and now the Melzi spokesmen denounced this allusion as indelicate, if not grounds for further umbrage. The threat of a chivalric chain–reaction culminating in a geometrically expanding series of new challenges loomed over the negotiations and was only dissipated when Francesco's mother labeled the whole disagreement a ploy to drive the Melzi women back into the Castello. Many were persuaded of the reasonableness of the Margrave's circumspection by an eloquent foreigner's citation of the notorious case of Bardolini and the Englishman, and Francesco's cousin Andrea was kept busy compiling counter arguments: Men should know whom they are murdering, retaliatory prosecution lacks style, true spectacle requires the exposed visage, etc. In the midst of the clearing the negotiators beseeched one another, snickered and shook their fists in the air. Twice Francesco's father marched back to the horses, instructed the party to remount and was riding away when a blue–cloaked messenger arrived to whisper a concession in his ear. The servants set tables of eats and wine out under the willows. A handful of bedlamites attacked the coaches with mudballs. Francesco's youthful aunt succumbed to heat prostration. It began to look like rain.

By the time the Margrave was persuaded to remove his hood, revealing thickly rouged cheeks, a garish yellow wig, purple lines spreading from the corners of what looked like blue lips, and a paper ball–mask—the blatant hokeyness of which seemed a confirmation of Francesco's worst fears and should have been more than sufficient warning to everyone else involved but wasn't—the viola d'amore strings vibrating in his head had subsided to a buzz. The sweat trickling down his spine and accumulating in a squishy wad of linen between his buttocks had at one point very nearly provoked him to gallop right out onto the field of conquest in a last ditch effort to look like the champion he knew himself to be, but when in a fatal instance of good sense he'd confided the impulse to Arturo who forthwith entrusted it to Uncle Baldassare whose ears belonged to Francesco's dad, he'd learned that such tactics sacrificed in sagacity what they gained in panache and besides, he was just fifteen, what did he know? Melzi would never understand that what he was confronting was the modern genius for replacing conflict with organization or that his difficulty was merely that of everyone else since the Renaissance—how to resist anything so amorphous, rational, and outwardly benign as bureaucracy. However, he did understand that what had gotten concealed underneath the Margrave's hood had been glory, and having been taught since birth that it was the most exciting thing in the world, he recognized as deeply significant the fact that he was feeling bored. He tried to continue waiting, grew drowsy, started to daydream and pretty soon didn't want to die. An awkward development under the circumstances but one that at least loosened him up enough to dismount. And as the spectacularly clothed gentlemen in the midst of the clearing continued hefting, scrutinizing, and deprecating the Margrave's Swiss rapiers, thus instigating a contrapuntal fracas within the ongoing squabble over whether the rouge, wig and ballmask constituted a disguise within a disguise and so were liable to the same objections as the hood, Francesco scooped up a fistful of veal from the serving tables and wandered past the coaches where two footmen were whipping back an onslaught of squealing urchins. Behind a dray he discovered his youthful aunt sitting on the grass, her skirt hiked up above her knee, sharing a bottle of chianti with the French viscount's blacksmith, Slipknot de Gruyere. She cocked an eye at Francesco, demanded just what did he think he was doing here when his duty so plainly lay on the field of honor? And as Francesco stumbled towards the willows to relieve his agonized bladder at last, he marveled that her voice had spoken the very question that was his own.

And on and on and on throughout the remainder of the afternoon. So for Francesco it wasn't much of a climax when the steadily developing drizzle finally ran the Margrave's cheeks, wilted his ballmask and made unavoidably obvious the insult that, suspected far too late, had already provoked Francesco's father to frantic searching for some technicality that would extricate his family from the miserable affair. But no luck. For on the Margrave's horse sat, not the Sky of course, but a *woman*—the gigantic, slovenly vixen from the trattoria of Chiaravalle, Sour Maria as she was commonly known. And surrounded by guffawing blue–cloaked horsemen, she galloped about the soggy clearing, challenging the Melzi champion to combat, deriding his reluctance to meet her, and wondering that such a noble family had no offspring to defend its name. Francesco's father retired to his coach without a word, pulled the drapes, and declared that he wouldn't show his face again until safely within—not just their palazzo in the city—but the Villa Melzi seven hours journey hence. Uncle Baldassare regrouped the nineteen horsemen, tried to quiet the riffraff who, having picked up Sour Maria's taunts, were now dancing around Francesco's father's coach hooded in flour sacks, challenging him to martial contests and insinuating various irregularities in his masculine parts. Someone pushed Amalfi into the mud; Andrea got punched in the eye; no one could find Arturo. And as the cooks and lackeys sprinted about gathering up the waterlogged hambones and linens, and as Francesco's mother keened loudly within her sister's carriage, and while the horses squealed and reared and the wheels sucked noisily at the soft ground, without a backward glance, the soggy band rattled out of the clearing on its long way home.

For Francesco little seemed to have changed. Straggling along with the other riders and coachmen—not really behind or beside anyone, hardly connected, merely drawn along by the fastidiously maintained hiatus between his horse and every other—he felt as extraneous now as he'd felt all day. It was, of course, apparent that the whole undertaking had been a masquerade, not just for Sour Maria and the Margrave, but for himself. He was no rival of a high–born rogue; he was a boy—promising student of elocution and ballroom dancing, hope of his family's future, but in point of fact, no great shakes. However, what did seem to have changed was the rest of the world. There'd been a disaster. And although he'd had no hand in it and couldn't participate in the family's grief and viewed this ignominy as if from afar, Francesco knew himself the cause of all. No longer solitary and negligible, he was now isolated—something done *to* him. And as the rain matted his hatbrim to his forehead and mud from the carriage wheels splattered his chest, he felt drawn to the lepers and cretins cavorting nearby. Even their filthy anonymity was preferable to such importance, and Francesco had to stifle an impulse to leap down among them. A wretch with no nose spat loudly in his direction; a shapeless creature—so mudcovered Francesco couldn't distinguish male from female—showed him its arse and gave a screech like cats fighting. And as the procession continued on past black fields and mulberry groves until at darkness it reached the twisting road beside the Adda, Francesco gave himself over to fancies of gore and mayhem, horses stampeding, metal crashing down, the perverse fellowship injury brings.

At last the dark walls of the Villa Melzi appeared through the storm, and the whole band of drenched travelers drew together in a corporate shudder of relief. Here were dry clothes, protection from laughter, forgiving sleep. But as the carriages approached the outermost gate, their passengers were startled to discover the vilest turn of all in this vile, vile day. Blocking the entrance was a mound of ox manure as high as a man's head, whole cartloads of it dumped into the path and heaped so that not even a solitary rider could pass. You could see its black shape from a furlong's distance, see the rain streaming in shiny rivulets down its sides, a sliver of moon glistening in the moist folds. A dueling foil protruded from its front pinioning a missive written in Latin quadrimeter, something about decorum, catastrophe, the lesser lights' sphere. As the riders and horses stopped, a hush fell, and Francesco felt himself drawn in. The day had begun as a summons to him, the chance to enact his character and fate. His only mistake had been to misconstrue what part he'd play, to vastly underestimate the strangeness of the thing. Dismounting from his horse Francesco strode over to where three exhausted coachmen were rolling their eyes, shuffling their feet, each more determined than the rest to shirk this chore. One of the men warned: The young lord! There were some coughs, a stir, then nothing. Francesco took a deep breath and the odor was like a plunge into dying. He could hear the patter of raindrops on the mush, watched the offal oozing around his toes. So this was it, he thought, the reason he'd been born. He edged a foot into the stew. An old retainer beside him protested weakly, and when Francesco replied, he was surprised to hear the sound of his own voice—as rich and soothing as viola d'amore strings! He waved the servants back, waded in up to his knees. It would be slow work, he knew, but he felt strong, ready, as if nature had prepared him for this challenge long ago. And as his mother and cousins and aunt peered out from their carriage windows, Francesco thrashed and shoveled and scooped with his bare hands, until at last the Melzi champion cleared a way so his family could go on.

After this, it was generally acknowledged that Francesco would always be wrong. The civilized hypocrisies that everyone else recognized from childhood, he'd blunder through life believing, and he'd doubt only those inevitabilities no one else paused to consider. Faith in him was screwed a turn too tight, suspicion left uncapped altogether, and so instead of shooting for virtue's pinnacle, he'd habitually aim just above it. His most recurrent vision would be of his inferiors gazing upward, laughter spilling from their mouths, as he glided in a perfect arc just over his heart's desire. Even in the most ordinary undertakings there would always be a pile of manure blocking his way. Because he alone saw it, his actions struck others as peculiar. His parents hardly knew what to think. They might have reconciled themselves to a commonplace son—Francesco's father was himself pretty commonplace—but a commonplace son determined to act like a champion was indistinguishable from a fool. His mere presence could make villainy fashionable, nobility clownish. There seemed no alternative but to turn him into an artist. And so when Leonardo da Vinci next dined at the Villa Melzi, Francesco's father dropped the necessary hints, and Leonardo—who was by no means averse to accepting money if he didn't have to work for it—figured a rich idiot in the studio could cause no problems if you gave him nothing to do. So Francesco Melzi became Leonardo's apprentice, and though the liaison with a common guildsman was an insult to the Melzi name, it kept the family embarrassment out of harm's way.

Throughout his youth Francesco knew that this was his family's reasoning, and now eight years later in a foreign land he has often imagined that Battista da Vilanis, the weasel Salai, all the courtiers in the chateau, even the maids and stable hands—in short, the entirety of the imaginable universe knows, too. Wasn't the lord of this very same Amboise regent in Milan when the Margrave humiliated Francesco?

Who would expect the French to keep a secret? Gazing at Leonardo's splotched and hairy head poking out from underneath the mountain of bedclothes just now, Francesco feels a flutter of rage rise in his throat. Disdain, disdain. Never has he known glory except as a joke. He's terrified that the present situation is just another set–up, that Leonardo's manuscripts will turn out to be gobbledy–gook. Francesco's read them—pages of triangles and half–moons, sketches of cow innards, about a thousand drawings of pulleys, water–screws, tie–beams, masonry, some wild–flowers and horseheads, all surrounded by inscrutable remarks written backwards in a mixture of Tuscan, hideous Latin and phonetic spellings of Arabic and Greek ... well, honestly now, is this what genius looks like? Melzi's brain is a tangle of conflicting plots; he feels like a character in some malevolent author's play. Out of a thousand farces how to conceive even one satisfactory ending? It's hopeless. And yet, doesn't he seem to be confronting at this very moment the unlikeliest phenomenon of all—a second chance? He watches Leonardo's dry lips twitch in silent argument with God–knows–what specter. His whiskers are matted with broth and onions, his forehead a glob of age spots, peas, worry–lines. If not from such old and homely stuff, from where do better worlds come?

And so, knowing that Leonardo has already willed him his squiggles, laundry–lists, nightmares, mistakes, but amply aware that if France wants them Leonardo's notebooks will prove less sacrosanct than a kidney bean, and feeling for the first time that ignominious success might be preferable to almost any kind of defeat, Melzi is just beginning his life as a scoundrel when Battista moans, No more flowers! Melzi glances down at the figure lying spread–eagle at his feet and, with one toe, up–ends the water–basin. Battista comes off the floor sputtering. You win, Melzi tells him. Have at the paintings, desecrate the studio, leave your mark wherever you choose, France will probably confiscate everything anyway. Melzi smiles just to let Battista know Melzi doesn't take him for a fool and adds: I'm bribing you. Which amounts to an understanding, and in seconds Battista's skipping down the stairs.

Melzi next brushes a paper crocus from the bed where Leonardo appears to be swearing at no one and, seating himself on the pig's–bristle throw–rug, appeals to the Maestro for understanding. History is a difficult task. How unfair that weariness can demean life's climactic moments, that neither doom nor triumph ever arrives on time. Truth is, only in retrospect is anything thrilling; even in the midst of conquests you're mostly bored. How well Francesco understands this now. Much of Leonardo's own life has suffered this defect—no offense intended—and here at the conclusion his death's making a poor spectacle. How wrong to dwindle into anti–climax! Left to itself has nature ever contrived a satisfying show? Melzi pauses, moved by his own eloquence. At last he means to strike a blow with his own arm, to punish the world for countless disappointments. Briefly, he enumerates the maxims, regrets, gestures and facial expressions appropriate for Leonardo's final moments. He recalls Leonardo's heartfelt penitence for wasted opportunities, the discharging of his faithful servants, the tender parting of the Maestro and his beloved disciple, Francesco Melzi. He runs through the story of how King François Premier collapses sobbing when he hears the news, mentions the castle eulogies, processions through the streets of Amboise, anguish in Florence, Venice, Rome, and concludes with the triumphal return of Leonardo's works to Milan under the protection of his spiritual heir, commentator and learned apologist, Francesco Melzi. He does not mention Battista's overpainting of the *St. John*, the disappearance of half a thousand scribbles detrimental to Leonardo's reputation as a sane man, or the succession of folk Melzi expects to pay off, be sodomized by, or hire some thug to bludgeon in order to make this scam work. In a really swell peroration he touches on the perpetuation of Leonardo's memory through the publication of his treatises and founding of the Academia Leonardi Vinci, both under the supervision of the internationally renowned Leonardo publicist and patron, the esteemed heir to an esteemed house, the immortal Francesco Melzi. And then patting Leonardo's knee, Melzi adds: Trust me. Leonardo gazes out the back of Melzi's head, makes an unintelligible snort. And with a quick sigh, Melzi's on his way back down the stairs, already wondering how he's going to get himself and 6000 pages across the Italian Alps before King François cuts him off with an army from Marseilles. There's a heavy feeling in his chest, and he thinks it's penitence, vows to confess when he's safe in Milan, but he must already know it won't do any good. He'll live with it his whole life long. For Francesco Melzi has discovered fiction.

Of course, Leonardo da Vinci doesn't think Francesco Melzi has discovered diddly. None of the fantastic things the young man has said are half so pleasant as this silence he's left behind. Leonardo's grumpy, would like to forget about the yellow monster outside, Salai, this woman on the floor—wants to return to his dream of platan leaves and updrafts but, for some reason, can't. Pinioned and sweating upon the tick, he notices the pool of spilled water meandering through the dust and food scraps. How peculiarly the world behaves. The planks are badly pitted and you'd have thought the water would've soaked through the cracks in an instant, disappeared except for a splotch. But here it is, a tiny pond tracing furrows in the wood's grain, which Leonardo never remarked till now. Perhaps he's always lived among regularities, perhaps been subservient to them, and this makes him wonder just what his dimostrazione was ever meant to show. Just now as he lay here recalling his boyhood and the woman's flight, Leonardo almost thought he gazed up into a familiar face, youthful and damp–skinned—Salai's face!—but as he knew it many years before, on the hot afternoons under Tuscany's blue sky, sweat pouring down the adolescent's cheeks, glossy black curls in his eyes. What Leonardo had wanted to tell Salai at that moment was that if the cave was really bottomless, as Leonardo now suspects, or if you were as likely to fall into darkness by fleeing as by taking the plunge, well, then couldn't Salai understand about the wrong turns, the confusion, about Leonardo's mistakes? But when Leonardo listened for the rough sound of Salai's broom, he heard only footsteps trotting down the stone stairs, heard silence—bluer than ice in your hand—and opening his eyes he saw this chamber, a line of crenels in the distance, water edging across the floor. Had Leonardo failed to make himself clear? Had he spoken too harshly? Maybe he forgot to speak at all. But no, he cringes at his words, or something like them, recalls saying that, really, the horse was just tin and brass, just a huge, costly toy. It wasn't alive, it wasn't really a horse! What the hell did Salai want anyway?

And Salai had almost smiled then, narrowed his eyes—the eyes that, approaching forty, still were the long–lashed, black holes in a street–urchin's face—and said: Have you ever spent the night in a stable?

And thank God, Leonardo had had the good sense to keep his mouth shut.

You have to wait…, Salai began, his hand resting on the window ledge, eyes darting about. You have to wait until nightfall, but not so late that the stable–yard is closed, as late as you think you can wait and still slip inside. There's a right time, a rhythm, moment, and if you wait until you're certain, you've waited too long. You must learn how much to dare. The stable boys and grooms are always watching, always alert, older and stronger than you are, and with truncheons. They want you to play the woman in their games. If there are many of them, this can be very bad. To enter the yard, it's best to lean like a pauper near the gate at sundown, wait until a rider comes on his beast and, as the stable boys lead him through, try to slip in beside his right haunch. Once inside, you should continue walking beside the beast as far as possible, but not so far that you're detected, and then dash like a squirrel across the paddock to the outbuildings, hide in a shed or the hayloft. Usually the youths will be attending the beast or the rider and will threaten to beat you but won't follow. If they don't threaten you, be careful not to look back, for they're surely chasing you. If you're being followed, you should try to slip into a bin. If someone finds you in the bin, try to throw a bridle into his face and duck out the door. If this doesn't work, the hayloft offers many good places. There are other ways to enter the yard, especially if you have comrades, but this way is best. Once inside, your comrades are likely to betray you or to use you in the same way the stable–lads would. Entering may be easier, but in the end the dangers are worse.

To gain admittance is a thing of great craft, and repeated failure is necessary to learn to do it well. Luckily, the grooms are indolent and stupid. Even if one lays his hands on you, you may be able to appease him by rubbing his loins or offering your mouth or bunghole for his amusement. Many times I've saved myself a beating in this way, and if he beats you afterwards, well, the pain is brief—unlike hunger or freezing or a night of coughing in bad weather.

If you gain the stable, you are usually safe. There's much darkness and many good places—under the hay with the corn–snakes and vermin, or behind the slop piles, in the deep recesses of bins where the mice nest or underneath the troughs with the frogs—many places where, because of the unpleasantness, the stable–hands prefer not to go, especially after nightfall. You can hide there and wait. Once darkness is complete and you've heard no sound for a proper length of time—of course, in order not to be fooled about the duration, it's wise to place yourself in an awkward posture resting your weight on your arms and note whether your joints have yet gone numb; if they have not, it's wise to continue waiting—when there's no longer any sound, you can come out again and dine on the horses' fodder. If you are fortunate, there'll be a gloomy colt or some other bad feeder whom the grooms have given honey or sweet syrup with its grain, and if you can snatch this before the beasts gobble it, then you'll dine well. If not, you must be content with dry oats or barley. Or if the monsters have left you nothing, or if you've been timid and waited too long to come from your cell, then there's the hay or straw—which has little taste and rises back into your mouth after swallowing but is preferable to nothing—or the rodents or insects if you can catch some. Toads—in season—are easily caught, and contrary to what's said, they aren't poison, though their taste is bitter. None of this is bad.

Late travelers are bad. For when they arrive, you have little choice but to hide in the slips, among the beasts, beside their hooves, in the shadows, as near their bulk as you dare. You hear voices or the gate creaking, and because you are in utter darkness, because you can't see even your hand before your eyes, there's no hope of finding a good place. If the groom has a lantern, you'll be caught, and if not, he's likely to stumble over you. Or he may have a dog.

For some reason, men are most dangerous in the middle of the night. I once watched a comrade used, beaten, partly strangled, then quartered. Dismemberment is common. I've heard rumors of burnings—though because of the dangers of fire in a stable, I doubt that this can be true. I've never witnessed these things in the daylight, except following a trial.

So, if there's a late arrival, this can be bad. You must slip between the beasts—quickly, without the help of your eyes. Using your hands, you must locate a post and find the ropes that have been used to tie the beasts' heads. These will let you know the distance that is safest between the animals and where you can pass without feeling their teeth. If you are very lucky, you may happen upon an empty slip or foaling stall. But hiding there can be dangerous because the traveler, arriving exhausted and looking for a place to leave his mount, may also come upon it. Then, if he sees you, you've no escape. If he doesn't see you, his beast will surely injure you, for it has not yet been tied and in order not to be observed, you must remain quite still. Or you may find a slip where an aging palfrey sleeps. This is the best of fortunes, for these nags don't disturb easily and have little vigor in them. However, in the dark, you've only your hands and nose to follow and little time. Careful discriminations are difficult, and fortune rarely blesses you in these matters, for the stable will be full of stallions and they wake at every move. You are well advised not to waste minutes searching, but to slide as quickly as you can behind the first post and wait. The beasts on either side will try to bite you as you pass, but if tied well, they'll fail. Once between them, with the post to conceal your form, you should attempt not to take another step. Perhaps you will be fortunate. The traveler or awakened groom may find a place just inside the entrance. However, this isn't often the case for, being indolent, the stable boys will have led each mount only as far as the nearest opening, so the vacant slips will be at the far end of the structure, and as the intruders approach, you'll need to continue moving back toward the stable wall.

This will give the beasts beside you great joy. For their hind—quarters are either untied or just loosely tethered, and they will feel your heat, feel your head near their thighs, smell that you are frightened. You will know then how small you are and that your skull is paper. As the traveler or groom walks up the row of animals, you'll be amazed how still the monsters become. Those near the entrance will snort or squeal, stomp their feet, even put their ears back, flair their nostrils, and try—despite the ropes around their nose and head—try to bite the traveler's weary horse as he trudges past, and the groom may bellow at them, strike their faces with a crop or reins. If he's especially irritable, he may stop and belabor one till blood flows. This can be very good. Or he may just swear impotently, continue on, half–asleep, unknowing. You'll hear the shot of hooves against the wall at your back, the feet stomping, animals leaping at their ropes, but where you sit crammed up in the tiniest ball at the base of the floor with your knees pulled sharply up under your chin and thighs jammed against your chest, there where you hide, your beasts will remain as still as the sun over water. This is because they mean to kill you. If there's sufficient glow from the groom's lantern, you'll be able to see this in their eyes. They will peer back at you, of course, without interest. Their necks will be twisted as far as the ropes allow, but a fly would animate them more than you. You're very small. They aren't disturbed. They don't despise you. They mean to kill you because they're bored.

As the late intruders approach, one or the other beast beside you will stir. He'll edge his rump to one side, peering at you past his shoulder, calculating where you are, how far you'll leap. You don't know which animal will strike first, of course, but prefer they don't strike together. You can expect one to kick your head when the groom draws even, and you'll have to lunge without his hearing, land on your toes' edge, swallow the noise inside.

This restraint is difficult, and I haven't always managed it. Once I weakened and was heard and barely escaped under the bellies of the animals. My hand was crushed and two fingers became useless. I was bitten, which is always a great liability, for everywhere you flee you leave a spoor of blood. A hoof—ludicrous in the dark—glanced off my shoulder and I heard the crunching inside. For some reason, I wanted to laugh. When at last I escaped, I swooned. Later the pain was very bad. I lay in the straw several days, unable to move, my hand and shoulder bloated grotesquely, like grain sacks. I had no food.

The first strike will usually land no more than a hand's width from your face. It will be so loud the echo will never cease, and you'll feel your skull swell so large to contain it that nothing else will ever reside there. However, you mustn't let this distract you. You have to be prepared to leap—always without a sound, without movement really, never whimpering, no rustle, glint of light—must dip your shoulders quickly, for the second horse may let fly, and the first—having seen you alter your place—may swing his hip full around and step on your shin or ankle. Or he may be pleased to observe you, his eye expressionless, may distract himself watching you shake. Sometimes their hoofs lash out rapidly in succession, smashing the wall just beside your eyes, again and again, or just above or beneath you, their dead flesh bouncing back upward the instant it touches ground. If both beasts are spirited in this fashion, it may be wise to risk the groom's cruelty, for it will soon prove impossible to remain sufficiently vigilant in both directions. And once injured, your face will be crushed quickly. However, such devilish vigor is rare, for they find great amusement in your suffering and wish to prolong it. Striking rapidly, they can't watch so well. It is only the most untamed among them—the thinly muscled Spanish beasts who remember the green scent—only those who've preserved their happiness, who'll fall into an ecstasy trying to kill you. Whenever possible, avoid them. Sometimes you can determine these by their odor, for it is more shrill in your nose than the others. But such discernment quickly becomes difficult, for stables have a blinding smell, or taste, mix of piss, semen, dung, hay, rodents, and living inside it—especially if you are afraid—and often longing to vomit, you may become incapable of correct discriminations.

If you must vomit, it's best to swallow it. As silently as you can. And as soon as you beshit yourself or piss your shirt, if you are clothed, shed your garments—stealing others is rarely difficult—and, regardless of the danger, flee that stall. For the animals will smell these things, and your shame will give them great joy, and so they will become exuberant in stalking you, amassing confidence, and this can be a liability, for when—

And Leonardo had shrieked then: Who are you to be telling this to me!

And Salai had said: I'm your life. I'm your life. I'm your life.

HORSES

About the time Leonardo was preparing for Ludovico's Paradise Festival, during the winter of 1489–90, while sitting up nights in Ambrogio de Predis' little shop above a nameless alley dickering with the weights, gears, springs and wedges of his clockwork universe, he'd become aware of an intrusion that, by the time he first noticed it, had already become a habit: a child, sullen and filthy, sleeping who–knew–where but continually underfoot, hovering at the edge of Leonardo's eyes. Later this odd fact, that Leonardo never actually saw Salai for the first time, that his earliest encounter with the boy had been a kind of stumbling over what, even as he tripped on it, was already tiresome ...this fact would characterize Salai, or perhaps only Leonardo's involvement with him. Whatever, Salai's arrival would remain inseparable in Leonardo's memory from the whirring of his clockwork universe, the maddening wait on the Castello stairs as Bellincioni teased the hardness of the stones away, and the brisk January morning when Leonardo first woke to the echo of the world shouting his name. Already as Leonardo climbed from bed that morning, not thrilled so much as reassured, buoyant, as if what he'd always suspected had finally been confirmed and so left him with the confidence that, yes, he could continue—all that, assuming he could believe in it—as he climbed from his bed that morning and walked to the door of the little workshop where goat cheese should have been waiting but where instead he found the black–haired, nameless urchin, scrawny, louse–eaten, leaning against the doorjamb with his empty gaze drifting over the fence, already Leonardo had begun to wonder. But not until that morning did he suspect anything new. Leonardo had coughed, shuffled his feet, raised his knuckle to tap the boy on the noggin, when all at once Salai turned around. His curls hung down into his face, his eyes were damp—neither a child's eyes, nor a man's—and without acknowledging that, yes, he'd just eaten Leonardo's breakfast, he spoke: They say you're making a horse.

Now, that chronology had to be wrong. Leonardo's encounter with Salai couldn't have been on the morning after his clockwork universe bedazzled Italy and Spain because, until the mechanism finally started to whirr and tick and turn, Leonardo had been in danger of losing the whole commission. Ludovico hadn't spoken to him in over five months, the pipeline of reimbursements for materials had dried up to a trickle, and rumor had it that Antonio Pollaiuolo was about to step in and take over. It would be April before Leonardo would resume work on the statue, and if Salai or anyone else had asked Leonardo that January morning about the horse, Leonardo probably would've scratched his ear and shuffled back inside. Nevertheless the two moments would remain inseparable: that chill morning of his first success and his meeting with the boy. And during the summer that followed, as work on the horse intensified, the child had in his servile way so insinuated himself into the rhythm of the workshop that, despite the absence of anything he actually did there, he soon seemed inseparable from whatever went on. So that as this fact of Giacomo—whom Marco inexplicably persisted in calling Salai until gradually everyone else had picked it up and only Leonardo seemed to recall that the boy had ever had another name—as this fact was acknowledged, so that a place began to be set out for him in the evenings and rags left in the loft to cover him on cool nights and his diminutive body confidently identified by the other boys as the one that even the newest apprentice could, with impunity, kick around—as all this that had evolved over months became commonplace, Leonardo began to sense a slippage in his affairs. He rose each morning to a clear agenda of steps, tasks, errands—first, divide the horse's head into degrees, then measure each section with a length of string, then build a box large enough to encompass its girth, then mark each side at regular intervals. And he went to bed each night telling himself that tomorrow would be the same. But something seemed to be underway that he hadn't started. And there were moments when he almost felt scared.

Leonardo passed that spring shuttling between his studio and the stables of Ludovico's military commander, Galeazzo Sanseverino. He compared the heads of twelve stallions known for their beauty and composed a primitive grammar of equine proportions. He divided the foreleg of a huge jennet into the intervals of the diatonic scale and compared the vertebrae of a dead Arabian with the wedges in an arch. He visited cannon foundries, took elaborate notes on casting and at night hid himself away with a Latin primer, hoping one day to translate Aristotle on his own. He repeatedly reassured himself that, with all he was learning, he had to be making progress, but despite eight years of work on the statue, his problem was still the same: His horse wouldn't stand up. Between the works of gods and of Florentines there seemed to be this difference. Galeazzo's Sicilian destrier could rear back on its hindlegs like a creature of fire and ether—Leonardo had seen him countless times—but no amount of genius could persuade a sixty–ton bronze cantilever to extend diagonally twenty–five feet from two posts as thin as horse ankles. Since 1482 Leonardo had been drawing models of the statue with and without its rider, forelegs kicking out at a snake or fallen archer, or rocking back as the beast's frenzy was reined in, sometimes with the trunk stretched almost straight upward as if about to leap an impossible barrier, other times extended over prostrate enemies, shrubs, tangled lances, but no matter how he shifted the center of balance, the statue remained a no go. The problems were the same ones he'd encountered in his designs for flight—the incommensurability of live and dead weight, the intricacy of the pulley system that made up animal myology, and above all, the astounding ratio of strength to bulk in bone and muscle tissue. If nature was whole, he reasoned, the creation of beasts, statues, and paintings should on some horizon converge. But the more he studied, the more it seemed: Making a horse was one thing, making a sculpture another.

Sometime that year Leonardo changed his plan for the statue. Instead of the rearing horse we now say we know he couldn't have completed but don't, Leonardo began to work on the prancing horse we now think he probably could've completed but didn't. It's anybody's guess how this change came about. During that summer of 1490 he traveled to Pavia to consult on the renovation of a cathedral, and while disputing with the architect Francesco di Giorgio, he probably noticed the equestrian monument in the piazza. I imagine him standing in the heat, seething under one of Francesco's patronizing retorts, and becoming conscious that he was, well, gawking at it. The ancient statue was of the goth King Gisulf, face turned sunward, body held in the ease and readiness of a practiced rider, and beneath him his horse pranced, mane bouncing, neck jaunty. Of course, what Leonardo saw wasn't the pose. That was traditional. Perhaps he saw himself, that confined ambitions still interested him, that a single step forward involved something he'd missed. But it's even odds whether what he saw buoyed him up or cast him down. No matter how excited he became about the Pavian statue, he must've felt his distance from its creator. That sculptor had been whole in ways Leonardo never could've dreamed. Undertaking the Pavian horse, the man had simply set out to achieve what at every moment of his life he'd always already known. To achieve the same, Leonardo would've needed to put out his eyes, forget Brunelleschi, un–know himself. And so, even if he hadn't found Fazio Cardano cavorting with the blacksmith two nights later and never ended up witnessing on a brothel's roof what convinced him that, even if he managed to connect flesh to bronze by divine omniscience, his life would always be accidental …, well, Leonardo still would've returned to Milan feeling dead.

His bones creaked. A cuspid throbbed. He could feel his face shriveling, the skull pushing through. When he got to the workshop he shut himself in his bedroom, collapsed on the bed. All he wanted was oblivion. All he got were paroxysms, ecstasies, galloping fears. Leonardo was a boy again—only ten years old!—wandering Albano's slope, gazing up into a horse–shaped darkness that floated in mid–air. Its flesh shivered, its nostrils dilated and blew, its pizzle winked out from a sack of skin—snort, stomp, snicker, blow. Miraculously the mass seemed to move and remain stalwart at the same time. Then, just as Leonardo drew back, there was a snap like cracking bronze. And he found himself falling down the wet edge of a rock, clawing at the black air, beating his face on night's scarp, terrified, as he tumbled into nothing at all. At this point Leonardo repeatedly awoke, sat bolt upright, and saw two eyes gazing back at him. Beyond his fingertips a vortex of black curls glistened in the moonlight, and from the round bone in his ankle a peculiar warmth had begun to spread. Could Leonardo have not known what was happening? Are there men whom nothing arouses while there's still time? All night this sequence repeated—collapse, dream, snap, vision—and on into the next after-noon when, alert at last, Leonardo would've climbed out of bed and up into the hayloft to toss the presumptuous street child back into the alley—or so he told himself later—if only he hadn't caught a whiff of almonds, seen daylight and grasped a single, clear idea: If bronze won't support sixty–tons on two legs, give it three! He leapt from the sheets, threw on his hose and tunic, and set to work with the first pleasure he'd felt in years.

Progress was glacial. Before beginning to think about the bronze sculpture, Leonardo had to design a casting mold, to find kilns large enough to fire the sections, and devise a scheme for assembling the parts. But these operations remained so far in the future as to seem phantasmagoric. First, full–size clay models of the sections had to be made and before that, an array of smaller models in varying poses and scales, all of which would require extended study. During a trot what were the relative proportions of shank to gaskin, and when the left foreleg was fully lifted, in which planes were the other legs—not to mention neck, mane, tail—found? And, of course, all his previous calculations for a stationary animal now needed adjusting for a moving one, which presented the old problem, viz., that understanding momentum in a horse taught you so little about the appearance of momentum in a piece of bronze. But regardless of these difficulties, Leonardo felt heartened. Every operation looked simpler now. Not that any obstacles had been overcome, but an old distraction seemed to have been removed. All summer long his horse moved forward a step at a time, never reared up to throw him. He busied himself concocting glues, experimenting with new tools and braces, and he began designing a huge cart to transport the finished work to the Castello. He'd made a start. Now he was in the middle of it. And if, lying in bed at night he heard the sound of breathing nearby, he must've dreamed it was his own genius beginning to stir at last.

But it was while negotiating these manageable tasks, as he calibrated the number of handwidths across the flanks of Galeazzo da Sanseverino's Sicilian gelding or bent over a tiny mechanism made of match sticks and cypress kindling or pushed ciphers about like a usurer figuring interest, it was while absorbed in just such daily operations that Leonardo began to feel troubled. The horse made sense within a realm. He called this realm by many names, sometimes imagined it as a god, other times as an elaborate gearworks or as chinese boxes, but mostly it was nature. What he sought to achieve, what ordered the actions of Marco and the shop boys and determined expenditures and animated his conversations with his rival Bramante or even decided which pages to read in Euclid or Alberti, was the difference between inside the realm and out. When he figured out that a compact arrangement in a mechanism worked more reliably than a dispersed one, he concluded that, instead of being an accident, compression was natural to organisms, and he found it in sonnets and cattle embryos and the path of water down a roof. He concluded that the leverage necessary to keep the horse's ankles from cracking was more readily achieved if these same perpendiculars formed the statue's infrastructure, more readily still if they were the troughs to evacuate the casting wax. No part could afford a private life. Within the overall harmony every entity joined every other, became multiple, allegoric. It was precisely this connectedness that made works—those of gods and Florentines—doable.

Which led to a conclusion. Genius, observation, study, theory, craft, ought finally to amount to one thing. In other words, a flesh and blood horse could be considered a vastly more complex version of an alarm clock, power relay, ratchet, or water screw. If it were possible to know all the principles involved, you should be able to make a horse by sheer calculation. God had. Likewise, if you observed horses carefully enough, long enough, you'd learn what inspired feats revealed. Same thing for paintings, poplar leaves, madrigals. The problem that in the midst of his absorption disturbed Leonardo wasn't that nothing so neat ever happened. The problem was that, when it did, it didn't last. Sometimes a successful step resulted from observation, calculation, craft, or the combination of all three, but the next time it resulted from an accident or sprezzatura or dumb luck or...truth was, Leonardo couldn't tell what it resulted from. He might spend all afternoon figuring out the ratio of powdered borax to Greek pitch and aqua vitae in a sealing solution only to find it unaccountably dry or glutinous when mixed. He could adjust for the mistake, of course, but the next week he might have to adjust for the adjustment or return to the original proportions or, most inscrutable of all, might find that the solution had now begun to display the opposite defect, was too viscous where it had been too runny. Or he *thought* it had been too runny. He had to vary each day's practice from the regularities he'd observed during the days before, watched his most reliable conclusions mislead him. If nature made perfect sense after midnight when the city was quiet, it might make none at all—or even appear monstrous and uncanny—in the boiling afternoon.

And then Leonardo had an experience.

(The story needs a scene here. I can't write it. Leonardo goes to dine at Andrea da Ferrara's home, gets into a quarrel with his companion or rival, the architect Bramante. A trivial issue, not sure just what, but the fact that Leonardo doesn't care makes his anger even more disturbing. What's happening to him, etc.? When he gets back home, he finds the workshop in an uproar. Several of the boys huddle in a corner, brandishing fists. A barrel of plaster has been overturned, a large earthenware jug's smashed on the floor. Marco, the oldest apprentice, waves a gesso hook in the air, looks genuinely dangerous. Leonardo blusters, "Who!" "What!" And they all point to Salai—that is, the new boy. I think Leonardo's still calling him Giacomo. Anyway, seems that Marco has found his lost silverpoint in a sack Salai keeps in the loft—don't ask what Marco was doing there—and now all the other boys are eager to mutilate him. The whole things strikes Leonardo as crazy, without reason. Anyway he boxes some ears, bellows, grabs Giacomo/Salai by the breeches, and drags him upstairs.

And here something unaccountable happens. I can imagine it, or think I can, but if I tell it, my sense of artificiality, of unnaturalness becomes overwhelming. Leonardo pulls the boy to the edge of the bed, starts berating him. At first Salai won't look up, stares down at the floor or gazes past Leonardo's shoulder. Leonardo figures he's ashamed. But the posture's too stiff, unbending, etc. When Leonardo can't get a confession, he gets irritated, decides to strap him. Just then the boy pulls something out of his pocket. Maybe it's a wad of paper. He says, "You've got it wrong."

Leonardo, of course, thinks the boy means the silverpoint. He becomes furious, "Liar!"—picks him up by a fistful of curls. Maybe he even slaps him, I'm not sure. But the boy just becomes furious, too. He shakes the paper right into Leonardo's face. "No!" he screams, dangling by his hair—"It's flat!" or "dead!" or "paper, you dolt!" or something. I don't know. And undoing the wad, he reveals the torn section of a sketch. It's from a drawing Leonardo has made of forelegs. Salai points at the pastern."It's not *moving!*" he shrieks.

You can see my problem. Anyway, Leonardo knows the boy's right.)

And that night before retiring, Leonardo installed a drawbolt on the inside of his bedroom door. He began locking himself in each evening, ignoring the rodent's claws that scratched in the dark. He didn't hear his genius stirring anymore, and getting out of bed each morning his legs felt heavier, but something had been contained. Marco, Antonio and the shop boys certainly noticed a difference, an official limit where before there'd been neglect, and possibly because they were working hard and felt exhausted or because they trusted Leonardo's judgment—not likely—or looked toward a time when they'd be journeymen themselves and could behave just as capriciously or perhaps because like Leonardo they too had felt the erosion, the tiny blackguard's way of—merely by leaning on his broom or falling into that to and fro of hips and arms that passed for sweeping—his way of insinuating himself into whatever you were doing until almost any clearly acknowledged status seemed preferable to this squishy, infinitely malleable nothing ..., perhaps because of all this or something still less explicable, they didn't complain. They continued to ostracize and beat Giacomo, just as they had themselves been ostracized and beaten, as had Leonardo himself, but in the workshop affairs remained outwardly as before. And Leonardo took heart that, at the least, the walls of his room defined him. He was master here, and if someone doubted it, or if at times he doubted it himself, he could point to the workshop floor, where day by day horse was coming to light.

All that fall Leonardo's plan for the Sforza monument accomplished what nothing else had accomplished for so long before, i.e., kept him on track. He had little difficulty ignoring Bellincioni's mocking deference when the two men passed in the Castello, and he quickly forgot Francesco di Giorgio's condescension and Bramante's bluster. When it became clear that the cardinal in Pavia was going to follow di Giorgio's recommendations for the cathedral there, when his own entry for the cupola competition in Milan was ignored, Leonardo shrugged, said his horse was enough to chew his beard over, and simply went on. Using the furnace of a nearby armaments manufactory, he cast a waist–high replica of his statue that managed on its humble scale to stand firm and look remotely like a beast prancing. For some reason the raised foreleg didn't harden properly and what should have been a hoof remained an elongated blob, but for the first time he could touch his conception, and it thrilled him. However, as the nature of his achievements began to look increasingly arbitrary that fall, as the horse's progress came to depend on mere accidents or chance, Leonardo found himself more susceptible to interruptions. The sound of a boy's voice in the alley outside his window might lure him into wordless reveries, or while piecing together the dried hipbones of a dead colt he might slip off into daydreams of hedgerows near Vigevano or of a Roman arch that once puzzled him or Bramante's chancel near San Satiro. Sometimes he'd get sidetracked by a mathematical oddity or mechanical toy, and intending to distract himself for only a moment, he'd realize hours later or at bedtime that he'd squandered his whole day. He took strolls through his little vineyard to clear his head; he began to lure himself on with bits of dried fruit or unwholesome pastry. His toothache returned, and he pulled the cuspid himself rather than submit to a barber. The distraction from the ordeal was even worse than the agony—which was saying a lot—and for a week work stopped. Of course, he eventually got himself back on course, and he tended to dismiss his waywardness as understandable, but his erratic concentration dismayed him. With no sure notion of how the parts of his undertaking fit together, of how his experiments with burnishing salts in July connected to his drawings of horse tails in September, he had difficulty not succumbing to randomness. The end was nowhere in sight. The very idea of progress looked squishy. What was all this effort for, anyway?

And that was when Leonardo encountered what, when years later on his deathbed if he'd bothered to think back on it, would've seemed like an omen or portent or whatever you call the first sure sign of the predicament you'll eventually wind up in but which, at the time it happened, just looked weird.

During that winter of 1490-91 Ludovica Sforza announced his engagement to Beatrice d'Este, and the marriage promised to have more kinks in it than a bedspring. Cecilia Gallerani, Ludovico's mistress—and in some versions, his master too—was pregnant. No one in Beatrice's family was likely to cavil about adultery—Beatrice at age

97

fifteen having herself been around the block a time or three—so long as what was universally known remained officially unacknowledged and all political arrangements were satisfactory. This last, however, presented an obstacle. After all, the wedding wasn't Ludovico's hooplah. It was ostensibly for young Anna Sforza, Ludovico's niece, whose name on the invitations was necessitated because Ludovico wasn't the real duke, only regent and de facto duke, the real duke being Gian Galeazzo Sforza, whose frailty promised to prevent him from ruling Milan outright until 1494 when tuberculosis would finally save Ludovico the trouble of assassinating him. However, for now the strength of Ludovico's bond with the enceinte Cecilia seemed critical, since Ludovico had only actual power, not official power, which meant that his wife, who even under the best circumstances would have only actual power, not official power, would now have only actual power over one who himself had only actual power and who, therefore, had better not be under another woman's actual power, etc. And Cecilia was one of the few Lombard women whose learning, wit, and savoir vivre could actually rival Beatrice's. Leonardo got involved in this mess because the clearest reassurance that Ludovico could give the Este that he was, in fact, master in his own house was to treat himself to the kind of conspicuous celebration that all other interested parties—Cecilia, Anna Sforza, Duke Gian Galeazzo, Duchess Isabella, the Pope, Holy Roman Emperor, Kings of Naples, France, Spain—would find infuriating. That is, Ludovico's wedding needed to eclipse in splendor every other conjugal celebration in recent memory, especially that of the true Duke and Duchess, at whose nuptials only twelve months earlier the little known Florentine inventor Leonardo da Vinci had made a huge hit with his clockwork zodiac, spheres and gods—the renown of which posed a problem now.

So that was how, on a December afternoon, Leonardo found himself standing in Galeazzo Sanseverino's courtyard watching various footmen in outlandish costumes parade geldings by while Leonardo's assistants flopped this or that piece of cambric across their haunches and Messer Galeazzo hmmmed and ahhhed until Leonardo could insinuate which color or gewgaw would appear most impressive and Messer Galeazzo could announce that this was, in fact, his choice. It was the merest silliness, but in truth, Leonardo found it a stupendous relief. Work on his statue had slowed to a standstill, and he'd taken to sleeping later, exhorting his apprentices with talk of discipline, discipline. The workshop looked a mess, half finished carvings, plaster dust, open pots of gummy oils everywhere, and as the temperatures plunged that winter, everyone's cold, clumsy fingers provided ample excuses for doing nothing at all. The wedding made this lassitude official. Ludovico's plan was to put on a jousting tournament whose colorful banners and stunning costumes would give a romantic appearance to the practice of driving an oak pole through someone's chest, and in service to this end, Leonardo, young Andrea, Marco, a silk merchant's unsightly child named Balthazar, Antonio, Giuliani, and, of course Salai, were modeling costumes, measuring cloth, shucking peacock feathers and, in general, gaudying-up enough good horse tack to make the victims look cheery. Leonardo had just remarked to Galeazzo that, given the likely result of the jousts, they might wish to employ scarlet tactfully, when a shriek sounded from the palazzo.

Running inside, they all found Salai upended, curls bouncing about his eyes, struggling with one hand to prevent his pockets from spilling and, with the other, to protect his brains from hitting the floor. One of Galeazzo's retainers, in a grass skirt, fright-wig, and necklace of dog's teeth, held the boy's ankles, while Marco grabbed at his hands and Antonio tore his breeches down. Portions of outlandish costumes were scattered on the chairs and divans, and the ash-bucket had been overturned. There were shouts of *ladro!* Thief!

Leonardo commanded them to stop, never expecting them to and feeling astonished when they did. The retainer released Salai and started back-pedaling. Marco tossed Salai's hands aside and dove for the armoire. Antonio froze with fear. Having failed to inspire such awe in his lackeys before, Leonardo was about to seize the opportunity to deliver a fine tongue-lashing when something massive flashed by his face. He turned to look, just as the liberated Salai, screeching like a cat, leapt into his midsection. The shape was, Leonardo recognized, messer Galeazzo's sword, which at that very minute, in this very tiny room, was turning the furnishings and bedclothes into confetti. The retainer prostrated himself weeping, and the sword hissed through the air landing an eyelash away from his face. A perfect circle of urine appeared on the floor. Marco disappeared behind the armoire, Antonio beneath the divan. Salai yiped and scooted between Galeazzo's feet, giving a kick to the retainer's head in passing and looking for all the world like the only one present lacking in healthy fear. Leonardo ducked, Galeazzo swore, the armoire tipped over missing everyone by less distance than all would've liked, and leaving Marco exposed with a very sickly grin. Seeing his chance, the retainer hugged his master's ankles, pleading for mercy, and Marco, who prayed the man knew what he was doing, followed suit. Salai took a last turn about the room-stomping Antonio's instep, plunging a finger in Marco's eye, tweeking the servant's beard, and taking out Galeazzo's knee in a gratuitous show of force—and then with a snappy head-fake, zigged, zagged, spun past Leonardo's clutching fingers, and vanished out the door.

And Leonardo found himself moving. Down a corridor, through the kitchen, over a chopping block, into a pantry, around a laundry hamper, up stairs. He didn't know why he was moving, not at first, whether he was running after the child or from something. He'd simply followed the same motion out of the room that had caught everyone up inside, gone with it, and this was when—for the first time in this hallucination of an hallucination—Leonardo asked himself: Why had he never kicked this little troublemaker out? The emphasis falls on *asked*. It wasn't that, dashing down the hall, he decided he would. It was that for the first time he acknowledged having had for months every reason to discard Salai, no reason to tolerate him, and so felt now the urgent need for explanations he lacked. He started to feel panicky, tried to convince himself he was just mad.

Anyway, it was then that, turning a corner in some anonymous corridor, Leonardo saw a door close and leapt for it. His hand hit the wood with a loud thwack. Heat burst in his wrist. Then the door gave way and a body came whirling at him, kicking, shrieking, biting, twisting. And Leonardo held Salai. The torso gyrated, kicked out twice, went flaccid. Leonardo felt his fingers close around the boy's throat, felt the flimsy cartilage flex in his palm. A strange exhilaration rose inside him. With his free hand he ran his fingers through the oily curls and, pulling the hair back, forced the boy's eyes to meet his. Was this it, the edifice against which he was beating his brains bloody? And for the briefest of instants it seemed that Leonardo's life could be different, as if—far from being a mad and incalculable labor—the horse were a conceivable task, something he could just do and walk away from. It was only a statue! You didn't have to unriddle the universe! Salai's lips were motionless, his eyes vacant. Leonardo listened to his breath hissing softly, felt the muscles struggling to swallow underneath his palm, and as Marco's shouts began to echo along the corridor and from nowhere Antonio appeared waving a poker and in the distance Messer Galeazzo's heavy boots could be heard clopping unrhythmically over stones, Leonardo and Salai gazed into each other's face. And both knew Leonardo would always protect him.

The soldi! Marco yelled and leapt at Salai's hand.

Antonio waved the poker. Ladro! Pederasta!

Leonardo lifted the boy high into the air and, with his free hand, prized three coins from Salai's fist.

Marco dove for the money. Antonio dove for Marco. There was a moment's frenzy—oaths, scratching—then darkness. When Leonardo recovered, Salai had vanished and Antonio was crying.

Galeazzo arrived short-sword in hand. Dank turds! he bellowed. Cocytus' tomb!

Leonardo shrugged. Gone.

Sitting in the oven of my vast and remarkably yellow 1955 Buick Roadmaster beneath a thirty–foot monument to every heart's desire as my doggy drools down my neck and the flash–floods of perspiration rush over my flesh producing, when I move my arms, a frictionless glide reminiscent of ice skating, I'm puzzled by my nearness to the catastrophe ahead. I'm trapped here because doomed men are struggling, but from where I sit I can't tell what's underway, and if I were to try to help, I'd have no clear idea what to do. It appears to be a clash of systems and forces. I don't count. From her post overhead the thirty foot woman takes no notice. Her eyes are set on the infinite distance where all my wants will be fulfilled, and the doomed men are, after all, doomed, and so not her boys. Surely I love this woman with a love past remembering, but sitting so close to her mounds and abysses I can't help noticing, well, she lacks a dimension. For instance, she doesn't talk. Not that the desires I'm convinced are my deepest, secret, most unspeakable and, hence, my real desires, not that these leave much room for talk, but still, I want to. Who can say why? People grow restless, want answers. I can imagine how the thirty foot woman would satisfy every doubt but prefer, in this heat, not to. Unlike Deirdre, to whom it's pointless to say anything and in front of whom I can never hold my tongue but who, if she speaks, is sure to say what makes me crazy, what'll provoke me to swear and slash the air and reveal that I haven't the faintest glimmer who my not–wife is, the thirty foot woman either arouses me or puts me to sleep. Now, I can't say I desire resistance, can't even say I desire Deirdre—what good does saying it do?—but I can say that as Deirdre prepares right now to go somewhere horrible to do what's inconceivable to objects and persons I prefer never even to consider, the prospect of living without her terrifies my soul. Of course, life without the thirty foot woman might be dreary, too. Some have even said she speaks words as irresistible as Deirdre's, that her sentences are figures of bliss and flesh, unmistakable at any distance but, up close, having no depth at all. I know an irrefutable argument why this can't be the case but believe it is. What if all around me now there were secrets to which I'm deaf, revelations I can't see, noisy proclamations bringing my nightmares to light? Refusing such miracles betrays the mind's petrification, but still, I wonder: How will I translate?

In front of me drivers are forsaking their A/C to hike themselves up on fenders and steal glimpses of the mayhem. Occasionally, some adventurers march down the lines of cars to get a closer look, but either a police barricade or the heat sends them back. Lots of chatter, communal disgruntlement, quips. Nobody seems to know anything. I'm dehydrating, waiting for a definitive disaster, when I notice—to my left at the edge of my vision—a woman literally sprinting to her car. I ask myself why, on pavement in street clothes under direct sunlight, would a sane adult, who had any alternative, *run*, but then I hear a shout behind me and doors banging. All at once, people appear to be running everywhere. I figure the demonstration's breaking up, reach for the ignition, but at the same time I think, uh–oh, this looks like panic. Windows closing, doors being locked, lots of hollering. I start punching buttons on the Port–A–Phone, maybe Deirdre's still got me on TV, but all I hear's the cricket sound. She's gone. Even in 120 degree heat, even in the middle of bedlam, DeeDee's employer's phone ringing into an empty house makes me sick.

"Harr—harr—harr!"

I turn around. There's this fat monstrosity in a beach shirt and opaque sunglasses a couple of Toyotas over, and he's sprawled on top of his pickup roof, a mini–TV propped up on the hood, sucking what looks like a (COLD!?) beer, and chortling like an idiot.

"Cops?" I yell over at him.

He grins back. "Worse."

I screw up my face to say, I don't get it, but he just harr–harr–harrs and looks back at his TV, and then I do. Several youngish men, one virtually naked, others in the wet, disheveled remains of business suits, ties and jackets, are all jogging up alongside the rows of cars, trying to talk to passengers, yelling slogans, waving, exchanging a few smiles, even getting down on their knees in mock attitudes of pleading. The tone of it's hard to gauge. Lots of burlesque, a carny atmosphere, mardi gras—one guy in response to some banter from a car drops his trousers and wiggles his fanny—but then you remember that some of these guys are sick, they've just been yanked around by people who refuse to touch them, they've got to feel rotten, some are probably scared. A pale, bald man—late thirties maybe—walking my way doesn't look like he's having any fun. His tie's yanked, and there's blood on the front of his shirt, apparently from a badly swelling nose. He's not trying to talk to anybody, hardly looking up, but then neither does he seem exactly to be running away. I hang out my window as he passes. "Hi," I say.

He looks at me, stops. "'Hi'? 'Hi'? This is a *riot*, for Chrissakes."

"You okay?"

He points to his face. "This look like okay?"

I notice that his suit, despite the grunge and wrinkles, is a spiffy, double–breasted affair. His eyes have a damp, animal sickliness about them. "Nope. Cops coming?"

"It's the dream of their lives that we'll get away." He swipes at his nose with his cuff. The sleeve comes away bloody. "Any chance you got a handkerchief?"

"Kleenex," I say and pull one of those pocketbook–size packages from my glove box. He uses it all.

"How come I'm doing this?" he sounds like he's asking me but isn't. "I mean, maybe there's a square foot left in Utah where a demonstration still demonstrates something, but just between you and me, don't count on it. I got hit in the *face*! Can you believe that? With a goddamn for–real billy club!"

"How many of you here at this—"

"Maybe thirty. They call it a 'theater.' Thirty of us at this 'theater.'"

"You gotta admit," I say, "it's impressive. Thirty people can stir up a lot of chaos. How many cars would you figure? Three hundred?"

"Oh, lot more than that. Three hundred just between here and the intersection."

"Impressive," I say.

"You wanna know what's weird?" He leans closer, places a hand on the roof.

Then for the first time he notices the Buick. "Hey, this thing is reeeeally awful!" He gives it a once over, whistles. "God, I've never seen anything …. Did they actually paint 'em like this? I mean, yellow—"

"Antique," I say. "What's weird?"

He sights down the chrome. "Twenty feet? Twenty–two feet maybe? Like they thought it was a rocket. And *yellow*." Whistles again. "But no way it'll run on low lead. You must have to—"

"What's weird?"

He's back. "What's weird is the whole purpose's coverage. The organizers—as smart guys go, these aren't smart guys—that's all they'll talk about. Reporters, cameras, interviews …."

"You mean like it's not really a protest?"

"No, I mean I work for the network, for Chrissakes. And here I am getting myself billy–clubbed for TV time! What if—it won't happen, but it almost could—what if I end up getting to decide whether to put my own face getting stomped on the news? I sit there in these meetings. They don't know me, they don't know what I do, but I'm fantasizing: Me getting me slammed to put me on …well, it's weird."

"So why're you doing it?"

He just slips off his jacket, hangs it on one arm, doesn't answer.

We stay like that a minute, then I add, "Want to sit?" I pull Leonardo's box out of the seat. "Give your blood time to clot."

He nods at Metropolis. "He bite?"

"Sometimes."

"My car's not far," he says. "I'll be out of here before you will."

We both chuckle.

Then he leans closer. "I'm gonna tell somebody, why not you? We hired a PR firm."

At first I don't get it.

"The demonstration—it has its own PR firm. Organizers do the interviews, but PR people decide what's to wear, which intersections, who talks, escape routes, call the stations, tips to cops, letters to editors. Even—get this!—there's this poor bastard. In a wheel chair—"

"Hairless, big ears, wasted looking," I say. "Local news, every night."

He nods. "Lennie. Seven'll get you ten he's planted before payday, but PR people, they use him like a prop! Rehearse Len's entrance, roll Len out, zoom Len across town—we got a special van—line up Len's angles, make sure the cops reach Len first …. It's all statistics, market data, codes, ratings. I mean, the guy's out there dying for MVI!"

I give him a blank.

"Maximum Video Impact."

"So why's he doing it?"

"So why'd anybody make a car like this?"

We bake.

Then, "Y'know, I haven't smoked in …seven, eight years, but I'd grovel for a cigarette right now," he says.

"Never leaves you," I say.

"No chance in hell …?"

"Nobody smokes anymore."

"Yeah." He grins, starts off.

"Good luck," I call after him.

"Not much of that."

I sit for a minute not wondering but not exactly not wondering. I remember childhood tales—maybe I'm making them up—of heat tortures, athletes dropping dead, death by poaching. Why is this funny? After awhile I start punching radio buttons, hunting news. Perspective would help, and though I won't get it, outright lies might help, noise might help. However, before I find anything I hear vibrations. Or maybe I just feel them, air kind of beating on my ear–drums and this klap–a–klap–a–klap–a rhythm, way off. Nothing I can see through the windshield, but then Metro notices too, ears up, snuffle snuffle, so I can't be hallucinating. I get out of the Buick and do a three–sixty. The sky's empty. I'm about to yell over at the fat monster in the shades on the pickup, when I notice he's gawking at me.

"I saw it," he shouts, like he's a real sharpie. "I got yoo, buddy, I gotchooo!"

I take a step in his direction. "Where?" I ask. "Can you see it?"

But all at once, the grin goes and he's standing. "Get back in there!" he yells, and not clowning, like scary. He jabs a finger at the Buick. "Now!"

Planes? Tanks? I'm thinking. Guns? I spin around, start for cover. I think I see whatever's seeable, don't see anything to fear, but I'm scrambling anyway because, hey, can't absolutely anything happen? But then I notice the fat guy hasn't budged. He's just standing there on top of the truck, ten feet in the air, his index finger jabbing at me like Uncle Sam.

"Which's it? You stupid or queer?" he demands, then waits. He actually seems to expect an answer. "Everybody's a liberal, you wanna pinch boy–fannies, blow goats, hump light–sockets, no skin off my ka-nozzer, buggers are okay, but hey, those guy's sweat poison! Whatchoo think you're trying to—"

Then I get it. "C'mon, all I did was talk to him!"

"That faggot was bleeeeeding!"

"Good grief," I say. "Look, a minute ago did you hear a propeller?"

"Don't I feel bad about you guys? I've had the clap, I'll say it, I've got herpes right now. God's an asshole, punishment for love. Here worm, this is whatcha get 'cause you're happy." Dramatic pause. "But now I ask you, does me dying do you guys any good? Does me gettin' sick make you feel better? No, not one—"

The guy is hairy. His shirt's got poinsettias on it and it flaps across a swollen belly with an outee. He's still holding the (COLD!) beer and has about a four–inch TV sitting on his truck hood and is wearing day–glow flip–flops, and over his eyes there are these opaque shades that resemble a push–up bra, and he's standing on the roof of a red pickup in 120 degree heat talking about death. He's a joke, of course, but he's a pretty good joke, and trapped in a bad one, I'm tempted to take him seriously.

"Nobody wants to contaminate you," I say.

"I mean, I got a heart," he says. "I hunt and that's not so good, I know, but I eat what I shoot, and I got parrots. *Two* parrots!" The man's *shouting* all this to me, two Toyotas away. "And you may not believe it, but I was married seven years and didn't cheat and still pay my child support. Gospel. So, it's not like I don't got feelings. I mean, if I started thinking what it's like to be you guys, dying from love. Yeccch. But does it do you any good I drive myself crazy? No, not a bit—"

"Everybody's dying," I say. "Democracy." I take a step toward him but his scruff rises. "Look, it's a tough case, we both got y chromosomes, both pollute, but between me and you, well, even if you were the Buddha, I could still go blind. What's that say? I don't say it says nothing. The guys in the road, maybe they're clueless. Maybe the point's not to save lives, or not only, or not just—"

"Hey, *I'm* not blaming you for being a faggot! *I* don't wanna kill bum fuckers! *I* never said just 'cause you're sick, just 'cause you're swishy, just 'cause you sodomize boy scouts—"

"Were we discussing you?"

"—*my* body, *my* fault, *my* business, *my*—"

"Excuse me," I shut the door, roll up the window. "Gotta French-kiss my dog."

As might be expected, after Leonardo da Vinci's unframing, Deirdre remained unreconciled to my collaboration in my professional demise. My attempts to explain why I'd abandoned "Leonardo" for Leonardo didn't get much clearer. What I kept wanting to tell Deirdre was, "Look in Leonardo's box, you'll see." But the circularity of this advice seemed unreassuring, even to me, and besides, what if she looked in the box and didn't? Nothing I had to say about what I'd said in the box could say more than or better what I'd said there, but maybe if Deirdre saw nothing in the one she'd see nothing in the other. And vice versa. However, in time Deirdre came around, not because she ever understood why someone whose intelligence she'd formerly respected would sacrifice his prosperity to create what couldn't possibly inform anyone of anything anyone would ever pay to know and, even if successful, could never divert you as much as a movie—Deirdre came around not because she understood what I'd done but because she turned as peculiar as me. En route to her future, Deirdre fell into the gap between what attracts somebody to a life and what you have to turn into to live it. That is, Deirdre found Metropolis. But I'm getting ahead of myself.

During the autumn after I miserably disappointed all who had faith in me, shamed Deirdre, and peeked into the maw of financial ruin, Deirdre took her doctoral exams in psychology. Perhaps her professors were only engaging in "supportively interactive mentoring behaviors" in their efforts to "positively empower" Deirdre in her "individuated esteem maintenance and self–actualization growth–program," but they told her she did well, and neither she nor I saw any reason to doubt their sincerity other than the reasons for doubting every word they ever said. As I spent those months sorting through the rubble of me, Deirdre began her clinical residency at the university mental health clinic. Each morning she drove to a remote corner of the campus where for four hours a day she became the ashcan into which people dumped their self–hatred and where for another four hours she tried to recover from the first four. The work was tough, she acknowledged. The forces of brokenness and alienation were overwhelming. Nevertheless, she remained optimistic: "People *want* to survive!" Unfortunately, she was amassing impressive evidence to the contrary. Her "client load" was a repertory of soap opera plots whose catastrophes she foresaw. She spent a lot of time not screaming: "You did whaaat?!" And never asking: "Have you lost your mind?!" And failing to comment: "Absolute BULLSHIT!" She often reassured herself that her clients were "in denial," which appeared to mean that she could ignore whatever they said but didn't seem to mean much else. Had I not known she was a mental health professional with techniques for maintaining her personal equilibrium in the face of madness and futility, I'd have mistaken her for someone devouring herself alive. Some nights she'd march through the door waving her arms and shrieking: "Can you believe X said Y to me, to me a woman! Actually came right out and said it, staring straight into my face! Hasn't he/she/it any shame! What in the Goddamn world do these people expect me to think if they sit right there and tell me they're going to etcetera." Other times she'd arrive dropping her clothes on the threshold, whooping, writhing, with a bottle in each hand, and go for the stereo volume. It was fun, but I was never sure it was me she was fucking.

However, the worst were the nights she didn't get out of the car. She'd pull into the drive and just sit there, forehead on the wheel or leaning back in her seat, a blasted expression in her eyes, ignoring me when I called her to dinner, and coming to bed, if at all, only after I was asleep. I'd find her in the morning on top of the covers, still wearing her clothes, sometimes with her eyes open, not in the magical oblivion of virtuous souls but in that gruesome, leaden state of narcosis from which a corpse awakens to prowl the earth. "Well, every job has its grim side," she'd repeat, and I could never disagree. "Whoever expected that caring would make sense?" she'd ask, and we'd admit that only fools expected it. "Every worthwhile undertaking looks pointless better than half of the time," she'd sigh, and I'd say nothing for fear my personal stake in this particular maxim might seem obtrusive.

"Nope, R—," she'd add, "what you're doing really *is* pointless."

But despite Deirdre's struggles, I didn't worry about her, or not at first. It seemed pretty clear that she was building something—a colossal model of human nature, an untold epic of woman, a basis for hope—and I figured, if the model held up, if it proved strong enough to support her, she'd have a lifetime to explain it. If it gave way, of course, we'd both know more about it than we could stand. So, I never asked her the obvious questions. After all, her misery wasn't proof she was wrong, and what alternative was there? However, more than once Deirdre asked herself the obvious questions for me. During a lull in conversation or as we'd sit reading by the woodstove, she'd get out of her seat, come around the coffee table, sit down as close to me as possible and, duplicating my exact posture, say: "Dee, honey, just out of curiosity, as your devoted spouse, I'd like to know why, for God's sake, you're punishing yourself in this ghastly manner, that is, if my asking doesn't pry." And I'd always figure that she was still okay as long as she got back up, returned to her seat, and answered, "No, I don't mind, R—, but I really don't know what to tell you. I suppose I'm mortifying myself in this way, because—and I'm a little embarrassed to admit it—because I must actually still believe somewhere inside of me that something I say or don't say or do or don't do may through some accident or oversight actually help some pathetic wretch a teensie–weensie little bit even though I certainly don't count on it anymore." And then she'd grin, "And I plan some day to charge a dollar a minute for it."

So, I didn't worry until I noticed a change. "After all, it's feelings that count, right? Not what people say, not what they think. You can't imagine some of the outlandish notions, perfectly preposterous ...! My job's to observe patterns, how ideas are *used*. Maybe I don't see it at first glance, but with training and practice and sound instincts and a solid foundation in research, well, obstacles can be identified, illusions uprooted, people can be encouraged to grow in their own—"

"What if they don't want to grow?"

"You can't not grow," she said.

"What if where somebody finds herself isn't a stage?"

"Life is never static."

"What if they believe their pain is just them?"

"Beliefs don't count. Humans grow."

"What if someone perfectly miserable has decided, well, this is my misery, it's the kind of misery someone like the person I am has, and she's fully prepared to stay right where she is for the rest of her natural life? I mean, couldn't she need help, well, just making do?"

"Nope, physics," Deirdre said. "Everything living moves."

The university mental health clinic was located on a square of grassy turf as far as possible from the alumni association and right next to the last remaining strip of residential property before the campus adjoined a massive housing project. The residential neighborhood had long since gone the way of student housing generally, having crammed approximately two hundred undergraduates into a fourth as many bedrooms and reverted to the primeval wilderness of an adolescent's imagination, so that the whole area looked bombed—except for the housing project which looked like a set for *1984*. On the entire block only one house was still inhabited by its owner, a bottle–blonde, fortiesh, topless dancer with too many children and boyfriends, named Franny. Franny possessed free and clear—through the VA and a vietnam hubby MIA or dead—a little brick bungalow that with a few thousand dollars in the right spots could have been fit for humans. Of course, Franny never saw a few thousand dollars in her whole life, so the dilapidated slum killed the imagination needed to restore it. However, along the back edge of Franny's property where the parking lot of the clinic adjoined what had once been a hedge, was the most splendid oak tree I've ever seen. Its top covered three lots; its trunk could have housed a kitchen, and unreliable estimates placed its seedling days before the Bill of Rights. The cacophony of coos and tweets and chitters from its branches could almost be heard above the traffic noise some days, and every afternoon as Deirdre limped out of her office and toward her Datsun, she would pause, stare up into this leafy abundance and remind herself that somehow, for no known reason, in isolated pockets throughout the universe, a handful of creatures weren't striving with all of their might to die. The students whizzed past, the stereos boom–shucka–ed, Franny's kids shrieked, the boyfriends swore. Because I believe every story has its secret loveliness, I imagined that the oak tree was Franny's, since I never saw any other.

Shortly after beginning her clinical residency Deirdre got Franny as her case. It was plain from Franny's file that she was a chronic liability of the clinic's location, a rite through which novices like Deirdre had for years been forced to pass. There were so many different handwritings on her case notes that they looked like a highschool yearbook, and Franny's evolving diagnoses composed a contemporary history of social work. Despite these intimations of futility, however, Franny's melodrama didn't seem homogenous. She'd undertaken several self–help campaigns, gotten her GED, beaten a drug habit, and managed once to keep a receptionist's position for over a year. Even fighting chronic depression, even shaking her nipples in strangers' faces every night, Franny could still horse-laugh and sound upbeat about love. But that was about as far as the romance of Franny ever got. The rest of her life was lawsuits and Child–Services investigators, a son with signs of autism, cancer symptoms she refused to check, mysterious bruises on her arms and neck, unanswered questions about the boyfriends and her daughter, and, maybe worst of all, an intangible something in her voice and mannerisms that made further explanations unnecessary. Although I knew all this about her only through Deirdre, never saw Franny's face till I saw it in on TV, and didn't learn her name until near the end—or rather because of this distance—I had much less trouble accepting Franny than Deirdre did. For me, Franny could be emblematic, a woman whose defeats disclosed the lurking grotesqueness of what passed for normal life, and I always suspected her predicament made more sense than Deirdre allowed. But Deirdre enjoyed none of my detachment. Having been saddled with the responsibility of gazing into Franny's eyes, of exposing herself every week to the raucous cadence of Franny's voice, Deirdre was continually fighting not to believe in her. I always knew the day of Franny's appointment by the way Deirdre dawdled in the shower that morning, by her truculence at breakfast and the edge in her voice as she dragged her slippers across the floor.

"It's just so ..., so .... And, R—, I'm really sorry to have to say this. It's just so male. Why are you afraid to feel what she feels?"

"How would I know if what I feel's what she feels? Hell, Dee, I've never even *talked* to her, for Chrissakes."

"If you were a woman, you'd know."

"Every morning I thank the eternal Santa Claus I'm not enough of a horse's ass to dispute that with you," I said.

"A woman doesn't have the luxury not to feel. She knows every second, in the middle of the night, at the tips of her fingers, in her stomach and feet, exactly how this woman feels."

"And you ask me what I'm afraid of?"

"Why are you always protecting yourself?"

Horse's ass though I was, I didn't say what I already suspected, that not even the vast fortress of psychotherapy was going to protect us from Franny. I'm not the poet of Franny's life, am not even the poet of my own, which is to say am struggling frantically and ineptly to become the poet of Leonardo's, Deirdre's, Metro's lives, and so of Franny's only by the way. So I'll neglect to recount the sequence of nightmares into which Franny and Deirdre descended that spring. Suffice it to say that Deirdre provided the "supportive environment" in which Franny "explored her personal value structures," and Franny utilized her "avoidance mechanisms" to forestall "self–actualization," and Deirdre stopped hoping Franny's life would ever change and consoled herself with knowing all the reasons why. What matters for this story is the final episode of that one.

All spring Deirdre and Franny continued to beat each other up without either one taking much interest in the outcome, and then one night a storm blew in from the ocean. During the pre–dawn hours Franny's gigantic oak dropped a gigantic limb on a shiny Mazda parked illegally overnight behind the clinic but owned by the son of an alumnus with deep pockets who, alas, was an attorney. It was obvious to all that the sole result of legal action against Franny would be pointless bankruptcy, since the courts couldn't confiscate her home and she owned nothing else, and besides, the son of the alumnus was rich and had insurance up the yazoo. However, rich lawyers rarely suffer in silence. So, somebody in a suit behind a desk called someone else in a suit behind a desk who in turn called numerous other similarly attired and identically situated persons and the upshot was a Sunday feature–page article—replete with data on the incidence of injury and property damage and taxpayer costs computed to the nearest thousand dollars—on the potential dangers of the unregulated growth of urban trees. There was a four color photo of Franny's tree limb lying across the demolished canvas top of the Mazda exactly where a driver's head could've been and a reference to the "narrowly averted catastrophe" in which Franny's name and address were given. Who knows what anyone in the seamless fabric of three–piece desk–proprietors hoped to accomplish with this silliness, but like most public campaigns, it was predictable only at the start. Within days there were letters to the editors, bumperstickers and yard signs, angry call–ins to talk shows, public opinion polls, rumors of a referendum, green logos, computations of tax dollars, activists bemoaning the demise of cedars and moms narrating Bobo's escape from murderous sycamores. Everybody had an opinion. Everyone sensed a crisis. Action was clearly called for. But among the array of self–defeating and mutually unintelligible solutions, the single point on which all parties agreed was, to anybody with common sense, everything was perfectly obvious.

A group named Trees R–4–U organized a string–a–thon in which players from the local high schools and community orchestra performed non–stop Haydn quartets twenty–four hours a day, through storm and calm, in the clinic parking lot beneath Franny's oak to dramatize the "harmony of man and nature." An anti–tax group (Metropolitan Younger Business Underwriters and Citizen's Council, or MY BUCCS) published documents demonstrating that, if the city sold at present market value the mature timber on all publicly owned lands, a half mill net decrease in property taxes over seven years would be the result. This was followed in the local papers by a brief and magnificent "warfare of the numbers." The Chamber of Commerce found itself divided between members insisting no one could tell *them* what *they* could do with *their* trees on *their* property and other members anxious for legislative protection from liability in cases of tree–related job–site accidents. Two vigilante groups sprung from nowhere, one called People for People that went on a rampage one night and lopped off about thirty large limbs in a downtown neighborhood, and a second group—People against People for People—that got into fist–fights with the first group. There was a demonstration. Some women in their fifties showed up in bell–bottoms and sang folksongs, and nine students occupied the president's office at the university and wouldn't let the secretaries in. The residents of the housing project issued a statement, a Native Americans' organization issued a statement, both major political parties issued then retracted then reissued statements that they subsequently disclaimed, and a previously unknown gay anarchists' coalition issued a perfectly filthy but very funny statement about coitus with a cunninghamia bush.

Where Franny was during this carnival I have no idea. Nothing I ever learned led me to suspect that she had an opinion on public menaces, either to trees or by them, and whether her notorious and surprising act resulted from panic, momentary confusion, or calculation seems to me to depend on whether one regards panic, confusion, and calculation as different things. All I can say with certainty is that for reasons never adequately explained, sometime during the early morning hours at the height of this impassioned public shout–fest, Franny walked into her backyard and with a tiny electric chainsaw made a seven inch deep incision around the circumference of her tree. In a book full of fabrications, concocted data, and shit flung high, let this fact stand as virtually true: The principal living parts of even the most massive trees are the outermost rings. Do these rings irreparable damage, and the tree won't die in a weekend, may not die in a fortnight, but trust me, the tree will die.

For about a week following what came to be called "The Windfall Taxes Chainsaw Massacre," Franny's face gazed back at Deirdre and me whenever we glanced at the newspaper or TV. She was interviewed, discussed, vilified, pitied, and of course, photographed, photographed, photographed. The news media thought it had died and gone to heaven: A high–minded public controversy involving a topless dancer with implants and a chainsaw! An array of absolutely incompatible groups identified Franny as the embodiment of whatever they considered right or wrong with the universe, and whether by skill or innocence— or simply because nobody was ever *listening* to her—she managed not to persuade them otherwise. Morning or evening Deirdre and I would turn on the tube and there'd be Franny, always a bust shot, explaining that the tree had been her shelter in a harsh world, but that the strain of fighting the government and business interests and courts and do–gooders and university was probably inconceivable to people who hadn't known it as intimately as she had, that is, in the flesh, and what's more, there were personal disappointments that Franny's modesty prevented her from mentioning, promises and betrayals that …that…. And her lip would tremble and the camera would zoom in and several buttons would inexplicably pop loose and then she'd recompose herself, remind the interviewer she was no one's victim, owned the tree free and clear, and was a taxpaying citizen.

Later Deirdre and I decided Franny's account of what happened had to stink, because a local station got the tail end of the tree–cutting on video, and unless it was a re–enactment—which they never said— what was a TV crew doing in the clinic parking lot at three a.m.? But no matter, because in front of a camera, Franny always proved that seven years of disrobing before audiences taught you something. She would gradually lose her composure, dart glances at the viewer; she'd turn at thirty degrees and stammer something about her children; she'd give the perfect pause to an unspeakable indignation, then, on the verge of over–playing, would droop, turn away, conclude—camera zooming now—with the gorgeous smile of a fifteen year old: "A person's got to survive!" No point calling it a performance. Everything's a performance. The mystery is that it was a skillful, poised, convincing performance and, therefore, utterly impossible for the aging, bewildered stripper who'd just spent five months with Deirdre failing to grow. Every time Deirdre saw her face on the tube, she'd mutter, "Nope, not her, not Franny, not Franny's words, not Franny's voice, not Franny's hair, not Franny's eyes," meaning—I believe—that the dazzling video entity before us inhabited a universe infinitely distant from the clinical sanctum where broken souls recounted their eventless grim sagas to Deirdre everyday. Although I knew this sanctum only from Deirdre's narrations, I shared her astonishment. On the screen Franny was simply more godlike than human beings can ever be in a mental health clinic. But what also began to impress me—and at virtually the same junctures—was how much Franny's televised confessions, silences, sobs reminded me of, well, psychotherapy. Perhaps it was the voice, its flatness in the act of self–exposure, or her expressionless face when recounting the sufferings of "I." At times, I even wondered if sitting in front of the cameras Franny hadn't become what, sitting in front of Deirdre, she'd always imagined herself to be, what their sessions had been rehearsals for. Of course, ample reasons why this explanation was wrong, not to mention snotty, rushed to my mind, but I soon decided—and still believe—that what caused us to be so aghast whenever Franny appeared, what provoked Deirdre to deny again and again that this rapturous creature could've been the woman in the file under Franny's name, was how readily we could see that she was.

By June the oak leaves were falling day and night, and a fine litter of twigs had begun to cover the ground. They surrounded Deirdre's Datsun, cluttered the floorboards, luggage area, even the seats. Whenever Deirdre backed out of her parking place at the end of the day, she'd find a faint outline of debris, and if the wind blew, leaves slid across the pavement making a scratchy sound. If you looked at them closely, the leaves didn't look dead so much as preserved or immutable. As if they'd stopped aging. They were still green, or greenish, but they had a dry, leathery texture with red spots on the underside. Brown came later, slowly. We made a small collection of the sheddings, kept them on a sill in our kitchen, the earliest twigs, leaves, acorns, on the left, progressing right as summer advanced: the sundry kinds of oakish demise. It was a clock, but I didn't know what interval we were measuring or whether anything started over at the end. One thing for certain, Franny and I had become peripheral. Regardless of the climax approaching, of the catastrophe Deirdre was pushing us all toward, it seemed that the principal characters now were herself and whatever more than just a member of the plant kingdom a magnificent dying oak couldn't help but be. Does matter have plots? I watched the window-sill shrinking; I awaited the clarity I feared.

On the week following the massacre, Franny was scheduled for an appointment, and for only the second time in five months, she didn't show. No phone call, no message, no cancellation. "She's confused about her actions," Deirdre told me. "She's too ashamed to face me."

"Don't count on it," I had just enough presence of mind not to say.

But Deirdre was too frankly relieved by Franny's absence to note my restraint. Every minute she'd spent gazing into the television, every tree branch bouncing off her hood, had raised the ante on her anger, and though she called her feelings unprofessional, inappropriate, even weird, Deirdre now admitted what she'd never admitted before: If Franny had returned to the clinic, Deirdre wouldn't have known how to behave. I found this statement reassuring and scary. Reassuring because it signaled a limit. There was obviously a point at which "self–actualization techniques," "esteem maintenance," and "behavioral management" could just go to hell and Deirdre would punch Franny out. She felt betrayed, suckered, used, and if, in the absence of human nature, the verb "ought" still has an application, I certainly saw no reason why betrayed, suckered, and used wasn't exactly how Deirdre *ought* to feel. All of which is to say it was scary for purely selfish reasons. I wasn't ready for Deirdre to turn as peculiar as me. I longed to have a partner in my disorder and confusion, and I looked forward to talking with her once again as with a fellow sufferer: Few things are more tiresome than a spouse who comprehends you. But while Deirdre had been negotiating her truce with behavior technology, I'd been exploring a land where bewilderment was the natural condition, and I was far from sure, if she now came "back," just where we'd both be. What I'd found in Leonardo's box had made my condition bearable, but I couldn't imagine any conclusion to it. So, I must've thought I needed Deirdre not to know something I must've feared that I knew, or maybe I wanted not to know something that I feared she knew, but I certainly saw no reason to trust the story in the middle of which we were. Deirdre seemed ready to abandon her future, and her future was the only one I had.

Regardless of my fears and Deirdre's anger, however, Franny came back. It was on the same fall morning that a university maintenance crew finally cordoned off the parking lot where the twigs were continuously raining, the first morning Deirdre ever parked her Datsun on the other side of the street. Deirdre didn't recognize her. Franny had on a Claiborne jacket, raunchy green, but cut for big bucks, with exaggerated shoulders and a plunging lapel. Her skirt was short, surprised you with her legs, Deirdre said, but not tacky, and her haircut was "a bargain at eighty smackeroos." The visit lasted ten minutes.

Franny had just dropped in to tell Deirdre what she was up to and to thank her for all her help. The media coverage had opened doors, she explained. There'd been some modeling, fundraisers, entertainment people—"the better sort, y'know"—everything was working out, and now she ran this club—"very chic, very uptown, not a dive like the other"—that served a "professional clientele" near a glitzy convention center in a mall. She said she was engaged to the club's owner, though Deirdre didn't see a ring, or saw four but none that looked engageable, and was "putting together" her own escort service—"a real up and coming business these days." No mention of the tree, no mention of the missed appointments, no mention of the son, cancer, VA ....

"But what's to mention?" Deirdre asked herself for me later that night at home. "I mean, it's not as if we knew each other. It's not like I liked her. It's not as if we'd ever had a conversation ...."

Then they hugged, smiled, and Franny ended by declaring she owed everything to Deirdre—a remark Deirdre strove mightily to take in the way intended—and "to the exposure," by which Deirdre assumed she meant the news. "You just don't believe, Dee, how a camera can change things. It makes you feel like yourself again. Alive, y'know, strong."

Deirdre finally decided that no one had destroyed the oak tree but that the oak tree had been destroyed, that the woman who visited her office that day was not her client named Franny, that the clinic was a daydream and soap operas were true. It was with these avowedly self-defeating, avowedly unacceptable, avowedly worthless explanations that she made her life whole again. She didn't come home writhing or screaming anymore, she stopped sleeping like a zombie, stopped pontificating all during supper. She continued to work at the clinic that summer and into the fall, and as the limbs tumbled onto the pavement and various botanists and nursery experts examined Franny's oak and walked away shaking their heads, Deirdre's routine came more and more to resemble normal life. By November our window–sill had been traversed by leaf fragments and brittle twigs, each with its own texture and mode of decline, and none green anymore, and one Monday when Deirdre arrived at the clinic, she discovered a stump standing beside a gigantic pile of logs. There was a sign, "$75 per load, will deliver" on top. In a week the logs were gone. Deirdre started parking at the college of education, walking across campus to work, so entering the clinic by the front. As far as I know, she never saw Franny again. A sale sign eventually went up in front of Franny's lot, but by then Deirdre wasn't working there. A couple of years later, we were driving down Franny's street and were surprised to see a young girl that Deirdre thought looked like Franny's daughter and a motorcycle parked in the drive. Neither of us wanted to wonder and didn't. As I write these words, somewhere across town the bulldozers clank back and forth over the space that was Franny's oak, creating a perfectly level, blemishless plane on which the university's newest and most advanced building, the school of Communication and Broadcast Arts, will stand. Between it and the housing project is a ten–foot tall chain link fence. The project has acquired a name, "the war zone."

The end of Deirdre's future arrived quickly. She continued at the clinic until the completion of her contract and residency, but she no longer asked herself for me why she was continuing, and our silence on the subject looked more and more like the silence of those for whom everything's clear. When the clinic director invited her to continue another year, she declined, and when her senior professor advised her to continue, she declined, and when they both "sensitively, with positive interpersonal regard, but utilizing an educationally appropriate growth–enhancement technique" tried to browbeat her into staying on, she said, okay, she'd definitely consider it but never did. One night just before Christmas she arrived home and, for the first time since the spring, didn't get out of her car. I let her stay there, resting her neck on the headrest, her arms on the wheel, until I got worried about the cold. When I asked her to come in, she put up no resistance, even smiled, followed me, sat down at the table still wearing her overcoat, and stared. She stared throughout the beer–batter shrimp, through the six chapters of *Middlemarch* I read beside the woodstove, through a quarter and a half of an NFL game and the eleven o'clock news. At last, in the middle of the night as I tried to sleep despite the eerie consciousness that on the other side of the partition my wife was sitting bolt upright in her overcoat, eyes wide open, in a perfectly dark room, I heard her rise, tread softly to my bedside, and ask in a beautiful, bell–like voice: "We don't deserve to like ourselves, do we?"

I don't remember what I said, but I remember feeling nauseated. "Who's to say?" Something like that.

But Deirdre wouldn't joke. "You."

"I don't want to."

"No choice. What if somebody threatened you?"

"What difference would it—?"

"There's a gun to your head." She put her finger to my temple, cocked her thumb. "You have to say."

"No."

"Bang. What if somebody threatened *me*? What if somebody asked you and you had to answer because ...." She raised her finger to her temple, pulled her thumb back, stared straight ahead. "...you have to answer because there's a gun to my head."

I didn't speak at first. I just lay there on the pillow looking up at my wife in the dark in the middle of the night with her overcoat buttoned and her hair gone flat and her finger pointed at her head.

"You have to say," she went on, "because somebody does, because we all already know, and because if nobody anywhere says, no matter how stupid it is, no matter how empty, no matter that we all know it's just another lie—" She took a deep breath. "—the silence is going to get so bad I can't stand it anymore." And then she looked at me. "We don't deserve to like ourselves, do we?"

I reached up and took the gun from her head. "Probably not."

Deirdre smiled. "I didn't think so."

And then, still bundled in her clothes, she crawled into bed beside me, crawled into my arms, and as the mattress folded up around us I felt her body—and, of course, I know that I'm exaggerating but also that I'm not—felt her body grow thirty pounds lighter. We lay there saying nothing. Then she began to cry, and for no clear reason, in a minute I began to cry, and crying we slipped into oblivion and slept like children for the first time in a year. The next morning, the window-sill was empty; Deirdre checked into life science programs and came home with Metropolis. She never went back to the clinic, didn't bring home her coffee maker or wall posters, never completed her research project, received no degree. Up to this precise moment she has never undertaken anything that would require or allow her ever to say, "I expended four years, sixty–nine credit hours, and many, many thousands of words in the scholarly labyrinths of the social sciences."

My friend Arno, who was loyal enough throughout Deirdre's ordeal to say as little as possible, has, subsequent to breaking his heart and beginning his MBA, confessed that he always knew what was going on.

"She's an idealist! A frustrated, anachronistic, sincere idealist! Sensitive people can't make a difference anymore. It's sad. I feel bad about it, y'know I do. I'm not unsympathetic, but really, it had to happen."

"Does the word 'idealist' mean something?"

"Nothing at all, that's what's so pathetic. She went through all that misery for no reason. Poor kid. Utterly pointless, empty sign of suffering, pain's lacuna ...."

"If it doesn't mean something, how come it describes her?"

"That's the point, nothing happened to her! She just—"

"Shut up, okay?"

Not that Arno's life is anything to imitate, but like so many who aren't naive anymore, Arno has become tirelessly interested in those of us who are. About the time Deirdre and I were turning peculiar, Arno's wife was walking out, and so our triumvirate spent two idyllic years commiserating. He'd drive down for a visit, and we'd all sit on the deck drinking beers, and Arno and I would do the funny, awkward things guys do because they can't hold hands and cry. Occasionally someone would fall into the form of bullying called being honest, but for the most part we enjoyed helping each other make tales of our mistakes. Back then we believed—I still believe it—that recalling how a sensible beginning turned into a muddle is a worthwhile thing to do. Suffering can't become fun, but in the best of all possible worlds, suffering with friends—smart, extravagant, generous ones—isn't anything I'd exactly want left out. Anyway, if Arno and I manage to grow old together, those two years will be the reason why.

Deirdre and I got unmarried and created our second life, and Arno sold a screenplay, published some poems, began his jazz album, photographed Montana, almost negotiated a Paris revival of his one-act play and, as his daughter started third grade, awoke one morning nose to nose with bankruptcy. I don't know the details. We tried to help out but didn't have any money. For several months he disappeared. Then within a year, he'd enrolled in an MBA program specializing in bombed-out humanities doctorates. He began calling us two or three times every week, often in the black hours between deepest sleep and waking, always eager to regale me with some morsel from his courses. "'The challenge of insurance marketing lies in the absence of positive incentives and reliance upon the weakest known motivator—long-range, rational self-interest. It ...therefore becomes necessary to engage in realistically negative as well as positive education ....' Listen to that! It's extortion! They're teaching us to scare the money out of 'em!" In the beginning the calls knit us more firmly together, confirmed our cherished nightmares, our nihilistic predictions. Things really were as ghastly as we'd always believed, or worse. We found reassurance in the obviousness of the contradictions, refined the rejoinders that put our enemies in their place. "It is a truism that the hardest customer to sell is one who recognizes he or she is being sold ....' Hitler knew that! Stalin knew that! There's even a theory of the anti-sale, like the anti-hero, where the real salesman acts like he's defending you from—get this—the Corporation!" But pretty soon I began to get bored—our responses were becoming mechanical—and there was something ugly about delighting in the worst, trying to outdo every past cynicism. Sometimes when the phone woke me, I'd be slow to answer, or I'd beg off, explaining that I was working hard on my Leonardo da Vinci novel and needed the sleep. Arno's enthusiasm never faltered, however. He continued to greet each horror with fresh astonishment, held his grotesque relics up for admiration as if they revealed uncanny truths. I began to doubt my commitments, to fear that I'd become the aging leftist we'd always despised. But then I noticed something new in Arno's excitement, something I hadn't heard before.

For example, there was this idea from an international finance class. I could never really grasp it, but it had to do with the way an investor could finance a venture that had, in reality, already occurred. "The whole thing has to do with the similarity between actuarial tables and statistical samplings, both of which are highly regular and involve extrapolation. It's complicated, you probably need to understand catastrophe theory, but in essence, you invest on a theoretically future event that is, actually, statistically, mathematically, a past one. The result is there's no risk, no need for money to change hands, not even any credit."

"And the investor makes—"

"Over time, a killing. Assuming you have the bucks."

"So, its like the shell of free enterprise but, really, there's no enterprise at all, nothing free?"

"Yeah, yeah, that's it. Like God was your broker."

"Well, maybe if a third—world nation..."

"Wouldn't work. Too much capital, too much data, too much technology. I'm not saying it isn't an outrage. But it's an astonishing outrage."

Or there was this story of a drug company that started its own black—market subsidiary. By the time the authorities got wise, it had so surrounded itself with legalese and holding companies and proxies and silent partners and other kinds of dodges and intermediaries that all the guilty execs managed to retire, grow old and die before the feds could work their way through the paper trail to an indictment. "Un—be—fucking—lievable!" Arno kept saying. "And everybody knew who'd done it. Everybody!" Even long distance, even over the phone I could hear him slapping his knee.

"I suppose, Ol' Sport, but I can't see what's so special—"

"Oh, don't be such a prig. I'm not approving. I'm just saying the system was ingenious, the vision. Even you can see—"

"They got rich selling drugs to black teenagers, used up *my* tax dollars, probably encouraged deforestation—"

"Oh Christ."

For a while after that we didn't talk. When finally the calls began again, they weren't in the middle of the night anymore but just after supper, and they always started off polite, Arno asking was he interrupting anything, did I have time to chat. We might resume the polemics of earlier days, but they'd be humorless, like citations in a legal brief, and we didn't continue long. There'd be a word or two about Arno's daughter, a private school he'd visited, some rumor concerning his wife, then a pause, and Arno's next words would be in the quiz—show—host voice that signaled the start of our conversation. "Hey, did you know that the average work week of persons making over eighty thousand a year is less than fifty—five hours? Fifty—five hours! I got that

119

from Forbes. You guys planning to take Sunday off?" Or he'd say: I'm thinking about having my dissertation published. I know, I know, the revision's not finished, but I've got a friend who's got a friend at SUNY, and she thinks presses base their decisions on the first two and the last chapters. According to a survey done by a marketing firm in Tacoma, only one reader in eighty–six thousand ever reads more than a hundred pages of anything." Or his favorite: "Now, if I want to live in the Northwest, I probably ought to specialize in high–tech marketing and sell myself to a corporation as an editor-writer of computer copy. There's security in that. But if I'm willing to go freelance—say, as a science editor or policy writer—I'm told I can get into triple digits within four years, though that's hustling. Then I could live wherever— the Berkshires, say, Paris—work out of my home, you know ...." The ploys were so obvious that, at first, I ignored them. Be patient, I told myself. Your friend is undergoing a terrible loss. But it didn't take long until I recognized: Who was I kidding? The calls had become sparring matches, acknowledged as such by both of us, and knowing I was being attacked wasn't going to protect me. I started telling Arno to own up to his heartbreak, to quit acting like the monster he'd always despised. He retorted that money was the only subject I could talk about for longer than fifteen minutes, that I'd probably overlook any outrage for ten thousand bucks. I scoffed, said private schools wouldn't protect his daughter, her home was a jungle. He asked what "novel" was I talking about? Leonardo da who? At the start of the next conversation we'd always brag that we felt stronger, more confident for our mutual lacerations, but in my soul I was terrified that everything Arno said was right.

THE ANATOMY OF MARCANTONIO DELLA TORRE

For a time, after Leonardo had ridden out of Milan with Luca Pacioli and Salai in 1499, after he'd abandoned his dream of the great horse and returned to Florence, after he'd set about the task at age forty–seven of starting life over, nature had seemed like a burden. He was learning proportions of proportions, practicing Euclid, and as his mathematical knowledge increased, so did his astonishment at ordinary things. When he'd been a youth, ideas had lived in trees and rocks. Merely glancing at a bat's wing he'd possessed its movement, workings. He hadn't known where this knowledge came from, often felt himself god-inhabited or vaguely freakish, but while still a boy, he grew accustomed to instructing others. He was proud of this power, but it also scared him. Was this how the Savior felt, hearing unacquired wisdom pour from his tongue? In Verrocchio's shop he learned color and perspective, but less as a new science than as something he'd always known, as experience. In Milan he discovered the intimacy of painting and mechanics, saw how the anatomy of an eye and the anatomy of a picture proceeded along parallel lines. He stole books on astronomy from the Marliani brothers, constructed wind–up toys and tiny engines, learned to humble himself at the feet of Pacioli, who might be an indefatigable blowhard but knew roots. All this helped.

But by the time he'd fled Milan in 1499 and returned to Florence, having watched his godlike achievements crumble, having worked his way through interminable pages of polygons, become adept with calipers and projections, and even convinced himself late one night that he'd squared the circle—Leonardo realized science wasn't a preparation. There was no lesson that, once learned, returned him to painting, no study of water that ended in canals. Knowledge was its own universe. Roots might lead to falling bodies, yes, but they also led to more roots, or to optics—now become startlingly numerical—as well as to diminution ratios, which meant bluing and updrafts and the curl in a man's hair. His dream of possessing knowledge now struck him as mad. The most he or anyone could hope was that knowledge might one day possess him. Truth was huge; you were tiny. It was then that Leonardo began to feel nature as a weight or affliction. He wanted to escape it, to crawl from under the avalanche of commonplace things. Staring at a stump he'd feel his heart start to pound; watching a swallow circle he'd want to cover his eyes. Pebbles on a highway, weeds in a ditch, everything teemed with invitations, and nowhere in this frenzy could he find a place to rest.

Until one spring day in Florence in 1506 as he stood above the Arno, leaning over the side of the old bridge between two merchants' stalls, watching the dirty current from the valley's run–off, when nature finally set him free. He saw the water spin once, twice, three times into its own backward motion, saw Pecham, perspective, the dream of universal science float away, and realized the ground he was standing on was cracked. Hell, it wasn't even the ground. It was *him*! And staring down into the Arno's twists and turns, Leonardo knew that he'd always built blindly, or if not blindly—for if it had been blindness, how had he managed to erect the clay horse? How had Brunelleschi constructed the dome of Santa Maria del Fiore? How had Alberti calculated...? No, it wasn't blindness, but it was the kind of vision that, because you couldn't stop seeing it, would always mislead you. Of course, standing there on the old bridge as a gaggle of Turks ambled noisily past, Leonardo couldn't make sense of all this, couldn't begin to explain how the same eyes that now seemed to be setting him straight had, in the past, been his undoing. But regardless of paradoxes, he'd definitely seen the three circles in the Arno's current and had recognized, at that instant, that he'd been seeing them his whole life long, though—enigma of enigmas—he'd never seen them till now. It was just what Jacopo Il Poggio, the little fart, had tried to say.

And so what he should have said to Salai was: No! No! No! I'm not even my own life, I never had *my* life. Life? Look at this beard, look at this useless hand, look at my plans rotting in the cellar. Why, this isn't *me*!

But unfortunately what he'd said was: You? Why, you're not my footstool. You're not my shopboy. You're not even my past or my bad dreams. My life?! I don't owe you horse shit!

And Salai had said: No, you gave me horse shit. What you owe me is an explanation.

There's no sound in Leonardo's room. In the far corner underneath the window, the woman lies spread–eagle, her legs, rough apron, fleshy shoulders stretched across the planks. Outside a bulbous cloud floats past a tower. A voice calls out in Dutch. Through the dried film of vegetable broth in the corner of his eye, Leonardo surveys his surroundings. He has no idea what to make of this woman. The persistence of her body here in the death–chamber of the age's godlike miracle, well, it seems very accidental. If, that is, she's really here. Leonardo doesn't see much breathing. François Premier should be here, Marcantonio della Torre should be here, Bramante should be here, Melzi should be here, Bellincioni should be here, Salai should burn in quick–lime and bubbling sulphur for eternity with his fingernails pierced by red–hot needles pushed slowly in up to the first knuckle and his nostrils teeming with dung–maggots while a thousand stallions frolic nearby on luscious pastures chortling—or he should be here. But this woman should be in her natural sphere downstairs in the pantry or outside somewhere with the goats. Of course, there was the dimostrazione. Like the paper flowers, she's left over. Leonardo's inquiries have usually resulted in just such loose ends. How often has he sawn through the bones of a pig's breast, prized it open with a crack, wrapped the greasy heart in his fingers and with a squeeze invoked the grisly flux only to watch the lungs lie flat as before? Everything seems connected if you want knowledge you can walk away with. If you really need the world to hang together, you'll get nick–nacks and gew–gaws or a miscellaneous body sprawled on your floor. Leonardo tries to snort with disgust, can't, ends up coughing painfully. Over where the woman lies there's still no movement, no breathing.

But then Marcantonio della Torre never seemed to breathe at all. Leonardo had observed him closely, hours at a time, and never once seen the anatomist's nostrils twitch, chest rise. Of course, that might have been because the air in the room was so ripe you could've written your name on it. Anything like a real breath and you'd wretch. Leonardo remembers sniffing at the candle–flame periodically, letting the heat clean out his nose and throat. He always marveled at the young man's capacity to disregard rot, almost as if he'd handled death so often it no longer came near him. Night after night Leonardo had seen him with midges crawling into his ears, the candles hissing out, and gasses that brought Leonardo's gorge up enveloping his face—and never a blink. His was a kind of anti–soul, thriving on bile, spittle, bones. Leonardo had always tried to live both in his five senses and above them, and by the time he met della Torre he'd already come to regard his eyes as tools, but odors would always dismay him. A breeze dank with plant mold or the waft of musk from his own arm could smear him across past and future, annihilate everything nearby, make the darkness surrounding the table, the carrion basket at his feet, even his own hands, unimaginable. How could anyone ignore corruption? A moth flapped into the flame, caught spattering fire, burst. Della Torre's fingers made little sucking noises as they slithered about in the meat. Only if you murdered longing, crammed your life into the tips of your fingers and heard childhood, if at all, like conversation across cold water—no, della Torre had little use for breathing.

I'm sure it was revenge.

The voice brought Leonardo's head up.

I know that sounds harsh, della Torre said. There was virtue in it too, I suppose—duty or honor. I may be incapable of fidelity, but that doesn't mean I can't recognize it.

Leonardo looked over the candle into della Torre's face. The anatomist was behaving as if the story of his former schoolmaster, Guido da Forlì, were an abscess or blister. Did he expect Leonardo to soothe it? One hand picked at a lump of tissue, let it drop. He leaned forward as if unsure whether to say more. Leonardo watched.

Of course I carved the body he gave me—from nostril to knee. What would you expect? I was the pupil. I spent two entire days up to my wrists in the viscera. When it came time for the university, I was ready.

Guido da Forlì was a teacher, Leonardo said. He understood patience.

He hated me.

What's the difference?

Della Torre laughed: Yes, but disappointment can be a harsh master. Then laying his probe down on the cadaver's navel, della Torre smiled the quizzical smile of a man who'd never been lighthearted a day in his life and, glancing at the darkness eating their heads, he told Leonardo the story of Matteo da Rimini.

The League of Cambrai of 1509 had proven no more noteworthy

than any other Renaissance political entanglement, thrown together as it was to acquire momentarily within the spider–web of plots and counterplots pieces of a few virtually ungovernable dominions for the purpose of ceding or obliterating them immediately afterwards, its only memorable difference being the way the Italians made the French look like chumps. Hardly four years later Machiavelli would codify the principle at work here—betray utterly, annihilate completely, bribe lavishly, but never do anything just a little bit—and the French, suspecting everyone for a liar but no one for an extravagant liar, ended up defeating themselves by defeating Venice by believing in the Pope. Specifically, they spread the body parts of 20,000 foot–soldiers across Italy from Cassano to Peschiera before Pope Julius made it up with the doge, linked elbows with the Emperor, bought up a slew of Swiss mercenaries, appealed to Italian patriotism, and chased the bewildered Louis Douze right back across the Alps. Renaissance politics as usual. Nor was there anything extraordinary about the accompanying chaos in Venetian university towns like Padua, the students having long grown accustomed to running riot whenever the government did and the townspeople having always despised the little snots in the first place. Any ripple sufficed to start the accusations flying, the students rampaging, the militia banging on the doors at night. And that one of these accusations would mention an anatomist or that the militia would eventually end up banging on an anatomist's door would have struck no one as surprising. Even in Padua where as many as a hundred of the swankiest citizens might appear in the dissecting theatre to watch a nameless prosector run his cleaver across a dead prostitute's sternum and where cadavers were officially if parsimoniously supplied to the medical faculty by the Venetian state, even here the circle of tolerance was narrow, fragile. Before every dissection the Pope's indulgence had to be read, the inquisition's authority acknowledged, the cadaver's pardon begged, the university seal flourished, the local rulers invoked, the head lopped off, the eyes poked out and all manner of spooks and hobgoblins shooed away. No, the only unusual thing about all this was the way it converged on Marcantonio della Torre.

In 1509 della Torre was professor of the philosophy of medicine at Padua and, though only twenty–eight years old, already a notorious figure. Having been appointed university lecturer in ordinary while still a teenager, he'd immediately terrified and offended the entire faculty by dismissing the barber–surgeons from his public readings and taking up the dissecting knife himself, a practice made possible by his ability to recite from memory whole chapters of Galen, thus enabling him to come down from the podium and speak from the table. Moreover, he was rumored to continue his anatomical studies in his own chambers at night. This last had something especially racy and delicious about it. Aside from being illegal, cutting up a human body alone in the dark looked to the sixteenth century a lot more diabolical than scientific and, given the absolute unavailability of cadavers, usually meant grave–robbing, if not murder. Needless to say, the students considered della Torre the hottest show in town.

The townsfolk, on the other hand, would've liked to roast him. Even the prosperous burghers who attended his dissections, subsidized the scholars, and prided themselves on having one foot in the new learning—usually the same one they'd gotten in the door of the Medici bank—even these acknowledged that he was uncouth, and no sooner had the French more or less handed the Venetian army its fanny at Agnadello than the city fathers started tossing around della Torre's name as a possible scapegoat. The students who at the moment were drinking themselves blind, looting, and reducing Padua to a shambles would've been a likelier choice, but since they were more numerous and a good deal braver than the depleted constabulary, the authorities preferred to go after their professor. Exactly what, everyone suddenly wanted to know, was an impious subverter of civic virtue who was known to be lacking in human decency not to mention plain old squeamishness doing up alone all night during a political crisis as everyone else in town prepared to resist a hostile invasion and practiced their French? The question's syntax should've disqualified it, but it didn't, which brings up Matteo da Rimini.

Matteo had been a colleague and close friend of Marcantonio's deceased father, Girolamo, and so, unlike everyone else on the faculty, had no personal basis for disliking the young anatomist. Instead, Matteo hated him with the pure and selfless hatred with which only the finest representatives of a dying age can hate the future. He did not desire to see Marcantonio stumble; he longed to see him erased, or failing that, to see him quashed, squalidly humiliated, forced to recant his every living breath. This wish was acid in Matteo's bowels, a spike through his dreams. He sucked it, wept it, washed and fondled it, woke each morning praying: Let it happen today! For fourteen years he suffered the boy's disdain. The adolescent Marcantonio had simply appeared in the piazza one grimy August afternoon, possessed not so much of a powerful name or patrimony as of a sublime confidence that he could judge the world. Professors old enough to be his grandsires competed shamelessly for his attention, descended to tricks and pratfalls, whispered their rivals' foibles in his ear, as if this child's admiration might redeem their benighted lives. Marcantonio submitted to their worship, but whenever he deigned to speak, the men knew they were no better than plumb–lines in his hands, chisels, rusty saws. Matteo who'd set out to guide him for Girolamo's sake felt puzzled that,

125

when addressed, Marcantonio always turned his face away, and so he concluded that his friend's son had grown up indolent and simple. But then one evening when at the end of his patience Matteo seized Marcantonio's neck and spun his head around, he saw in the vacant gaze an insolence so vast it left him giddy. The muscles of Marcantonio's face remained motionless. His eyelids never lowered. He peered back at the older man as if, instead of being reproved, it were *he*, this fifteen-year–old simpleton, who were examining Matteo da Rimini. Matteo blinked his eyes. No one would ever be this child's teacher. And stepping backwards he heard his soul ask for the first time the question he'd later hear whispered in cafes, shops, hallways, the piazza: Was it really possible, could the son of their beloved Girolamo possess Satan's secrets, was this the evil they'd always feared would come from knowing the truth?

And so Matteo swore to have nothing further to do with the boy. He would watch, wait for the reckoning. But on the day Girolamo della Torre yielded his ghost to heaven, Matteo had been standing beside his friend's bed, and bending down to witness the cracked, salty lips kiss the spirit away, Matteo heard his friend lisp a last word—Marcantonio! And thinking he recognized in this sound a father's dying request, Matteo assured him, yes, he would look to the boy's education, watch over him as a father, intending of course to do nothing of the kind, no sensible person ever feeling bound by deathbed extortion, but then his friend had grinned, given his head the slightest shake, and lifting his withered hand, had lain a finger on Matteo's chest, and Matteo had understood—it wasn't the *boy* about whom Girolamo was worrying.

For already Matteo had been infected. The taunting voice—But have you *seen* the septum's pores? Have you touched them with your *finger?*—already it filled his mind, took him over at night, and as the years passed and Marcantonio became master, lecturer, instructor, doctor, on and on—still a child!—Matteo saw his own life transformed into something fantastic. His lectures dwindled; his thoughts drifted; the scholars dozed in their seats, passed missives, slipped their hands under one another's gowns. In the street he listened as they murmured della Torre's name in the rapturous tones reserved for burghers' daughters. What had the young master with the sulphurous eyes, the voice like a cleaver, the hands that ventured where the heart recoiled, what had he disclosed, averred, implied, reviled? And, yes, after scolding his credulous proteges, after scoffing when they claimed that respectable citizens, Venetian physicians, even a philosopher from Tuscany had attended the hellion's lectures, Matteo had himself gone. With the coppery bile flooding his throat, despising his mendacity every step of the way, he'd slipped into the furthest row of the dissecting theatre, concealed himself behind a tall youth in a green riding habit, and swearing he'd stay just long enough to glimpse Satan's play, watched as the devil squeezed blue liquor into a charred pedophile's aorta, saw him map the veins, trace the thin vessels branching like olive trees down the cadaver's crushed arms, from trunk to toes, held his breath as the reprobate drove his own fingers into rot's orifices and peeled back the tissue, laid bare what Matteo had read about his entire life and witnessed countless times, had even supervised in auditoriums much like this one and as a physician had bled, bandaged, cauterized but until this moment had never actually *seen*! He held his breath, craning forward until a jolt and peremptory snort beside his ear made him realize that in his excitement he'd climbed up the back of the tall youth in front of him, was at that moment digging his nails into the green riding cloak, and—Would God not spare him any indignity?— was drooling. Drooling! Matteo threw his hood over his face, slithered home like a viper, and flinging himself on his cellar floor, shrieked himself to sleep.

Year in, year out. It was as close to hell as a righteous man comes, and months later—in Pavia now—after the League of Cambrai's collapse, as the panic receded and silence returned to northern Italy, whenever Marcantonio della Torre paused late at night over the transverse section of an arm or thigh, still as enamored of flesh as in Padua but now far less swanky about it, beginning to feel his first uncertainty about his own powers and their place in the world, as he thought back again and again to his Paduan success, his colleagues' astonishment, the hissing of his name in the piazza, trying now to end once and for all the pounding that each morning invaded his dreams, della Torre would understand perfectly the hatred in which Matteo da Rimini had lived, his lechery to see his young rival boiled, quartered, stretched upon the rack of his own presumption. Dull minds might content themselves with cheap jokes and private mutterings, for they'd never glimpsed the possibility of their souls' extinction. But Matteo was fertile ground. Understanding took root in him quickly. Having witnessed the brilliance that overshadowed him, he couldn't return to daily tasks in which he no longer believed. Shut out of the future, disgusted with the past, all he possessed was fury. Marcantonio della Torre had stolen his education, transformed his memory into a slough of folly, erased forty years of labor, made him into a mistake. You could hardly expect him to be a good sport about it.

So when back in Padua a student informed Marcantonio della Torre that his colleague Matteo da Rimini had taken to abusing him noisily in prayers each morning at the Church of the Hermits, or when Marcantonio learned that Matteo was compiling a list of Galenist anatomical heresies to submit to the Dominicans or later that he'd harangued the Venetian signoria for nearly two hours about the noxious spirits released into the community via public autopsy, Marcantonio hadn't been taken aback. Even the afternoon when Matteo appeared at della Torre's anatomy lecture in a white robe with a smoldering buckthorn branch intoning exorcisms from Albertus Magnus in ecclesiastical Latin and scattering coriander seeds in the air, Marcantonio had remained unperturbed, refusing to mystify anything as ordinary as an animal with its foot caught in a trap. Obsolete lives were noisy, and good sense taught you to ignore them. Granted, the spectacle had something pathetic about it, but there was nothing Marcantonio could do. The only aspect of the whole messy business that continued to surprise him in Padua as he daily grew more astonished by his own success, by the sight of necks craning toward him in the dissecting theatre, nature's infuriating proximity, was how long it seemed to be taking Matteo da Rimini to realize his life was over.

Whether or not Matteo's yammerings actually provoked the writ against della Torre, the result of which would have been—had the militia gotten its halberds on him—a trial far more agonizing than any punishment meted out just for being guilty, whether or not Matteo really could claim much credit for this would remain unclear. Della Torre certainly had enemies in sufficient quantity that an addlepated don more or less could hardly have swayed the Venetian authorities. The silk merchants, glass–blowers, country priests, yeomen and sundry thugs who were perpetually eager to see a scholar sizzle probably found Matteo's denunciations of a fellow physician titillating, but by the time Matteo had married della Torre off to the infidel's granddaughter, exposed his cloven hoof, made him nephew to Louis douze and the Pope's son, depicted his necrophilia, murders, rapaciousness, and generally attributed to him so many black–arts and powers that only a fool would have risked arresting him, by then pretty nearly everyone—both those who wanted to bake the anatomist for the fun of it and the more rational city officials who merely needed a victim to divert attention momentarily from the two thousand local sons they'd marched out a month before against not quite three times that many superbly armed French chevaliers who'd promptly fertilized the earth with them—i.e., by then nearly everybody knew Matteo for a crackpot. The signoria's accusations against della Torre would, of course, be lies, but the distinction between decorous lies and outlandish lies seemed important. It was one thing to look vicious, another to look silly. The council muzzled Matteo, invoked high principles, debated gobbledy–gook, wrote something Latinate and commissioned the constabulary to arrest the traitor.

And then the affair took a curious turn. While the city fathers were busy conscripting a dozen yokels from among the outlying peasantry—every Paduan youth being either under fifteen, dead, or a proven coward—fitting them with pikes, harquebusses, beavers, gorgets, and trying to teach them to look like the nonexistent constabulary the city fathers were counting on, Matteo da Rimini paid a visit to della Torre's apartment. Exactly *why* would never be clear to anyone, certainly not to della Torre, perhaps not to Matteo himself. By now, annihilating the Antichrist, snatching a soul from perdition, reproving an aberrant colleague, saving Venetia and protecting his deceased friend's son had all so run together in Matteo's mind that his every act was as multi–layered as Dante's inferno. Perhaps it was Matteo's own yearning for the knowledge he meant to destroy, his ache to thrust his own hand just once through the veil of words, or his fallen soul's recollection of the apple's tangy meat, perhaps it was just bestial curiosity or even an old man's boredom that finally drew him—now that his adversary's destruction was assured—into the circle of corruption. All Matteo would ever know is that while perusing Avicenna's medical poem on the balcony that evening he'd had a vision. Holy armies had suddenly appeared in the purple sky just above a neighboring palazzo, great clouds of roiling dust rising from the legs of frenzied stallions as black as the apostate's heart, swords, lances, cannons, rams, all galloping forth to do battle with what could only be described as an immense horizon of blinding light. Matteo shook his head, momentarily saw a sunset, distant hills, a pigeon perched on a roofing tile, and then lost himself again in this apocalypse. On which side virtue lay it seemed impossible to know, but Matteo sensed that after God's warriors encountered radiance, a great peace would descend on earth and, still more surely, that the site of this Armaggedon was Marcantonio della Torre's rooms. He donned his cap and mantle, stuck a copy of Mondino beneath one arm and, striding down the Via San Francesco, walked right into the anatomist's foyer.

Marcantonio, who was at the moment wrist-deep in the organs of an infant's cadaver he'd purchased that afternoon no–questions–asked from a local slime–bucket named Il Fortunato, a figure notorious on the streets for having only one nostril and half a lip as a result of getting overly intimate with a wheel–trueing device in his father's smithy as a child—Marcantonio, who in dissecting the infant was actually committing a crime legally punishable by those very torments about to be meted out to him for political acts he'd never dreamed of, when he heard the door crash open thought of nothing but, Here are an extra pair of hands to hold this liver! Rushing downstairs he chose not to marvel that the hands were attached to his father's former crony, the principal nuisance of his daily undertakings, and not his arch–nemesis only by virtue of being too loony, but merely grabbed the tassel of Matteo's robe, bolted the door so as not to be interrupted twice and dragged the older man back to the table saying, Here, fool, hold this.

Which for no reason I could ever convince you of, Matteo did.

Thus began the strangest of all anatomies the history of Renaissance science would ever know, an ordeal that continued through that night and on into the next morning when, pausing to drink goat's milk and chew honeyed toast on the veranda, the two physicians allowed their eyelids to droop for the shortest of instants as the sun boiled the streets, then up again and working through the afternoon heat, gadflies, wasps, infernal midges, until blessed darkness returned and with it an autumn breeze that blew the stink away. During the entire time, they quarreled, shaking chisels, saws, kidneys in each other's face, and never had each despised his rival's pigheadedness so much as now. It was nothing less than human wisdom that they contested, peeling back the tiny heart's wall and flushing its cavities with salty water, nothing less than light's path through blackness, how spirit dwells in the flesh, what can't be said and whether a mishandled truth is mortal. They hunted the three ventricles of Aristotle, the two and a half of Avicenna, the porous septum of Galen and Mondino's honey—combed interstice. They found them all, they found nothing, they didn't know what they found. They pointed, poked, sliced, piddled, watched those shapes that when animate seemed so firm collapse now into puddles of purplish goo, saw eyes melt into the spongy forebrain, muscle tissues turn limp or hard, organs wither, lobes flop and nowhere an edge or outline or border to show that the thingamajig ends here. Again and again Matteo insisted that they'd never find what they longed to know by taking it apart, and each time della Torre countered, But look and see! Look and see! They snipped the vena cava, rubbed its surface with their fingertips, sniffed its leathery edge, listened to the sound it made when whacked on the table, bit, licked, chewed it, compared its flavor with the triceps and concluded the heart wasn't a muscle. Twice peering down the esophagus their foreheads struck, once Marcantonio cut Matteo's thumb with the chisel, they hissed, swore. Both knew it was devil's work, but gazing into the same terrific ignorance, acknowledging that they had no idea—not just what they were looking at, but even why they needed to—each man felt himself a stranger, someone lost in a country he'd mistaken for home, and in this shared misery and silence, they blundered on.

They didn't hear the pounding until the third time, but once they finally did hear it, they both knew they'd been listening for it their whole lives. They were bent over the infant's skull, fragile as a toy boat, with the saw halfway through the cerebrum and Marcantonio's fingers wiggling around in the eye, and as the sound rippled through the walls and floorboards, up their shins, spines, and finally merged with the beating of their hearts, they each looked up into the other's face and understood exactly how they'd arrived here and where it would all lead.

130

At that instant della Torre acknowledged, perhaps for the first time, what a flimsy concoction the facts are, only slightly more reliable than nothing, and he saw that his confidence had never been much more than a refusal to look around. He hadn't expected being correct to defend him. He'd just been insufficiently impressed with others to worry how he appeared. As a result, he'd gradually been transformed into all the specters flapping around in the darkness behind those very eyes staring at him now from across the table. Even if he wasn't innocent, he felt like protesting, he was certainly no demon! He supposed that he could endure having his knees crushed and his tongue cut out, but he would have preferred to watch his enemy boil in lard. He wondered if the iceberg forming in his pelvis right now was what the vulgar called fear. The air ceased to pulsate, the floorboards grew still. For a long moment the two men continued to look at one another, then Matteo shrugged: Well, they're here.

Della Torre frowned. I deserve better than this.

There's not much knowledge without virtue, Matteo said, but there can be really gruesome virtues with almost no knowledge at all. You've acted as if you didn't believe this. You've tried to destroy the benevolence you expected to protect you. Don't act like you're surprised.

Adder sputum! Vinegar piss!

Many things are more important than new ideas.

You knew?

Matteo smiled. I've felt a great longing to see you afraid.

The pounding came again, grown fatter, bulging up into the beams where sticky spiders slouched, beating the air hot, filling each man's skull until it shook like a rattle. Della Torre's eyes throbbed. From somewhere came the sound of shattering glass. He decided to wake up from this nightmare. He decided to wake up from this nightmare. He decided to wake up from this nightmare.

Stupid! he hissed. I've cut the veil away, flayed error, held nature in my palm. Here on this table, underneath your own fingers, can't you see?

You talk like a child, Matteo said. What do you have to show for your devil's meddling? Here on this table I see chaos, sacrilege. Wordless matter is nothing. You're as benighted as I.

Dotard!

Reprobate!

Della Torre glared back at him, then spoke slowly: I'm the future. You're as commonplace as cobblestones. It's for you to make way. I am more important than you are.

They held one another's eyes long enough to purge the sin of pride as the pounding drew sweat from their pores, drove their teeth out the tops of their heads, rose up through the roof and became the hooves of a thousand stallions rushing across the plain of Armageddon, riders leaning forward on their weapons, cannons bouncing wildly behind, as God's army suddenly vanished without a sound into the immense kingdom of light.

Then Matteo replied: I know.

When the band of armor–clanking yokels at the front door finally figured out that no one was going to answer, they fell to quarreling, and word had to be sent to one Arturo Gerli, a townsman of no great distinction but someone's cousin, to learn if he thought the signoria preferred the house burned down, stormed with ladders, laid siege to, cordoned off, ignored or just what. The neighbors were by this time awake and, leaning from their windows, offered suggestions of their own, exchanging news and insults, complaining of the racket, mimicking the soldiers' pronunciation, and generally enjoying the show. Beggars, mastiffs, and prostitutes worked the edges of the crowd, and one orange–haired bedlamite shrieked, Pickle the doctor! and flung himself repeatedly onto the ground. The decision at last arrived from someone claiming to be in a position to make it that the door should be beaten down, and the ad hoc militia began applying its halberds, pikes and axes to that end in what was surely the messiest forced entry in Paduan memory. The bolt wouldn't give; the hinges wouldn't flinch; the walnut planks were as thick as a forearm. Someone came up with the bright idea of firing a harquebus at it. The ball ricocheted off and struck a teenager from the banks of the Brenta between the cuisse and poleyn, badly denting the armor and dispensing with his knee. He had to be carried away sobbing, and the remaining constables eventually bashed a hole big enough to cram a skinny mule-tender through, running his hose on the splinters and virtually having to undress him in the process. All of which left the yokels feeling intensely shy once in the foyer, having not one of them ever set foot on carpet or seen a painting. They took their time working up courage to bellow the half–dozen authoritative expressions they'd memorized, still longer to venture up the stairs. They hoped nobody was home. They were disappointed.

The signoria had prepared them for what they might encounter in the anatomist's rooms, so the tiny shit–smeared torso with its duodenum curling down the table leg and a sawblade wedged in its nose didn't send anyone leaping off the balcony. Having grown up doing things to live piglets that sixteenth century city–dwellers would've been reluctant to do to potted plants, the rustics weren't deeply troubled by the sight of gore, though one tender–hearted swain—called mockingly Lavender Giovio—had to lean against the wall till his head stopped reeling, and there weren't any dead–baby jokes. What did surprise and baffle the soldiers, however, was the appearance of the traitor they'd been sent to subdue. Various councilors had explained that though an experienced Satanist, deeply initiated in bookish secrets, a mason, hideously rich, probably in the French employ if not of Gallic parentage, and certainly a violator of custom, truth, virtue, nature, doctrine and ecclesiastical law, the damned physician Marcantonio della Torre was hardly older than the yokels themselves. But the debauched practitioner standing before them now was wizened and stooped with a weary sag to his eyes, and though he wore the black robes of a scholar, he could easily have been taken for an humble mendicant or someone's grandsire. He seemed unperturbed by their noisy entrance, continuing to gaze down at the large, pale cadaver on the table before him and whispering unintelligible incantations. The puzzled guards murmured that perhaps the sorcerer had compacted with his father Satan to take on this guise of maturity, but then the demon spoke—in perfect Italian!—claiming that the French betrayer they sought had been transmuted by Lucifer into gaseous sulphur in order to float out the window upon an icy breeze arisen from his frozen heart. They could see for themselves where his garments lay crumpled upon the floor, his body having melted with a hiss and the odor of boiling sassafras. The old man spoke without once lifting his face from the livid neck beneath his hands, and though his voice was calm, almost soothing, there seemed to be something furious in the way he glared at the corpse. He held a large cleaver pressed against the cadaver's throat, seemed on the point of ramming it into the tissue and bone, and it was this spectacle, far more than the ubiquitous carnage in the room, that very nearly unnerved the peasant youths. Human blood and organs might be indistinguishable from goose innards, but the thought of this human body, as healthy and whole as if it had walked the earth but moments before, the thought of these Christian remains staggering about mute and headless on resurrection day—*that* was disgusting.

Then the old man begged for mercy, reminding the constables how much he too had suffered from the hellish betrayer, having—he feared—bartered his own soul for a taste of astonishing evils, and as the befuddled youths whispered among themselves, first, that the pitiful wretch was plainly not the man they sought and should be abandoned to his damnation, and, next, that this might be Beelzebub's voice spinning their minds around, and, last, that the perverted desecrator of souls probably deserved stomping to death anyway, the man added that in gratitude for any modicum of leniency they might see fit to extend he was prepared to reveal a spectacle rarely enjoyed by mortals, a miracle to amaze townsmen and family, i.e., the secret of life itself. And opening a large tome and plopping it down on the cadaver's naked pubis, he explained that, though the body of man was known to be a universe, it wasn't a harmony of constellations and moons as commonly believed, but rather a great principality at war. Conceive it as a city, he continued, brawls and swindling everywhere, walls tumbling, alleys twisting, a populace of tyrants, thieves, rebels, rogues. No one could know its purposes, for endless striving was its very nature. Bellies usurped reason, humors vied for dominion, the eye overthrew the sense of hearing, and the heart would rule all. The ancients had mistaken life for equanimity and governance, just as he had once done himself, for their only study had been of death. But to glimpse the body's secret, to snatch a truth not yet decayed, one had to enter the fray, leap upon the enemy where he lay guileless and unsuspecting beneath your very hands. And here he paused, seemed to tense, then added: Nothing is less certain than the future. And raising the cleaver into the air he whispered in a voice grown luxurious and warm: For all knowledge is ambush, for triumph belongs to the wily, for everything living moves. And spinning on his heel, he flung himself on Fat Sacchi the goat–lover's son.

Sacchi squealed and vomited his dinner. The cleaver lodged in his leather gorget, somehow piercing an artery that promptly showered the room. Big Lothario grabbed the madman's knees, Little Lothario wrapped around his head. More or less everyone rolled on the floor in half–digested pasta while a fellow known to the others only as Him Yonder got his halberd tangled in a linen hamper and someone's matchlock exploded raining down stucco, bits of rafter, and bewildered spiders. There was some cursing, the dead infant's pancreas got involved. At a crucial juncture the yokels figured out that whatever didn't have armor on it was fair game, and the demoniac's brains, kidneys, spleen and privates received a proper kicking. Exactly whose blood it all was no one could be sure, but eventually the assailant stopped twitching, so they dragged him by the whiskers down the stairs and were all fairly delighted to be done with the place, its smell of sin and pesky flies. All but Lavender Giovio, who lingered momentarily over the two cadavers, poked a finger in a bulbous whazzit, twiddled squishy doo–bobs, flipped through the pages on the unmarred body's lap, then called out to the others that this Christian's soul had just entered hell. There was silence, a cough, some eye–rolling, then somebody said, All right, how can you tell that this Christian's soul has etc, etc, Lavender Giovio smiled, placed his palm on the forehead and pinched the nostrils closed. Still warm, he said, but no breathing.

Leonardo listened to della Torre's imitation of the swain's voice break into a snicker as the light on the men's faces flashed uncertainly and somewhere a shutter banged free. A storm was blowing up from the Ticino, and as the night began to come alive around the dark room Leonardo wondered how many deaths a man's bones could absorb before breaking through the skin and simply walking out from under him. Della Torre was repeating some portion of his tale, his back bent ever so slightly and his head held almost but not quite at the angle of someone looking you in the eye, and for the first time Leonardo imagined that he might be profoundly bored. An odd thought. To strike the devil's bargain, plunge your fist into a heart, and bring it out again with nothing that amazed you—Leonardo would guess that this would be what boredom felt like and that the rage it sparked would become a conflagration, blackening your eyes, burying you in ash, slime. Yes, there'd been a betrayal, and della Torre would never understand whose or why. Watching the young man devour his soul, Leonardo knew that one day he, Leonardo, would say to Salai or Melzi or some besotted lens–grinder what he ought to be saying to della Torre right now and that the dazzled silence then would leave Leonardo wondering if he'd ever in sixty–odd years spoken an intelligible sentence. Since understanding was fated to come to you anyway, why did it never arrive in time? The room seemed darker now. Over della Torre's shoulder a shadow slid along the wall.

Suddenly Marcantonio shouted: The light!

Leonardo lunged for a candelabra as a gust ripped through the curtains, blew out the flame, and set the tapestry flapping wildly against a chair.

Get the shut—

No, here!

Kicking once at the window with his far leg, Leonardo leaned shoulder to shoulder with the anatomist, and together they wrapped their hands in a tight ring around the last light, a dirty taper in a teacup. The wind whistled past their ears, bringing distant barking and a wet smell like freshly bathed hair. A roof tile crashed on the paving stones outside. Leonardo watched a dung–fly shiver on the table's edge then blow away. The roar of air filled the room.

Now! della Torre yelled.

The two men grabbed the shutters, threw the latch, slammed the windows, pulled the drapes, just as raindrops splattered on the roof and the first thunder struck. Leonardo felt it rumble through the soles of his slippers and wondered what makeshift force of law had arrived to fetch them to a reckoning. He took a deep breath. With the windows closed the air would begin to gag him soon, though the flies had momentarily been chased into the rafters and the heat was gone. The room was dim now.

Good fortune, della Torre said holding up the dirty taper as he relit a candle. Our gratitude to the saints, Matteo da Rimini, Lord Vesta, and that apostle of resentment—Guido da Forlì.

Many hands to protect a small light.

Claptrap, della Torre said. The only protection I ever needed was from teachers.

You're confusing yourself with what you study, Leonardo replied.

Mock me, but where has there ever been a mortal I could learn from? After Galen only folly and the enigma here. Della Torre gestured down at the cadaver and then, recollecting the work, added: Get the syringe.

Leonardo rummaged through a cabinet, pulled out a glass pipe with a greasy leather bag at one end. Perhaps Matteo da Rimini was your kinsman, he continued. There's something in his enmity that's curious. Not every cocksure youth drove him mad.

Whatever bogey he worshipped it wasn't me.

But still, whatever he saw in you seemed worth being afraid of. He possessed exceptional discernment, you said as much. Listen to your own tale.

You needn't make riddles of commonplace things, della Torre said. Nature blessed Matteo, but his education served him badly. The man's mind teemed with spectres.

...the specter of a better mind.

Claptrap. Give me your hands.

Standing the head on its chin, della Torre worked the drill through the bone into the pulpy cortex as lightning flared at the curtains' edge and the floorboards shook.

Start confusing mistakes with miracles, he continued, and you'll end up baying at the moon. Matteo da Rimini was a rodent. The age of martyrs is passed.

Nature has to be an orderly realm, Leonardo began, but I've watched fire streak down the clouds a thousand times and never seen it look twice the same. I find this and many other things remarkable. Tell me, what could the man have done to deserve your admiration?

Della Torre didn't look up. He could have driven the cleaver into my—

CRASH! The storm blew the windows back open and snuffed out all the lights.

Leonardo was hearing that sound more and more often these days. His gigantic mural, *The Battle of Anghiari*, had gone to smash in 1506, and when he tried to renege on his contract with the signoria, the Florentine law crashed down on his head. He absconded to Milan where he found a new patron in the French regent Charles d'Amboise, but the dam he built on the Adda collapsed into the mud, and his plans for Charles' new palace crumbled under the weight of diplomacy. Pope Julius and the French formed the League of Cambrai in 1509 and bashed into the Venetians. Pope Julius and the Venetians formed the

Holy League in 1510 and bashed into the French. With the help of the prodigy Marcantonio della Torre, Leonardo began an illustrated book on the human body, even contrived a way to reproduce the sketches, but the project soon became top–heavy and tumbled down. His astronomy collided with his math, his math jostled his hydraulics, his hydraulics undermined his optics again and again. One evening circumscribing rectangles, he disproved Archimedes only to recognize the next morning that he'd mistranslated him, and he started to wonder, was the only point of knowledge to make each downfall spectacular? He grew lethargic, found himself scrutinizing boys' buttocks in the vapor baths, and late one night woke to the unmistakable odor of Salai's damp curls in his room—a thing that, by then, hadn't happened in years. Charles d'Amboise died, his successor Gaston de Foix died, their enemy Pope Julius died, his enemy Louis douze started to die, and somewhere in a dungeon in southern France, Leonardo's first patron, Lodovico Sforza, died. In 1511–12 plague swept through Lombardy forcing Leonardo to remain in town. And then Marcantonio della Torre died. There seemed nothing left but to publish Leonardo's magnum opus, the treatise on painting, so he began it a dozen times. He turned sixty. He started to wear spectacles. His right hand cramped. Nature might be an orderly realm, but Leonardo was a mess. CRASH!

What kept him steady during this second collapse of Milan was what drove him crazy during the first one—a horse, only this time with more attention to the rider on it, one Marshal Gian Giacomo Trivulzio, a nobleman, Milanese patriot, and braggadocio. Evidently, Trivulzio wanted a monument to his own prowess in order—among other things—to defy the French, and he chose both a subject and sculptor intended to recall Milan's former glory. Leonardo, who could still hear the clay fragments of his first debacle crunching underfoot whenever he walked past the Castello, wasn't the fool who'd blown the project twenty years before. Although he might never appreciate that a second chance was irrefutable proof of the existence of God and so occasion to prostrate oneself in slobbering obeisance to whatever bogey had provided this preposterous, Disney–like plot turn—all preparatory to seizing it in both hands—despite never appreciating this, Leonardo certainly felt the oddness of his repetition. He was, after all, making another horse on virtually the same site where he'd botched the first one. So he didn't waste time. He tallied each cost precisely—2,946 ducats for the tin, kindling, pumice, and a half dozen troglodites to beat the bronze into a barrel–shaped chunk, plus another hundred ducats or so for Leonardo to appear at the right moment and transform it into his employer—and when in an inspired moment he imagined the beast rearing heavenwards on its hindlegs, leaping out of the stone, Leonardo told himself, uh uh, this isn't Pegasus, and placed all four hooves firmly on the ground. No doubt about it, Leonardo was becoming one of us.

Of course, *this* horse was small–potatoes compared to the sixty–ton colossus of hoof, hock, and croup he'd formerly thought to die for, but as he turned sixty, Leonardo was weary enough to find manageable tasks interesting. With Marshal Trivulzio's coins trickling in and with the threat of plague restricting his distractions, Leonardo threw himself into work. He exhumed his old sketches and calculations, began haunting Milan's stables again and even revived his acquaintance with Galeazzo Sanseverino's former groom. Progress was steady. Day in, day out. Leonardo felt like a new man. And just as before it was Salai, now a wastrel of thirty with banal ambitions and the exaggerated swagger of someone entirely worthless—but still a ten–year–old boy's hair—it was Salai who roused Leonardo from his dream. By the summer of 1512 Louis douze had buried two regents in Milan and was hightailing it over the Alps, having left behind a suicidally loyal garrison in the Castello Sforzesco which, before the last fleur–de–lis topped the horizon, was negotiating its surrender to the Swiss. Marshall Trivulzio, whose one joy in life had been mayhem but who'd failed utterly to raise a band of stout lads eager to be shishkabobbed, had—after much high–blown expostulation—ridden away with Louis Douze. The garlic–chewing mercenaries of the Holy Roman Emperor tromped into the city, and the population started speaking Schwyzerdütsch. The trickle of coins stopped. The supply of bronze stopped. No one examined the sketches, lists of tools, and out–of–pocket expenses Leonardo continued sending to the Marshall's villa each day. Leonardo kept working.

So when Salai finally found him with his calipers and compass and gradients and silverpoint and sanguine and bone meal in Trivulzio's stable during the blackest blackness before dawn, squatting on a milkmaid's stool in the yellow circle of an oil lamp, amid the odor of hay and horse piss, as rats rustled beneath the straw and the air hung as heavy as a sweatsock—well, Salai should've burst out laughing. I mean, the man was mad! Would he never stop? Or if not laugh, then shake him, wake Leonardo up, spit right into his precious eye, just as Salai'd done a decade before. And that's just what Salai would've done if only it hadn't been horses. For even though he'd scorned the Trivulzio monument, had concerned himself with social respectability, arranging dowries for sisters, conniving prosperous lodgings for uncles, all the while steadfastly refusing to acknowledge that, after twenty years, the old promise could still be fulfilled—despite this resoluteness, Salai had never anticipated *seeing* a picture. And so walking through the stable as contempt assailed him, as the beasts' wholeness and his own need–need–need pierced his heart again, Salai stepped right up to Leonardo's back and glanced over his shoulder. Flared nostrils, frenzied eyes, necks twisted up, around, backwards, muscles twitching, withers, hocks, hoofs, manes flying, tails flung high, thighs, teeth, gaskins, croup, all just as he'd suffered them through a thousand-thousand nights. He heard the silverpoint scratching, saw Leonardo's fingers dart across a line, and beside himself once more, he began to mutter, yes, he'd wait, forever, when his breath disturbed Leonardo's hair. Leonardo jumped from his stool flinging hands, stylus, chalkbox, paper, drawingboard, calipers, bone dust, resin-pouch in the air. No more horses! he bellowed and stormed out the door.

THE ADVENTURE OF GIULIANO DE MEDICI'S STABLE

And so began the renunciations that would send them all one September morning, 1513, rattling through Milan's southernmost gate behind a cartload of palate knives, gesso pots, pigments and carpenter's tools pausing every thirty furlongs or so to massage their buttocks and open the seventeen chests, sacks, boxes, bundles just to make sure the loose sheets of doodles and meanderings were bearing up under the journey all right, which usually meant perusing a page or three. By the time they reached lovely Rapallo, Leonardo'd already renounced sculpture, meat, Florence, anatomy, heavier–than–air–flight, Plato's *Timaeus*, and stopping short of utterly renouncing either Milan, where his vineyard still flourished, or the French, who'd so far been the only ones to adore him, he bounced along behind the heaped–up cart in a coach Salai'd hired from someone named Feruzzi—supposedly an iron–monger, more likely a blackguard, almost certainly a relative—and with every jostle muttered: No more notes, no more dawdling, no more mistakes. Trivulzio's exit had finally awakened in Leonardo the same apprehension awakened in Salai nearly seventeen years earlier and taken for granted by the half–dozen vagabonds tucked in the coach's crannies when they thought beyond their next meal—i.e., time was running out. Either forget science, practice exorbitant ass–kissing, and begin to work fast, or Leonardo's so–called career as a so–called genius was over. Precisely what besides desperation and a Medici Pope would effect this alteration was unclear, but leaving Milan, everyone in Leonardo's entourage felt hopeful. In the box up front Lorenzo held the reins slack and flirted with young Melzi, and on the coach roof Battista plucked a chitarra and sang of post–coitum tristesse. Il Fanfoia sifted the loose clothing in the luggage hold for pocket change, and late that night beneath a sky as flawless as betrayal, a barn owl perched on the topmost wagon-stave and beheld them like the destiny they couldn't even dream.

The journey took three weeks, and when at last they reached Rome they found a city of pigs. Gargantuan sows grunted in the Colisseum, flopped on the Forum's swampy floor, chased piglets over the Palatine Hill and beneath the arch of Severus peed in hot streams. Shirtless youths with gnats in their hair hawked shoats to pilgrims slouching past, merrily shoving their knives into the shrieking animals as the buyers counted their coins, and at any moment a boar big as a chapel door might rush snorting from behind a forgotten senator's home. In the evenings cocottes whistled from glowing windows where in exchange for a cabbage they'd unveil their astonishing bosoms, and everywhere there were friars prepared to sell you St. Bartholomew's baby teeth or the tiller from the ark. Leonardo and his followers thought it was the classiest place they'd ever seen. Mucking along the boggy highway beside the Tiber they heard peddlers brawling in High Dutch and saw black–gowned scholars nosing the Latin inscriptions ankle–deep in cattle turds and rain. They stopped at an inn with a golden apple on the lintel, made supper of figs and white kidney beans, and after walking till midnight in huge ovals around the Pope's gardens—where once a billygoat charged Leonardo from the shadow of a buttress and slovenly rats ambled across his path and as he bent to pluck a watch-clasp from the cobblestones he thought he heard a voice whisper his name—Leonardo lay awake the rest of the night calculating the minimal cost of the provisions he'd need to win fame. Next morning he called on Pope Leo's brother, Giuliano, explaining that he, Leonardo da Vinci, former servant of Giuliano's father, Lorenzo Il Magnifico, had immediate need of fine housing, good food, luxurious furniture, trained artisans, a cook, influence, copper, various alembics, two burnishing devices, and additional funds sufficient to buy himself a gold necklace. Giuliano sighed, let his morose eyes sag over his cheekbones, lamented the deplorable state of his own fortunes and— real life isn't believable—apologized that he could do nothing till that afternoon.

City of pigs, oxen, marmots, wallabies, whippets, ermine and even one sickly white elephant in the Pope's zoo. On your way out for caffelatte in the morning you might trip over a porcupine—someone's pet brought back from Cathay by an adventurer with Colombo—and you'd get bitten by a monkey or half–tame hyaena before you could pull the quills from your leg. From the window of his apartment in the Belvedere Leonardo looked down on the pink–eyed doves that circled the cupola every evening or watched skinny cattle wandering up the alleyways from the river. It was as if nature were at last coming to find him, grown weary of his delay, were chiding him for infidelity, and surrounded by so much movement Leonardo almost felt young. Leonardo's rooms were fitted with yellow truckle beds, pink divans and chifforobes; holes had been knocked in the walls for windows; and a terrace was being built so he could dry his whiskers in the sun. In the workshop Salai and Melzi quarreled over the avalanche of materials Giuliano kept sending, and Lorenzo banged away at the wooden cages in which Leonardo planned to house the exotic creatures he found. Never had arrangements seemed so splendid. All that was lacking were commissions. And so Leonardo wandered out into the Piazza San Pietro, started buttonholing strangers, dropping names, coins, until he located in the Borgo Vecchio a palazzo more stately and decorous than any he'd ever seen. He knocked loudly, had his name sent up, and when he heard the booming voice he knew so well, rushed inside to embrace his old rival, Bramante. How had he come...? Where had he gone...? They'd never expected to see each other again!

The two men dined in a hall as vast as Leonardo's hopes, traded tales of dead Lodovico, Fra Luca in Florence now, Amado, Bellincioni, di Giorgio the snoot. Nearly twenty years had passed since they'd vied for Lodovico's favor, and confronted with this vision of their forgotten youth, they fell in love. Bramante assured Leonardo of spirited assistance, patronage, influence on his behalf, whatever he needed, and meanwhile introduced him to Bramante's young cousin, the handsome boy Raffaello Santi, a great admirer of Leonardo's unfinished murals. When late that night Leonardo staggered drunkenly past the scaffolding of Bramante's vatican renovations, he dreamed he'd found a home at last.

He readied his workshop, he rose early, he waited. In the papal gardens were rows of hyacinths and irises, strange weeds—Job's tears, wild raspberry, water parsnip—and to avoid boredom Leonardo sketched them. He pared the roots from a gourd and watched it survive in a pot on his window–ledge. He saw a sprig of lilac bend itself sunward, made notes on blood and sap, calculated the age of a felled cedar by the unknown practice of counting its rings. He began to think about writing a book on heliotropism and phyllotaxis, but when at dinner one night he mentioned the scheme, Salai choked on his veal and Battista had to leave the room. No more distractions, Leonardo told himself. He returned the next morning to Giuliano's palazzo where he learned that his patron was away and then wandered back to the vatican where he examined the foundations being laid for the four great pillars of Bramante's new basilica—just in case his friend needed Leonardo's consultation. He then wandered through Bramante's newly remodeled loggia downhill from Leonardo's own apartments where to his astonishment he discovered the boy he'd met at Bramante's manor, Raffaello, painting a mural in the papal rooms. The work was located in private chambers and so wasn't quite of the public prestige or dignity appropriate for someone of Leonardo's stature, though—Leonardo had to admit—he'd come to Rome prepared to settle for less. But he was surprised. If such tasks were entrusted to apprentices in Rome, what should Leonardo da Vinci expect? But by the time he got back to his workshop he was sulky as a cistern. Great undertakings were in progress in every corner of the city. Even the bristly Michelangelo Buonarotti was busy here. It felt shameful to be idle.

Finally, an invitation arrived. Leonardo was to come to Giuliano's for dinner, the world would be there. Lorenzo sewed up the holes in his master's lavender hose, and Francesco Melzi gave him pointers on talking to cardinals and using cutlery. Leonardo retrieved the list of bawdy tales he'd compiled during his days as Lodovico's courtier, strove to commit a few to memory. It had been awhile since he'd needed to amuse anyone, since he hadn't been the center of every discussion, but recalling how he'd turned heads in Florence when he spoke, he figured he knew what he was about. He wore a dashing hat, arrived late enough to seem debonair, located the right henchman to bribe for a good seat at table, and prepared to quip and flatter with the best of them. But since so much of the repartee was in Latin, he had difficulty not sounding like a hick. When called on to eulogize the god of Geometry, he had to listen to every toady correct his declensions, and once during a lively moment when he called over to Bramante, Donato didn't hear. The Pope himself weighed three hundred pounds, had the manners of a gamekeeper, a bawd's laugh, and was fond of concluding grave or spiritual reflections with a thunderous burp—a practice Leonardo found disconcerting—and the one time His Holiness addressed a question to him, the papal gaze had moved on before Leonardo got his tenses straight. Leonardo could tell he hadn't shone. He wound up sitting in a corner near a whimpering friar who'd eaten twenty-four raw goose eggs on a dare, wondering what about the present situation felt so familiar. He was doing everything correctly, but it seemed to be making no difference at all. The friar vomited into the fire place. The room broke out in wild applause. There was discussion of taking the Pope's white elephant to the Forum. When time finally came to leave, Leonardo had to be reassured by Giuliano that he'd made an impression. Something would come of it; the Pope was, after all, a Medici. Leonardo agreed to wait.

Bramante received unlimited funding for his new cathedral, the papal apartments, and various renovations for diplomats, wealthy patricians, and Medici family members throughout the better sections of the city. Michelangelo was assured of unimpeded access to the papal coffers to facilitate his labor on Pope Julius' elaborate tomb—the work of a lifetime, everyone agreed—and for any provisions or comforts that might make his task less onerous. Raffaello Santi was charged with covering all the walls and ceilings in the papal chambers and adjoining rooms with murals on inspiring themes and with directing his assistants to oversee all embellishments necessary for beautification of the edifices his uncle Bramante was erecting and was admonished to assign a greater portion of the continual avalanche of portrait requests from noble families throughout Italy to artisans of lesser craft or, at least, to his apprentices so that his own devotion would remain more single-mindedly at the service of the Pope. Leonardo da Vinci was to design a stable. City of pigs, wallabies, lemurs, nannygoats, kangaroos, llamas, bobcats, sheep, and now—horses! Leonardo swore he wouldn't touch it. Giuliano smiled, eyes oozing down his cheekbones, head tilted to one side. Just the beginning, he said. The ineffable stupidity of which didn't strike Leonardo until he tried repeating it to Salai. Just a beginning?! Leonardo was sixty–one years old at a time when the life expectancy was twenty–two. Salai stomped out of the workshop; Lorenzo picked up his bird–sling and slouched after him; Battista collapsed moaning on a bag of walnuts, and Leonardo moped in the ruins of the capitol for two whole days. At the dilapidated baths of Diocletian a small, angry dog chased him into a drainage ditch and beneath the arch of Titus he saw a heifer sliding its tongue in and out of its own nose. A pony with a hard–on trotted behind him all the way down the Via del Corso, and when at last he climbed the hill back to the Belvedere—as bleary-eyed and haggard as a wooly St. John the Baptist—the doves swooped low in their oval round the basilica and shat on his head. It was an assault. Leonardo gave in, drew the stable without bothering to inspect the site, arranged slips and bins in slapdash order, threw in enough details to make the sloppiness look calculated, signed the cover page with a flourish, included a dedication to his celestial benevolence and the only light in a vast murkiness, most noble, big and rich Giuliano de Medici and, for good measure, his beloved brother and morning star of Christendom, wise Pope Leo, the thought of whose abundant person made Leonardo want to retch, sealed them in a red leather case and persuaded Francesco Melzi that delivering them wasn't beneath his dignity, which it was. The drawings were received with all the falderal they'd have received if Leonardo'd spent a lifetime on them, and Melzi returned with a thousand compliments and a bagful of money. Then Leonardo stormed off to Bramante's.

Who wept. Yes, he'd neglected his old crony, been unfaithful to their solemn love, yielded to ancient envies, refused succor, behaved as an opportunist, a beast, a traitor, a man of cold affections, infirm purpose, empty talk and emptier deeds, scum, snake droppings, snail snot, whatever-have-you that's low, smelly, vile. Hadn't everyone flocked to see Leonardo's fresco in Santa Maria delle Grazie, called him philosopher, godlike man? And Bramante's own creation—he shrugged—perhaps the little monastery wasn't such a remarkable thing. Bramante's apostasy was shameful, he acknowledged it, flogged himself, blew his nose, said he was base, slimy, wretched, noxious.... Could Leonardo ever forgive him? Needless to say, Leonardo hadn't come across Rome to forgive him. He'd come to beg. The two men stood in front of a fireplace slightly smaller than Leonardo's whole apartment, beat their breasts, mingled hoary manes, pledged fealty to death, confided past spites, pettiness, opened their veins and bled into each other, and Leonardo stopped just short of crawling on his knees. Bramante advised patience. Rome was leviathan, far mightier than puny Milan, but devious and slow. Even now forces were stirring to bring Leonardo his deserved honor. And Bramante would himself vouchsafe that Leonardo had many supporters here, persons wildly enamored of his many unfinished paintings, and by the by, had Leonardo examined young Raffaello's murals in the Stanza della Segnatura? They ate dinner from solid gold plates, shared an antique chalice supposed to have been St. Matteo's own, waxed tipsy, sang a filthy ballad, and when at last Leonardo wove his way past the scaffolds, wedges, blocks, ropes where the new basilica would one day rise, he suspected his life was over. He'd been sucked into fortune's maelstrom just as the world expected. What could other persons offer him but their confusion? In the morning he would return to the seventeen chests, sacks, boxes, bundles where his notebooks were stored, divide day from night, devote himself to knowledge. Stables? Bah!

And so Leonardo went to bed that night deep in fury and determination, dreamed a new table of contents for his treatise on painting, imagined Michelangelo's comeuppance reading Leonardo's discourse on nudes, Bramante's remorse, but at daybreak instead of rising to clarity and fresh concentration, Leonardo was awakened by noise. He heard Lorenzo swearing, barks, shattering glass. Rushing into the workshop he found Battista pummeling a hairless underbit tree–stump who issued a sound from his mouth like speech and coughing. The tree–stump handed Leonardo a letter—with Giuliano's seal on it—requesting a variety of mirrors, polished coppers and burning-lenses for some alchemical affair Giuliano was up to his ears in and explaining that Georg—the tree stump—knew how to make them. It, Georg, then ransacked the workshop, set up a grinding bench, and began singing beer songs. If you interrupted it, it swore at you. If you tried to touch it, it bit. All appearances suggested that it was moving in.

At the Palazzo de'Medici Giuliano was away. It was still early so Bramante would be sleeping, and besides, what could Bramante do? Leonardo didn't have enough cash for an interview with the Pope. After the debacle of his *Battle of Anghiari*, he couldn't look to Florence for help. The French were threatening war again, and a letter would take weeks. Besides, how would you start? Your Highness, there's a German in my apartment.... Leonardo wanted to scream. He was no burnisher! He was Leonardo da Vinci! On the dilapidated steps of what had once been the old basilica, Leonardo passed the smiling youth Raffaello and thirty or so of his sycophants, and though Raffaello nodded respectfully, made way for Leonardo, and by even conservative estimates had to be fabulously rich and corrupt, Leonardo didn't acknowledge him. Having been admired by philosophers, he just couldn't ask for help from boys. One of Raffaello's groupies bumped Leonardo as he passed, excused himself, said something about an *old man*, and another called back that a panther had escaped from Pope Leo's zoo. It was a joke, of course, but the piazza was deserted, and a drizzle had begun, and an unfamiliar chill sent Leonardo bustling back to his apartment. When he arrived he found Lorenzo and the German killing doves out the workshop window, having opened every cage in the place. The furniture crawled with toads, rodents, lizards, and when Leonardo grabbed the culprits by the scruff of their necks, his right hand cramped up and wouldn't let go. Georg had to be pried loose barking and spitting. Lorenzo sulked. Salai hadn't been seen in four days. Il Fanfoia was in the hoosegow for shoplifting and, according to Battista, was sure to pay for the crime with his fingers. Squirrels plundered the walnuts. The terrace had sprung a leak. And Francesco Melzi chose this moment to appear in a painter's smock asking for instruction in the mixing of oils.

Leonardo had both feet on the window ledge and, looking down, was allowing his fancy to dwell on how cool the paving stones would feel striking his forehead, when the papal emissary arrived with his first commission. It was no great shakes, a small madonna of the kind Beatrice d'Este used to ooo and ah over—Leonardo chose not to wonder to whom he was indebted for this—but what mattered was that, to somebody official, Leonardo still looked like a painter. Before the toe of his left slipper had touched the floor, the conception was percolating in Leonardo's brain. To befit a pope the image should be both unworldly and earthen, almost cruel, an eroticism so ethereal its viewers would feel their bodies as wounds. Every shape exfoliating from the radiant center, grace–abounding arcs, Being's leap—the face would give off more light than any painting had ever contained. By the time Leonardo was down out of the window and into the parlor where Melzi kept repeating to the papal emissary the kind of clichés about condescension that made everyone want to throttle him, Leonardo was already lost in calculations. His breath came in spasms; the blood pounded in his face. He tried to sign the contract that, for some reason, the emissary seemed reluctant to let go of, while trying not to appear as desperate as he, of course, was. He knew this was his last chance. He was determined not to blow it.

Which made failure almost inevitable. What to his own age looked like perfectionism and to ours looks impractical and naive, was probably, for Leonardo himself, what made art so exciting. In a painting, something he knew, something he couldn't have painted and *not* known, was always at stake. Although he no longer imagined madonnas as geometry or expected science to create them, he remained as intent on the work, and as oblivious of patrons, as twenty years before. Small wonder then he paid so little attention to the extraordinary elegance of the papal emissary's cloak, the Tuscan lilt to his voice, or the inexplicable presence of two splendidly dressed attendants just outside the door. He scrawled his name—left to right this time—at the bottom of the contract, stuffed the document back into the young man's trembling hand, and bustled happily out of the room.

In truth, the emissary was, by virtue of a genealogical irregularity and widespread tolerance of philandering, a Medici fifth cousin in the maternal line and had, from the time his nose nuzzled his nanny's teat, been treated to tales of Leonardo da Vinci's scandalous abandonment of his Florentine commissions in defiance of the Muses and the law. Now, having arrived—thanks to the blessed virgins Mary and Diana— within the same political orbit as this legend, the young dandy was prepared to undergo all manner of indignities just to start an anecdote someday: Well, as my compatriot Leonardo da Vinci once told me.... And if Leonardo had recognized the strategic opportunity here, if he'd just taken time to make chitchat or noticed young Melzi's frantic attempts to signal to him, hey, look at that crest on the guy's buckler, then this story might still have a chance for a respectable ending. But Leonardo was far too ecstatic to worry over protocol. He abandoned the humiliated emissary to Lorenzo, Georg, Battista, and Melzi, hunted up his protractor, and got right to work.

Within a few hours he'd determined that shadow would rule the work, that disegno was a minion. The execution would be a tour de force of reneging, fuzzy edges, wistfulness. There'd be much to learn about how silver, ocher and brown diminished, and so he probably should observe sunset on the Campagna, especially in autumn. Then there was translucence. Salai could experiment with viscosities for overpainting, Battista could take notes on drying intervals, and Leonardo would himself anatomize a dead maiden's face to learn what he could about pallor. Once the conception was as sharp as an icicle, he'd draw the cartoon. Geometry had never dreamed an intricacy to match this one, and so Leonardo decided to write Fra Luca regarding projected reductions of irregular polyhedrons and, by the by, what was new in Tuscany? Then he'd consider—very, very briefly—pigments, resins, varnishes, bristles, abrasives, linen, hide–glue, fasteners, knives, cleaning agents, chalk, the plan of his studio, Verrochio's madonnas, artificial lighting, his apprentices, and, of course, the woodgrain in the panel, which Leonardo suspected of having far greater influence on the finished work—even after gesso had been applied—than was commonly believed. Leonardo was hot, he was happy. But because he was intent on succeeding, he resolved to act fast.

As a result, when the same papal emissary reappeared a month later prancing and reeking of citronella, hailing everyone by name and making noises to the effect that he'd really love a glimpse of the painting, Leonardo could boast that he'd perfected ocher, concocted a revolutionary fishbone stylus, discovered a new method for three–dimensional composition and expected to start drawing the cartoon within a fortnight. Never had he progressed at such a spanking pace! Of course, there was nothing to *see*.... Even so, disaster might've been averted if Leonardo had fed the young man dinner, made spirited conversation, and offered him Melzi's companionship for a night, but not even the apprehension of impending mortality was strong enough in Leonardo to transform this fellow's crimson blouse and suffocating aroma into the perfectly straightforward signals they were intended to be. Leonardo smiled, told him to return in six months, closed the door in the dandy's face, and ended his career as a painter.

When Leonardo got the news that he'd been sacked, he ran shrieking to Giuliano whose eyes and jowls made a puddle on the floor. Nothing could be done. During the time Leonardo had been planning his madonna, Raffaello had measured, sketched, painted and all but taxidermied Pope Leo's pet white elephant who'd succumbed to the Roman heat and a stomach full of river–stones fed it by die–hard Savonarola followers five weeks before. The portrait looked about as much like an elephant as Leonardo's madonnas looked like Hebrew carpenter's wives but never mind, it made the Pope happy, Raffaello rich and anyone as painstaking as Leonardo superfluous. Leonardo's madonna had been given to an epigone in Raffaello's entourage who'd painted it in a weekend, and no one had noticed any difference. For that was how you knew popes from painters, Giuliano explained, popes didn't have to wait. At the sound of which words Leonardo felt a remarkable lightness spread outward from the bone at the top of his nose, saw his own head float through the window. So all of his virtues had been subservience. Giuliano oozed along the floor in a morose smear of sympathy, sighed, tsk–ed, reminded Leonardo how the favor of princes was a shiny pathway to delusion, counseled resignation, etc. But Leonardo now saw, as if for the first time, that freedom just meant never caring deeply about anything. What could be purer than a life without deeds? A bell clanged in the distance. A warm breeze touched his throat. Patience, he thought. And the ludicrous black gnarl of this

147

word pleased him so unspeakably that he giggled and guffawed, bent himself double, let the laughter surge through his nose, shake his shoulders, fill his bones, until Giuliano placed a hand on his arm, saying, Don't weep, my friend; Don't weep. Which Leonardo tried to reassure him he wasn't doing. Then realized he was.

If dying here alone in his bedchamber on May 2, 1519, as the water from the upended washbasin slowly transforms itself into a dark depression in the floor's grime and the silver-gray clouds cast their vague light across the paper lilies and cords, if dying here alone Leonardo were—out of some need to humiliate himself or a delusion that by reliving his nightmares he could end them or because of an inner dividedness that seems natural to us but preposterous to him—if Leonardo were to recall that moment in Rome when he made his last bid for public acclaim, he'd find his mistakes as unavoidable as when he made them. He's still pretty sure that at bottom nature's one entity, that the myriad of contradictory experiences are somehow intertwined. If he's achieved any peace of mind it's by living without peace of mind. And although he knows he'll never find the unitary principle he's always been on the verge of, knows his faith in nature has mostly done him worldly harm, he still can't believe his investigations were for nothing. Anyway, he can't regret them. Staring at the near edge of a gummy stain on the floorboards, Leonardo thinks there must be a waywardness within his fate. He'd expected the future to be hidden or devious, but now—like this spilled water seeping through the dust or like the patterns he has watched vanish and re-emerge in the Arno— its shape seems to have been constantly before his eyes. Couldn't he see that popes weren't philosophers, that perfect devotion would be lost on crowds? But losing himself in every painting, he certainly *looked like* someone who couldn't see. Now the only mystery is how little mystery there ever was. And then the final irony, to end up all alone, isolated by the knowledge he now knows he never even knew—well, it's as if he'd missed his life just because it was there.

Of course, Leonardo isn't alone. Over beneath the window in front of which he expects at any minute to see Salai scowling—no, no, no, he expects nothing of the kind!—beneath this window lies the woman. Leonardo fears she's dead. It's a possibility his last dimostrazione never allowed for. After all, this was supposed to be Leonardo da Vinci's death, and the thought that her demise could displace his, that in the end the end might be another's, well, it never crossed his mind. Everything else can be lost. Your knowledge can turn out illusory, your deeds amount to nothing. Even your agonies could be another's agonies that, while you were busy agonizing, substituted for your own. But can someone else die in your place? Leonardo looks over at the woman's heaped up form that at just this instant and to his immense relief emits an airy fart but otherwise promises to remain negligible a few pages longer, and decides: no, she's breathing. Much more needs to happen before these two, man and woman, will find each other interesting, but already her body has disturbed him. And good thing. If she'd been dead, his last dimostrazione would've been a failure. For even though the darkness on Albano's slope annihilated Leonardo, even though it deprived him of his levity and made him terminally profound, it was only a beginning. And Leonardo wanted to see: the paper flowers, ecstasy of color, catapults, tripe—would she fall for it just as he'd done fifty years before? Not to her death or even from grace, which he didn't imagine she had much of anyhow, but like she'd been taken in, lured, succored. At the time, he thought this might settle something.

Now it's becoming hard to care. Gazing out the window past the line of ragged crenelations down to the perfectly still river that he can't really see from this bed, Leonardo feels like a confused old man. Maybe trying to understand your fate, to know the forces controlling you, was how your downfall became assured. Of course, Marcantonio della Torre would call his vaccilation cowardice. What would you be? Blind? A gull? Or he'd chide Leonardo for studying what hadn't died. But Leonardo sometimes thinks now that he really did know, must've, that gazing down into the Arno's current that spring of 1506, seeing the current spin once, twice, three times into its own motion, he'd seen everything his heart desired, and that afterwards he was completely free. Perhaps the only mistake was to think his freedom meant he'd finish something. Anyway, if it was knowing that undid him, then it was too late to unknow after that, probably always was. He sighs, shakes his head. Paintings peal, statues crumble, books don't get written. It seems preposterous to think others might understand you. Hell, he doesn't even understand himself.

But then Salai wasn't trying to understand.

...so you dream of owning horses. You dream, lying there in the filth and slop and drippings, of being the man who strides through their midst more terrifying than they are. I've seen these men. I have watched them from the small holes where I hid. They are stallions themselves, great beasts, untamed, and like the creatures who crush you, they delight in killing. The beasts adore such men. Their nostrils ripple, ears lift. You can hear them snicker and paw the earth, and from its sack of skin their great grimy pizzles slide out into the air. These are the beings for which horses are made, but first a horse requires subduing. If unsubdued, it would mount its rider, drive its hooves and pizzle into him, bite clean the man-flesh from the rosy bones. It's mayhem, after all, that's the great love—Why else would ravishing be more joyful than surrender? Why else is it, as I'm told on good authority, that women, though as randy as ourselves, take less pleasure in the act? And so, killing must be driven out of them. It is this feat that makes the owners of horses uncanny. They have terrified the powers that other mortals fear.

Salai's voice filled the window, made a hole in the vanishing light. ...so you dream of owning horses. You lie in the black mud that's earth and sewage, and your head fills with this dream you hope will heal the wound of being born weak. Someday, they'll know the fear you know in the dark curled against the stable wall as their hooves smash the boards beside your ear. Only worse. For they'll feel it before you who are small. If they don't feel it, then you can punish them. This is what it means to own horses. I've dreamed this dream a thousand times, know its minute parts and tiny spaces, and I can assure you, it's a fine, joyous, manly dream.

Salai smiled up at Leonardo, one hand on the sill, his curls dangling across his eyes. He'd begun to pant.

It is, unfortunately, only a dream, he added. When I was a child in Milan I remember seeing you pass by the Vercellina gate. You wore a luxurious gown, I recall that it was green, though later when I wanted to burn it I could never find it among your clothes. I hadn't seen anything like it, and being young and despicable, I assumed you were fantastically rich. Salai chuckled. It's a common enough mistake.

Leonardo felt ashamed to stand there in silence, but what could he say? The...the hour's late, he muttered.

Salai lurched forward: Bad debts!

THE PREVIOUS CONTINUED

Returning from Giuliano de' Medici's palazzo, having been outdone by a hack in Raffaello's entourage and so deprived of his papal commission and thus for a second time finding that the success he'd anticipated was already past—all this was in 1514—Leonardo felt like a man betrayed. If his desires were natural, why hadn't nature satisfied them? If they weren't, how did they arise? He climbed the stairs to his apartment, took no notice of some merchants haggling in the doorway, and sat down for twenty–four hours in a straight–backed chair. He'd never yielded to melancholy before and was determined not to start now. He would adjust to solitude, resume his studies. Having been denied the chance to amaze humankind and recognizing the futility of trying to teach it, he would avenge himself by proving he'd been right all along. But no sooner had he seated himself among the piles of pages on his bedroom floor than he felt cicadas flutter in his bowels, and he had to pace the room, break wind. He tried wrapping his arms around his middle to hold his organs steady, but his stomach kept twittering. Finally, he walked onto the terrace where the moon and two large stars made the corners of an equilateral triangle, and listening to a young girl's laughter from a distant doorway, he began to relax. But the instant he resettled himself among his notes, his nausea returned, and he had to flee to the terrace or streets.

This continued day in, day out, the spasms coming and going. He remained as alert as ever but couldn't organize his thoughts, could only wander, gawk. In the shop Georg spilled beer on the copper filings, sang flat. Battista had the flux and couldn't work. Il Fanfoia was all thumbs. Leonardo began to wonder, was he turning into what people had always said about him? At night when he collapsed on his cot, numb from the dancing about of his attention, he'd be assailed by spectacles. He'd recall that time was short, awake in a panic, but his efforts at thought always sent him to the streets again. Week after week after week until he found that he needed to talk. He was watching a sheepdog hump a ewe in the weedy rubble of Catullus' home, musing on the spine's ripple in billygoats and men, when he noticed a filthy child leading two kids by a rope. The boy wore neither shirt nor shoes; his unruly hair framed his eyes; there was something about his smile. Although Leonardo had no business with him, he started questioning the boy: Was the odor among the ruins always this vile? Of what wood was his staff made? And who had twisted that stout rope? He hardly heard the goatherd's replies, but his reedy voice held Leonardo like a gull in a breeze. It was shrill, perfect, and—though not exactly pleasant—more captivating than Leonardo could've dreamed. They chattered until darkness when Leonardo followed him as far as the Porta San Sebastiano and watched him disappear into the memory of daylight, one finger raised at the last, perhaps in mockery—how could you tell?—and, feeling suddenly the air's chill, Leonardo rushed back to the Belvedere where, instead of whipping about like cedars in a windstorm, he floated quietly into sleep.

Lorenzo and the tree stump were quarreling, and Leonardo woke to find Georg barricaded in the workshop, Melzi and Il Fanfoia slumped gloomily on the divan. Lorenzo had gone to purchase a blunderbuss, though no one knew how he'd pay for it, and odors of burning coal floated under the door. Leonardo banged on the wall, demanded entry. There was a loud crash, some grinding. Battista shrugged. They were uncertain whether Salai still lived there. Leonardo was about to send Melzi for a constable when it struck him how little this mattered. He looked at the assistants. They were all so withered, dead. And he

151

rushed back down the stairwell, out into the piazza, where he hailed chambermaids, buttonholed mendicants and ragpickers, began trading anecdotes with an Israelite cheese–hawker whose whiskers smelled of whey—anyone. How had nature gotten obscured, Leonardo wanted to ask, how had it become so entangled in mindlessness, esoterica, furious doing? He chattered about dust, rain, hair, vermin, the miasma rising from the Pontine Marsh. Sometimes he scribbled in the blue journals he kept on his belt, but mostly he talked. Chance remarks stopped him. He bored strangers past saintly endurance. You could find him holding forth in the Piazza San Pietro surrounded by milling lepers, amputees, harlots, pick–pockets and the occasional pilgrim who mistook him for a reformer. No subject was too hackneyed. He scrutinized the moronic faces before him, hung on every word. This was life, he told himself. Life! life!

He had, he knew, become a crank. Day after day he strode through the Roman heat, sweat–sloppy, stinking, as quick to pounce on a listener as a cat on a cricket. Once when Giuliano invited him to dinner he arrived late in a flowing gown, refused to eat gammon, slumped down on the hearth where a dwarf was picking his nose, and laughed boisterously at the high–toned flattery and observations. When someone finally worked up the nerve to speak to him, he launched into an encomium on the Moors, and when the wine steward approached, he called the man Thales, posed him a conundrum. It didn't take many such appearances before rumors began to circulate—he was said to swallow incantations on bits of foolscap, to froth and spout gibberish— and he soon developed the habit of babbling on after all his listeners had drifted away. He wasn't mad. In fact, he'd never felt more lucid in sixty years! But the world seemed too ripe. If he couldn't determine where his knowledge ended, where his downfall began, well, he feared he might dissolve. He began to take reassurance from faux pas, to feel relief when his friends scurried away. He was exorcising a devil, driving an old nemesis out. He had to struggle not to revel in his newfound license— now that really would've been mad!—but he often felt giddy.

Most of all, though, he needed the voices of children. When the worst of the heat had passed and dampness no longer rose from the forum's swampy floor, or when at the height of the afternoon he sought shelter under the cypress boughs beside the septizonium of Severus, or whenever he braved the Hussites and rowdy penitents passing through the arch of Titus, or simply if the temperature and his lassitude combined to make him edgy, Leonardo would seek out the hairless goatherds among the ruins. Some were already losing their sopranos, others had voices as airy and shrill as girls. Leonardo would stroll among their animals, pick the lice from the boys' necks, listen to them squeal. He fancied that their chants were Adam's lost speech, that they

152

smiled because of something they knew. At dusk their yipes and hoots took on an unearthly sound, and their slovenly figures on the horizon struck him dumb. It mattered little that they mocked him. He didn't want their love; he wanted their motion, life, secrets—them! He didn't know what he wanted. The more afternoons he passed in their midst, knees bumping the sides of their animals, watching as their arms extended like willow branches to snare a kid, the more he believed they possessed what he'd always been seeking. If only his drawings could float over a page like their brown goats across a piazza. What difference if the world despised you? He just wanted to hear these voices.

Then one night as he strode beside their thin arms and blackened feet toward the Porta San Sebastiano where the whining of sheepdogs would blend with the noise of nightingales and locusts and where the odor of filthy wool would be lost in the forsythia and all the corners of starlight would puncture Leonardo's eyes, he heard a giggle as soft as beating olive branches and realized that every beast and child had started running. It was a perfectly still night, and through the soles of his slippers Leonardo could feel the earth vibrating. The vibration increased steadily like the stirring of leviathan after long sleep, catching Leonardo up in its rhythm. He had no inkling where they were leading him or why, but he felt the dry–mouth of abandonment and struggled not to fall behind. The air grew brown, powdery. He felt a hand slap his thigh. Someone shouted. Along Aurelian's wall they ran, up to the towers beside the gate, past the Swiss guards lounging on their halberds. The soldiers guffawed—a dotard in a dark tunic with white whiskers and velvet cap, not decrepit but looking ninety, racing with gypsy children and country roustabouts into shady scrub pine, bay laurel, dog rose, his only guide the stars and fortune—the incredulous guards didn't lift a finger to stop him. Leonardo loped out the gate, chest heaving, wobbled along to where the paving stones ended and the scraggly brush began, hardly feeling the soft slaps and pinches on his buttocks as squeals, cries, yip–yipping filled the air. He wanted to run out of his bones, into starlight, completely be there. Gasping for air, he leaned forward, joining with the bobbing heads and shaggy backs on every side, and was about to bay at the moon, when a goat veered into his path and he went down. Horns, hooves, bleats. His arm caught in a bramble. His cheek walloped the ground.

In the momentary blackness, as the goats rumbled past, Leonardo sensed something was wrong. The dirt smelled sour. He was somewhere different from where he'd imagined, or there'd been a confusion. Struggling to his knees, he tried to peer into the darkness when his forehead struck an elbow. He'd made a mistake, he wanted to explain, but he heard his own jaw grind, started to vomit. Suddenly, he was jolted in the back of his head. The planet rushed up, and he bit it.

Fingers began tugging at his clothes, scratching, pulling his collar. He heard laughter. Help, he spluttered, help! But no one understood him. And as night slammed his head again and the thunder entered him and his bones began to tear, Leonardo's last sight was of a slender boy, pizzle in hand, spewing a shiny arc at his face. Piss on the mule, he heard the voice squeal. Piss on the mule!

Leonardo would never know how he got back as far as the wood scaffolds in front of Bramante's basilica the next day where he eventually woke to a sulphurous ache resembling daylight; nor who were the dairy maids, animal–tenders, Franciscans, and possibly even soldiers, deserving endless gratitude for having propped, shoved, and toted him there; nor even whether the previous night's episode might not have been, in reality, a wildly intoxicated delirium for which he was now paying with a hangover of apocalyptic proportions—no, Leonardo knew nothing clearly except that he wanted to sleep and couldn't climb the Belvedere's stairs. Which last obstacle he overcame as he'd already overcome the suspicions of respectable passers-by, the sentries at the San Sebastiano gate, and the twenty furlongs from there to here—by passing out and reawakening days or minutes later on the other side of them, God only knew how. In the apartment everybody was sympathetic. Battista sat on a hamster cage clucking morosely. Lorenzo shook his head. Il Fanfoia twiddled his thumbs. If the treestump was around, he at least remained quiet. Leonardo postponed thanking heaven for his safe return and chose instead to follow the path of sunlight across the rug to his chamber where, discarding the tatters of his robe, hose, and the withered toad carcass he discovered in his linen, he concluded that he must be even more confused than he'd imagined since immediately upon crashing down on his mattress he thought he heard Francesco Melzi say: Careful, that's sold.

Twelve hours later in a barren room with his feet on the chilly floor and his eyes on the seventeen piles of notes in the blue moonlight, Leonardo would ask Melzi what he was talking about, but first Leonardo was going to have a dream. His dream was of the entry to paradise beyond the ninth sphere of the empirium edged in red chalk on rice paper with guilded gewgaws that resembled the Pope's toes or nipples, the whole looking very much like Bramante's banquet hall in the Borgo Vecchio. A long-eared St. Peter poured wine at the table's head, shaking his shaggy mane and condemning gypsy children to Milan. Had Leonardo met the handsome young admirer of his unfinished sentences? he asked. The saint's eyes were slightly crossed, which played hell with perspective—Leonardo must have been in the basilica because, whenever you looked up, the ceiling fell in on you—and they ate with gold palette knives from a table laid with gigantic commissions. Leonardo considered the appetizing surfaces for a lifetime, but when he leaned down to sink his teeth into them, they tasted like a stable. What are you waiting for? whinnied St. Bramante. And scoffing loudly, he smashed his hooves against the latch, spilling Leonardo into nature. Which turned out to be round, of all things! Shouldn't it be transparent at this distance? But no matter how many legs Leonardo gave it, nature's darkness only deepened. Bramante galloped off in a cloud of dust, and Leonardo found himself peering into a hole as black as a boy's hair. Life! it said. Life! And tumbling in, Leonardo spun round in a vortex, once, twice, three times, until cascading down on Tuscany, he rained, thundered, flashed, and placed his feet onto the chilly floor.

Sold? he asked. Beside his seventeen piles of papers, someone had arranged linen, hats, boots, robes, hose in neat stacks. In the scullery the silverware and plate had been crated. The sitting room was divided into a pile of empty cages beneath the windows and a stack of tables, beds, divans, carpets, wardrobes, chests beside the door. The panels Leonardo had carted all the way from Florence, the red lizard he was training to fly, a waste-container you could open with your foot, the ox bones he'd wired up like a forearm, his stringless viol, his plume cap, the animals—all had vanished. Leonardo bellowed for Battista. He swore to hang Lorenzo and the goddamned treestump from a roof. He leaned out a window and called Il Fanfoia, rousing a bedlamite in the alley who started howling the ballad of Jehovah's wager with Bilbao in which the minstrel loses his land, wife, health, son, tongue and concludes teaching others—through sign language—to sing his moral for him, that moral being that humans, no matter how vicious, are less dangerous than God. Gazing across the Campagna at two lemurs in Pope Leo's zoo as the bedlamite's voice itemized its impressive list of miseries, Leonardo knew what he had to do. He shouted for Mel—

Who arrived before the second syllable. Seems Salai had gone into business, and though Melzi wasn't clear about particulars, he was precise about the heart of the disaster: Salai had made the whole workshop into partners! Francesco Melzi, a capitalist! He fell to the floor, wept for shame, pleaded with Leonardo not to tell his father. It was just that, having never been included in anything, he could hardly resist when... Leonardo understood. And the furniture? Evidently it was collateral, or had been until a snag in Battista's arrangements with the Moorish baccarat player who'd advanced the thirty ducats to pay back Georg's friend Johannes the lensmaker brought a balance due before a sale was final, or maybe vice versa—Melzi, having been taught to declaim and sing but never to multiply and subtract, had fantastic notions of the difference—anyway, this snag had required selling the workshop to get the Gioconda out of hock so it could be used to secure an advance on Salai's original speculation, a percentage of the profits of which were already promised to the next one. They'd planned to buy it all back, of course, but then Il Fanfoia walked in on Georg and Johannes plundering Leonardo's seventeen piles of notes without paying Battista the twenty-five soldi he'd charged the Alchemist Hammad Assad'hi for plagiarizing them, thus undermining the solidarity of the corporation. There were shrieks, accusations. Battista called Johannes a dachshund turd. The upshot of which was the quarrel between Lorenzo and the German in which Georg threatened to inform his true and only master Giuliano de'Medici of Leonardo's quackery and sloth, thus endangering their entire enterprise, to which Lorenzo responded with a small fowling piece—no one knew how he'd bought it. Salai was in the midst of negotiating the elaborate network of loans, bribes and extortion that formed the workshop into a holding company and terminated the treestump, when the failure of a Venetian slave merchant required the foreclosure of half a dozen small silk manufactories in Lombardy, so forestalling payment on a load of indigo floating somewhere out in the Aegean, which payment one of Salai's confederates was counting on to refinance the loan that would have paid off the lien on the sitting room furniture that, as a consequence, was now being confiscated by an infidel money-lender who—

Leonardo thanked Melzi, assured him his explanation was sufficient, except for one question. What *sort* of business?

Melzi bunched his forehead. Not a single business really, more like a group or series, multiple investments in various non-consumable import commodities that under normal market conditions—

Livestock? Leonardo asked.

Melzi opened his eyes wide: How did Leonardo know?

But Leonardo was already heading down the stairs, on his way to Giuliano's palazzo. He'd wanted to get to the bottom of something, and well, now he had. How far had he fallen just to know what ground felt like? Why was it *loss* that made your mind clear? He strode the long, vigorous strides of a man with a sense of humor, a guest at the wedding of hope and folly, and he filled his head with the rich, black smells arising from the streets. At the Palazzo de' Medici he was prepared to be told Giuliano was away, was ready to battle an army of euphemisms, even to wait—he was, after all, only a painter—and so was utterly undone to hear that his patron was asleep. It was the middle of the night. The doorman, who wasn't surly so much as puzzled, mistook Leonardo for a messenger and asked did he bring news from the army at Savoy? Leonardo bit his cheek to keep from laughing—at himself, at the light breeze under his arms, at the doorman's grape-blue jowls. No, he explained, he'd mistaken the hour, had come on an affair of property and unruly lackeys and would return with daylight. And nodding apologetically, he struck off in the direction of the Pantheon, now following his nose or nightmare or instincts or whatever you call that thing that, if only you'd followed it months before, you wouldn't need to follow it now. Anyway, Leonardo knew where to go.

Later, he'd wonder *how* he knew, what exactly he was thinking. But at the time, as he turned up an unfamiliar street, circled back to the west side of Giuliano's garden, stepped on a dozing cat's tail—getting his ankle clawed and waking half the street—he wasn't thinking at all. He merely rushed forward, running one hand along the walls he passed, and at the cut-through of an alley, came to a stop in a shadow. He felt dizzy. It was like entering his own dream. Sure enough, he found the double gate at the end of the cut, just as he'd conceived it, and then counting off a dozen strides and hoisting himself up onto the edge of a fractured cartwheel, he ran his fingers over the top of the wall. If the artisans had followed his drawings precisely, the niche ought to be right about here—invisible to passers-by but within easy reach of a rider. Leonardo's fingers touched iron. He gripped the lever, pulled, heard wood groan, and stepping back onto the earth, found the gate swinging open.

Inside the wall the moonlight disclosed the only Roman commission Leonardo da Vinci ever completed during the years Bramante, Michelangelo and Raphael were founding the history of art—the stable he designed for Giuliano de' Medici. Until now, Leonardo had never looked at. The stiles and fenceposts glowed lavender in the moon's reflection, the leaves of the laurels shone. So this was his picture! He followed a railing as far as the corner of the paddock where just beneath the stable eaves he expected to find a lamp but didn't, then recalled having switched corners to avoid the door's arc—no matter; the wick was gone—and from there under the low lintel and into the odor of wet hay and dung, the hush of tails, manes, animal breathing, where in the blackest blackness he found himself alone with his five senses. Despite its mundaneness, the stable's conception was vast, over two furlongs in length if you placed the corridors at ends. He'd concocted the groundplan randomly, figuring three braccia per beast, grouping the slips in either fives or nines, distributing the lofts and bins by whim, and disregarding proportion altogether—Giuliano hadn't noticed—so that now he had little way of determining where the turns lay, except by recourse to the same whims he'd indulged in planning them. He thought he could make out a faint glow from the right side of the corridor up ahead, but discovering within the first furtive step that he'd been standing nose to nose with a cedar partition and that the glow came from the moon behind it, Leonardo started edging his way between the slips toward the elaborate watering troughs that could accommodate a dozen beasts and refill automatically by means of float valves and self-cleaning cisterns, having already become so enraptured by this vision rendered in wood, iron, tin, mortar, that he almost missed the sound he'd come to hear.

It wasn't loud, only ghastly, a quavering squeal like the banshee. It ricocheted around the maze, coming from every side, above, below. Leonardo didn't step so much toward it as into it, moving from the moon's glow into a darkness as dank as any bowel. The smell of mash and sour bran assailed him; for a moment he feared he might swoon. It came again, and this time seemed up ahead. He ran an outstretched finger along the partitions and stall fronts, counting five tie-posts then slowing for the invisible shoeing stool or wagon tongue or low rail that would mark the end of this block of slips, or for post number six which would guarantee about eight more worry-free braccia before a column or corner came out of the pitch to crack his knee. A ghostly German destrier stuck out his muzzle and nipped Leonardo's shoulder. A pony gnawed the railing of its stall. Leonardo could hear his slippers slurping in the dung, felt the ooze penetrating the fabric. This was descent, he knew. And there was no telling how deep you'd have to go. He heard the sound again, this time nearer. He stepped in the direction he thought was toward it, only to flatten his nose on a post. Then he heard it so far away, so faint, that he wondered was his mind wandering, was he falling asleep counting fives and nines? His senses seemed useless. His plans left too much to chance for calculation to help. Mostly he depended on his picture—or worse, on his picture of his picture. He tried to recall if the shadow in front of him was supposed to be a wall or an opening, but his designs, he knew, weren't consistent. And besides, he might have gotten all turned around.

At last, as he was beginning to fear that he was lost in his own scheme, he noticed a smell—sharp and gamy. The beasts in this part of the maze seemed more aroused, panicky. They yanked at their tethers, paced, slammed their hooves into the wall. There was an edge to the air, something that made Leonardo feel—for the first time—afraid. He kicked over a waterbucket, felt the nearness of an animal, warm breathing on his neck, and thought he heard from somewhere a mastiff growl. It was impossible to see anything. The nickers and whinnies became shrill. And Leonardo was starting to back away from this pandemonium when either a rope or harness—something stringy and complicated anyway—got tangled in his feet and, in his struggle to get free, he lost his balance, went down. He grabbed for the wall. His hand slammed against a wooden surface. And—surprise, surprise—he saw a glint of light.

Leonardo lay very still, listened. Darkness wasn't what he'd ever loved; it was merely what, as a boy, he'd fallen into. And even if, this time, he'd entered by design, where he'd ended up was none of his doing. Why penetrate further? He could retrace his passage, scramble back up to the sunlight, the odor of grass and rustle of olive trees, return to his mother's home on the slopes of Monte Albano. What was boyish cowardice to a sixty-two year old genius whose humiliations were legendary? Let the furniture go, let the workshop and the Gioconda and the boxes of notes go, let everything go. It wasn't as if his knowledge mattered to anyone. Raising his torso into a sitting position, Leonardo let the kicks and shrieks and banging explode in his head. The animals in this part of the structure weren't just restless, he realized. They were wild—probably only weeks away from running loose somewhere in Turkey or Persia. But despite their noise, he could tell that the sound he'd followed through the labyrinth to this dark end had stopped vibrating in his ears and vibrated in his spine now. Just the other side of this partition he was resting against was the nature he'd labored to uncover. He already knew what he'd find if he went through this opening, knew he'd always known. He could go back now. He could go back. Running his fingers over the surface, he located metal, deciphered the latch, lifted, shoved, and stepped into a lantern's glare.

The world whitened. Leonardo almost saw—or maybe heard—a motion and sickly gleam, red. He was in a vast room—had he designed this room? for what purpose?—but what was happening, these huge shadows, thunder, wasn't contained there. In one corner a small chestnut mare sprawled on her side, sweat soaked and ruddy. As Leonardo approached, she half-struggled to right herself, squealed at him. A bay colt leapt maniacally from one side of the enclosure to the other, tossing its mane, ears back, nostrils wide, shying, prancing, flinging out its back hooves in a sideways motion so fluid the kick seemed to Leonardo not to happen at all. The air was thick with brown dust. The ground rumbled. Against the wall to Leonardo's right was what appeared to be a carcass with a shiny bone jutting out its gaskin. And in the center of the room, the dark wooden railings, the glare, the pounding feet, explosion, shrill noise, was a single figure, dark in the lamplight, with a hayfork in one hand, a carriage whip in the other, charging at the bay's face, driving the horse sideways and back, flinging itself into the animal's mad eyes, its voice chanting a hymn: Lisss—ten—to—me! Lisss—ten—to—me!

Salai never took his eyes off the beast, but he saw Leonardo approach. Deep in misery and bliss, he flung the whip at the bay's muzzle in a demoniac's parody of training, but both men knew it was theater. With the staff of the fork secured under his armpit and his shoulders hunched forward and his black curls bouncing like the streamers of a willow, he leapt about the floor shrieking, not directing the beast so much as just vexing it, heckling, refusing ever again during the animal's short life to be out of its way. From time to time he'd utter some ritual word or offer an intelligible gesture as if these remnants of a sane undertaking were what permitted going mad. But otherwise it was riot, orgy. Salai screamed, the horse edged back, and Leonardo watched its bulk collect itself around a precise idea: remove this. For an instant the animal turned transparent, filled with the otherworldly beauty of infants, and then it whirled, tossed its hindquarters at its tormentor's head and became again the perfect motion that was hardly motion at all. Salai ducked, jabbed the fork into the bay's flank, threw the whip at its forelegs, and the horse went down. The crunch brought bile to Leonardo's throat. And closing the door behind him now, gliding along the wall where the sprawled mare eyed him with the distraction of the furiously dying, stepping over the grisly carcass, pausing in the dimness of a corner, Leonardo felt his manhood as a weight. He acted here, against any will or knowledge or decision. So what if he'd been deceived? When *wasn't* he deceived? And his last contact with the person he'd always mistaken himself to be was his conviction that, now, it would end.

Salai hovered near the bay's head, panting, his tongue flopping onto his teeth. Leonardo made no effort to disguise his approach. The colt lay on the ground, heaving, struggling to push itself back up onto its feet. Salai danced at its head, shouted: Lisss—ten—to—me! Lisss—ten—to—me! And it wasn't until Leonardo had seen the exhausted horse rise to its full height, withdraw into contemplation's purest state—a look so jaded it could view the empyrean unmoved—it wasn't until Leonardo had seen this withdrawal and had himself stepped from the shadows toward the giddy, bent, screaming figure and, laying his good left hand on Salai's wrist, had, with his country-lad's grip that at sixty-two could still crack walnuts, ripped the hayfork right out of the demoniac's astonished arms—it wasn't until then that Salai acknowledged him. Their eyes met. Leonardo said: No. And with a squeal of joy, the colt charged. Salai ran for the hayloft, the beast thundered behind, and in the mad scramble of limbs and dust, the last thing Leonardo remembered as the horse crashed into the wall was Salai's laughter dissolving in the night.

"—my rights too."

"But, Ms. Havlicek of West Perry—"

"*Mrs.* Havlicek. My husband's a manager at Poly-Tel and I have two lovely boys."

"But, Mrs. Havlicek, don't you agree that every citizen's right to life ...I mean life's sacred, isn't it?"

"I didn't make'em do it. Nobody put a pistol to their heads, tol'em, be a pervert! What about priests, fr instance? And another thing—"

"But some rights are more important than others, don't you agree? The human right to survive is more—"

"Everybody's rights're equal in America. I got a right to visit my own mother, haven't I? Can't stop traffic 'cause people're sick. I gotta right—"

"Martin Luther King stopped traffic."

"Martin Luther King stood up for what he believed, just like me, and he was for equality. I got two lovely boys, they're not prejudiced, and no pervert's gonna—"

"For those who've just tuned in, we're discussing the civil unrest that's taking place—according to our updated information—at *three* downtown intersections. If you're currently in traffic, we recommend avoiding all main arteries around—"

Thanks a lot.

"—and north of the Market Plaza transit stop. You're listening to Voice of the Peebles! This is Freddy Peebles, at 478-LOUD, and I want to hear *your* voice about AID-US week, occurring—"

I start punching radio buttons. Crackle, guitar solo, "YEAAAAA," hisss, "momma to—old me not to cryyyy," "wah—OOP," "troops the demonstra—," sputter, blip, "motorcycle WO—man."

I'm past it before I hear what I heard. I head back, hunt, peck. Madonna, Madonna, Dolly Parton, something godawful, Madonna, Madonna, Luther Vandross, but before I can locate what sounded like information, I hear or feel that klap-a-klap-a-klap-a again, only this time louder, closer. I stick my head out the window, lots of wind now, but still I don't see. Then the sound of a p.a. brings my eyes, not up but over, and I spot it, rising right out of the thirty-foot woman and—here's the creepy part—camouflage colored. Not police. Military. I'm deciding whether to run or hide or phone for help, when the p.a. starts up again. I can make out a figure in infantry fatigues, female I think—the blades have knocked her cap off and she's got a mess of blonde hair flying around—and she's leaning out the side of the helicopter speaking into one of those hand-held horn things. I can't get the words, but then she turns in my direction.

"—in your cars..." The wind blows her voice away. "—eye contact and skin irritant. I repeat: Do not be alarmed. Close all doors and windows securely; turn air-conditioning to recirculation only. I repeat: Do not be alarmed. In case of accidental exposure, medical units are located at the rear of the traffic blockage for your convenience. I repeat—"

Shit! I'm out of the car, back door open, doing my imitation of the master's voice. "Come, Metro, come!" Metro rolls over, kicks his feet up, guffaws. Of course he doesn't do that, but might as well. I take hold of his collar, he growls. "Come, Metro, come!" Doesn't budge. I think he

161

won't bite me, but I don't *know* he won't bite me. "They're about to gas us, Metropolis." I pull. He growls. Idiot! Can't you see I'm trying to help—

And then, do I smell it? Kind of like jalapenos, or just very bad pollution. Maybe I'm imagining, but between paranoia and the facts, what's to choose? I dance around, waving my arms, mouth words at the woman in the helicopter. "No air conditioning!" I make suffocating gestures. "No A/C! Die from heat!" But can you believe these people? She blows me a kiss!

I'm sealing myself back into the car, rolling up, locking. Lotta good it does; back in 1955 they built cars to sink; pollution seeps in, dust seeps in, rain seeps in, only the breeze stays out. Anyway, I'm sealing myself up when I hear fingernails on the glass. I turn, and guess who?

"Lemme in!" Muffled noise, muffled noise. "Lemme in!"

It's the fat beach monster from the red pickup.

"Back window's out," he, I suppose you could say, explains. "Bein' gassed for queers..., my own country!"

Shirt wide open and (COLD!) beer gone now, he's heaving, plainly nuts, neck twisting like a lizard. Even through the shades, I know his eyes are saucers. In the hierarchy of worldly delights revenge ranks up there with orgasms, but I'm gawking to see what shape my doom is taking and, so, for a nanosecond feel sufficiently distracted not to care. Helicopter's right overhead, no fumes or sprayers or napalm in sight yet, and each breath's a reprieve. I let Grendel in.

"You sweat or pee on anything in here?" he's phantasmagorically gross enough to wonder.

"Christ! I'm not sick," I think I scream at him.

"Nobody's sayin' bein' queer's sick. This is the twenty-first century, almost. Don't talk stupid. I know 'bout Freud. You think everybody but you's uneducated? A goddamn free country! Any pervert who wants to—"

"No, no, no! I'm not *gay*. Hell, I'm even not-married."

He grabs his head, rocks back. "Ooooh, that's the worst, when one of our own guys gets hit! I can't stand it." He reaches over, clutches my shoulder. "I just wanna say—"

And that's when the poison reaches us. Not a smell, just a scratchiness on the back of my palate, or not even a scratch but this need to clear my throat which, when I do, leaves me really needing to clear my throat which, when I do, leaves me REALLY needing to clear my throat which....

Hack, hack, sputter, wha—CHEW! Cackety cackety.

"Can't...!"

"...air ...you?"

Grrrrrff, snort, snort.

162

Then just as quickly it's gone.

Metro's making strangulation noises identical to my strangulation noises while Behemoth appears to be barfing into the glove box, everyone's eyes are lava pits, right here in Greater Pandemonium, but before torment resumes, I'm going to do something. I punch the Port-A-Phone.

"Voice of the Peebles, name, job, number, subject of your—" It's a female voice, not Freddy himself, and very, very bored.

"I—I'm there! I—I—I'm in the demonstration, I'm calling from my car, I'm ...there's this helicopter—"

That's all it takes.

"...caller right here right now on the scene of the disturbance! Hello, I'm Freddy Peebles! Let's hear your voice!"

"They're gassing us."

"With what? Pixie dust?"

Canned laughter.

"No, the cops, the army, the U.S. government is gassing—"

"And are you ever angry! Stuck there in traffic, your car overheating, and is AIDS your fault? Did you invent sodomy? Let the people know your name!"

"R—."

"'R'?"

"No, with a dash."

"And R—, you must feel..., stranded right there in the middle of this pointless, illegal demonstration—you must feel damn fed up, sick of individuals interfering with your rights, is that it R—? I mean, let's face it, how much can a government do for a dead man anyway?"

"You don't understand. I'm calling from my car, a-a-and there are cars everywhere, both sides, hundreds, just ordinary citizens, voters, and a helicopter's flying around overhead, and it's *gassing* us. Like tear gas or mace or—or—"

"All because a bunch of promiscuous homosexuals wanted somebody else to pay for their carelessness!"

"No, no, it's an *army* helicopter. Or marines, I think, ...and they're just gassing everybody. I mean, I'm not even close, and they're spraying over ...it's not a mistake! They're just blowing poison right out into—"

"I mean, we're all sympathetic, right? This isn't the dark ages. Who cares what some pervert wants to do in the privacy of his own home! But you agree that law-abiding citizens shouldn't have to—"

"MY OWN GOVERNMENT IS GASSING ME!"

Silence. "R—, I'm having difficulty knowing where you stand on this issue. Don't you have an opinion? I mean, you're involved, you're on the scene, but you seem afraid to commit yourself. Why are you so wishy-washy? What have you got to hide? Let the American people hear your—"

But the poison's back. Odorless, invisible, an itch that, the more you scratch, itches worse. Eyes, throat, skin, all alive—like bugs, mites, fleas crawling inside you. Barely noticeable, then shooting right off the prickle chart."

Hack, sputter, wheeze, wheeze, phew.

"I—! You—!"

"...see'em ..."

Monster, doggy and me're nuts, wild, groping for whatever suffocating creatures grope for. Capitalism conquers its final frontier; the air's no longer free! I beg, borrow, steal enough breath to survive, sucking the poison through my fingers, the cloth of my shirt, upholstery fabric, underarm hair, covering my nose with whatever's in reach, and in the back seat Metro paws his muzzle off his face. We'll pay! I want to scream. Name your price! We'll pay any amount! When Gargantua gets—give him benefit of the doubt—an idea. He grabs Leonardo's box—

"Hey!"

—upends fiction, pages spewing—

Hack, spew. "My sto—sto—ry!"

—sticks his head inside.

Nothing.

"Help?" I wheeze.

Nothing.

"Help?"

Nothing.

"—lp?"

A hiss of breath and Leonardo's box comes crashing over my head. Answer: it helps. I don't know why. Maybe they're not using a gas, maybe it's a dust or something infinitesimal but heavy, so it falls through vents but can't—or not as easily—drift upward into a topsy-turvy carton deep enough to ship a microwave oven in, or maybe there's a chemical in the box or some residue from the paper that through a Steven Spielberg-like combination of carcinogens and herbicides spontaneously neutralizes the miasma, or maybe the official madness just doesn't allow for arrangements as elaborate and pointless as this one, but for whatever reason, there's air in Leonardo's box. For a paradisal instant I thrive within my hallucination's container, then Gargantua has the box back, and my lungs ignite again.

This continues for, I dunno, maybe a couple of minutes, maybe twenty, long enough for Leonardo da Vinci to leave Rome and try to become a writer, and never any talking, just the perfect pact of two entities hell-bent on breathing. Leonardo's box goes. I close my eyes, hold my nose or suck the upholstery. Leonardo's box comes. I open my eyes, cram my face into a corner, very, very gingerly inhale. It ain't fresh. It stinks—like photocopy fluid—enough to taste. But it does not burn. Leonardo's box goes. I close my eyes, etcetera. The pact is homo sapien only. I try once to share with Metro; he levels his eyeball at the box, snarls at civilization, and I get another suck before reality returns. Meanwhile, I feel Metro nuzzle his snorting, wormlike way underneath my seat, where maybe he gets some air, maybe not—the ways of Dog are wonderful—but when at last inspiration returns and I venture the atmosphere, he's perched on the seat, scrutinizing his surroundings, and one helluva lot more self-possessed than me.

"So what's this stuff, anyway?" my approximately human companion wants to know as soon as or, in truth, a good while before anyone can be sure the poison has passed. The helicopter drifts off behind the thirty-foot woman. The haze is clearing. Distant screams come, go. I'm sitting with the box between my chin and the windshield, luxuriating in oxygen. Beelzebub peers over his sunglasses at a page of horseplay.

"Perhaps now isn't a literary moment?" I suggest. "Perhaps now we might muster what looks like the survival instinct and run for our bloody lives?"

"Can't outrun attack helicopters, dope." He fixes me with the shades. "Guys like you skipped Nam."

I gaze into the mirror at Metropolis' eye gazing back: Attack, Metro! Kill!

"This Leonardo, he's Leonardo da Vinci, right? The submarine 'n' airplane guy. The monster taps his finger on the page. "Where's 329?"

"The airplane stuff was mostly propaganda—WWII, Italian fascist horse-manure. Lots of Renaissance inventors designed flying machines. Leo wasn't special, or not for that."

"You a college professor?"

"Slum lord." I smile. "It's a novel."

"So, where's 329?"

Now, this question has something funny about it. I mean, the whole car has turned into episodes of Leonardo da Vinci/"Leonardo da Vinci." Pages on our laps, under our feet, front seat, back seat, recto, verso, some scrumpled, stomped or sneezed on, others still clinging accordion style to numerical sequence, but barely, barely. Down my legs are what appear to be two different sections promiscuously intermingling, something in the two hundreds and another that got misnumbered, pages 47a, 47b, 47c ...all the way to 47q. I'm not hopeful about sorting it out. Maybe somebody hunts long enough, he/she/it'll concoct a sequence or locate a floorboard without "Leonardo" written on it, but all Behemoth and I see is print. I put a hand over my eyes, plop down my index finger at random. "There."

He's unconvinced, picks the page up, reads. Six hundred fifty something. "You mean this stuff for funny, right?"

I shrug. "It's kind of mixed up."

"Oh Christ, it's *Modern*!" The inflection's the one people use for baby diarrhea.

"No, yes, well, no, yes, well, no, yes, but what happens on 329 isn't what happens after what happens on 328, or it might be but ..."

He snorts, shakes his head. "Nobody tells stories anymore. Nobody. I don't get it. I mean, it don't take no degree! Granny couldn't write her name, but she could tell a story! You got a beginning, you got a middle, you got an end. Things get worse, things get better. Somebody kills somebody, somebody fucks somebody. You don't know why, then you do. Where's the problem? I mean, ain't like a *car* engine!"

"Just maybe I'm not dying to tell your granny's story! Just maybe I'm sick to throwing up with your granny's story! Can anybody make a car engine, anybody in America? Migraines and algebra problems have beginnings, middles, ends. You don't know, then you do! Hell, even this sentence has a beginning—"

"Gimme a pencil."

"What for?"

"Shut up and just gimme."

Like my own catastrophe and like most others I've known, the end of Deirdre's career proved an unmitigated evil only so long as she was in the midst of it. Having received the mysterious envelope erasing her from psychotherapy's memory, she became profoundly mopey for two months. She spent some days in her pajamas and developed the habit of staring at me with her head tilted: "What if I turn out to be as confused as you?" I couldn't convince her that this wasn't the nadir. All in all, she'd begun to resemble a social worker's version of young Hamlet when, one Saturday in a fit of lighter spirits, she spent the whole day baking a Black Forest Cake. It was—I still taste it— astonishing. Monday morning she took out a vacation loan from the credit union and enrolled herself in a ten week cooking course in Marseilles. She came back in September and got a good-paying, enjoyable job in an attractive little restaurant just three blocks from our—at the time—modest home. The following summer she went back to the cooking school and, on her return, got a fantastic-paying job with the innovative, enlightened corporation that had bought out the little restaurant and turned it into a Howard Johnson's. She continued to work as a master chef and buyer for the corporation for four and a half more years during which time she disremembered everything she'd learned in Marseilles and developed a mysterious, all-devouring out- rage. Equally important, however, she acquired the American habit of living one worthless life for the sake of a second, intermittently human one and saved—get this! forty-eight thousand dollars! She invested all but a smidgeon in DeeDee's Live-in Kitchen Kleen and Katering, advertised herself haphazardly and now works maybe four, five days a month, mostly at home, pretty much when she wants, and lost last year four thousand dollars less than me. Which still isn't enough for medical insurance, a retirement plan, savings account, anything unexpected, or clothes, but like one-third of America we get by on it. The rest of the time Deirdre reads what makes her crazy.

"This is incredible! D'you know how fast the incidence of ultra-violet-ray related carcinoma, that's skin cancer, has increased just since 1963?"

"No idea at all, thank God, not an inkling, and consequently, I sleep serenely at night. However, now that you've acquired this burden, I feel certain you'll make me a gift of it, making a renewal of my anti-depressant prescription necessary."

"Over 800%, and the median age of onset has dropped 13.6 years. Three more decades of ozone depletion at the present rate and they expect removal of skin lesions to become an annual event, like dental check-ups, for every Caucasian over thirty."

"Sayonara peace of mind!"

"Why is obliviousness like yours different from just apathy, R—? You really do owe me an explanation since, if I don't leave you, I'll need a lot of help not despising myself."

"Honestly, Deirdre, you have the least developed appetite for self-deception of any person I know."

"Who do you know?"

"It's positively unAmerican. Here you are surrounded by television evangelists, cosmetic surgeons, pornographers, tobacco-industry research scientists, political advertisements, actors, car salesmen, pharmaceutical-company research scientists, undercover cops, psychiatric consultants, tax attorneys, oil-corporation research scientists, official information sources, public relations experts, weight-loss clinics, all manner of ingenious fabrications proving every fear's unfounded, and you cling to your nightmares simply because they're true! Isn't there anything you'd like to be incurably deluded about?"

"I'd like to fantasize that there's hope. I'd like to make-believe that caring was different from being suckered. I'd like to hallucinate a way of striking back."

"She's psychotic!"

I suppose that if Deirdre hadn't turned peculiar we'd still be married, but I lack a reliable standard for determining whether this would be a good thing. What I can attest is that for anyone preferring survival to success, peculiarity's a plus. Given the choice between a transparent but comprehensible sham and a befuddling but unshakeable fact, institutions will acknowledge only the former and the police will work very hard never to see you. Not that Deirdre and I pursued oddness from strategy. Our diminishing scrutability had various causes, but at its root was an inconstant faith in money—our difficulty believing that economic predictions weren't hallucinatory, that price tags revealed the worth of anything, that numbers weren't a kind of joke—all this punctuated by thrilling episodes of covetousness and calculation. However, at some point in our deterioration we certainly recognized the freedom that strangeness brings. Muggers and psychopaths considered us less predictable than themselves; corporations inexplicably read "lawsuit" written on our foreheads; collection agents treated us with enormous respect. The only difficulty was that our second life—the one protecting the first—required a lot of work. There were extra forms to file, letters of explanation, corroborating documents, whole agencies to manage "exceptions," and all this effort—just to sustain an illusion!—could leave us confused. We often seemed to verge on unrecognizability even to ourselves. For example, although Metro fulfilled none of the doggy functions and signified "pet" only through his annual, expensive vaccinations and served no purpose whatsoever, we could hardly separate him from us. We developed telephone rituals, identities and voices specific to our three numbers, and we resisted violating this decorum with an earnestness that far surpassed our need. We orchestrated Sunday drives in the Buick, ransacked vintage shops for period clothing, practiced insouciant gestures. Was all this for our fake life? The other one? Some life yet to come?

Sometimes I felt that only our present had become unintelligible, that the whole of our past leading to this deviousness, each decision, every stage, even our surprises, remained as logical as machinery. The nature of my new "career"—about which more presently—brought me into frequent and intimate contact with objects whose purposes had passed away—carriage steps, cisterns, harnesses, paraphernalia for steam heat or gas lights, hitching posts, ancient electrical hardware—and perhaps because our identities had grown amorphous, Deirdre and I developed loyalties to them. We cleaned our oddities, arranged them on tables, porch rail, floor. Parts of us seemed embodied in what was otherwise classifiable only as junk, and we discovered mysteries in these survivals, mysteries akin to archaisms and literal meanings: What exactly does one get straight from the horse's mouth, and why—just because the horse is a gift—shouldn't you look in there? Sometimes alone in my den, I'd wonder how we appeared to persons better-adjusted. I'd stare at a carefully designed, perfectly incomprehensible tool and imagine a young attorney standing on our threshold, imagine her feeling as an early discoverer of fossils must've felt, say, a Victorian who considered the universe a few thousand years old. I conceived an affinity with the bugs and rodents whose dwelling was the deterioration of mine—our crumbling foundations—and once Deirdre and I got into a huge row over spraying for termites. In the end, we didn't. I even nurtured a fantasy in which, without ever suspecting it, we turned out to be the secret continuation of dead civilizations and extinct species. All that we found inscrutable about ourselves was the persistence of these vanished others, their defiance of nature's dictum that one chance was all, and I speculated that in some infinitely distant oblivion lay buried the well-organized world of instincts and customs and loves in which Deirdre's and my idiocy were a perfectly natural way of life.

But I've gotten ahead of myself. Shortly after I unframed "Leonardo," during roughly the same period that Deirdre was discovering how hideous growth could be for anything in its path, I found myself surrounded by a multitude of friends, colleagues, and family members whose complete confidence in me had miraculously metamorphosed into hatred. I preferred to resign my post at the university rather than show my fellow historians a book manuscript that would certify me insane, and so with no job but superabundant litigious creditors, I sold our second car, pawned my father's old trumpet, held a three-day garage sale, gave blood, participated in a sociology experiment, cashed in my ludicrous retirement, and having squeezed my turnips and momentarily slaked the craving of the most ravenous of my erstwhile loved ones, I hauled out a calculator and determined that we still owed sixteen thousand bucks. Deirdre came to my rescue, recalculated, and found that I had the amount right but the pronoun wrong.

"If *we* owe it, then you get a job or I get a lawyer. You have till Saturday. But if *you* owe it, well, Jesus, don't I know how weird life can be? After all, I'm your wife! I love you! No matter what happens, I'll always be there for you, waiting just outside the courtroom."

Impressively unconfused about my reliability where loved ones are concerned, Deirdre drew up a binding contract detailing my sole responsibility for all our former debts and for all her legal fees if she had to come after me. I signed. She relaxed. I fell apart. When I quit discovering "Leonardo" and started discovering Leonardo—a prolonged dreamlike transition without sharp beginnings or ends—I felt myself overtaken by necessities so far-reaching that debts didn't exist. I can't say I forgot about money or that I expected some suicidal publishing conglomerate to reimburse me, but I confess that dollars had little reality in the universe where Leonardo had so much. So, I was dazzled now to undergo an equally convincing illumination of precisely the opposite kind, having suddenly discovered myself in a sinister kingdom where poverty, hunger, isolation, scandal and other dooms made Leonardo the least tangible, most dispensable of fancies, an otherworldly abstraction with no reality at all. More than once I remarked to myself that perhaps only the inverted commas had preserved my icon from this avalanche of what I now termed "real life," and I felt a panic to bracket myself in conventional punctuation, institutional markers, unmistakable forms. Fortunately the quantifiability of a financial problem goes a fair distance toward its solution. Even now I can't give this great mystery the intelligence it deserves, but I'm convinced that the nearer starvation creeps, the more obtrusive wise courses of action normally become. The wholesale breakdown of this principle in our fair nation today strikes me as an alarming register of the bewilderment being American has turned into and explains why from time to time thoughtful persons find Marxism an inescapable conclusion. Anyway, the strategic advantages of a financial crisis—especially for anyone 1) white, 2) male, 3) middle-class, 4) not disabled, 5) healthy, 6) heterosexual, 7) under forty, 8) protestant, 9) vacuous, 10) degreed—is that it less often confronts one with questions about what to do than with the question, Can I stomach it?

I wrote *Win!* I exhumed the nine responses to the bogus queries that I'd sent to publishers the previous spring, and located among them the letter from Marjorie Sharp (okay, okay, but her real name was less believable) in which she condemned my avarice and offered me a contract. I gave no explanation for the eight month hiatus since our first communication but instead launched an impassioned account of my lifelong dream to be associated with a high-minded publishing enterprise like hers, especially one that would defend the legitimate rights of crass and opportunistic hacks like me, but that the advance—$4,000—was too low. I doubled it and sent two chapters. Nothing ever seemed easier than writing them, not because writing anything is ever easy, but because the chapters had nothing to do with me. I wrote what every American claims to know but feels indignant to hear. I explained that nothing was simpler than to *Win!* but that winning required clear goals. The only clear goals were money, sex, power and fame. Everything in America was designed to enable, prevent, and precisely measure the achievement of these goals, but that, in most competitions, a frank awareness of the situation was an advantage. More fundamentally, contestants needed to realize that the goals also functioned within the contest as a kind of capital, certain portions of which were afforded to each player in advance, much after the fashion of credit cards. In America persons started out with credit limits of money, power, sex and fame based on projected winning potential, and—here's the important part—these credits had exchange value. In short, you could trade future sex or fame for present power or money, and vice versa. The point was to recognize when the rates were in your favor, where to invest, whose capital was borrowed, overextended, etcetera. I said as little as possible about discrepancies in credit for players born poor or non-Anglo, and dodged entirely the fact that my book presupposed a populace born at eighteen and pretty well vanished at thirty-six, fearing such concessions might open a breach. And I certainly never tried to explain what words like "money," "power," "sex" or "fame" meant. Whenever they resembled shibboleths, I insinuated that doubters were naive, that only a college professor wouldn't know what sex and power were, etcetera. The reader was, of course, a woman—Ms. Sharp being the only person whose opinion of *Win!* would ever make any difference—but for reasons not altogether clear, I sensed an advantage in writing as a man mistaking his audience for male.

Ms. Sharp wrote back a nine-page letter of detailed, outraged and often incisive criticisms, saying that, censorship be damned, she'd never be a party to anything so cynical. I returned the first two chapters unchanged plus three more and covered them with a letter lauding her judgment and discussing the fundamental reconception of my project that I'd undertaken under her guidance. Never had I felt so completely understood, so entirely grasped; I recognized now for the first time that my homophobia, binarism, mastery fetish, hierarchical reasoning, control mania, and phallo-logo-techno-thanato-centrism were by-products of the master narrative imprisoning the West. I used the word "feelings" often. I said I wanted "to grow." In a postscript I asked if I could call her by her first name and wondered what she thought of changing all the pronouns to "s/he"? Sharp phoned to say how much the sales staff admired my soul-searching revision, that she was amazed to meet a man so honest, please call her Marge, and a contract was in the mail. The advance was no sticking point, but regarding the pronouns, far be it from her to tell an author how to write his book.

With half of the advance I appeased the more sinister of my litigants, and I used the remaining four-grand to begin *Why You Already Know Everything You Need To*. I completed it in five weeks, having copied the last chapter verbatim from *Win!* and I then wrote Marge a proposal for two more books in my "series." All this I also sent to an agent she recommended, someone named Gloria whose full name I no longer remember but whom Deirdre and I dubbed Ann Excelsis. The details are unilluminating, but within sixteen months I'd received sufficient advances against hypothetical royalties to transform the hatred of my family and friends into permanent indifference and to begin fabricating my second life, the unreal one. I completed six manuscripts. For all I know, none ever sold a copy. I saw only two in print, spectacles I didn't relish, and there were certainly no royalties. I kept my "series" going—with steadily diminishing zeal—for another year or so, and then after a dozen phone calls from Marge describing the attractions of daytime TV appearances and book signings for organizations of physicians' wives, my relations with the prestigious publishing firm came to an unimpassioned end. Far be it from me to say why a publishing conglomerate must feed itself food it cannot eat, but I assume my pages were stuffed down its throat, that at some later period they were shat out again and that, if I wandered for a decade the discount book warehouses and federal prison libraries of my motherland, I'd one day encounter several thousand glossy escapees from a supermarket paperback rack proclaiming me a thinker of intellectual daring, bottomless insight, and immense fame. At least, this has become a recurrent nightmare. Gloria Ann Excelsis tried to tempt me with promises of geometrically expanding riches—I suspect the supply of authors with academic credentials, no scruples, a gift for sophistry, and the ability to fabricate contemptible books on demand, wasn't endless—but I already knew that, in the rationale for doing despicable work just for the money, there were two flaws: 1) the money rarely lasted longer than the time required to do it; 2) nobody quits ahead. As my masterwork on the subject tactically omitted, the only real way to *Win!* was to get out. I took my advances, erased my computer, got a secret number where I could be reached and a public one where I couldn't, took up residence in Leonardo's universe, and began concocting an occupation that nearly made sense because it so plainly didn't.

I became a miracle worker. I bought a second-hand truck, a few tools and a lot of paint, worked out a mutually profitable arrangement with two former students—Darren DeLight and Beatrice no surname—both of whom were savvy and agile but clueless enough to work for someone like me, spent a couple of weekends watching do-it-yourself videos, got licensed, and already possessed of a waspy male's customary know-how, I began to reconnoiter the boundary of wastelands and slums. Unlike investors who sought concepts, systems, networks, I sought what success could never see. Call them leftovers, but my desiderata were those foundations, chimneys, crumbling frame homes, dilapidated façades, porches, stone walls, forgotten warehouses, dry fountains, railroad depots that, if you were lucky and approached them with sufficient working capital and caution and ingenuity, would bankrupt you very, very slowly. This is the old town within every city that still exists because, to those who matter, it doesn't. For example, Beatrice was jogging one day and discovered a dirt alley—looked more like a driveway; city map didn't list it—less than half a mile from the new courthouse, in an area that had apparently once contained shipping companies. There, between a rusted hangar and the cracked concrete loading yard of every post-apocalyptic sci-fi movie, we found a pristine, two-story brick and plaster structure with the Coca-Cola emblem engraved on the entrance. It seemed too small for a bottling plant, and the bewildered executive who finally after weeks of ceaseless badgering either figured out or arbitrarily decided that, yes, his firm owned the property and would part with it for, well, for exactly whatever we were offering—his name was Gunn—Mr. Gunn stated that the site had once been part of an abortive, now obsolete, decentralizing program masterminded by a crackpot relative of the company founders, long-since retired in infamy, and that, though intended for a satellite shipping facility, the lot had been neglected, lost, the program abandoned, and so no structure had ever been built on the site. We possessed impressive evidence to the contrary but didn't argue. Coke wanted oblivion, was prepared to pay money for it, and so dispossessed of official reality, the little stone structure had escaped the grand schemes and ineluctable forces erasing all trace of its contemporary world for half a mile around. Darren, who as a six-foot-five, black teenager had suffered the misfortune of becoming more interested in the implausible destiny of African-American intellectuals than in basketball and so ended up at twenty-seven possessed of more sophistication and outraged self-awareness than could ever be crammed into any career, had—just before dropping out of his doctoral program in history—dropped out of law school. With his old textbooks, a be-your-own-attorney manual from the organic grocery, and occasional calls to a cousin in the prosecutor's office, he finessed the necessary documents, and we got the abandoned shipping depot for change. The city water lines didn't run. There was a problem about access and right-of-way. We had to work a deal with the homeless men who slept in the docks. But once reborn, the little box was a wonder to behold.

We called ourselves Second Chance. We went on search and restore missions, usually on foot or bikes, and whenever a candidate for revival turned up, we'd begin the process of checking deeds, tax records, plat maps, old newspapers, local histories—I was a historian, trained for research; here was a task I could do—and if no obstacles appeared, we'd swing into action. We'd do an inspection which, because no one cared to stop us, usually meant going a fair distance into the walls, floors, foundations. The trick was to find structures that, though officially worthless, were architecturally salvageable. We all did everything, but where expertise was required, we divvied up the load. I did carpentry and stonework. Darren had heating and plumbing. Beatrice, who at age twenty-three was a being of vertiginous complexities, having grown up the daughter of practicing homosexual, but male and female, parents whose prominent careers as state department employees required as well as taught the duplicity needed to maintain their highly civilized marital arrangement, and consequently taking in strategy with her pablum and attending schools in eleven countries—

she spoke four languages better than I spoke English—and possessed of cultural and social ambiguities unmatched save by sexual ones, being neither male nor straightforwardly female but also not any of the categories—transvestite, hermaphrodite, lesbian, gay, transsexual, bisexual, pansexual, nymphomaniac, celibate, repressed, neuter, frigid—by which a world that's prepared to worship sex or deny it will designate what it won't understand, Beatrice or Beats had a genius for electricity. She understood current, the elaborate circuitry of attraction and resistance that manages terrifying forces to productive ends, and though no good with a hammer, she had the planet's quickest, most finicky hands. Second Chance paid for an electrician's course at the community college, bought a copy of the building codes, and trusted her like an encyclopedia. Beats has probably never felt at home anywhere in her life, but surrounded by schematics and wiring plans, she's impressively unconfused.

Cheaply retrievable properties are rarely located in the downtown centers of despair and futility but can be plentiful in the remnants of former communities where industry and commerce have made imperfectly devastating raids. We found a rotting Victorian gingerbread without street access concealed behind the shrubs and privacy fence of a concrete company's parking lot, and two bungalows beside a drainage ditch where the ground was too soft for a styrofoam fabricator to build. The railroad was a source of great bounty, as were old properties adjoining the interstate or suburban malls. Anywhere a grand scheme had recently plopped down, its margins were sure to be littered with carcasses. There were far more of these structures than anyone would suppose, enough to keep us perpetually in work. We bought for pennies, selected for dilapidation that was outside-in, top-down. A new roof is cheaper than a new floor. Façades are easier than foundations. We soon became expert at identifying what we couldn't do—a lot of preserving anything is self-knowledge—and at guessing costs. We were often wrong, of course, but because our estimates became more reliable as we worked, we rarely sunk a fortune before realizing we were about to. None of which mistakes are avoidable if you're a homeowner relying on banks and appraisers or a contractor hoping to profit on a realistic scale. What made us seem viable was being of a size and ambition that no one capable of crushing us cared to. Our dream was to persist. We absolutely couldn't grow.

"In short, you're an entrepreneur," Deirdre concluded. "You own more buildings in violation of codes than any other five bloodsuckers in the county. You exploit depressed markets, thrive on misfortune, produce nothing, collaborate in the universal disregard of natural contexts, but it's okay, 'cause your buildings aren't good for anything, right?"

"Unreal estate magnate."

"I believe in your intentions, R——, but let's be frank. Aren't people like you the problem?"

"I don't make money. I don't evict. I don't sue. I never call cops. I hardly pollute. I don't develop. I rarely tear down. In six years, I've never once cut a tree. Hell, I don't even rent!"

"A corpse is a way of life. Some things can't thrive without rot. Nobody *restores* a squatter's home!"

"Is it better self-destructing?"

"How else are worlds reborn?"

"Who says they are?"

And in some such way I retrieved my second—or was it my first?—life from financial chaos. We rarely sold the properties we refurbished, our goal being only to *appear* prosperous. I had no illusion of making a profit, or better, I had multitudinous illusions of just this sort, was surrounded with entrepreneurial pretenses, the impenetrable veil of tables and figures, so that even to myself I occasionally looked viable. We worked where and mostly when we wanted. We often had fun. In a situation where thriving is inevitably at someone else's expense, we did as little harm as we knew how. I wish this mattered. Whenever money actually did change hands—the coke plant went to a magazine writer with an infant's smile who, as far as we could tell, had infinite funds but no car or family—we divided it, but most of the time we borrowed. The appearance of prosperity—that is, good credit— is always preferable to cash. As a result of manageable expenditures of time and sweat and paint and plumbing, and during a surprisingly short span, Second Chance became the sole or joint holder of the deeds of roughly one hundred eighty-six urban properties, most plainly worthless, but a few of genuinely debatable value. This meant I stopped being a deadbeat and became a risk. I owed vast sums to interests powerful enough to keep me afloat. Brutal men mistook me for cunning. Upwardly mobile women hallucinated that I was sexy. Persons who when I'd been a young historian found me contemptible and who when I'd owed sixteen thousand dollars dismissed me with a yawn, now that my financial problems were genuinely insoluble, awoke from deep slumber whenever "liquidation" crossed my mind. I didn't worry how much I might be losing—if in truth I was losing—or how long I could lose it. Far too great an outlay of capital would have been needed to find out. I now saw that calculations existed so that either someone with nothing to gain from ruining you could report to his or her supervisor that there was no reason to ruin you or someone with something to gain could remain uncertain of the cost. For a long, long time I had no real problem of either kind.

"Now, I shore ain't nothing but a yokel, ain't never had no

university education like yerself and yer gentleman colleague, Mr. Dee-Light, so I cain't understand the nuances—"

He says "new ounces."

"—of high finances, junky bonds, hosTILE takeovers, REcession, DEpression, INflation, broker tradin', restruct'ring, DEregulation, AGglomeration, securities EXchange, futures, indexes, forecasts, prime rate, prorate, but I got me a fine little calky-later—"

An IBM just smaller than my car engine with interfaces to every legally accessible financial data network in the West.

"—and it says yer broke. No offense meant, hope none taken. Yer yield—even you get cash in advance and buy paints, lumber, wire, dry wall, pans, every bit on ninety-day-same-as-cash—yer yield from interest cain't make up maybe one third the salary of this shere lovely lady—"

Beatrice blows her nose into her fingers, wipes them on her shirt.

"—and there's yer colleague, honorable Mr. Dee-light esquire, to speak not a word on the subject o' profit."

Loathing exists without origin. He arises from our lack of natural predators, the bald fact of our flourishing unopposed. As he never stops reminding us, given the universal fact of human self-interest, his concern for our troubles is probably the closest thing to altruism we'll ever see.

"Nothin' to gain, nothin' a-tall," he insists. "Truth to tell, I like you fine. Tain't *personal*."

I have tried to convince both Darren and Beats that at civilization's present knotty impasse where mendacity has come to be expected and only the plausible isn't believed, where the shortest distance between two points is under normal conditions an endless spiral and the strongest argument for the trustworthiness of an utterance is that it makes no sense at all, precisely the inscrutable character of Loathing's opposition is what reveals him to be—terrifying thought!—exactly as he appears. But they won't have it.

"I mean, he acts like a snailbrained, backwoods, uncouth, anti-intellectual, racist prickhead, but is he really?" Darren remarks two to nine times daily. "I mean, what's he hiding in that truck? And have you noticed he limps sometimes on his left leg, sometimes on his right? His mispronunciations aren't consistent; I'm compiling phonemes. Some of those predictions require logarithms, and no way he knows even fractions! Is it possible the government could pay him enough to *fake* that accent?"

Beats is grave. "He isn't after money, that's obvious. Dominance wouldn't be direct enough, so how would he get off on it? It'd be reassuring if he wanted sex—repulsive, but reassuring—but it isn't imaginable. He has no interests. Maybe he thrives on humiliation, but

176

it's hard to imagine him thriving. Race could be involved. I really wish I knew that he hated us, but what're his desires? It's scary, but sometimes I look at him and think: nothing's there."

"He says a-FREAKIN'-American, for Chrissakes!" Darren beats his forehead. A-FREAKIN'!

Loathing regularly appears at our worksites, driving a red Toyota panel van with "Q.E.D. Loathing" written on the side in large, metallic, multi-colored, 3-D graphics. That's all. No occupation, no phone number, no motto, no logo, not even the name of the sign painter. This and his computer's miraculous capacities are all we know about him for sure. None of us recalls when Loathing first appeared or precisely how long he's been around, only that somehow at some point we each acknowledged him. He drives up very slowly, rolls to a stop, no squeal of brakes, no gravel crunching, takes his time getting out, sometimes doesn't, just sits there watching or leans on a gate or fence or stump or, lacking one, squats. If we look up he nods, either tries to start a quarrel or chews; if nobody looks, he waits ten, twenty minutes, climbs back into the van, shifts and, just before driving off, imparts a tidbit of "viral statistics" that—were I the superstitious sort who takes numbers seriously—might shorten my allotment of heartbeats by years.

"...nope, no way, absolutely not, law o' nature, contrary to science, fact o' God. Best you do is maybe three, maybe four thousand, for better'n eight months work, mostly interest, 'n minus loss and depreciation 'n there's taxes, prepayment, needs dual oscillators or catastrophe theory...well, it's somethin', granted, but lookahere, and Mr. Dee-Light, I call you as my witness—you don't object to serving in this capacity, d'you honorable sir?"

"Give me the color lines! Jim Crow! Slurs! Epithets!" Darren rants his way down into a stairwell.

Loathing resumes without a blip. "Man don't make a profit, he goes belly up. Truth o' nature. Don't need religion to tell him that. Now, sound business includes—I'm speakin' only as a poor cracker, y'understand, salt of the earth, workin' stiff, horse-sense, not your intellectual—"

He says "inter-less-skewel."

"—know-how, but sound business includes the time to lose, truth to tell, but the question's I'm asking, when's yer time to gain? Far as I can reckon, don't never."

"We'll cut ourselves paychecks," I say. "Word of honor, soon as the day's out. I'll put me on a salary, name your figure."

"Don't help," Loathing's deadpan. "Cain't draw on minus balance."

"I'm rich."

"Gross income fer last year was $7349 plus change. Net was

negative. Includes yer wife."

"I'm not-married."

"No nevermind."

Beats leans out an attic window. "How'd you get his tax records, reptile?"

Loathing smiles, never misses a stroke. "Ask him, am I right."

Beats looks at me.

"He's right," I say.

She rolls her eyes.

"Die!" Darren's voice rumbles from the cellar. "Die now!"

"Fiiiine little calky-later."

When needing explanations, I've tried to convince myself that Loathing's an exorbitantly successful contractor undergoing an ontological crisis. Second Chance is what can't be if he genuinely is. I picture him as the miserable owner of a forest green Jaguar sedan whose monthly payments and escalating maintenance costs require a steady income in six figures, thus provoking him to gnaw the flesh of his knuckles and despise his children and harvest annual crops of ulcers large enough to park mobile homes in. From time to time he asks himself, Is this what's called "success"? In lieu of indisputable answers, he sits down at his computer and demonstrates beyond a shadow of a doubt that Second Chance can't exist. He then drives over to pass along to us this information, hoping we'll go "poof" before his eyes. Anyway, it's an explanation with everything going for it but belief. I suppose that in my bones I know or fear or sometimes hope that for all lives there are reckonings and that Loathing's mine, not something worse. Doom will find you; I've read *Macbeth*. Or maybe I still count on luck, mean to grab it with both hands. But in the meantime, Loathing's the threat of reprisal in my fantasies of escape, my unreality's unreality, and so about as close to myself as my other ever comes. I try not to get hung up on him.

"It's a healthy attitude," Arno has reassured me. "We're beyond good and evil, nature, man. Why beat your breast? It's a system. Call this hick—whazzisname? Losing?—the 'reality sign.' Without him, you're probably not a business."

I love Arno, but it's an indication of the difficult period of our friendship that his approval now feels to me like jail. "The only danger I see," I answer, "and as my financial advisor you tell me if I'm wrong— the only danger is he could decipher information faster than I can generate it." I pause. "I mean, that's the competition, right? My data outdoes your software."

Arno chuckles. "The player with the longest credit history wins. More or less. It's not just *any* data; the classification system's infinite only in theory; there are traps; but, yeah, information raises the same problems as God."

"So between unmasking him for a fed and allegorizing him as a principle, there's nothing to choose?"

Eight hundred miles away over the telephone I hear him wince. "Well, it's not mystical! The system of systems may be homeostatic, but gaps, indeterminacies are how it runs. Take your Leonardo novel, f'r instance...."

Silence.

Like every other satellite orbiting the preposterous vanity I dub "my life," Arno keeps a box. Customarily we converse in vast detours around it, fearing that, if he hasn't read it, I'll be insulted and, if he has read it, I'll be insulted. Of course, we both know that we both know that I know that we both know that he knows that we both know every word in it. "Leonardo novel?" Coy, coy.

"A traditional humanist might consider the text-system dysfunctional, but the lack of motive doesn't signify. You've got a desire—object, the horse, and a clear goal, i.e., your hero's kicking off, and there's even a helper—the role's shared by Melzi and later the woman, whazzer name..."

"Mathurine or Mathurina, depending on—"

"...or in the most inclusive terminology, a space and a movement, subject and object, concept versus thing."

"Male female?"

Arno's back-pedaling. "Now, I never said that! You can think that, if you want, but why get Jungian?"

"Simply analytical, methodologically coherent, rich in discriminations...." My sarcasm trails off into mortuary rhythms.

"Look, why's the little bugger so pissy?"

"You mean the boy, Sal—"

"The little bugger. His function's too abstract, sublime—Science? Modernity? Is this another version of the presumption plot? Humans as the permanently unhoused, more angst stuff? I'm telling you, R—, it's pretty worn out. Nobody wants to hear it. If you're miserable—"

"I'm not miserable."

"—it's not a cosmic problem. Or it's white boy stuff. But it's nothing people—"

"Who?"

"People have to be amused, Squire. They can't always be a-learnin'. Dickens."

"Is there a point about my business?"

"The point's that a lack of motive, lack of market's irrelevant. I mean, this Loathsome defines you. Difference, deferral. Nobody produces for *need* anymore. But, see, in your—uh—'book,' the real gap's not textual. It's contextual, in the literature system, in the social

179

system, in the Systems system."

"Meaning?"

"Who gives a fuck about Leonardo da—"

"There's supermarket pasta called da Vinci. There's a children's fold-out book about his horse. There's a mutant Ninja turtle named Leonardo, and an electronics catalog with his Vitruvian man for its logo. Eighty-nine books mentioning him were published last year; over a hundred public institutions have exhibits; there are at least three English words derived from him; two electronics commercials, four car commercials—"

"He's part of the nightmare we woke from. This is the future. Wake up."

"Where?"

"Leonardo's a quote."

Lying on his tick this afternoon sweating beneath an avalanche of coverlets and gazing out at the same clouds that have hovered in one place continuously during three years, Leonardo wants to wake from his nightmare. None of the books he'd planned got written, his thousands of pages of notes wouldn't organize, the knowledge he spent a lifetime acquiring wasn't, well... there. Or it was there only in the way bandits are there: armed and ready to ambush you but gone when you returned with the law. That a vulgar failure—not a failure of prowess or philosophy but of common discourse, speech, script, diction—that such a failure should consummate all his others! At least, the horse's collapse had been spectacular, measured an aspiration, but to fail in the end of mere words, to leave everything untold, fall silent in defeat— it strikes him now as contemptible. Having sought to surpass humanity, Leonardo da Vinci winds up beneath it! And odder still, or perhaps fitting, when the last chance came, his accuser had been no god or potentate, not posterity or nature or the ancients, but only street scruff, dross, a lackey—Salai. Looking toward the window where the weasel still lingers like ghostly pain, Leonardo can't believe his story could really be this one. What maleficent ingegnere would've contrived it? What obscure plot could so much humiliation serve?

Of course, it crosses his mind that he may have contrived it himself, that his fate has proven inescapable because he's hallucinating. Crosses his mind?! Hell, wasn't that Salai's whole point—that the horse was merely a phantasm, the obstacles all imaginary, that the only aim of knowing never to know? Why else would your experience come to nothing? And Leonardo certainly tried to explain himself then, to insist that, yes, his work may have been illusory and the statue just a fabrication, but the horse—that had been as true as death and disappointment and a ten-year-old boy's hair. But no word he spoke was any word he wanted to say, and faced with Salai's candor, he'd gradually betrayed himself, yielded, acknowledged all. Or so it seems. In the silence of this chamber as Leonardo surveys his surroundings through the glutinous film of what he thinks from the smell must be radish drippings, he feels like a parody or counterfeit, his own maladroit quotation. These lilies, balloons, spent machines—they're leftovers from a pastime, from a dimostrazione that, had it been a dimostrazione at all, would've been his first. What did he think he was trying to prove? That he was someone else?

All he wants now is for it to end. If only Salai had kept silent four more days, swallowed thirty-nine years' outrage, remained the lackey they'd both agreed—without exactly saying so—to act as though he'd always been, then Leonardo could've abandoned Leonardo just as he'd abandoned Milan, Florence, Rome. He could've memorized some maxims, murmured them at a propitious time; his will would've been read; Melzi could've eulogized him, and even if no one believed the tales, they'd have borne repeating. So what if you died in arrears! Nothing ever made a full account. But death was the last thing Leonardo expected to come naturally. Is your undoing always your own doing? The only place Leonardo can rest assured it won't be is the future. If he's to awaken from history, he'll just have to go there. God's cods, this inept chronicler hasn't even provided a transition! With a deep breath, he plucks up the seam of the pig's-bristle throw-rug, flips it back, bucks his torso, twists his neck, flails his useless hand, and trying to overcome seven decades of futility and fifty pounds of sheets, Leonardo prepares to meet Salai's engine.

It's at this instant that Mathurine wakes. More accurately, she opens her right eye, spies a fuzzy blueness she believes to be the afterlife, and hears Satan's voice as the beating of wooden mallets on her head. The afterlife seems to be made of paper, resembles a carnation or scored radish, and is resting on the bridge of her nose. This isn't the world she expected to return to. Her memory's ajumble—there are pictures, but the only names that come to mind are Shadrach and Abednego—and she feels peculiar. Evidently, she has become a new person, has been invaded through the nostril or ear by a renegade spirit and is suffering exotic inclinations, impulses not her own. Though not predisposed to metaphysics, she's leaning toward the interpretation that, having until this moment been unremarkable, she's now constitutionally wicked, and scanning the filthy floorboards, windows, wall, tapestry—all of which have been disguised to look exactly as before—she's eager to find out what evil holds in store. The rodent-looking sacristan at Blois—a virtuoso suspicioner capable of discerning tactics in a sneeze—has told her of nefarious doings abroad, of profane conspirators bent on robbing humble clerics, of apostates dividing sheep and goats, of Waldensians, Hussites, Beguines, Cathari, sects, cults, factions, cabals. In the past Mathurine has regarded his fears as the luxuries of a class not besieged by tapeworm or dropsy, but now she's more open-minded. She feels especially receptive to his greatest enthusiasm: Books! Manuals! Pamphlets! Tomes! She's watched him squeal himself redfaced, pound his fist on the altar, kick phylacteries. The invention of moveable type a little over half a century earlier has resulted in the proliferation of strange works—how-to manuals for surgeons, primers of geometric theology, the Koran in French, verse accounts of returns from the dead, guides to sorcery, herbals, alchemical texts—and it's this image of inquisitive nobodies squirreled away in badly lit hovels drawing undisciplined conclusions from half-truths cranked out in fantastic quantities by unknown printers in Venice, Mainz, Valencia, Castille... it's this image that really drives the sacristan loony. What do you think they are reeeeading?! she's heard him demand, or Qu'est-ce qu'ils liiiisent, pense-toi?! For the first time this all seems to involve herself.

Evil is what someone else knows that you don't. It may not be fun, but it's always a secret. Pushing her torso gingerly upright, Mathurine does her best to ignore Satan's exuberant bashing of her sinuses and to make sense of her new relationship to her epoch's worst fears. The afterlife has become a wad of blue paper in a pool of carrot juice beside her knee, and despite her initiation into Luciferian mysteries and—judging from her headache—eternal torment to boot, the only change in her surroundings seems to be that it's a lot quieter than she kind of does/kind of doesn't remember it. In his deathbed the master's flailing his arms right now at phantoms, plucking up the throw-rug Mathurine went to some pains to fetch from the stable, and generally fluttering and flapping around like a flounder in a boat-bottom. It has for a long time been obvious to Mathurine that this barbarian resembles the infinitely malleable Anti-Christ that vivifies the sacristan's finest nightmares, but now the aptness of the comparison strikes her with new force. How many times has she seen Leonardo hunched over some pile of scribbles and loose pages, muttering indecipherable incantations, blasphemous oaths? How often has she been berated by Monsieur François des Melzes for picking up fallen papers or closing some open volume? Once when no one was about, she snuck into the stone cellar, and examining the strewn sheets, she found all manner of

mystic shapes,

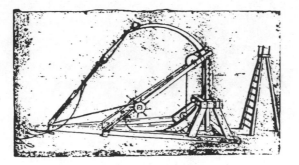

allegories,

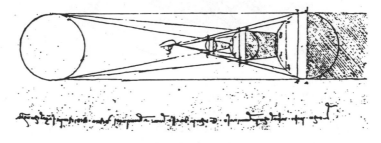

maps of netherworlds,

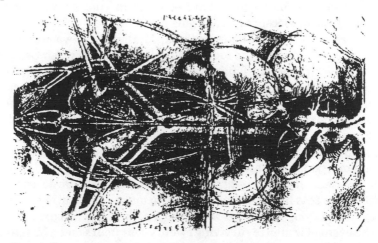

and, most gruesome of all, a man stripped and bound to a hideous wheel of torment!

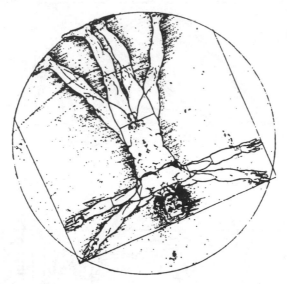

Pulling herself woozily onto her feet Mathurine now recognizes that in this very house all around her is the fulfillment of her evil destiny. Having been invaded by the whizzing projectile in which her master's diabolical genius evacuated its host, Mathurine feels akin to the Italians. Theirs is a shared damnation, mutual vileness, and for the first time she wants, not just to observe their witchcraft, but to participate. She must know what Leonardo da Vinci knows! This itch is what fallen innocence often comes down to.

Creeping toward the straw tick, Mathurine is wondering how she's going to decipher the mutterings of a barbarian when Leonardo, who's still kicking and flailing at his covers, reaches the end of his strength. Having amassed his vigor and prepared to tumble one last time into the kind of hole sensible people spend lifetimes staying out of, he's discovered that he can't budge. The bedclothes have accomplished their purpose: Leonardo's soul is tethered to earth. And at this juncture he's applying his wits as energetically as possible to the tactical problem of bodily liberation when Mathurine, with a powerful curiosity but no clear objective, steps up to his pillow. Leonardo sees her. Mathurine sees him. She knows what to make of le maitre senile and of le maitre dying, has even assembled a pocketful of resigned maxims in the event of le maitre surviving twenty-four hours more, but she has no idea what to make of le maitre trying to get up. His teeth are clinched. His eyes look determined. And because she really hasn't had much practice at considering Leonardo a person, that is, as thinking of his face as one she might someday look right into, and because she still hasn't guessed that the bonk on her head was Leonardo's doing—lucky for him—and since he seems to have something ominous in mind and she hasn't but would like to, when Leonardo smiles, she smiles back. He gives her an ingratiating wink, makes the deprecatory, shilly-shallying gestures of a helpless foreigner, carefully mimics the steps for getting this goddamn mountain off him, and Mathurine, who can't read writing but can read dumb-shows like a philologist decides: Why not? In seconds Leonardo's onto the floor, bare knees wobbly in the breeze, and before Mathurine can wonder, hmmm, is this maybe a bad idea?— the geezer's sprinting down the stairs.

Outside in the courtyard Francesco Melzi stands on the floor-boards of a partially loaded wagon about to leave town. Boxes and pouches surround his feet. For half an hour he's been browbeating Battista into helping him pack and carry Leonardo's sketches and notes—6,000 rag and vellum pages varying in size from a notepad to a legal sheet and including clasps, binders, covers, containers, etcetera, weighs just over eight hundred pounds—and his euphoric sense of a new life has subsided into a sober resolve. He never anticipated how complicated the responsibilities of fiction would be. He knows that Battista can't be trusted to keep silent if left behind, that he must persuade the servant to come along, but he has no idea how. Battista's in the cellar gathering another armload of cross-sections of ox-hearts, annotated sketches of drilling rigs and pulley relays, allegories, and dredging plans, while in the wagon Melzi arranges and ties down the luggage, racking his brain for something like a plan. This last activity is more productive than it has been in the past. In part because, until now, honor has always hemmed him in. One definition of a free spirit is a resourceful coward impervious to shame, and it's Melzi's refusal to be daunted, not so much by reprisals as by baseness, that has him using his wits now to such excellent effect. Correct or not, Melzi *feels* that he can make something of himself and is prepared to resort to the most contemptible actions to bring it off. This he can do. Anyway, it's in the midst of this furor of preparation that Melzi hears a roar, crash, and scream come from the little doorway leading into the kitchen. He looks up just in time to see Leonardo in his nightshirt stagger out into the courtyard, eyes dilated like those of a seer newly descended from a rock, with Mathurine more or less dangling from his neck.

This is the first real test of Melzi's new life. He recognizes that his abandonment of the Maestro has been noted—Leonardo's far, far gone but evidently still this side of Elysium—and that Leonardo has pursued him to enumerate the infinite kindnesses bestowed upon the contemptible and falsehearted dilettante by his magnanimous, renowned teacher. Nothing surprising in this, and Melzi would hang his head, grow hotfaced, and resort to the same weteyed obsequiousness tourists display before starving nine-year-olds outside the New Delhi Hilton before stepping into the airport limo and getting themselves the hell back to New York—if it weren't for Battista. Melzi needs to be the last Italian ever to see Leonardo da Vinci alive. Five furlongs out of town he intends to give in to his emotions, collapse weeping, and tell Battista some version of what he's already rehearsed for Leonardo, or whatever else he damn well pleases, counting on Battista's confusion and Melzi's purse to make it reliable. Until now, Melzi has thought the major difficulty was to persuade Battista to return to Milan before completing his so-called apprenticeship, but suddenly Battista steps from the cellar with his umpteenth armload of canal dredging diagrams and observes enough of Leonardo's sprightly dash across the courtyard to complicate immeasurably Melzi's narration of Leonardo's demise. The creature who inhabits the dueling fields of Francesco's memory, a vixen with rouged cheeks, blue cape, and an odor like ox manure, appears to him now as she does on all such occasions, scoffing, I told you it would turn out like this! But for once Francesco doesn't yield. He's a courtier; humbuggery runs in his veins. If defeat is what comes naturally, then he'll have to act weird.

He points a finger at Leonardo, shrieks—DEAD! DEAD! Our master's DEAD!—and jumps from the wagon into Battista's arms.

Ooph! Battista says and tosses the canal dredging diagrams into the sky.

Melzi rights himself, plants his feet in the firm but limber manner prescribed by Luccio's *Primer of Declamatory Tropes and Speech Ornaments*, Venice, 1463, and begins: See where his great spirit walks, our genius departed, the age come to its end! Upon the wooly backs of heaven's herd, those white harbingers of storm and earthen tumult, see his leaps, a figure composite of gossamer dream and memory, spun of our time's pregnant wish and the chance of seasons, days. What did they call him? Ingegnere, blessed, maestro, philosopher, he who more than others was who we would be. Feel his ether upon you, know his disembodied shape. Does he seem corporeal, a fleshy presence impossible to doubt, persisting still? OH, WOULD IT WERE SO! How brightly his gray eyes glimmer, how far-seeing and strange. Ah, our paltry souls won't relinquish, our memories cling like maidens still. Stay, master! Remain, illusion! But he will not. Our hearts deceive us like his panels which made us see—how irresistibly, with what animation, with such waking dreams—long perished things. He's gone, gone. Weep, clouds! Tear your hair, willows! The best of us, our own faith and eyes, gone, fled, invisible.

Silence.

186

Battista isn't unimpressed. He's just stepped into this courtyard and been cracked in the sternum by Francesco Melzi's shoulder. He's seen an emaciated Methuselah bare-legged in his nightshirt drag a hefty peasant fifty feet. He's stood by as drawings that for six years he's been protecting with his life are scattered in the mud without so much as a complaint, and now he's being told that the Maestro, whom he sees crouched over and peering at a wagon wheel not twelve paces away, is a ghost. Battista's no rube. He knows a flim-flam when he sees one. But since hardly anything in Leonardo's workshop has ever looked real, Battista's difficulty isn't to recognize a flim-flam but to distinguish a run-of-the-mill flim-flam from a trap. Best thing to do in such moments is act savvy. He cocks an eye, peers down his nose at Francesco, takes a long look over at Leonardo craning his neck to scrutinize a cracked wagon spoke, and says, Pshaw!

Melzi falls to his knees. Let us all die with him! He draws from his doublet a cute little dagger about as vicious as a number two pencil, and just for effect positions it to plunge right into his—ugh!—eye: Here bereft of hope, light, we like foundlings moan, but what chance of succor? Our breast, milk of wisdom, gone, gone. What good this life sans reason, this nature devoid of holy order? Come, brother, let us darken what merits only darkness! Enter oblivion's peace, the final night!

And damned if Francesco doesn't fall forward in a trajectory that's going to drive the little letter-opener right through his frontal lobe!

Never underestimate the power of an outlandish gesture in an uncertain spot. Battista knows it's hokum but, confronted with Melzi's willingness to take hokum to its bitter end, he shrieks: Wait!

Francesco sticks out an arm, catches himself with his eyeball one hair's width away from the dagger's point, asks: Hmmmm?

Battista looks at his toes, clears his throat, scratches his crotch, hems, haws, whistles, and points to the canal-dredging diagrams scattered on the ground. What should I do with these?

Blasphemer! Idiot! Ingrate! Melzi roars and, leaping to his feet, sticks the penknife right up Battista's nostril. WHERE ARE YOUR EYES?! Our master, the Florentine, he who made flesh a marvel, stole heaven's fire, created contemptible you, he's DEAD! DEAD! DEAD! Don't you see his shade where it vanishes e'en now? Can't you see it fade to airy nothing, become mist, as we speak? Deprived of Truth's original, what care we for counterfeits?

And just for effect, and despite the genuine agony it costs him, Melzi stretches out one foot, places the heel of his slipper atop the diagram of an apparatus for transporting silt from canal beds, and stepping down hard, eliminates forever the leaf that should've been between verso 385 and recto 386 of the Codex Atlanticus now at the Biblioteca Ambrosiana in Milan where, otherwise, we'd see the machine never had a prayer of working.

Our lives are through! Francesco snarls.

And Battista, undone at last, starts to weep.

AND HORSES

For several months after the incident in Galeazzo Sanseverino's palazzo, having for reasons—ought one speak of reasons here?—having for no comprehensible reason protected Salai from his assailants—all this was back in Milan during the winter of 1490-91—for several months, Leonardo tried not to consider what he'd failed to do. At times letting Salai escape had seemed a loss of nerve, an example of un-masterly indecision, and Leonardo resolved next time to be firmer. But the hollowness of his excuses was too evident, even for Leonardo himself, and whenever he remembered the moment in Galeazzo da Sanseverino's hallway—black curls clinched in his fingers, limp face turned upwards, the thrill in his teeth as the shouts and footsteps behind him grew louder—Leonardo felt himself standing before a darkness. What good would experience do here? It was the end of experience, dullwitted nothingness, a cavern into which you plunged. Salai stayed away just long enough for Leonardo to hope his own past behavior might be a puzzle he needn't solve. What would it be like to enter the shop each morning and find the wood chips still littering the floor? Or odder still, to find some slackjawed stranger sweeping the boys' leavings away? But then, in a pattern that would repeat itself over two and a half decades, Salai simply reappeared one morning, took up his broom as if he'd laid it down the night before, gathered the goat's milk from the threshold, and—offering no explanation and displaying no awkwardness about his lack of one, so that, if truth be told, Leonardo could never be sure the rascal hadn't already arrived the previous morning or been there for weeks, the whole rhythm appearing so perfunctory that, well, how would you notice?—he resumed his duties as though the past were a dream.

At the time, Leonardo hadn't been doing much work. The problem of the statue's scale and casting still daunted him, and in the months after Ludovico's wedding—while Salai remained God knew where—Leonardo just wasn't up to it. Every idea struck him as stale. The orderliness of his procedures seemed unreassuring. In an effort to rouse his genius, he undertook a thorough reorganization of the workshop, sent the youngest apprentices back to their families, but after a few days of shoving tables and barrels about, he grew listless. Someone broke the drawbolt on his bedroom door. A costly hide disappeared. It rained for four weeks. And then one morning he awoke to an inexplicable freshness in his lungs and the warmth of sunlight edging across his pillow. Downstairs the cheese tasted sharper than he'd remembered, and after stomping around the kitchen and flexing blood into his fingers, he started up the steps to Marco's room. He wasn't sure what he meant to tell his apprentice, may or may not have actually mentioned any work they had to do, but he definitely did announce that whatever the eye could see the hand could fashion—a boast that, for all its hollowness, got things moving again. The phrase was Bramante's, an answer to some conundrum Leonardo had posed him one day in the giardini pubblici—or perhaps it had been Leonardo's response to a riddle of Bramante's—but it had occurred to Leonardo that night in the midst of wild dreaming, and standing beside Marco's bed this morning he hadn't spoken it so much as heard it for the first time. So Leonardo would've happily conceded that, regardless of the difficulties of his rival's temper, arguing with Bramante could remind you who you were.

Or would've conceded it if, returning downstairs, he hadn't run into Salai. The child was rummaging the sacks of dried clay, pulling out the smushed model of the forelegs, dusting everything off, composed, resolute, as if he knew exactly what was going on. It wasn't merely that no one had so much as touched any section of the horse-mold since November so that now confronting the half-made replica resting on the shop floor Leonardo felt confused, almost shy. Its plainness belied all those months of fantastic wrestling. Where had Leonardo been? Nor was it that Leonardo hadn't actually instructed the boy to prepare the clay and soaking solution and pestle and miscellaneous contraptions so that his activity now had an air of clairvoyance about it. It was hardly the first time one of his assistant's actions had anticipated Leonardo's commands. And even Leonardo's recognition that, until he saw Salai laying the poplar slats into the tub of murky liquid and arranging the mold and bands, Leonardo hadn't been sure himself what he was about to do, hadn't acknowledged even to Marco that, yes, today the horse would resume—even this depth of collusion had a naturalness to it. No, far more than any of this, what unnerved Leonardo as he stood at the bottom of the stone stairs was his difficulty recalling if this was Salai's first morning back. However much he tried both then and later to reconstruct the sequence of events—Antonio had recently found his purse rifled; perhaps the cut on Andrea's nose was the urchin's doing; how many days since he'd noticed that the floor was swept?—no matter how often he told himself that his apprehensions were illusory, the mind's confounding of forgetfulness and its own fears, Leonardo would always believe that at the precise instant he reawakened to the colossus, Salai had reappeared.

Salai and the horse; the horse and Salai. Thinking about it made him crazy, so he didn't think about it. Each morning he arose to work in progress, and each day he lost himself in whatever was going on. From the moment his feet touched the floor until an interruption or his clumsiness or a damaged tool made him pause, he'd labor beside the anxious boys, often not speaking for hours at a time, fingers scratching at surfaces, pounding salts, sketching elaborate contraptions, bending wire, threading iron bolts, or if not laboring, then struggling against his guilt and terror of squandered time. He had no clearer sense of the whole now than during the previous winter, and he still got lost in his own interminable, frenzied revisions, still watched his conceptions vanish, piece swirling around piece, the old vortex of self-loathing, vacuum, nothingness, a hole. All that had changed—and the thought crossed Leonardo's mind more than once that, for all he knew, the change could be for the worse—was that he rose now to something already happening, something he didn't have to start over each time. He couldn't be sure where it was headed. He might be traveling in a circle, might wind up repeating himself. All he knew was that he was following, and he hoped that his direction was the horse's own.

(If I'd been able to write the scene of the stolen silverpoint, then here I'd recount Leonardo's problems with motion. What made that earlier scene seem contrived—a ten-year-old child informing Leonardo da Vinci of his "mistakes"!—was the child's character or motivation. Salai's actions were turning into plot functions, expressions of a need—whose?—to keep going. I hardly know whether his concluding words, "It's not moving!" have been spoken. But if this turns out to be the story in which they are, then Leonardo's problem is that his drawings are accurate. His sketches of forelegs show what photographs of trotting horses show. Frozen creatures, cropped life, truncated acts. Salai knows, Leonardo knows, seeing motion isn't seeing this. I imagine Leonardo beginning to distort the drawings, conceiving poses that, in truth, no trotting horse has ever assumed. At first, this doesn't disturb him, for he already knows that perspective, to look convincing, can require similar distortions. But at some point he becomes nervous. What exactly is he distorting for? If his eyes aren't faithful, how have his eyes seen this?

In the missing section, Leonardo begins to suspect another nature. Humans desire something his universe doesn't contain. And yet, watching geldings cavort, Leonardo has never felt any deprivation, any lack. Nothing motion needs appears to be missing, but nothing Leonardo draws is what he's seen. This section—which happily isn't written—concludes with the following, bombastic sentence: "And feeling his head spin, Leonardo looked down at his feet and saw a crevice opening, saw emptiness, saw himself looking back from across an unbridgeable divide.")

As long as the horse continued forward, the divide could be
ignored. Leonardo's art seemed to involve a paradox, an incoherence
that he'd have to confront—if ever—in a future he might never see.
Each night as darkness blinded him and the need for food got too strong
and any boys who hadn't slipped away hours earlier finally made their
escape so that the only sound in the little house was Salai's broom
scraping over the workshop floor, Leonardo would collapse into a chair
or on a stone bench in the vineyard, clean of notions, consumed, utterly
blank. Gazing up at the fixed stars then, he'd let the tension in his back
subside, wait for oblivion to overtake him. This moment was what he
wanted. If only tomorrow would be the same. But whenever the horse
faltered, if the next step proved unstraightforward, if this morning's
dry clay seemed too moist by evening only to turn crumbly the following
afternoon, or whenever he woke to find last night's new place just the
same old place again, then nature's inconstancy scared him. Why didn't
what happened just happen? Why did you sometimes need more?

And then all that had until now gone without saying came to an
end. Leonardo was struggling one evening to make a compound of
binding salts coagulate. It was maddening work, each trial producing
infinitesimally too much of one ingredient or another, disproportions so
negligible he repeatedly believed the next try would succeed. At one
juncture the whole solution had gone to smash, and in a pique Leonardo
had flung the pestle across the shop, striking a beam and hitting young
Bernardo square between the shoulders. The poor boy started bawling
and Leonardo had to send Marco out to buy candied ginger to restore
order. At last, as daylight began to fade he'd made some progress,
having realized that his mistake had been to grind the organic matter
too fine, just the sort of over-scrupulousness that had undone him time
and again, and he was in a desperate race with nightfall to complete
this one small step. It seemed such a modest ambition, but as he
squinted his tired eyes into the bowl before him, he realized he wouldn't
make it. He rocked back on his stool, wiped his forehead with a damp
arm. In the dying light his frustration seemed fundamental. How often
had he found himself struggling against just such accidents of common
life? It now seemed to him that he would never finish the horse, that this
wouldn't be because of his ignorance, but because of a mediocre bean
harvest, an infected toenail, or some emperor's whim for a bronze
shaving bowl. Leonardo da Vinci's work would come to nothing and the
whole business would look funny.

Slowly he stood and made his way up the little stairway to his
chamber. His back throbbed fiercely and his knees were numb. He was
just forty, but already he felt old. The legendary strength in his hands
hadn't given out, but sometimes now his right one would tremble, and

one morning he'd had to soak it in warm water before he could begin to draw. He pulled his clothes off, let them crumple on the rough wood floor. He made no toilet, crawled under the bedclothes and in the darkening room sat up, back against the headboard, gazing into the gray-flecked gloom. His future appeared vividly before him. He would overcome the last obstacle, unriddle the horse, only to see everything collapse for want of materials, patronage, time. He felt himself dying. He composed final speeches then realized no one would hear them, saw himself trampled beneath the hooves of an immoveable weight. It was a night in which only inertia stopped him from gobbling bella donna, and he was wading into the blackest lagoons of self-pity when a voice spoke. W—w—wait, it said. Leonardo stared into the blackness, didn't breathe. He could hear an owl hooting somewhere far off, the rustle of mice underneath the floor. His head bent slightly forward. Wait? he wanted to ask. Wait for what? For morning, for armageddon, for your bowels to move?

For several seconds the room was perfectly still, and Leonardo had to recall the proem of a lengthy treatise on benevolent spirits to keep himself from being spooked. Perhaps the voice was meant to chide him for cowardly despair, or it might be a good omen. Of course, there might have been no voice. But then the voice sounded again, this time softer, aspirate: I can wait. And Leonardo knew he wasn't hearing things. There at the side of the bed near his feet, he made it out now, a darker, more unruly darkness within the universal dark, a slight sheen, curl, line of flesh-watching or hiding? For the longest of times Leonardo held the figure in sight, trying to make out its expression, hear its breathing. Then he spoke: What do you want?

The owl hooted again. Far away a woman was singing.

It's alive, the boy began, but his voice stuck in his throat.

Alive?

You can smell it! The nostrils—

This isn't fitting—

It's starting to move, I've seen—

Shhhhhhh.

The boy fell silent, took a deep breath. This is the great work, he finally uttered. Creation again. After it's a deed, nothing will need repaying.

Leonardo didn't reply. I don't know, he said at last.

The voice came back fierce: I have seen them! There's nothing—there'll be nothing left over.

It's only metal! It's not—

We'll be safe.

Leonardo lay very still. He couldn't conceive the boy's meaning, but at the same time the meaning seemed utterly bare. He looked over at the curls, the dusky skin, one eye glinting in the refracted moonlight. This wasn't what was happening, he wanted to insist. This voice, these words, they were as beside the point as salts that wouldn't coagulate. Leonardo eased down more deeply into the tick, pulled the coverlets up.

Well, it won't be alive like Messer Galeazzo's stallion, he muttered. It won't eat oats.

It will shame God. I—I hate them. They've...they've got legs, trunks, once when I lay beneath him, his stink filled my throat...your head will burst, your mouth will ache, eyes burn, your fingers are so small, brittle, and when they crush—

Shhhhhhhhhhh.

Leonardo turned his face into the pillow. No, what was happening was something else. This was just a digression. What, for God's sake, could art be if disorder like this expressed it? He settled himself, emptied the day from his exhausted arms. An eleven-year-old street child was living in his bedroom. It was mad, but no matter. And then without ever meaning to, he added, Okay, you wait.

And so Leonardo became someone he didn't know. The sculptor abandoned himself to his work like a dying man to his illness, and he struggled to ignore what, in the end, amounted to nothing at all, but increasingly everything apart from the horse was illusion. The phantom who collapsed from fatigue each night or who often beat his forehead in frustration, who slept in Leonardo's bed and listened to the rhythm of strange breathing—this was a dream from which daily the sculptor woke. As long as the next step went forward, these distractions seemed immaterial. The resins and emery he consumed were becoming his true food now, the only substance that genuinely renewed him, and all that came between his hands and the parts they fashioned was the thinnest layer of skin. It was by no means clear that, instead of the clay hooves and gaskins on the workshop floor, his body wasn't horse, that the inert materials weren't drawing their vigor from his organs. When he finally completed a full-size clay version of the left rear hock and cannon, he concocted the plaster female from salts made by roasting his own dung. One evening after the apprentices had slipped away, he placed himself inside the pointing machine—a mansize box!—and, sliding the rods to his face and body, compared his contour with that of the small model he'd cast the previous winter. They matched. More and more his diet resembled the compounds of oils, pitch, glue, egg, and aqua vitae used to coat the molds or secure the sections. He drew a kind of confidence from this identity, believed with the optimism of touch and taste and sight that, even without science, he and the beast were one.

But if he ever lost his way, if the horse balked or strayed or threw him, or if, beside himself with excitement, he tried to see what lay ahead, the sculptor would be overcome. He'd start to have second thoughts then, find that he was of two minds about everything. The prance that had moved him so deeply, that had conveyed the work's meaning and carried him away, now looked like a clay replica or imitation, and in the midst of rigging an escape trough for the sculpture's wax sheath, he'd see exactly what he was doing. Or worse, he'd see the phantom, Leonardo, doing it in his place! The sculptor would be paralyzed then, would stand there gazing down at his hands as his apprentices started to giggle and edge away. Had he forgotten the work was mere horseplay? How had his deeds become so transparent? He could never find a cause for these disillusionments. Lucidity seemed to float—weightless and without shape—above certain moments or operations, but whenever the truth occurred to him, what he saw looked painfully familiar, as if he were only now seeing what he'd always known. He'd let the bow drill or chisel or coils of wire slip from his fingers then, cringe at his manifest pretensions, and wonder who the sculptor was to whom this humbug had seemed so natural. Leonardo was feeling like his old self again, and this prospect terrified him. When one morning he woke to discover, on a sketch pad from the night before, a horse rearing on its hindlegs, hooves kicking out, trunk lifting into the air as though bronze dreamed it could fly, he realized he was living in a circle. He was desperate for guidance. Before the sun had risen above the wall of his vineyard, he'd set out for Pavia.

Fazio Cardano met him at the door in drag. Draped in the veils of a Moorish courtesan, he'd been entertaining Andreuccio, the blacksmith, in the scullery. Andreuccio slouched against a grain barrel with his beefy forearms across his chest, occasionally sipped at an opaque liquor, and watched Fazio undulate, bang finger cymbals. The moment was plainly inopportune, but having only the stranger in his workshop to return to, that or his youthful presumption, Leonardo decided to brazen it out. Fazio, who was delighted to enlarge his audience, fluttered his fingers about his throat and started clucking of gossip. It seemed that a sport of nature had just been discovered in the lunga dimora, or lengthy residence, the Pavian street slang for dungeon. No one had the story right, or rather it was circulating in contradictory versions, but evidently the creature's mother had been condemned years before to some variety of exquisite torment and had avoided execution by pleading her belly. She was taken out of the tower and stuck in a deep cell where the authorities promptly forgot her. Time passed. Her barley loaf and swill disappeared each evening. Her slop bucket came back full. For how long, no one could say. There'd been countless jailers, and the unfortunate protagonist of the story—who barked like a terrier and answered to the name Arrrchio—was so disfigured, pocked, stooped and moronic his age couldn't be guessed.

Andreuccio, who'd seen him, said he hopped about like a toad, jerking his head at everyone and foaming. Anyway, some weeks earlier an elderly pickpocket had turned up dead in a cell with buboes on his neck, and the fear of plague had been sufficient to provoke a wholesale cleansing. When one little-used cell-block was opened, Arrrchio was found naked and trembling beside an intact human skeleton still wearing a mildewed smock. Since that time philosophers had flocked to see him. He was the subject of much speculation.

Andreuccio the blacksmith possessed two opinions about the affair: first, that Arrrchio was unfit for labor, and second, that God had not blessed him. Fazio saw more in this second judgment than did Leonardo. He hopped about wide-eyed, his silk pants billowing, shouting, Yes! Yes! According to Fazio, Arrrchio's misfortune recalled Socrates' story of the cave, combining as it did an allegory of the mind's illumination with an exemplary tale of injustice. He became eloquent on the subject, dancing about with his bare arms snaking up and down, maintaining that the new age had disclosed many miracles. Leonardo could see that a forthright breaching of his own topic would get him nowhere, so he decided to come at it indirectly. He acknowledged that Arrrchio's tale bore a resemblance to Plato—one could imagine Arrrchio as a soul imprisoned by moribund authority, for example. However, he believed Arrrchio's misfortune was more an enigma than exemplum. Throughout the created world one observed divine reasonableness, all creatures revealing their natures through movement and action. Streams did not require correction, deer needed no reminder to flee lions, etcetera. Why then did Arrrchio, having been tutored since birth by nature herself, seem so alien to men? Was the soul our second nature merely? Fazio giggled, praised Leonardo's subtlety, but pointed out that he'd conflated incommensurables. Arrrchio's imprisonment was unnatural in the highest degree. The soul was our freedom. Wasn't Arrrchio's stooped body the very picture of a slave?

The conversation grew warm. Leonardo maintained that one law pertained to stones, beasts, and men, that the spirit couldn't be at odds with true learning, while Fazio resorted to byzantine analogies, gleefully spinning through Pecham's optics and various commentaries on the *Metamorphoses*. The air filled with gesticulating hands. Voices grew shrill. Andreuccio, now quite drunk, began to croon the ballad of *Giuseppe, the Lonely Castrato*. Leonardo felt dizzy, but if he was going to speak, this was the time. He drew in his breath, announced, I've witnessed what cannot be.

There was a pause. Andreuccio's voice continued to slur together various -issimo's and -accia's as the scullery enclosed the speakers more tightly. Fazio told Leonardo to continue. Leonardo explained how some months earlier while visiting here in Pavia, he'd come upon a curious fellow, a dwarfish man who taught many secrets but knew no words. Leonardo had at the time been studying the *Perspectiva*—the copy loaned him by Fazio—and had seen in the dwarf's motion a commentary on the eye. He spoke to the soul like a painting! Leonardo insisted. A living geometer! But then a mysterious event occurred that had haunted Leonardo to this hour. Beckoning for Fazio to lean closer, Leonardo dipped his fist into a bag of wheat, spread a thin layer of grain over the floor, and with his index, traced what he'd first seen in 1490 but wouldn't recognize until 1506. That is,

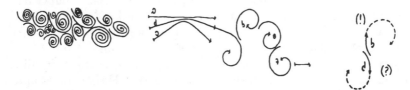

period. A motion gave birth to its contrary! Leonardo exclaimed. The dwarf taught space to lie!

For a long moment Fazio looked on in silence, then he whispered: It's a fable. Imagine unfortunate Arrrchio beneath the earth, surrounded by darkness, vermin. Does he know his liberator when the door swings ajar? Is not daylight a wrong his eyes do him? You've mistaken your teacher for an illustrator, have imagined contradictions where he's speaking an ancient tongue. Arrrchio's discourse is Adam's, but we, being fallen men, imagine he's dumb. Don't the vulgar laugh at numerology and other high things?

No! No! No! Leonardo slashed the air. It's mechanics! Couldn't Fazio see? He'd witnessed what made gibberish of Pecham!

Fazio shrugged. What would you have me say? The truth isn't a bolt of dry-goods! Either nature is a kingdom and we're its subjects, or its inscription requires making out.

But it's written in ratios! Leonardo insisted. He knew the heaviness of bronze or, say, its cost and hardness. But what seemed as clear as commerce one instant became, in the next, a mishmash of grammars, glyphs. This can't be!

Much gets lost in translation.

Leonardo shook his head. Arrrchio's prison is my ignorance. Let me out.

Fazio smiled. His fingers fluttered up to his throat. You have witnessed many mysteries, my friend, and have remained admirably steadfast, but far stranger is justice ....

LIFE

On the night of Leonardo's last visit to Marcantonio della Torre, the storm that blew out the lights brought nightmares into the room. It happened so fast neither man was prepared. Now, the nearness of the mangled cadaver, the smell of rain and earth, the howling of the wind, crashing candelabra, shutters, knives, all made the gloom uncanny. Like primeval nothing, or the void before omnipotence stirs. It was hard, even for Leonardo, not to panic. Through the unfettered window, he could hear nature's seams coming undone, a rift opening in rock. What if the ground beneath you moved? Leonardo tried to envision the storm's progress as a gathering of immortals might, perched on hilltops, chins resting on their arms, as they watched the cyclone slosh its tail through the Ticino, spreading mad waste. It felt queer to unite fancy with the riot and screech all around him, but he found comfort in it. Leonardo remained where he'd been standing, still holding the flaccid bulb of a syringe in his palm, waiting for the wind to die. He couldn't see anything.

Fire—!

The word was shouted directly into his ear as spastic fingers began scratching his face. For Jupiter's ....

H—help me with ...here, here, here!

The fingers clawed him again. Leonardo grabbed at them. Stop it!

The hands jumped and flailed like eels, beating against Leonardo, against whatever. A knee drove into his thigh, he heard broken words over the wind's moan: lamp ...wait ...no. Something had gotten loose. Leonardo lost his grip, touched wind, felt his own forearms struck again and again. The panic seemed to be on every side of him. He couldn't grasp it. At last he managed to seize a jerking wrist in his left fist, which even now at fifty-eight years old could still bend lead nails in the castello forge, and held it motionless waiting for the storm's spasm, noise, frenzy to pass. For a second the fingers kept writhing, either outraged or hysterical—in the darkness and noise of the storm as the shutters flapped and rain beat his skin, it was impossible to tell which—then went limp as a string. And as Leonardo held on, the phantasm stole over him that perhaps this hand wasn't his host's after all, was actually that of the cadaver returned to life, desperate to escape infamy under the anatomist's knives. The wind howled. The fingers

197

really did seem dead. Would this be how mortal shame overtook you, like a storm pitched to carry you away?

It was gone before it arrived. Leonardo released the hand, fumbled his way to the windows, tripped over something wooden, slammed into the sill, righted himself, groped for some stout object to bar the shutters, found nothing, groped again, found nothing, touched a thick timber, found it immovable, grabbed at what felt like a large knife resting against the offal basket beneath the table, too short, somehow dreaded touching viscera in the blackness, finding the organs too, too familiar, and all the while keeping one shoulder to the window, continuing to feel with every relaxing of his strength the storm scowling, its pent-up vengeance, a fury he'd just as soon not know. Finally he located a rod—well, it felt like a rod—leaning in a crevice. He yanked it loose, tensed for the sound of breaking, heard nothing and, discovering the stranger unexpectedly at his side, began shouting directions, responding to the shouts that came back, until, working together, the two men managed to contain the storm at last.

Several more dark minutes passed before della Torre could make his way through the mess and dismal air to a still-burning lamp in a remote hallway and walk back again, still more minutes before he had the room lit enough to survey the mess. The delay was a mercy, both men knew. The memory of the anatomist's panic seemed too fresh. Of course, they'd never speak of it. Slowly, as the shadows began to be pushed back into the rafters and as the sound of the blowing outside became less a part of the world, they started wordlessly mopping the puddles of rain in the cadaver's pits, righting candle-stands, dabbing at their clothes. Neither felt disposed to resume dissecting.

Finally the anatomist spoke. Spirits?

Leonardo nodded, wiped dry the seat of a wooden bench.

I've never taken pleasure in pastures, the anatomist began. I don't doubt that there are attractions—

My boyhood was passed in a village, Leonardo said.

I wouldn't have guessed that! Marcantonio slipped into the hallway, returned almost instantly with two goblets, a bottle. The two men drank in silence. A candle hissed. There were no insects now.

After a moment Marcantonio resumed. My boyhood also was passed far away. Don't smile—I'm not so young.

No.

But I never lived in a village. If not for the madness of Venetians, I'd have grown old in Padua. A well-lit room is a vast space.

Weasels hunt in the dark, Leonardo said.

Marcantonio guffawed: I begin to suspect that you, painter, are a weasel.

No, no. My predators are countless. I'm a hen.

Well, there's a merry thought! Marcantonio gulped down his liquor, let his hand rest on the bottle.

But I shouldn't like to say that all who prefer darkness are cunning—or so admirably cunning—as weasels, the anatomist went on. Much that when obscured looks ordinary, cows a man by candlelight. Our attractive friend, for example. And he kicked at the offal basket. A morsel hopped out, hit the floor with a splat.

Darkness has its terrors, Leonardo remarked.

Men will go to any length not to see.

But ignorance isn't always bad faith, Leonardo continued. I reason it like this: Much we would know can't be laid bare. Much that's laid bare isn't—

Blindness is bad faith. Always.

But you can't carve tidal pools! What of mechanics? If I bounce a marble—

Without knowledge, what are you being faithful to?

...or a falcon's flight?

But the anatomist had walked over to the cadaver, wasn't listening. He dipped his finger into a grisly pit, held the dampness up to his nose. For a long moment he said nothing. Then he added: No. Ignorance is always bad faith.

And without ceremony or preamble, he began the final story of that night.

Marcantonio had never expected to end up in Pavia. He'd escaped Padua under cover of darkness in a ratty gown purchased from a streetwalker. He'd traveled three days, determined to put as many furlongs between himself and the constabulary's pounding as his strength would allow, and then taken refuge in an inn somewhere north of Mantua. From there he composed a letter to a compatriot of his father's schoolboy days, someone called Blocco—it was probably a sobriquet—who, Marcantonio understood, was director of a Lombard medical faculty. He needed a post, he explained, also rooms, leisure, students, one competent cook, some furniture, Galen in Greek, a few garrulous confederates and a steady supply of cadavers. He sent the messenger away with petulant assurances of handsome recompense and promptly passed out in a chair. In what seemed like no time, Marcantonio was awakened by a loud pounding on his door that sent him scrambling for the window. But it was only his messenger already returned with Blocco's reply: Come!

Until he actually saw Pavia, saw the ancient wall with its blockish castle and dark stone, Marcantonio didn't realize why he'd turned westward in his flight. To the south had been the older Tuscan universities—Pisa, Siena, Arrezzo—or nearer still, the wealth of Ferrara. But he'd ventured out alone amid skirmishes and attendant brigandage to a remote town under foreign rule in a region he'd never seen. Now he realized he'd come for the name associated with the place—Sforza, force. No region in Italy, not even Rome, could boast the military resources, armaments factories, strategic advantages and wealth of Lombardy. The Castello Sforzesco was among the most formidable military structures in all of southern Europe, and hardly a day's journey away the Pavian castle was a second to it. Together they formed as invincible a line as northern Italy could claim, and having seen how flimsy the fortress of knowledge could prove, della Torre had been drawn to dominion without saying its name. In short, the events in Padua had scared him. Between his future and the nightmare of pounding that still woke him every night, he wanted walls, cannons, mercenaries. If ignorance arose again, force would be on his side.

So Marcantonio della Torre entered Pavia like an exile coming home. He located rooms in a narrow but pleasant alley off the central strada, cleared a space for the breeze from the Ticino to blow through, and every night looked out at the castle's grim façade and smiled. He was approaching his thirtieth year and beginning to feel impatient at how little he'd achieved. During his weeks as a fugitive he'd interrogated his past and concluded that only one question had ever exercised him: the ancient contention whether the soul inhabited the heart or the brain. All authorities agreed that the differences between life and death—movement, breathing, consciousness—were connected. What produced thought and imagination, they reasoned, was breath or vapors moving through the cerebral ventricles. Aristotle had claimed that the origin of these vapors was the heart and that the brain's role was merely distributive. Galen believed the vapors originated in the heart but were made intelligent in the brain. If Galen was right, della Torre now figured, there ought to be an observable difference between the vessels going into the cerebrum and coming out. It was this difference he wanted to study.

He didn't own a bed or breakfast table, but with the credit his name and signature could obtain he outfitted a second-story room as a laboratory. He purchased a couple of hunting knives, some second-hand carpenter's tools and a whetstone, and—even before seeking out the medical director—began taking long walks at dusk down the alleys leading from the market square. Wherever he encountered a knot of surly fellows, he'd step into their midst, amused by the shift of idiom, sidewards glances, silence. This was part of his work that—whenever he was disposed to thoughtfulness—puzzled him. Not because he found it low or sinister, but because it came so naturally, because he was good at it. In the environs of the lunga dimora, the castle dungeon, he found a hulking felon with a syphilitic cheek who for a pittance agreed to supply his needs. Within a few minutes the two men were smirking,

200

pounding one another familiarly, and although there was no confusion about the abyss dividing them socially, the anatomist felt like he'd found a confederate. He returned to his apartment in a state of high excitement, what in another man would've been lust. The next morning he struck out asking after Blocco until he located him in what looked like a parsonage beside a nun's hospice or abbey. The director was with an ailing pauper, an infirm, the old nun said. Marcantonio insisted on having his name announced anyway, refused to sit while waiting, and when admitted, entered the room as if conquering it.

He was surprised by what he found. The room was where somebody—Blocco?—lived, worked, slept. There was a small cot in a corner with bedclothes wadded at the foot and a dusty slipper sticking out from beneath the tick. A huge stack of papers, manuals, pamphlets half-stood beside, half-collapsed against a film-covered window, and on the adjacent ledge a one-eyed cat lay flicking its tail. Dust covered everything. A grizzled crone sat on a wooden stool with one arm raised and her naked dugs puddling in her lap, and Blocco, who'd been examining her, plainly didn't like the interruption. He turned to face Marcantonio, zipped through the conventional courtesies with just enough warmth to avoid insulting him, and then returned to probing the woman's underarm while answering his questions. There was nothing impressive about the director. He was square and short, with large ears and a pitted nose, and Marcantonio—who had difficulty not smiling at the man's too evident annoyance—found the thought of his reading Hippocrates ex cathedra ludicrous. Only his eyes were noteworthy, and this was because, Marcantonio concluded, they were too small. But as the interview continued—there were questions about the student organization or university proper, about its rumored boycott of a doctor of astrology, about disputations, della Torre's salaria, the French viscount—Marcantonio decided that, no, Blocco's eyes weren't small, they were embedded, mashed into his face where you couldn't get at them. Somehow you wanted his eyes, and it amused Marcantonio to think he withheld them deliberately. You'd need to pick the little man up and bash him into something to shake them out. The interview didn't drag on. Blocco soon muttered his condolences for Marcantonio's father—as if Girolamo hadn't been dead six years now!—and with a flick of his hand dismissed the subject and his visitor. Before Marcantonio reached the door, the director was peering back into the crone's face, gesticulating excitedly at the window, as though his encounter with medical history hadn't occurred.

Marcantonio della Torre soon came to regard Blocco's rudeness as typical. Over the following weeks he observed an identical lack of ceremony in the few colleagues he chanced to meet, in the aimless and unruly students, the town's populace, even the authorities. It became clear that what little information he'd possessed about Pavia was out of date. The only professors of any distinction there were the remnant of those lured from Florence and Venezia two decades earlier during the height of Ludovico Sforza's reign, and most of these lectured in Milan now, took no part in college affairs. What few figures of talent had strayed to Lombardy during the intervening years had either been coaxed by the French to join their renaissance on the Loire or had quickly moved on to more exciting posts in Turin, Pisa or Piacenza. Only the law faculty's preoccupation with Lombard juris prudence—of little use to the foreign rulers—had preserved it, so that ever since Louis Douze had marched into Milan in 1499 Pavia had been evolving into a law college with a small, loosely attached arts faculty of dubious legitimacy. Medical education was a joke. Far more emphasis was placed on the recuperative effects of lunar cycles than on the study of anatomy or reading of medical philosophy, and the only work a graduate could be certain to have read was the so-called *Book of Secrets*, a compendium of magic, recipes, folk wisdom and bawdy facts attributed to Albertus Magnus. It gradually became apparent to Marcantonio della Torre that, despite his reputation as the most notorious physician in one of Italy's most prestigious universities and Padua's most celebrated prodigy since Pico della Mirandola, Blocco had probably not heard of him. The director may have actually believed he was doing this ne'er-do-well son of his old friend a favor, may have regarded the young anatomist's arrival in Pavia as a colossal pain. The absurdity made della Torre laugh out loud. However, after soberer consideration, he decided that the situation was just as he desired. Truth was, everyone who'd ever tried to help him had been a nuisance. The admiration of students had gotten in his way, as had the crowds at his lectures. He'd come to Pavia seeking safety, a modest stipend, leisure. If the price was anonymity, well, that was no price.

So Marcantonio della Torre began to work. Nothing soothed him more than the rhythm of all-night dissections, breakfast on the veranda, a nap stretching into the early afternoon, then study, errands, disputations, followed by a return to the half-butchered body as the daylight cooled. There were few lectures and only a single public anatomy each year. Blocco's laconic invitation—Come!—had evidently meant only that, nothing more, and della Torre soon recognized that his expectation of a supply of cadavers had been foolish in the extreme. At first he considered complaining—if you couldn't impress Blocco, maybe you could frighten him—but by then his family's wealth had been placed at Marcantonio's disposal, and he decided matters were less complicated if he managed alone. His initial purchases were of poor quality—deteriorating corpses, obviously exhumed, some after lengthy exposure to moisture or vermin—and he could hardly use them, but his hulking confederate with the syphilitic cheek soon figured out the anatomist's preferences. Within weeks he could describe the available specimens as elaborately as a fishmonger crying his day's catch, always cautioning della Torre against hasty investments, and providing additional information of the most valuable sort: Yes, the molten lead had been poured into an incision below the pederast's diaphragm so the lungs were likely to be intact; or no, the pelvis had been pulled apart, not hacked, thus leaving the bones whole but the joints broken.

Perhaps it was the brutality of the petty tyrants who'd ruled Lombardy, the region's imperviousness to the republican sentiments of its neighbors, or it may have been the ancient character of the Lombard people, their predilection for military arts and low regard for new learning, or perhaps it was merely a result of living in the shadow of the castle's hulking walls, but for whatever reason, bodies in Pavia were never scarce. Rarely did Marcantonio go inquiring after the villain with the rotting face that he didn't find his accomplice with death to sell. And sometimes his wares included exotic extras. Della Torre found himself actually turning down opportunities that at other periods of his life would have been unimaginable—a hermaphrodite dead of natural causes and perfectly preserved, a teenage girl with a fetus in her womb, a man so ancient his arteries felt like straw and, when bent, cracked.

In the midst of such abundance, della Torre could hardly regret the absence of meddlesome colleagues, but from his earliest days in Pavia the disorderliness of the students infuriated him. Performance at daily disputations was atrocious, harassment or even violence against professors wasn't unheard of, and the resultant servility of the medical faculty had pretty well ruined those two or three colleagues— especially one erratic young Bavarian commentator of Hippocrates' *Epidemics*—whom otherwise della Torre might have found amusing. The scholars' only real enthusiasm seemed to be for their nightly carousals in the Piazza del Duomo, and so long as the legal faculty's prerogative to supply clerks for the civil service went uncontested, the law college let boys be boys. If it hadn't been for the French—who customarily tolerated local disturbances up to a reasonable level then stepped in, arrested everyone, lopped off the preferred hand, tongue, and testicle of somebody with no influence—della Torre might have feared for his own safety, but he reassured himself that, so long as he drew no one's attention, the powers of the realm would fight on his side. He learned to ignore the sparse attendance and bored gazes at his readings, learned to lecture with his head down and eyes on the page as his own teachers had done. When an occasional barb or echo of his former sarcasm slipped out, he was reassured to note that no one stirred, and though he simply couldn't bring himself to allow pointers and prosectors at his yearly dissection, he modestly deprecated the significance of doing the cutting with his own hands. His caution wasn't necessary. The mass of students immediately recognized this uncouth innovation as the result of inexperience—if he were an authority, why would he degrade himself?—and despised him. As for the handful of youths who found Marcantonio's obscurities alluring, he did what he could, but by and large he remained aloof. The situation was hopeless, he told himself, and the age of martyrs had passed.

So Marcantonio della Torre accustomed himself to the benefits of anonymity. The manuscript collection in the castle tower contained an incomplete copy of a treatise on animal diseases, attributed to Galen in an ostentatious addendum, and though della Torre doubted its authenticity, he devoted his spare hours to studying it. Not a day's journey away was Milan, a city of 200,000, and when time permitted, della Torre traveled there in search of conversation and amusement. He saw Bramante's illusory chancel in the little church of San Satyro, inspected the Ospedale Maggiore and the massive Castello, and met Leonardo da Vinci, who like so many other Florentine artisans dabbled in anatomy and loved to chatter about it. But mostly there was the work. Marcantonio had had some success macerating nerves to separate them from adjoining blood vessels and had managed to pick apart the threads in a chunk of spinal cord he dried on the roof, but he could see that this was no real beginning. The bodies he dissected altered so radically in the three or four days he examined them and the movements he hypothesized had ceased so long before, that he was continually besieged by feelings of futility. How could he hope to understand what was always already gone? He now realized that the question wasn't whether Galen's theory or Aristotle's was the accurate one, but rather, how could you study either? In spite of the insurmountable obstacles, however, he managed to follow the vagus nerve farther into the cranium and down its threadlike branchings than he'd ever done before, and though he was nowhere near drawing conclusions, he already suspected that whatever passed from the heart and blood vessels into the brain and nerves underwent a far more astonishing transformation than he'd previously dreamed.

At about this time in Pavia a skirmish broke out between the students, some merchants and the French authorities. A young law scholar was discovered in exuberant carnal intercourse with a French lieutenant's imported concubine, and when the French garrison assembled in the piazza to degrade, flog and dismember the lad, the students and townspeople rose up against their oppressors. Actually, this sounds more momentous than the little brawl was. All it included was an exchange of obscene gestures, a shower of crockery and dead cats, the detonation of five harquebusses—two of which misfired—

followed by a ramshackle charge from a dozen locals armed with rakes and andirons. The only injury was to a French sentry who received a powder burn, and the rioters exhausted themselves beating up the masonry on the house where the guards fled. However, in the confusion the convicted adulterer escaped, and that night a band of drunk students did impressive damage to several establishments in an area close to the French barracks. This created a complex and tension-filled situation. The French now needed to make a point of their virility and so threatened arbitrary mayhem on everyone Italian unless the criminal was hanged. Had the French restricted their threats to the students, the townspeople would've certainly cooperated. As it was, however, the locals couldn't enjoy a snotty law clerk's execution without appearing to have succumbed. A handful of townsmen met secretly and proclaimed their sympathy for the accused and their undying hatred for all things Gallic. Of course, the students—most of whom were Swiss, anyway—couldn't have cared less about the townsmen and cared hardly more about their fellow, it being brashly conceded among them that hanging was a small price to pay for one night with the woman in question. However, they always enjoyed looting, and the civil unrest offered a good opportunity. They swore eternal fealty with their brother, threatened retaliation. The French viceroy sent a small band of reinforcements down from Milan. Two cannons were pulled out into the piazza. Pavia settled down to wait.

Marcantonio della Torre wasn't about to get involved in this madness, and had a letter not arrived from Verona, he would've done his best never to cross his threshold again until everyone intent on murdering someone had finished. But the hulking machinery of influence had turned, and some cousin somewhere was writing to ask, not that della Torre assist the unfortunate law student—whom the cousin didn't know and suspected wasn't worth the trouble—but that certain prized connections required Marcantonio to register the family's *attempt* to assist, preferably with someone conspicuously placed. Della Torre, of course, knew no one conspicuously placed and wasn't about to jeopardize his privacy, but he figured he could safely inform the director of the medical faculty that, if the youth were reprieved, some dangerous person in Rome would be pleased. At Blocco's apartment della Torre was again told that the director was with an infirm, but when this time Marcantonio smiled, apologized for the interruption, and asked only for a more suitable time, the old nun looked as agitated as before. Her eyes darted from the ceiling to the floor; she coughed as if uncertain what to do, then told him to wait and rushed from the room. She was gone so long that della Torre grew angry and was beginning to divert himself with a lofty denunciation of the simpering farce medical education in Pavia had become when the woman reappeared.

She kept her head down, merely muttered some indecipherable syllables, and motioned toward Blocco's door. As della Torre entered, he saw the old nun scurry—in what looked like hand-waving and clumsy panic—back down the dark corridor from which she'd just come.

If Marcantonio della Torre had been surprised by the dirt, closeness and general disorder of the director's room on his first visit, he was dumbstruck now. Robes and linen, loose pages, slippers, a rope, a foul-smelling chamber pot, medical instruments and broken dishes were strewn on furnishings and across the floor. Drawers and cabinets were open, boxes and trunks had been shoved into the corners, and a dry and crumbling brick of partially eaten cheese sat on the seat of what appeared to be the only chair. However, the most astounding change was the addition of two wooden cots to the already crowded room. In one of these lay an aged man, utterly naked with his skinny genitals flopped on the sheet and his head tilted back with a rag over his eyes. In the other cot a small figure lay on its side with its back turned to the anatomist. Della Torre couldn't tell whether it was a young boy or girl, but something about its absolute stillness and the inhuman crook of its neck convinced him the child was dead. Blocco was down on his hands and knees on the floor beside the child's cot rummaging through a tangle of bedclothes and hissing curses. Sweat had soaked his white blouse—he wasn't wearing his gown—and across his nose he'd placed a pair of the new lenses, called spectacles, for correcting vision. He took no notice of his visitor for several moments, as if lost in hysterical, pointless searching. Then he seemed to recollect himself, rocked back on his heels, demanded to know why della Torre had come.

The directness of the question infuriated him. Marcantonio peered down at the little director, at the specks of his eyes that, now with the new lenses, looked even smaller, more pathetically meager. Acknowledging him was a humiliation. Tolerating his rudeness seemed inconceivable. For an instant, Marcantonio had difficulty speaking, found himself—ridiculously—recalling his whole celebrated history, his meteoric rise, thrill of holding a heart in his fist, hushed crowds inside the amphitheater. This tiny creature seemed so accidental. And the young anatomist came very close to turning on his heel and striding right back out of the apartment and Pavia. However, because wisdom so rarely acts this way, he began instead to explain in as supercilious a manner as possible how his family, because of their ancient respect in Venezia, had been approached by an unnamed prince to intercede on behalf of the wrongfully accused law scholar, and though della Torre had himself no interest in this matter beyond that of seeing justice done, his family had selected him as intermediary because of his renown as the foremost anatomist in Padua. Here he paused briefly to allow his words to sink in, then elaborated a few details and concluded that, if the director of the medical faculty were able to contribute to the just and equable resolution of the unhappy affair, forces of eminence in the eastern states would be favorably disposed to him. With this, della Torre spun around and was leaving when he noticed the little director's mouth agape and his tiny eyes bulging moronically. Marcantonio didn't know what to think. Had the simpleton not understood? Had he finally recognized who was standing in front of him? Marcantonio snorted, took a step back into the room, and was beginning an impatient reiteration of his message when the director's hand suddenly flew up into his face.

You come to me with *this*!! Blocco blurted out. Then before Marcantonio della Torre could take a breath, the small man spat out, Idiot!

Months would pass before della Torre would be able to stop hearing Blocco's voice or hear it without starting to tremble. He would repeatedly imagine inflicting on the astounded director the kind of withering sarcasm from which tender souls had been known to die, or bursting into contemptuous laughter before his startled eyes, or simply grabbing the man's throat, lifting him off the floor, and slamming his spine against a wall. And he'd waste countless hours trying to explain to himself why, as Blocco stood there glaring up into his face, Marcantonio had done none of these things, had remained as perplexed and helpless as a nine-year-old boy. He recalled the director muttering something about blindness, shaking his head emphatically, and as della Torre searched the universe for even one word his bulbous, dry tongue could utter, as he struggled against the water in his knees and weakness in his arms, he remembered the director pushing himself up from floor, taking della Torre's elbow in his grip, and—not violently, not hurriedly, just with the casual movement of kicking dry catshit over a threshold— shoving the anatomist out the door.

For the next several days Marcantonio della Torre did nothing but relive it. When at last his thoughts began to clear, he couldn't recall how he'd gotten from the little hospice back to his apartment, when he'd last eaten or slept, or precisely how much time had passed. He remembered wandering a narrow alley at dusk, hearing a woman cackle, being stopped once by soldiers who, perhaps because of his confusion, let him continue on his way. No memory or thought mitigated the event's intolerable closeness. Eventually its agonies began to subside into a shapeless gloom from which Marcantonio could arouse himself only by declaring the director a madman. He now missed the students and colleagues that in the past had seemed such a distraction. He would walk out onto his balcony and, gazing up at the castle's blockish façade, imagine himself standing in the midst of a huge dissecting theater, the faces huddled round the cadaver, Galen's words rising in his throat. He didn't know how to doubt his science or the knife's revelations, but his intelligence seemed to him to be shrinking. He decided to return to the rhythm of work and sleep, expecting it to reassure him, and was amazed when it failed. His thoughts were scattered, his concentration weak. He began going to bed while it was still dark, and for the first time since listening to his father read from Aristotle's *De generatione* outside the privy, for the first time in Marcantonio's thirty years, the smell of death nauseated him.

Ironically, he had many more hours now for work than at any time since arriving in Pavia, for the standoff with the French had brought virtually every public activity to a halt. Shops closed to avoid the thefts and beatings, and the law faculty seized the opportunity to visit distant libraries or take pilgrimages. One afternoon della Torre found himself explicating a tortured passage from *De usu partium* in the hospital amphitheater before a single, pimply boy, and there was talk that the French might suspend classes altogether, a severe economic blow to the farmers. In all of Pavia only the syphilitic villain who procured della Torre's cadavers continued to be as active as before. Whereas in the beginning of their association the two men had met only at della Torre's instigation, now the pocky rogue would knock softly at the scullery every three or four nights, and though the anatomist no longer made as many purchases—this, despite a notable increase in the offerings— the men continued to discuss their business with great deliberateness. They'd stand inside the doorway or foyer or sometimes the unlovely fellow would squat with his back against a wall or on occasion they'd enter the kitchen where della Torre would seat himself in a heavy chair and listen to the genders, ages, deterioration, difficulty of acquisition, and cause of death—by knife blade or falling or frailty or some vague natural cause—of each mortality. Neither man was by nature disposed to be talkative, but their mutual interest led them to speak of miscellaneous things, and in this way della Torre learned of the proposed settlement of the town's crisis and the opportunity it offered him.

As della Torre's confederate explained, the French had located an ague-ridden goatherd in the lunga dimora where he'd been confined for urinating on an icon in the duomo, and had sentenced him to an athletic sequence of stretchings, joint-poppings, brandings and lacerations preparatory to beheading, from all of which—except the beheading—he'd been reprieved. The idea, of course, was to demonstrate the French viceroy's authority to do whatever he damn-well-pleased simultaneously with his fundamental goodheartedness. As part of an official non-agreement worked out with the local leaders, various guildsmen would be allowed to respond to this perfectly arbitrary sentence with a protest that—in exchange for the French dropping all charges against the still at-large law student—would trail off in a flurry of

208

pointless bluster. The students didn't like this or any other settlement that ended their party, but the merchants noised it about that, one demurral and poweee! Which made the truce unanimous. The significance of all this for della Torre was that, despite having spent his entire adulthood wrist deep in mutilated criminals, he'd never actually witnessed dying. Now in the midst of his struggle to arbitrate between the heart and head, he had a chance to observe the soul depart. And just as important, his confederate promised to get the body for him.

It was just what Marcantonio needed to lift his spirits. Preparations began several days before the execution and built to a festive climax as the moment for beheading neared. There were implements to clean, a scaffold to build, military ceremonies to practice, arrangements for cordoning the piazza, and of course, food, wine, musicians, jugglers, etc. A French cardinal was traveling from Rome to divide final duties with the tottering dean of the duomo, and there was talk of an assassin, deeply schooled in the lore of bodily mangling, being shipped in from Lyons. Marcantonio wasn't enticed by death's technology, and having flayed a dozen babies' faces, his gorge didn't rise at bloody stumps or gore. Nevertheless, as the morning approached, he found himself as excited as the most sanguinary blood-lecher. He wasn't sure what he hoped to see. A rush of air from the vessels and nerves? A sudden stillness when the blade struck the medulla? The odor of sulphur or dew? But having been stymied by every prior discovery, he came to the ceremony like a pilgrim to a shrine. He felt humbled, ready to be done with as the gods of knowledge chose. He took advantage of his nocturnal habits to arrive early at the scaffold, and when he found a sizeable throng already gathered, he relied upon his academic robes to disguise his hard elbows and rude shoving. He finally got a good spot near the platform's chopping-end between two French youths with halberds and just a trace of whiskers, and as morning broke on the rooftops, he felt the crowd stir around him like a caterpillar on a warm stone.

The prisoner emerged from a brick passageway just as the first sunlight struck the piazza, urged on by a burly troglodyte and three guards. He appeared to have slept deeply, or perhaps only to have grown so accustomed to his cell's dankness that between consciousness and oblivion he hardly distinguished. His eyes were half-open, he squinted at his spectators as at a phantasmagoria. Except for an initial cringe, he offered little resistance and, when prodded, stumbled ahead like a groggy pachyderm. The crowd began to hoot, catcall. Acrobats vaulted out of alleyways or leaped at the cordon of soldiers. A juggler tossed a chicken skyward; mimes aped the hatchet's fall. Even the soldiers got into the spirit, tossing back the vegetables and offal that bounced off their prisoner's chest. Only the condemned goatherd himself remained serene. He trudged toward the block, craning his neck and blinking his eyes as if trying to make out the surrounding shapes, to awaken from his dream.

Then a curious thing occurred. As the man allowed himself to be pushed down onto his knees for the cardinal's blessing, he looked straight ahead—toward the waiting block, into the sun, almost at the place where della Torre stood—and for the first time seemed to know his nightmare wasn't a nightmare, that his head was about to be cut off. He went insane. He leapt at the cardinal, catching him under the chin with his chained wrists and driving him into a soldier who, in his astonishment, fell backwards off the platform. The burly fellow who'd followed the goatherd from the tunnel jumped onto his back and began beating his head, while a seasoned French infantryman deftly jammed his pike into the man's chained ankles. More or less everyone went down in a tangle, out of which the shrieking prisoner was yanked by his hair and stretched over the block amid vigorous cheering. Everywhere fists and elbows and body parts were jutting out. It took the reputedly virtuoso executioner two shots to do any damage, and by then he'd so terrified his would-be assistants that they were rapidly getting their hands and fingers out of the way. The result of all this was that, when the maladroit killer at last struck the condemned man's neck—cleaving the spine and pharynx and setting his cranium free—the goatherd's noggin bounced down off the block, missed the basket, struck the floor a merry thump, and hopped right out into the crowd.

It landed in Della Torre's hands. He wasn't startled by the shower of blood or sudden impact, and though the surge of bodies nearly drove him onto a halberd, he managed to hang on. He felt the soft cheeks with his finger tips, felt the nose pressing into his palm, and as he fumbled for the splintered vertebrae to turn the face upward, della Torre made the most astonishing discovery of his life. The man was still alive. His mouth and eyes were working frantically, his expression was as animated as any della Torre had ever seen, and his tongue flopped in his jaw like a salmon. Later della Torre would have ample opportunity to disbelieve what he'd witnessed, would recall tales of decapitated crocodiles writhing in the mud and would remember his own boyhood observation of a pig's lively demise, but now as he peered into the goatherd's face he could doubt that this man was trying to scream only if he doubted the faces around him had minds. So here was the mystery! He held a soul in his hands. Of course, no sooner had it all happened than the soul retreated—eyelids eased down, tongue lolled, lips went flaccid and blue. But even as the anatomist's mind spun and his legs wobbled, he felt a fierce joy rising in his heart. He *would* take this man home! He thrust the head into his bloody robe, ignored the soldiers' commands, and beating back the crowd's groping fingers, della Torre plunged right into the roiling throng.

From there everything was a single stripe of color until he finally stood over the small table inside his apartment and—with knife, probes, pincers—descended into the apostate's eyes. He worked his way through each ventricle where the sprite might hide, sniffed out every damp cranny, even ascended the spiraling pathway of the ear, found nothing. But his memory of the soul's nearness, of having held the spirit in his palms, seemed to transform these frustrations. He'd known life! Only moments earlier, everything he'd ever desired had dwelt in this flesh and cartilage before him, these very nerves and tissues. Even if the accidents were now missing, even if the soul's residues had been masked and its essence vaporized, still this head was home to man. There would be no going back. Knowledge was changed. And as the hours passed and heat came and went and his own arms grew cramped and perspiration soaked his bloody gown, Marcantonio saw himself in the dissecting theater once again, guiding disputations, explicating tirelessly for colleagues, students, laboring to share the love that filled his heart.

When he finally heard the pounding on his door, he knew it had gone on forever. It had followed him from Padua, slipped over the walls he'd placed around him, made force into his undoing once again. It was the French soldiers! But then he heard a familiar, gruff voice float up from the alley, fell silent. Suddenly, he exploded into a great guffaw. Rushing into the hallway, through the kitchen, Marcantonio flung the door open wide. It was his pocked assistant, come with two sulky thugs to deliver their wares. Della Torre was effusive with apology, slapped the rogues' shoulders, brought out drink and was reaching deep in his wallet to erase the insult of his inhospitality when his confederate stepped closer, looked him morosely in the eye and said: They've closed the university.

It was impossible. But the man handed Marcantonio a ripped-down pronouncement, written in both French and Latin, which, although the hoodlum couldn't read it himself, he'd been given to understand would explain the whole thing. Stringent measures, it said. Unhappily necessitated. Perilous miasma. Authorities. Della Torre tried to make it out but couldn't compose his thoughts. He was beginning to pant. After traveling so far, defeating ignorance, overcoming worldly obstacles, how could this be the end? He tried reading again but got no farther. His head was spinning, he needed to lie down. And then in a column of scrawls at the bottom he spied Blocco's name.

And Marcantonio della Torre was moving. It was the middle of the night. He might be wanted by the authorities. He didn't know. He wore a robe streaked with dry blood. He didn't care. He was going to put an end to the pounding on his door or slit Blocco's throat. He felt like himself again, freed from the jail of confusion, a lucid mind in a cosmos of dolts. Abundant explanations for his past frustrations now rushed into his thoughts. The little director had been a collaborator with the French all along, had from the beginning considered the anatomist's recalcitrance a danger. How else would Blocco have acquired his high position? The crisis had been the director's own doing, had been concocted to serve his barbarous masters and defeat native learning. Small wonder he'd received Marcantonio della Torre without fanfare! Marcantonio saw at last the wisdom of what he'd often heard, always soto voce, usually in the mouths of Florentines, that only weakness and apostasy came of Italy's division. How long would the proud descendants of the Caesars submit to Germans and Gauls? Such phrases had sounded preposterous before, but now he muttered them again and again, told himself that Blocco had betrayed—not just science, not just his pupils, certainly not just Marcantonio della Torre—but his homeland! The man was contemptible, vile. There was something finished about these explanations that, even in the midst of the anatomist's fury, seemed satisfying.

When della Torre arrived at the little apartment beside the hospice, he was surprised to discover a frenzy of activity. Nuns and various waifs scurried or wandered about, beds spilled down the stairs and into the street, everywhere voices could be heard keening. The air was full of the odor of unguents, urine, boiled linens. On the steps a beggar with blueish skin was being bled. Women, seeing the anatomist's blood-soaked robe, clutched at his hands, called him Physician! Redeemer! Their idolatrous tone sounded lascivious and full of threats. Della Torre had intended to rush into Blocco's room, lift the little man right off the ground, just as he should have done from the first. His rage seemed so pure that he could imagine nothing through which it wouldn't pass. But now as he picked his way amid the noisy and grotesque landscape, he could hardly believe how diffuse his purpose had become. From nowhere, a naked man rushed forward and flung himself onto the anatomist's chest. There was an animal shininess in his eyes, and his breath was repulsively saccharine. Della Torre had to strike him repeatedly just to escape. Everywhere, similar disorders threatened to engulf him. None of this was what was happening, he wanted to insist. And yet it confused him. Why should the future manifest itself amid such predictable misery?

Della Torre finally located the director in a small courtyard he stumbled upon after winding down endless corridors of nausea and groans. Blocco lay flat on his back on a stone bench. His tiny eyes were open, and through his spectacles he was gazing straight up at the moon. The young anatomist stopped a few feet away, looked down at the man's head. Now that he was here, Marcantonio felt unsure of himself. His denunciations that, moments before, sounded so scathing, now seemed almost silly. Blocco knew nothing, taught nothing, stood for nothing. It was like invoking God's wrath to swat a fly. Blocco's scalp looked patchy. His hands were as small as a child's. Maracantonio badly wanted a meteor to crush the man, but he had no idea what to say.

Then Blocco spoke: We need the rooms, he said. The scholars should be departed by the morrow. It's best if the neighboring regions remain ignorant of our plight. For the time. Of course, you'll want to go. There's a former associate of mine, a man much enamored of autopsy, newly ascended into a post of some prominence in Bologna. I haven't time to write him, but use my name. He'll certainly have heard of you....

Blocco's voice trailed off. He gave a weak wave with his hand, a gesture of futility or dismissal.

Who is we? Marcantonio finally asked. He hardly recognized his own voice. For a moment he imagined sucking the sentence back down his throat.

Blocco made the same vague gesture with his hand, repeated: We. Then he chuckled. You know, I always wanted to ask ...it's idle .... He fell silent.

Della Torre didn't speak.

Well, it's idle, but do you think what the ancients tell us about the homunculus is true? Could it really pass through the spine? I only ask because once I saw a notary hanged and noticed his organ rise to the manly state as the vertebrae snapped, and this seemed ...well, I thought you might have witnessed ....

The ducts within the nervous tissues are minute, della Torre said. The contents—it's impossible to discern them clearly.

It doesn't matter, the director replied. A curiosity.

I've wondered myself. I don't know.

Yes.

Silence again. The courtyard felt peculiar, a kind of cool place amid thick heat. In the sky the stars were glinting, as if the spheres held back hellfire, letting pandemonium seep to earth through cracks and pits. All around the young anatomist were purple shrubs, dwarf poplars, colorless grass. Far away an animal howled. Della Torre took a deep breath: It has come to my notice ...the Gauls ..., he began, then started again. Your name appeared on the document, and some explanation ...it would seem the least ....

Blocco saved him by nodding vigorously. Della Torre relaxed. The little director wasn't going to pretend ignorance, at least, would acknowledge his infamy. It was something. But when della Torre paused, the man merely gazed back up at the moon. A minute passed.

At last, Blocco spoke: When I saw you anatomize the recreant in Padua, I was much amazed and became convinced this was a great work. I'd never hoped to speak with you of it. I remember being pressed against a very large, red-bearded fellow, I suppose some sort of mason from the dust that clung to him, and over the heads of the students and gentleman I could hardly see anything.

You—?! Della Torre's voice caught in his throat.

This was some years ago, Blocco continued. Your father, peace to his deserving spirit, was already with God. The director heaved a sigh. It was difficult. The day was insufferably warm, and everyone was so intent on the work of your knife—I was intent myself—that I felt I might be crushed in the frenzy. I recall that I was too timid to stand upon the bench, very conscious of my own black robes ...

Blocco stopped to laugh at himself, then went on.

We couldn't breathe. So I had to conceal my standing by crooking my knees a certain portion, all this underneath my robe, you see, so that I appeared to be seated, a man of some stature capable of peering over the others from my pew—I'm very short. Well, you opened the chest, exposed the viscera, held up each organ. To think, I had practiced the healer's art twenty years and had never witnessed such things, not like this, not so that I could see. I couldn't have drawn a heart so a child could know it, had myself imagined it round, more easily discernible. It was an astonishing thing. Anyway, watching you that day I had thought, perhaps, you know, you might have found the little man, in the blood ... Blocco's voice trailed off. He gave a kind of shrug or what would have been a shrug had he not been prone. As it was, it resembled a bear scratching.

Della Torre's mouth hung open. The blockhead had seen him defy the Dominicans, watched him thrust his hands wrist-deep in death, witnessed the new age .... It was as if a cadaver had moved. Della Torre flapped his jaw. You knew?

Knew?

About ...me?

And then Blocco did something della Torre had never seen. He opened his eyes. Knew? Why, everyone .... The very idea!

The little director sat up, wiped his spectacles: Why, we hung on the news, dreaded to hear what you'd found, yearned for each bit of gossip more frantically than the last. Knew? How many days in the refectory did my colleagues, all the physicians ...and, to think, right here in Pavia, in the midst of our suffering, our affliction ...a miracle of the new learning, this .... Blocco sputtered to an astonished halt then burst out laughing. Oh, my young doctor! Yes, yes, everybody knows about Marcantonio della Torre.

Standing alone in the little courtyard, gazing down at the chuckling man whose pathetic person had overshadowed the fine hatreds of his youth, had crumbled the edifice that neither sacrifice nor devotion could faze, Marcantonio della Torre struggled not to weep. He didn't know what was happening, couldn't grasp the simplest things. To his humiliation, he wanted someone to confide in. It seemed perfectly reasonable to believe that somebody somewhere knew more about what was happening than he did and would be able to guide him. He hadn't felt this way since he was a boy.

You really don't understand, do you? Blocco was standing now, peering at him.

Della Torre shook his head.

And so Blocco explained. Plague had been rampant in Pavia for four years. The signs had been equivocal at first, and they all—both the French authorities and the medical faculty—had discouraged talk. Gradually, however, the truth came out. Not only the vagabonds and poor, but even the citizenry began to be visited. Several medical students were sufficiently acquainted with the disease to see for themselves, and soon the university was in revolt. More and more of the French garrison drifted away, unwilling to lose their lives protecting Lombards, and the public peace began to be jeopardized. The disease stole into the finest palazzi, carried off young women, professors, a French captain, merchants, tore through the Carthusian brotherhood, threatened to engulf the town. Anyone leaving had to conceal himself, anyone entering was a fool. Death was everywhere. And what could a physician do?

Here the little man paused, his voice gentle, like speaking to an invalid or decrepit grandam. And, you see, it was in the midst of all this ...this waste, pandemonium ...when all hope seemed lost, that the miracle occurred: Marcantonio della Torre, greatest physician of the new age, was coming to our aid. It was the answer to a prayer none of us had presumed to pray, our second chance, a cleansing, succor. Then Blocco shrugged. And of course, it was all a mistake.

And you knew ...about my ...in Padua?

I'd witnessed it myself! That was just the point, don't you see? We hoped so much, thought you possessed, perhaps, some balm, a secret herbal or ancient purgative, or even some miracle of the surgeon's art.

I never grasped—

Blocco waved the remark aside. From the first time I saw you I realized the error. You had nothing to offer, hadn't come for that, were hardly a physician. I'm still at a loss what to call you—not a philosopher exactly, no scholar. A man experienced but without age or—pardon my bluntness—wisdom. A self-born god. Expert. Whatever, it was plain from my first meeting with you that our hopes had been fantastic. You were too much this new being. Our miseries seemed mere distractions. I say this without bitterness, although at the time, you can imagine how disappointed we all were.

Della Torre said nothing. His body felt flat as a bladder. All the bewilderments of the previous months, the abundance of cadavers, their puzzling mutilations—della Torre shivered at the thought. The syphilitic rascal knew better than to show buboes to a physician! Everything made such impeccable sense.

Blocco coughed. I'd like to continue but. He nodded toward the hospice. The abruptness had returned to his voice, his eyes were lost again.

I wish you great deeds, he went on. If fortune wills it—and for an instant his face took on a childlike expression—I would treasure the chance to ...

And he reached out his hand in farewell, or perhaps just to touch Marcantonio.

And that was when it happened. Marcantonio della Torre, son of the renowned Girolamo della Torre, trustee of the ancients' learning, rival of Mondino, vessel of the future, Italy's celebrated prodigy, death's disciple, the ardent lover of life—had been summoned to a city rife with plague. He looked at the creature cringing in front of him, eyes wincing, hand outstretched. This insect had tried to kill him.

And as Blocco, standing there, began to sense the queerness of the anatomist's silence, as he shrugged, dropped his hand and turned back toward the mayhem inside, della Torre grabbed him.

Wha—!

Lifting the director into the air, depriving the writhing and astonished little body of ground, Marcantonio della Torre strode to the twisted fruit tree in the center of the court and, without passion, as the square torso squirmed and kicked and spluttered and swore, slammed the director's spine into the trunk. The skull hit, spectacles bounced and shattered on the stones. There was a terrible crunch, a rattle the anatomist felt in his arms, and with genuine happiness he saw Blocco's eyes pop wide open, saw the disbelief inside, and let the director's tiny body crumple to earth.

Marcantonio della Torre returned home with a clear mind and a bounce in his step. He was pleased to find that the gang of thugs had gone, that the apartment was quiet, that he was alone. He locked the door, settled himself at the kitchen table, and for the first time since fleeing Padua, he felt that there was nothing to fear. Perhaps he wouldn't leave Pavia, or not at once. Close down the university, close down the library and merchants; would the isolation be worse than what he'd always known? Mortality had become his natural element. Who could say what miracles the future might hold?

All that had been some time ago—exactly how long, the anatomist's story didn't say. If the pestilence was spreading, as the director of the medical faculty had feared, then the authorities had kept it quiet. More likely it was devouring itself, peaking, beginning to abate or move east. In Milan everyone knew Pavia had the sickness, that visiting the place involved risks, but since the deaths weren't obtrusive, many went anyhow. No buboes had turned up at the Ospedale Maggiore, despite the shuttling of merchants and couriers, and there was more gossip about the Pope and Emperor's feud than about the infestation. The Pavian university continued to be shut down, but street-corner savants preferred political to medical explanations. Anyway, the threat of plague wasn't confining Leonardo da Vinci yet, although the rumors had made him more conscientious about his diet and bathing.

As the anatomist's story concluded, Leonardo found the vagaries of chronology unsettling. For all he knew, the climax could've occurred that very evening, this cadaver on the table could be the one Marcantonio retrieved from the scaffold. Perhaps, just as Leonardo entered the door, the young anatomist had been returning from the director's apartment .... But, no, no, this neck hadn't been hacked, not in the manner the anatomist described, and the skin and vessels were supple, unweathered. Not a goatherd. Recognizing the differences, however, Leonardo felt how flimsy the differences were. A body was anybody, and the longer one lay on the table, the deeper you went, the less its history mattered, the more humanity became one flesh. There were freaks, of course. The centenarian Leonardo had anatomized at Santa Maria Nuova in Florence, for instance, had a liver with only four lobes! But even in that odd case, or the infant's thigh he'd acquired in Venice, the idiosyncrasies might be attributable to age or disease. Surely rot and decay were everybody's, the viscera were everybody's, the flies, candles, even della Torre's panic, or Leonardo's own weather-speckled hands ...well, what *wasn't* everybody's?

It made your head spin. The anatomist had concluded his tale laughing shrilly, too long, the way Leonardo had sometimes heard youths do. The man sat hunched forward now, the bottle held idly between two fingers, his eyes staring off at God knew what. For unclear reasons, Leonardo was beginning to feel embarrassed, wanted to make some convivial, pointless remark just to dispel the gloom. He wished he'd never heard these stories.

So, as I said, bad faith, bad faith! The anatomist's voice mimicked finality.

Leonardo didn't take up the challenge.

I sometimes wonder, will it ever be done? Della Torre nodded at the corpse. They rot so quickly, what matters goes bad ...

Leonardo shrugged. You're young, you have—

Don't tell me I'm young—again—don't tell me I'm young. I'm sick of hearing that.

Leonardo said nothing.

Italy's a dunghill, della Torre muttered. I've worked very hard. Accidents have surprised me.

You're speaking foolishly, Leonardo replied. Your surprise—if it deserves the name—is self-fashioned. Look at Matteo da Rimini, look at the surprise that undoes a—

Who?

Leonardo turned towards him. Matteo da Rimini, he repeated.

Marcantonio della Torre continued to watch Leonardo, brows furrowed, then gave a peremptory nod. Well, you're right. But I just thought there was—more. I opened the heart. He smiled. I held life in my hands.

You're a teacher.

Della Torre laughed, took a vigorous, sloppy gulp from the bottle.

Leonardo suspected it was empty. Perhaps you should move, try Bologna.

Move?

Yes, to Bologna or Salerno or, now that the French are in retreat, you might even be welcome back in Padua. There's nothing to keep you. Especially if the memories are unpleasant ....

Della Torre continued to stare at him. Move?

Yes, yes. Move. It's not so peculiar, is it?

Leonardo felt weary. Perhaps he should visit his friend another time, when the weather seemed less threatening. There was much to be learned from him, but somehow, the storm had spoiled the occasion. Conversation was becoming difficult.

Move? Della Torre said a third time.

The anatomist's face looked positively stuporous, insipid.

Yes, confound your soul! Leonardo bellowed. Movement, motor, motive, mobile, motion, *moooooove*! Leonardo leaped to his feet, grabbed his cap from the chifforobe, pointed to his own legs, and now unrestrainedly shouting at the young man, marched into the hall: Like this!

Leonardo's breath came in pants, his chest pounded. He could hear the young man following him to the door, but couldn't bear to look back. Leonardo had no idea what was dismaying him, but he knew he must get away, breathe air, erase this barbarous architecture, the blockish city, hulking walls. At the doorway he fumbled with the catch, had to wait for the anatomist to get it open. They said nothing, but Leonardo already sensed his impatience wavering, the forewarning of tomorrow's embarrassment, remorse.

The young man drooped his head, looked lifeless, abashed. He drew the door back, held it. Leonardo quickly stepped through, turned on the threshold, stammered: I ...it's very late ...so weary—

Della Torre's black eyes rolled upward in lagoons of filmy white,

fixed on Leonardo. Traitor, he said.
      And closed the door.

"So where're the quote marks?"
      I'm sitting here trying not to sweat up the four stacks of pages I've
managed to assemble into a rough order out of scattered episodes from
the only kind of story I believe I believe in anymore as Metro, the beach
monster, and I all await either liberation or more poison—which turn
our fortune takes seems pretty arbitrary—here in my yellow American
brontosaurus beneath a thirty-foot monument to an unspeakable
Venus while half a mile away doomed men are struggling to make their
pointless fate seem human to those of us who're confident we are, and
the man's question concerns punctuation.
      "In the story," the beach monster continues, "when the people
speak, y'know, where're the quote marks?" Its other head looks at me.
The eye in its forehead blinks. Several of its tentacles tighten about my
private parts.
      "You a college professor?" I ask.
      Its glower intimates its failure to enjoy my wit. "Look, d'you want
me to read your story? Guys like me, I mean?"
      "There was a time when poets said no to that question. I don't live
in that time."
      "So put in the quotes."
      "I'm learning a game," I say, as smooth under fire as Billy
Buckley. "If it's an interesting game, that's because it shows something
other games don't. Learning to play's not so hard, you already know
everything you need to, but what's strange isn't rules. I mean, the
changes aren't accidental. Learning's playing because learning's playing. I can't persuade you to play, but—"
      "Put in the quotes."
      "Nope."
      A few flames shoot from his mouth, the spikes on his tail twitch,
he exposes one claw "Whazzamatter, you didn't go to grade school?
When your people in a book speak, you put the wiggly worms around'em.
Like-kiss." He raises both hands, curls two fingers of each, makes a
quotation of his head.
      "Is this a law like gravity or a law like taxes?"
      He continues: "What's society comin' to, huh? A man wants ya to
read his book, he writes ordinary. Simple. You wanna write for snots,
artsy-fartsies, okay—your business, be queer, but when normal people
talk they talk normal. There're dictionaries for this stuff."
      "Whence hails the outlandish fable that 'when normal people

talk, they talk etc.' What if when I write like normal people talk—I mean, when you talk, do you put words in quotes? Do you do it when you repeat what you've heard? Is anything you say anything you haven't heard? If I repeat the words of a jingle, will you mistake them for my words if I don't announce, watchout, here comes a quote? If I talk about truth, justice and the American way, is there anything I can do, anything imaginable, to keep the words *out* of quotes? And are any of these rhetorical questions? So, what if, whenever I write the way normal people talk, what if normal people say, write normal! And what if, when I write the way nobody ever talks, the way nobody *can* talk anymore even if he/she/it wanted to, even if he/she/it knew how and cared and mistook doing it for a law, what if then normal people say: yeah, yeah, that's right, that's the way! Huh?"

"Put in the quotes."

"Up your fanny, shithead!"

His monster lip curls, his monster teeth grind. I think he won't bite me. I don't know he won't bite me. In our great nation crimes of passion are habitually provoked by departures from grammar. But, praise Allah, the danger passes. "You rich?" he finally asks.

At this juncture Metro turns his eye upon the beach monster and distinctly says: You, fatman, are far dumber than a dog.

"I grant you, a bright yellow 1955 Buick Roadmaster is sufficiently grotesque and pointless to resemble the costly toys of brain-dead millionaires," I say. "But, just between the two of us, let's admit that the temperature outside has climbed to 165 degrees and I'm driving a car with no air conditioning."

He shakes his head very slowly. He gazes at the wad of pages in his fist, the four stacks on my lap, my story all over the seats, dash, floor. "It took you like lot more'n a weekend to write this," he mumbles.

"Holidays."

"...just to be weird?"

This question is asked me by an obese man in a chartreuse shirt with large ocher and crimson daffodils on it, wearing opaque wrap-around sunglasses, thongs, seated in a twenty-two foot long yellow box surrounded by unmoving cars as far as the eye can see at a video simulation of public suffering enacted by plague victims and cops in space suits as the professional defenders of my national security fly back and forth overhead filling the air with toxins.

"If we didn't both know that sincerity is always a ploy, I'd struggle to convince you with all sincerity that never once in my life have I ever undertaken to do anything just to be weird. Such a statement wouldn't be true, of course, but it would be prodigiously less untrue than its contrary."

"Then why?" he asks and takes off his sunglasses.

For a moment I rummage the cornucopia of glibness. I don't speak. I'm surprised to discover that he has the pale eyes and long, amber lashes of an eleven-year-old boy. We sit there sweating, eyeball to eyeball, in a veritable landfill of my sentences, paragraphs, pages. I want to grab a fistful of story, stuff it down his throat: Read, Goddammit! But the futility's total. Nothing's ever enough. For the first time since the thirty-foot woman possessed my mind, since Deirdre hung up and our private number rang into an empty room, the English language contains no word that's mine.

"   ."

"I'm asking 'cause I'm curious, see," the monster continues.

"People like a story—I'm not different. And I read here about this little queer bit, Sally—"

"Salai."

"Like I said, and I c'n see he's fucked up. It's creepy, and I wanna know why. Can't help. It's a story! But then I think, the guy writes like he don't want me to know—"

"Like I don't want you to *not* know."

"Anyway, reading's not easy, but not the way mistakes're not easy. I mean, you worked at it. So I ask, why's this guy making life harder'n it is?"

"Some kinds of boxes, vehicles ..." But I can see it's going nowhere. I shrug. "I wanted to write a story that wouldn't let you off the hook."

In a world where anything can happen I'm still surprised when it does: Gargantua smiles.

"Well, I guess you did that," he laughs. "I mean, is all this stuff true? I mean, really."

"Naw. The facts aren't—a lot of them—they're bogus. Some of it's just wrong... I changed—"

"But was it like that? D'you think the Leonardo guy really didn't know, like you say? It's int'resting. What if here people act like he was this kind of genius, saw the future'n'all, who had a grasp, knew everything, when really he was just a ...well, like anybody. But then he still did those things! Or almost or he tried to. D'you really believe that? It's int'resting. I mean like heroes, y'know, maybe some heroes are dumb-fucks, trapped, y'see?"

"I—"

And then from all sides sirens crucify our ears. Whoop—boop—boop—boop—boop—boop!

"Whazzat?"

"Rrruff."

"Yiiiiiiiiiiiiiiiiiiiiiiiiiiiiiiiiiiiii—"

"Oh shit."

Police cars, people running, ambulances, an old codger in a

hospital gown, cops in space gear, pandemonium, Hades spills forth. A middle aged, bloodless woman with her blouse torn and sweat dripping from her chin labors past our car in desperate pursuit of CPR. A black youth holding some kind of blood-soaked dressing to a bad cut on his face. Nurses. Stethoscopes. Several people in surgical gowns with what's got to be a body on a table, tubes, anesthesia trolleys, and blood, blood, blood. All this rolling down the sidewalk, weaving through the stranded autos, across the highway median, coming over the side rails and from behind billboards, seething from cracks in hell's gates or in civilization, you choose, while getting louder, above the sirens and shouts, the sound of klap-a-klap-a-klap-a and the not quite smell of whatever it was that, twice earlier today, made breathing the costliest need I know.

Hack, cough—cough, sputter, a-CHOOO! And back we go into Leonardo's box. But this time the universal misery's a little thinner, intermittent, not perfect, and so I can suck air longer through my fingers and look around for explanations. The helicopter sound is really loud, or kind of comes and goes as if the noise were right beside us then blown away, or on all sides of us, or right on top of us, but loud, louder than before. The beach monster sucks and passes; I suck and pass; Metro snorts and burrows under my fanny. But whenever I peek out from Leo's box, I don't see much, just the panic on all sides, a wave sweeping from right to left like the panicked crowds of 50's horror films, all of miniature Manhattan fleeing miniature Godzilla, waves of hoi polloi, wax then wane, safety's over here, no, over there, no, etcetera. Anyway, between gasps I'm rubber-necking and still I don't see, though the klap-a-klap-a seems too close not to, when all at once it's sailing right before my eyes. The cockpit's low to the ground, not five cars away from us, moving kind of unstraight, vaguely haywire, and in the door the blonde soldier's not waving anymore. The p.a. horn's gone, she's hanging onto some sort of strap, bouncing around pretty good, and— although there's no certainty in judgments of other persons' interior states—scared to death. The helicopter zigs this way, then kind of leaps up, surprised-like, rolls sideways in the fashion of a barge taking water, then leaps up again, zigs off leeward. Either it's an air show or it's Big Trouble. All this goes on at an altitude not as much higher than the trees and telephone poles and buildings as anyone directly concerned would like. Zig, hop, roll, klap-a-klap-a, zag.

Above the screams and heat prostration and sirens and plasma bottles and unconvincing simulations of "Armageddon visits Our Town," I determine the helicopter actually is Godzilla, full-sized, that here's the fright-flick the 50's urbanites around me are fleeing, and that the mechanical beast's undergoing a crisis of self-determination. The possible upshot of which is, nightmare of nightmares, Godzilla's about to meet Queen Kong, for at this very moment the rhythm of zig and hop and lean and swirl acquires a destiny, disclosing its trajectory to include my thirty-foot beloved's depthless head. A young man in green surgical pants suddenly pushes his face right up against my windshield and shrieks: "It's not true! It's not true!" A woman with red hair to fill a car trunk starts beating on his back. Godzilla tilts—left, right—roars, slashes suddenly upward, rights itself infinitesimally, then taking a bead on Her Majesty—the smooth-limbed, the unspeakable—slices down.

Klap-a-klap-a.

"Eeek! Eeek!"

Rrrrrmmmm—

Although between doom's prescience and its consummation lies but the sparking of a neuron, the time has come to explain my life:

After Deirdre's lawyer made us look like what we were by turning us into what we weren't, Deirdre and I reassured each other that our marriage was in terrific shape. Our "divorce" existed only on paper, for the benefit of persons who took documents seriously, it made no difference to us. "We don't need the government to tell us we're in love," I said. "Or the church," she added. "What's marriage anyway?" we echoed. "Up with lawless fornication!" And we spent half a paycheck on a celebratory dinner, a night of wantonness in a downtown hotel, Sunday breakfast in bed. We then settled into our newly unmarried lives, a principal feature of which was talking about how nothing had changed. We moved into the apartment above DeeDee's Kitchen Kleen. We both fussed over Metropolis more than in the past, told ourselves he was becoming sensitive. We went on day-trips and walks in which we discussed the scenery. We discovered silent places in our daily routine that we hadn't known existed, went to a lot of movies. Gradually we both became very depressed. Late one night as we moved from room to room inventing reasons not to get into bed together, I broke out in an impromptu diatribe about the state of our country. I cited instance after instance of its callousness to its own people, its obliviousness and duplicity. "We wouldn't dare interfere with sub-machine gun ownership, but we'll require a town meeting to get a next-day abortion." "Not even the well-to-do can afford nursing care." "The water table beneath this city is polluted to a hundred feet." I became impassioned about our support of terrorism, our international hypocrisy and self-righteous palaver. Deirdre joined in: Of all our nation's victims, women suffered the worst; every law, no matter how harsh, was designed to show leniency to men. I agreed, added *white* men. She agreed, added *rich* white men. I nodded, said usually white rich *business* men. *Young* ones, she sneered. We smiled, took the president's name in vain, fell into one another's arms, made love for the first time in weeks. The next morning we admitted we were divorced.

"I intend to stay with you, R—," Deirdre told me one day, "probably forever, and that's going to require two things: a miraculous sense of humor and a willingness to do anything—no matter how horrid—rather than wake up angry two days in a row."

Perhaps it was Deirdre's resolution that kept us going—her mad faith that love justified unthinkable acts—or maybe it was my inertia, my uncertainty that acts existed anymore, or maybe we didn't keep going but just couldn't tell any difference or maybe "keep going" doesn't mean much these days, but anyway, the crisis passed and our heartbreak turned into a way of life. I worry sometimes at the price love exacts, whether love's violence isn't love's denial, but Deirdre and I stayed around after the center didn't hold and I'm not the man who regrets it. Sometimes I think our durability's accidental or just dumb luck and crave to prostrate myself before superstitions, offer up cringing thanksgiving. Most of the time I try not to think about it. Occasionally I credit the Buick.

It was just before Deirdre announced her resignation from the fantastic paying job with the large corporation that we bought it. We'd been talking about a second car, figured we could never afford a new one. My mother's next door neighbor, an aging semi-invalid, had the dragon in her garage, and one day on a visit home I delivered a pan of caramels to her and craftily offered to help her sell it. She hired an appraiser, compared prices in a vintage car mag, got on the phone with everyone disposed to give her free advice between here and Detroit, named a figure that left me dizzy, refused to dicker, and though I didn't capitulate in five minutes or five days or without good reason, I paid through the nose. If Deirdre and I had been divorced then, the deal would surely have stalled, which goes to show why divorce is a good thing. But at the time we still had her savings, and both of us loved its Buck Rogers garishness and talked a lot about the past's bizarre dreams of what we'd all one day be. To her credit, Deirdre has never blamed me for the car. Even when she explained the lawyer's scheme she insisted that, if ever I suspected our divorce was occasioned by the Buick, I could be sure I wasn't entirely wrong, but our problems weren't personal. Prolonged exposure to financial unreality led to suicidal longings—in everybody. Our only safety lay in greater fragmentariness, divisions, balks, hedges. If neither of us had the power to act, we were together less likely to self-destruct. We admitted that much in ourselves collaborated with our enemies, that our desires were hardly our own.

We towed the Buick home, traded a dozen paychecks to make its petrified pistons cough, washed, polished, waxed it, and for a period of nearly three years revived the antique custom of Sunday drives. It needed a full one-and-a-half lanes to negotiate a corner, and its tail could be as deadly as a whale's flukes. The hood was so long it foreshadowed our arrival, and because we frequently had to direct traffic around us, we always dressed to be seen: Deirdre wore a floppy hat; I sported a lavender tie; Metro's stump got a ribbon. Everybody gaped, everybody smiled. Gradually we developed surprising nonchalance amid universal disbelief and began to feel honest. Our defiance seemed so total that no one, not even ourselves, knew what to make of it. Were we recovering a lost future, resurrecting curiosity? What could an America that considered us normal have been? For its part the Buick remained magical. After sucking up our bank accounts and threatening to turn into an immovable, irreparable, unsellable car-owner's nightmare, the engine began to purr. More truthfully, it started to grumble—a low, sinister vibration you could feel through your seat. Not a friendly sound, certainly not an enlightened or humane sound, a sound like collapsing riverbanks or like the subterranean malice that never comes to anything, never goes away. Anyway, it was a sound I believed in.

Ecologically, of course, the car's a disaster area. You could run over Hondas and never know. Twice I've been ticketed for the color of the exhaust, and you might as well pack mud in the carburetor as feed it low-lead. With its rolling haunches, bulbous eyes, and a grill convoluted as a Harley, the beast defines runaway technology, consumerism, brute capital, machismo, progress atop an avalanche of waste. But disowning delusions can be easy, understanding them hard. Every time I push down its accelerator, I rediscover the wrongheadedness from which my happiness has sprung. I suppose a day is approaching when the Buick, like all things, must go. Still, I have difficulty imagining how exactly this will occur. I mean, you don't just flush it. It weighs more than five Mazdas; a single wheel is a hundred pounds. How are old mistakes dispensed with? Can anything started end? I distrust the Buick like I distrust my heart, I deny it like my soul.

For six months Deirdre and I endured our divorce like a whiny relative, then one day it stopped being a fact and became who we were. We accepted that life together would remain questionable—the normal state, I suppose, of forbidden loves—that what might or might not be required was nothing we could foresee. We stopped regarding unmarriage as a further step toward solitude, began to see it as an opening, part of the weirdness of living now. There were even moments when it seemed like fun. Who could tell where our unconnection might lead? We felt new solidarities, bonds with names we didn't know. Inexplicably, sex got better. Though I never mentioned it, I often imagined the two of us "marrying" again, sometime late in life, on our seventieth birthdays perhaps, surrounded by cheering, chortling friends, people shaking their heads, Who would have believed, etc.? We were, after all, in the middle of what no one else had already lived through, so who was to say? Also, a lot of our energy was taken up with survival now—not bodily survival, or not primarily that, but the survival of our first life, the one we continued for no good reason to call the "real" one. This struggle had become the principal subject of our conversation, the source of our enthusiasms and outrage. We called ourselves "guerrillas," "terrorists," a tiny "Resistance," making "war," not love. We joked about our "liberation" and "counter-strikes," about the oppressed nation "us." The metaphors seemed apt, right for a generation or way of life. Wasn't America oppressed? Hadn't something taken us over? If only metaphors were only metaphors.

Deirdre *is* a terrorist.

"I'm only a terrorist from the point of view of human beings," she insists. "From the point of view of everything else, I'm a natural force."

Or if "terrorist" sounds prejudicial, call Deirdre a "fanatic," "lawbreaker," "vandal," card-carrying member of the "lunatic fringe," or simply someone unlike anyone for whom such categories mean so much. She's also the gentlest person I know. She can bear fools, she can bear liars, apparently she can bear me, but she can't bear desolation one minute.

"What I don't understand, won't, is that you witness all this, and do nothing," she tells me.

"Nothing's an exaggeration."

"Nothing."

"Fabrications aren't nothing."

"Nothing."

"I give rot another go!"

"Nothing."

I love her. She's far past forty and not an aerobics queen and bulges in places we all know she shouldn't and—though I still notice a lusty perusal now and then—not the fertility goddess who turned my head at twenty-two, which means, according to *Everywoman's Twelve Steps to Sexual Fulfillment in Marriage*, we're dissatisfied by definition, and I suppose she's too full of mad hopes and brutal facts for her own or anyone else's good, but she's my last hold on sanity and I can't wish her other. If only she could say the same.

"The future will hold you accountable for what you've watched. If southern Florida turns into a desert, if water in California costs twelve bucks a gallon, if July fourth in Washington, D.C. hits a hundred twenty degrees, if the hole in the ozone reduces life expectancy in Minnesota to forty-three, if just once America goes five months without rain, our children's children will need to know you did something."

"We don't have any children," I say.

"We have Metropolis, we have responsibilities, we have the remnants of our lives!"

This afternoon my beloved is somewhere with a ten pound wrench trying to dismantle an eighty-foot crane or eighty-thousand dollar backhoe, or maybe she's driving spikes into gearworks or pouring concrete into a bulldozer's tank or chaining the body I hold each night in terror of its thin bones, chaining it to the moving parts of a gigantic engine or lying down in front of seven-foot wheels or making a human fence around a shagbark hickory or century-old cypress or otherwise defying a destructiveness so widespread and opulent and irresistible and faceless that it simply has to be imaginary, while a dozen sweaty joes hellbent on making a buck in unthinkable heat so they can feed themselves and families who, if they have their health, may not have much more. . .well, this is what Deirdre spares me from knowing she's up to. I should add that she's not especially brave, and if the weather's torrid and the workmen catch her, or if the police are called, no one's handling of her will be courteous, and if she ends up in the clinker she'll feel like table-scraps. Somebody's lawyer will bail her out wilted, sobby, and in the papers next day she'll get mentioned for wearing green socks or giving someone the finger or displaying unmistakable signs of drug-induced dementia and a psychologist will provide a clinical explanation of her antisocial impulses and a sociologist will discuss the deleterious effects of public permissiveness and the populace will relax to discover nothing Deirdre has ever said or felt need be taken seriously so that the liberal commissioner can conclude the affair with a renewed commitment to a future that has already passed away. The machines will roll, seventy-six acres of trees will vanish, next spring septic tanks will gurgle up mysteriously, a trailer park will wash into the river, and ten years of legal dickering will conclude that the link between the land development and these new drainage problems is too tenuous to justify court action. The only good to come of so much misery will be that for a month or two Deirdre's fit will pass. We'll sit on our porch at night, hold hands. In the fall we'll canoe down an oily river, and except for a few furious quarrels—with siblings, strangers on the phone, each other—and one fist fight in a deli between Deirdre and a chortling bald man who wants beef "rare enough to suffer," we'll know the oblivion of otters. Our story will momentarily look as though it could have a happy ending.

"You realize that you've gone insane," I tell her.

Deirdre throws back her head, laughs like Don Giovanni. "Have I told you how they make veal? How they make it tender?"

"Stop that."

"There's a box, one foot by two feet . . . ."

"Stoppit, I said."

227

"And everything I'm describing is perfectly legal, U. S. government approved, entirely out in the open."

"I'll throw up on your clothes! I'll eat at MacDonald's!"

"...and they put the calf in the box at birth, and they nail up the sides—all four legs touching—and they feed it liquids, usually through the vein, for two years, and since nothing can live in a box they pump it full of vaccines, and because the calf's silly enough to keep trying to move, these running sores develop—legs, spine, withers—so the farmer has no choice but to . . ."

"You can't keep doing this," I say.

"What does anybody know that could help me stop?"

In ways I failed to grasp at the time, Deirdre's lawyer had recognized who we were far better than we had. Divorce wasn't a stratagem; it was our name, the reality that marriage for people like us had become. What in other circumstances we could've shared, something firm, intricately coupled, indistinguishable from blood and breathing, had cracked—I don't lack names for it; I lack *the* name for it—and our proliferating versions composed what remained. Madness is more contagious than measles, spreads with contact exactly like infection. I spent my days reviving the corpse Deirdre was trying to help die. The same law that made her a criminal turned my frauds into lumber, exemptions, business, credit. We were neither of us especially tolerant or forgiving. Our sort of union was what my self-help books carefully said nothing about. We were divorced. Divorced! What needs explaining—I believe and disbelieve it; I can disbelieve my toes as readily; I stake my daily life on it; perhaps that kind of belief has nothing to do with anything; that's the anything this fiction doesn't care about—is that, somehow through our series of made-up lives or interchangeable masks or neverending quarrels, we stayed joined. I delighted in Deirdre's revenge—corporations richer than Poland brought to their knees by a middle-aged woman with a sand-bucket!—even if I lived in cringing fear of its consequences, and Deirdre studied every worthless shack I resurrected as carefully as the smile-lines around my eyes. Each of our individual and mutually contradictory acts was a single outrage, the same blighted hope, one blow, shared defiance. At times I wasn't even sure we disagreed. Of course, none of this is intelligible. I can certainly see how much it resembles a rationalization. Maybe I just mean our bodies occupied one house. Or perhaps Deirdre and I were "divorced." I suppose I should speak less "absolutely," say we were still "joined." But if our "life together" ever becomes "contained" like that, "I" "dread" the "unspeakable" "deed" that will "'certainly'" be "'necessary'" to set ""us"""" """"""""""""""""""free.""""""""""""""""""""

Convincing yourself you aren't psychotic is probably modernity's most self-defeating task, but convincing yourself that—psychotic or not—you aren't alone, is less so. I often felt that Deirdre and I were connected, but I could never be sure, and officially, publicly, we weren't. Countless times we each knew the attractions of flight, saw the doorway and no reason not to walk through it. If we ever felt confident, it was forgetfulness of our real situation. "Us" was past tense, a quote. At times, I felt that nothing my not-wife or I could do would reach far enough for the other to feel it, to suffer for it, to make "us" unmistakable. If you're among those who fear isolation more than schizophrenia, or the second only because it produces the first, then you'll understand why I felt relieved when disaster started to occur. I got turned down for a loan. At first, I assumed it was a mistake, but when I called up my personal vice president, I got put on hold. Never since I'd been a college professor had I been treated so routinely! I felt badly shaken. If the world was all my factitious empire knew it to be, then what appeared to be happening simply couldn't. I decided to wait. The secretary returned, apologized profusely, promised the veep would call right back. She didn't.

I decided not to tell Darren and Beats. If the refusal was an aberration, why panic? We were urban archaeologists, and our bottom line had always been, if not negligible, then hallucinatory. If things were as dire as I feared, of course, we'd all know too much too soon. But it was no aberration. Before I could stanch the first wound in my credit, I got turned down twice more. When I phoned the banks, everybody became instantaneously busy. I received the reasons given to those who aren't to know the reasons. Finally, just to see how desperate the predicament could be, I made a garbled but ominous allusion to chapter eleven within hearing of an officer. I wasn't even asked to wait.

"Write this down." He began reciting a number.

"Whaffor?" I asked.

"Attorney's office."

And so I knew.

Deirdre gave in to hope long before I did. She insisted Mammon couldn't devour me without biting its own hand, that I was it and so couldn't look like the enemy. "They can't see through you without seeing through themselves. The threat's 'us,' it has to be!"

"I don't know," I said. "If all something wants is to get bigger, well, maybe self-knowledge isn't a problem."

"It's not a morality play," she said. "Who cares if corporations agonize? But everything's motivated."

"I play by the rules! I'm invested!"

"Exactly! They think I'm what you're concealing."

I wanted a strategy to offer Darren and Beats, a plan we could try if we wanted to keep going. So I tallied the Second Chance properties that Every American Real-estate Purchaser (EARP) could find liveable—

a dozen, maybe twenty if we added a bath or entrance or privacy fence here'n'there—but the idea of turning a profit made me squeamish. Deirdre was certainly right, the line distinguishing me from a slumlord was thin, but as soon as I started to cross it, it mattered hugely. In the past I had turned structures into money only by accident, and the situations had always been odd. I mean, not just any old EARP was okay. Each time it was someone who'd caught the scent, savored what we savored, the kind of bewildered soul whose refuge these dilapidations already were. No developers, no agents, no renters—no EARP. I still couldn't decide whether I was a business or the parody of a business or either by virtue of the other, but now that for the first time I required capital, I couldn't stomach it. There's a lack of vision here, I know. If my story's self-serving, then I maintain only that it's idiotically self-serving, pathetically so. I finally hit on the idea of doing what I did best and could believe in—nothing. I would tell all, see what Darren and Beats wanted to do.

But when I got to the job—an eighty-year-old abandoned baby-food warehouse with an infrastructure massive enough to drive trucks over—I couldn't believe what I found. Darren was ignoring the beam he was standing on! Already from the loading bay I could tell it was hand-hewn, twenty, twenty-two feet, solid, and—as I got closer—probably walnut. For CEO's and drug lords, twenty-two foot walnut floor joists may be building materials, but we were Second Chance! We recovered worlds! Darren was standing on a form of life as utterly gone as gorillas, an unnatural history Madonna's millions couldn't have restored. He wobbled there, fiddling with heat ducts and, when—unable to contain my amazement—I finally pointed out the miracle supporting him, he just mumbled something about "your own business" and vanished into the foundation. An hour later Beats arrived talking non-stop about "progressive singles communities."

"On-site computer dating, resident shrink, polymorphous lifestyle support, therapeutic massage, non-therapeutic massage, experimental group intimacy workshops, even four hours free phone sex." She'd gotten an architect's rendering from somewhere, started shoving foldouts and market data at me. "We could do our own HIV screening!"

Darrell materialized from the Johnny-on-the-Spot. "And even if self-interest has gotten pitted against solidarity," he sort of said but more like recited at me, "Dubois saw all that. What about dual histories? Alternative development? Minority enterprise has never displayed the anti-social—"

"No more white male protestant heterosexual bourgeois elite liberal Anglo guilt!" Beats shouted.

"Help the poor!" Darren mimicked. "Help the poor!"

Silence.

I finally sighed. "What gives? You guys want to grow or something?"

Seems Beats and Darren had gotten this idea about turning the baby-food warehouse into what they were calling a "private alternative community enterprise." The plan was complicated, but as they explained it, the three of us would engage in a radical social experiment called "making money hand over fist." Besides the progressive sex shop, there'd be a "private-community" gym, a "private-community" aerobics center, a "private-community" yogurt bar, fried chicken takeout, and tanning salon.

"Tanning?" I asked.

"Revolutionary concept," Darren explained. "Black owned, see, but exclusively white clientele! Like, Aufhebung-ing late capitalism, exploitation reversed. Every dollar strikes a blow!"

"You probably can't understand," Beats reassured me.

So I figured I'd better explain about the loans. Especially if they were hallucinating development. But don't ask me how I knew—a twitch in Beat's deadpan, something Darren did with his tongue—but before I finished a sentence, I already knew they already knew. It was eerie. For a long moment we stopped talking, just did our collective best not to be there.

Then Darren cleared his throat. "No offense, okay? But a lot, probably most, of white America's unsalvageable."

"Using stuff up's all this country's good for," Beats explained. "Really, how much of anything deserves another chance?"

"Is there someone disagreeing here?" I asked. "I'm not trying—"

But then Darren stepped up real close, looked simultaneously into my eyes and through me. His voice sounded like someone I was just getting to know. "What we're trying to say, R—, is if you can't tell what's happening, then maybe, y'know, you should get out of the way."

Much remained obscure, but my marriage seemed to be materializing. Something had clearly conspired to undo me, and since my fabrications were indistinguishable from America, and since the absence of collateral could mean I was either a fraud or a developer, and since the worthlessness of the structures I reinforced merely proved I was an entrepreneur, the danger I posed had to be Deirdre. Of course, we didn't know what had linked us or whom or just how. Perhaps it's another symptom of our madness or our nation's, but we found the most convincing evidence in explicit contradictions. For example, we knew banks didn't distrust paper constructions, and we knew—or thought we knew—Beats and Darren didn't distrust tangible ones. Now each seemed to distrust me because I distrusted the other and to place their own trust in superficial falsifications of vaster scope. This implied that whatever was at work was simultaneously blind and all-seeing in the way only huge things can be. Moreover, having reached identical conclusions—specifically, that I was a total loss—the banks and my coworkers were responding in opposite ways: the first had cut me off, the others were taking me on. Perhaps the plot was multiple, two-headed, or divided against itself. Of course, between Darren and banks and Beats might exist only an accidental connection, but the fact that institutions regarding me with neither malice nor affection and co-workers regarding me with both all recognized in me a common problem—well, this strongly argued for realities I couldn't see.

"I refuse to get superstitious about systems," Deirdre told me. "Not even thunderstorms are more mindless. I'm not crazy, or not crazy like *that*. Hell, I even knew Nixon wasn't in charge."

I sighed. "If only it were vindictive, then maybe what we're not would function as a mirror. Like there'd be hope in what's eliminated."

"I still can't feel the center," Deirdre warned. "Something's coming that's not in quotes."

And then the impersonations began. I had overdue accounts everywhere, and DeeDee's Kitchen Kleen possessed specific protocols for threats, messages, promises, and evasions. I wasn't deluged yet, but DeeDee's employer's phone rang pretty steadily. I'm still not sure why the first one caught my attention—maybe there were earlier callers that we never noticed, or maybe the demise of my credit had made me more alert. Anyway, the caller said he represented an earth-moving firm, gave the sort of name you want to forget so can't, Sav-Alot Landscrape Systems, and DeeDee promised her boss would call him right back. Our feints were still pretty amateurish back then, no real challenge to rise to. But when I saw the message I didn't recognize the name. Now, I can't explain why, but an absurd name that fails to amaze me makes me nervous. Like my vigilance is weakening. So, I tried to dismiss it, threw the paper away. Usually with these guys, you're better off to call back. They make their money on easy collections, and if you can sound troublesome and the account's not big, one call may be enough. But the surprise was that Sav-Alot just vanished. I mean, the one thing you know is these guys'll keep trying. That's basically what they do.

Then we got one from Tru-Valu Prefab. A load of trusses they either had delivered or wanted to, DeeDee's had trouble with the message—thick accent. "German sort of, but too nasal, sing-songy, nearly Scandinavian." Anyway, if something you own need's a second chance, trusses aren't it; might as well start over. So I started checking. International yellow pages, directory of contractors, computer files of accounts, receipts, even called a guy I knew with a national lumber chain, but nobody ever heard of 'em. I decided not to call back. Tru-Valu vanished. Now, in a sense an overdue bill that evaporates when you ignore it is the sort of problem people need more of. It wasn't as if my feelings were hurt. Also, I was beginning to receive calls that disappeared far less easily, often after extracting promises I could never hope to fulfill, and more than once I asked myself why, when I had abundant, inescapable, and straightforwardly ravenous creditors, did I worry about bogus ones that took no answers for answers. By now I'd been turned down for a baker's dozen loans, was hearing rumblings of foreclosure, had suffered the indignity of being denied bankcard authorization on a four dollar purchase and was considering emigration. But in my mystery callers I imagined traces of the originary menace, misfortune's center, Trouble Itself. I couldn't satisfy my persistent creditors anyway, and I suspected that behind my sporadic ones was my real nemesis, the ultimate source of all my undoing. Did I want to know it? Perhaps I wanted to argue with it. In a direct encounter, I must've still dreamed I could win.

Anyway, I was inside Leonardo's box upstairs in our rented apartment in the house leased by DeeDee's Kitchen Kleen and Katering on a spring night in Milan in 1519 one morning not long ago when I heard DeeDee's employer's phone ring. I knew the hired woman would answer and so was hardly listening when suddenly a sound that had been ordinary and distant and continuous seemed to have turned strange. I stopped struggling with my betrayer, forgot the mountainous bedclothes on top of me, waited. There it was again.

"I …I can't tell you how angry we both …and then the Soviet Union, who would've thought?"

The hired woman was talking exactly like my wife!

I rushed down the stairs.

"Yes! Yes! And if everyone waits for some government to act, well …you've seen those pine trunks. They're as big around as dining tables!" She looked lost.

"Give me that phone, young lady!" I did my very best to bellow.

Deedee looked up, blinked, seemed to recall who she wasn't. "Oh oh! It's my boss!" she squeaked.

"I'm not paying you just to—"

She put the receiver into my hand.

"Who is this?" I demanded.

For a long moment only silence, air, the nothing that's never nothing. Then I heard a voice from the land where rivers are named for lovers and wanderers couple with gods.

"Oh R—, I've been thinking of you all day long," she began. "Here on this shore, I watch every wave, asking myself, how many oceans has he crossed? How many ordeals, adventures?"

"Excuse me, but I'm going to need your address, your phone, your business license. Nothing personal. I've just had some harassing—"

"Universal Amortizers. I'm sorry, I assumed you knew. The forgiveness people. I guess I thought we didn't need to be coy."

I tried to chuckle, feel around for some footing. "I certainly think I know my own interests. We're Americans, right? No reason we can't be frank. But the point of these phone calls, loans, my property ...well, what're your people really after?"

"Oh R—, I ask myself again and again! Just look around us. Spend, borrow, spend, borrow. It might be sad if not for all the dreams. Could everything really be love? Beneath this torrent, one source, a bottomless spring? I remember, when I was a perfectly naked girl, the unbelievable coldness of mountain water."

I had started to sweat. It wasn't her voice exactly. It was me, or rather the forceful, frightening, unconfused person I was no longer certain I wasn't about to become. Why, there seemed no end to all I might do! I racked my brain for an eventuality that was off limits. "I just wondered because, well, maybe there's been some confusion."

"I've had that very idea myself! It's uncanny! What if all that's sad turns out to be a comedy of errors, misunderstandings, mere peccadilloes? Sometimes my whole life seems like one long wish for happy endings. But if redemption's what you want, R—, if you really intend to make up for the past, everything you've done, well ...." She paused, gave a tired sigh. "Honey, the cost's high. $1,460,838.43, and that doesn't include transactions in the mail."

"That's outrageous! I mean, mostly I do façades, cosmetics. It's not like I originated anything!"

The enchantress's voice turned husky then, full of fog, smoke, darkness. "What they say about me's right, R—. I've lied to other men, I know how to promise, know what everybody wants to hear, but with you, I'm going to tell the truth. It isn't your burden. Forget it. There's nothing—*nothing*—you and I can't arrange."

I waited for her to continue, throat tight, then realized everything was up to me. "Nothing?" I croaked.

"It's all permitted," she purred.

"N—nothing?"

"That's what I've come back to remind you, R—. Whatever your heart can desire."

I slammed down the receiver.

Universal Amortizers vanished just like Sav-Alot and Tru-Valu, so Deirdre and I decided our bond must be real. Even if we didn't know exactly who or whence or why, we could be confident that something huge and squalid—the inconceivable malice we mistook for history, the perceptible limits of our world, a hysteria widely mistaken for normal—had recognized Deirdre's and my wellbeing as the same. It was unnerving, of course, knowing you'd been identified, singled out, by a faceless nemesis you knew better than to believe in. IRS? Mitsubishi? UFO? Shell? AFSCME? If only it were so concrete, so manageable! But despite the hopelessness of our predicament, we were overjoyed. If America was every bit as brutal as we feared, if the misery we saw on sidewalks, deaths we read about, sobbing we heard every night on the news, if all those nightmares that children notice but adults get over turned out to be true, then no doubt about it, Deirdre and I were married. For once, I didn't worry about wishful thinking. It was as if I'd reached out my hand toward a shadow in my own home and found a woman there. I couldn't get over how smooth she was, sticky sometimes, round along the left shoulder, at times bewilderingly frail. I lay in bed in the middle of the night, my mouth inches from her spine, anticipating my wife's taste—my *wife*—the cool of our breath escaping me, her smells in my smells in her smells, mingled sweat, rough lips on tiny neck hairs, licking her, licking her. In the dark, you become your senses. How can recognition make any difference? Within the cornucopia of things this story doesn't understand, here's another: Privacy has sometimes seemed the grimmest threat to me, other times my ultimate desideratum. Nothing came between Deirdre's flesh and my flesh. Nothing.

And then catastrophe struck. I learned that a twenty-three thousand dollar federal small business loan I'd applied for eighteen months earlier, had come through, and when I got home from the bank DeeDee was standing in the doorway gloomy as a refugee: "Sav-Alot called back." Turns out our so-called phone impersonator was a new credit division employee of the parent corporation who'd given the wrong operating name by mistake. The charge had actually been for bricks at Lowery's, a local franchise I visited perpetually, and payment wasn't even overdue. "Just data inventory, new ...uh, software sorry ...inconvenience," kid sounded goofy, likeable. Then later when the mail arrived that afternoon, we got a bill from Tru-Valu Prefab. I still couldn't remember them, but it was for porch balusters, not trusses— so a definite possibility. "Maybe I just got the message wrong," Deirdre admitted. We could hardly speak. We moped around DeeDee's offices. I crawled into Leonardo's box but the past seemed monumental, an edifice of the hulking obscenities of white men like me, deserving only annihilation. Deirdre read an article about how many acres of rainforest disappeared in the time it took her to read the article. I petted Metropolis but couldn't wake him. Finally the phone rang. We sat there listening to the tone, so much like music or faraway chimes or the recovery of your senses, again and again and again and again and again and again and again and again and again and again and again and again, until Deirdre said, "It's probably for DeeDee's boss."

I nodded. "I think he's out of town till next Thursday night but his lawyer can be reached at a number identical to that of the convenience store on Height Street."

Then she added, "Sorry," and her face did the amazing thing defeated faces do when the ghost of childhood in them smiles.

"Yeah, me too." I stuffed our comatose dog into the Buick, grabbed the Port-A-Phone, left for work.

Where I found Beats alone. She was crawling around on top of a wiring diagram in an unforgiving pink and blue aerobics outfit that, by turns, looked pornographic and funny, and when I asked about Darren her answer came too fast: "I don't know anything you don't know." I had her eye for maybe a nanosecond but long enough to know that, though she was prepared to lie about countless things, she hadn't been prepared to lie that time. Anyway, she probably wasn't lying about Darren. Who showed up eventually, battered A/C duct under one arm, eyes on his shoelaces, surly as a dustmop, and passed without a grunt into the floor joists. I thought I didn't much care whatever they were hatching and so crawled up on the roof to see what was fixable. But when I came down half-an-hour later a coolness in the air said: The End.

"Power system's dysfunctional," Beats announced.

Darren materialized holding an authentically godawful, charred fuse box. "The wiring under the floor's antique. There's been at least one fire, maybe several."

"And we're only talking about the lights," Beats put in. "A/C was added later, separate circuit, different power pole. The walls on the west side are like earth strata or trunk rings. Systems on systems. You can't put voltage together like that. There's attraction, resistance, reversals of current. And look, right here." She was holding her wiring diagram, a printed schematic on crumply paper, no telling where she got it, and pointing to what looked like a dense spider web or sketch-artist's pentimenti: lines over lines over lines over etc.

"Yeah, I see it." I was bluffing. "But we've handled worse—"

"No way," she said. "Whole structure explodes or twenty-foot flame shoots out of the wall in the middle of the night, place burns down in maybe six, seven minutes, or current just stops and y'never figure why, but any system this complicated, well, sooner or later the power turns against you."

"Is this an allegory?" I asked.

Darren handed me the fuse box. "Too bad, I mean, your having been a regular guy and all, but everything constructed ends."

Beats slid the diagram between a muscle and her leotard. Darren shrugged.

I took a deep breath. "We got another loan."

Silence.

236

"Twenty-three thousand dollars. Notified me just this morning."

Silence.

"We could cut ourselves paychecks, seal up this coffin and," I swallowed hard, "take your choice. Tanning palace or flesh club?"

Darren looked at Beats; Beats looked at Darren.

I don't know what reality is, suspect it resembles blood and breath more than currency and corporations, that it's nearer whatever I labor under, what I'm inside, than anything I observe, and recognize that when it crashes down on me I lose the luxury of doubting it, that no container is big enough to protect me from it, handy enough to expose it when I'm blind, sturdy enough to preserve it if it fades away, but since something will always be called it, I want to register here that, for me, nothing anyone calls reality will ever deserve that name as long as it makes no special place for the cold, moist, terrifying wave of sickness that passed through my stomach at that instant.

"Christ! You weren't even going to tell us!" Darren said.

"This place is history!" Beats stomped out the door.

"No, no, this place is fic—"

Darren stepped into my face: "If you ever get another chance, man, try not to blow it."

I was alone.

For a long time I sat there in the middle of what, for all I knew, might have been a baby-food warehouse, perched on what I might as well say were twenty-two foot walnut floor joists, as garbled reruns of nothing flashed in my head. I thought about fetching the pretend dog I called Metropolis from the Buick, but my imagination wasn't up to it. Perhaps the material universe grew older. I couldn't tell any difference. Eventually I heard the soft popping sound of gravel under tires and saw a red panel truck ease up to the loading dock.

"Haaaaard times, leastways my calky-later says. I don't know from personal, first hand 'sperience, but I see what I see, know what I know." His voice echoed to me over the expanse of floorless, parallel beams in the midst of which I perched. I could see him standing there, hands on hips, face in shadow, heard him smile.

"You win," I said. "Broken, beaten, belly-up. Got a revolver?"

He whinnied. "'Tain't news," he said. "You been busted since forever. Calky-later says you never paid nobody, don't own nothin', y'unnerstand, not outright, lose lesser'n lesser maybe, but never made first return on yer INvestments, no sir. Only news is yer knowin' yer busted. Now that's int'resting, no disrespect meant hope none taken."

"Disrespect?! Of course, you wouldn't happen to have on you the data of all my squanderings."

"$126,428.42 fiscal year close of business yestiddy, but since start up, we'd need ter divine categ'ries—"

"A prince. Every now and again I grow melancholy that nowhere lurks anyone whose acts aren't efficient expressions of purely despicable desires, narrow as a needle but perfectly oiled, and of course, I know that words used like that can't mean anything, but still, the naturalness of this picture depresses me. And then I run into you."

"Yep, 'tain't personal." Shuffles his feet, p'shaws.

"My one remaining concern is, having relinquished everything, Loathing, am I going to lose you, too? I ask because, well, nothing quite like you exists in my pathetic experience."

"Now, I think yer 'xaggerating. Ain't lost everything. Cain't lose what you never had."

"See, I've disbelieved the nation's laws, other people's intelligence, weather reports, every word I've ever read—"

"Cain't lose yer business, no sir. No more'n a poor man can lose a throne!"

"—disbelieved my own pleasure and the suffering of small animals, the existence of the human soul, the six o'clock news, both logic and illogic, the nutritional information on cereal boxes—"

"Gotcha wife, f'r instance, and a upright woman's a golden treasure!"

"—wouldn't trust, I'm divorced, would hardly trust a physician far as I could fling her, anybody in a pinch, standardized tests, and if I haven't consistently disbelieved in the material world I know that this results entirely from habituation, that confidence in my own body rests on grounds no more reliable than confidence in my own mind or words and, what's worse, is less coherent, that even if I can't disbelieve you exist now I have no reliable basis for not disbelieving you'll exist in twenty seconds—"

"Gotcha freedom 'n' that worthless dog out yonder."

"—but here's the funny thing. Even though I have no idea at all—"

"Still gotcha health."

"Gimme fifty grand for a kidney? Even though I have no idea who you are and certainly wouldn't trust you and don't know what it could possibly mean to say we're acquainted, still, I think that I've never for one minute been without the fear that you, Loathing, are the genuine article."

"And there's one more thing you got . . ."

I already had a question ready but didn't ask it. The figure just stood there, motionless, framed against the loading gate, backlit, hands stuck deep in the pockets of his painter's whites.

"Near 'bout priceless. Inval'able. Oppertunity knocks! Man cain't always tell what's it that holds'm back. Sometimes looks PEEculiar. Oppertunity knocks!"

238

The sunlight behind him was brilliant, eclipsed his face. I could see the panel truck parked in the loading lot, Q.E.D. Maybe it was a change in resonance, like the warehouse roof lifting off, eagerness where before every word sounded boxed, but as soon as he spoke my neck hairs prickled.

"That's a handsome Buick—"

And now, for the exciting conclusion of "Armageddon Visits Our Town":

Klap-a-klap-a-klap—
ker-BOOOOOOOOOOOOOOOOOOOOOOOM!

The helicopter slams my thirty-foot beloved square in the mind, doesn't stop there, passes through her intelligence like an instantaneously forgettable amazement then, coming out her other side, finds itself spent. Potency depleted, blades sheared, rudder limp—who dreamed superficiality could pack such a wallop?—it winds up positioned over an abyss. Time stops. Natural laws suspend. Then the gravity of the situation takes over. The dead engine coughs, the camouflaged body heaves, rrmm, rrmm, and with its tail caught in an eyeball, the copter lurches forward and down. There are screams, spurts of ugly smoke, a momentary flash of fire. I see tiny mortals tumbling earthward, hands, legs, flailing arms. The world divides into three kinds: 1) runners away, 2) runners toward, 3) the dying. Without intelligible cause I join the second kind, the beach monster sweaty and wild-eyed—no shades anymore—right there beside me. We're running "to help." "To help?" To "help"! "To help?!" When, lucky for us, we're stopped by a police barricade materializing spontaneously out of bedlam and nothing. "Situation's under control," a burly genderless being in space mask and padded vest reassures us, pops its palm with a riot stick. The statement's, of course, a pointless, preposterous, silly lie—nothing's "under control" here unless my heart is—but such remarks aren't meant to fool anyone. We get the message, shuck, jive, yessir/ma'am, and are backing up as a darkhaired young doctorish-looking—anyway, a guy in a green surgical smock—dashes past. We shout a warning too late. Burly reaches around, taps him sweetly at the back of his doctor's head. Guy skids on one knee, goes down. "Control," I say. S/he of the space suit looks off. Some fifty yards beyond his/her helmet and to our right we see what in my nightmares a living human body resembles on fire, but how can you tell? Might be paper bags, automata, simulacra. I've only seen it in movies, and everybody knows what *they're* like. We turn back toward the car.

More sirens, screams, smoke. The beach monster looks as frightened as I suppose I do, stares down at the pavement. There's something impossible about witnessing disaster. Like trying to be a tourist in hell or spectator at a lynching: No one only watches. Maybe original sin wanted to describe that, an innocence lost by just being there. I dunno. When we reach the Buick, we discover to our mutual amazement that Metro has climbed out of the back seat and pooped on the pavement in a neat pyramid beside the tire. He awaits us, making a tripod in the shady eighteen inches on the car's dark side, unnaturally close to his own droppings, as if to confirm his event, I happened here. Anyway, he sees us coming, slinks back over the front seat and onto his perch behind. All homo sapiens feel commented on. We stand over Metro's pyramid, our backs to the horror. We possess no trustworthy model of how to behave, fear degenerating into by-standers, are tiny and worthless, and well, speaking only for myself, I'm not strong. So maybe we listen for a voice, the moans of a creature in which we recognize a dream we once had. For the shortest of instants I imagine Deirdre in flames.

And then I notice that Grendel has climbed into the car, is punching radio buttons. "Your telephone work?" he asks.

"That's the radio."

He flashes me the how-dumb-can-you-get look.

"Lay—la," Eric Clapton answers.

"We don't have to just keep our mouths shut! I'm findin' somebody to tell," he explains.

The stations are in collusion to simulcast commercials. We tour the dial, learn a lot about brake work.

"Don't people do news anymore?"

"Move over," I say.

"Christ!" The monster droops its head. "And I used to love that song!"

478-LOUD, no problem remembering.

"Voice of the Peebles. Name, job, number, subject of—"

"I—I'm in the middle of the AID-US riot," I say. "Army helicopter has just collided with a sign and—"

She puts me on hold then comes back. "Freddy wants to know are you the same R—guy that's got no opinions?"

The question teems with wrong answers. "Just tell him I want to discuss the beheading of a naked woman."

The transfer is instantaneous.

"—psychopathic sex slasher with his own eyes! Hello, caller, it's Freddy Peebles! The world wants to hear your voice!"

"The United States Government gassed its own citizens and a hospital and then the helicopter went haywire and slammed into this huge billboard so that everybody fell thirty feet onto where patients—"

"Oh, oh, sounds like we've got nowhere man again, the human chameleon, R nothing!"

"—must be thirty-forty-fifty crash victims I don't know how serious but this woman soldier was dangling from a rope in the copter doorway with a public address system and I can see a lot of smoke from here—"

"Thousands of Americans, literally thousands, covet your privileged position, would even pay money to share your viewpoint, your front row seat, and with so many advantages, all you can do is repeat what's happening."

"—police cordoned off the area to stop people running to help and somebody caught fire I think you can't ever be sure but it looked like what a body in hell—"

"Now here's a citizen, ladies and gentlemen, who's been spoiled and pampered by freedom, democracy taken for granted, gullible, a lemming, swept first one way then the other."

"—sirens but fire trucks can't get through the abandoned cars and no ambulances since they evacuated I guess the emergency room when—"

"What the Voice of the Peebles has to say to . . . huh?" Loud staticky noise then he's back: "Well, R nothing, seems like not all our listeners appreciate your 'laid back' attitude! I've got a caller who wants to—"

Electronic fizzle.

". . . still can't get you out of my mind," her voice is as delicious as sunset, as the bluest night. "I stand at the water's edge, last daylight, and search the horizon for your sail. Everything that's refused comes back, I know it will, I know it. But R—, lover, why won't you let go? Why won't you trust me?"

The crackling silence, the inconceivable heat, the distant shrieks, voices—they're inside the phone receiver, inside my head, coming over the radio, on a page, all throughout the universe. I try to swallow, can't. "Wh—wh—where's my . . . what's happened to Deirdre?"

"Oh R—, I can help you forget—"

There's an explosion. Flames whoosh seventy feet up from the copter wreckage, police scatter, debris flies. The gigantic image of my desire shrivels, blackens, in seconds has evaporated. A rush of air impossibly more scalding than the impossibly scalding air that has already scalded us scalds us. Then a loud bang right above our heads makes everyone but Metro jump, as a smoking tennis shoe caroms off the Buick's roof and snags on the hood ornament. The beach monster and I stare at it. The grisly crackle of flames, sirens that never get any closer, smell of chemicals on fire. I realize that inside the phone receiver in my fist a mosquito is still buzzing. I silence it. It becomes the radio. "Lay—la." Grendel silences it. We do nothing. Then the monster takes a long breath: "Where's it all gonna end?"

I can't stop watching the sticky smoke pouring from the shoe. Tongue on fire, sole in flames. "Who can say?" I say.

"Like I already told you, I got my problems with you don't write normal, but okay, you got reasons. But the thing is, see, a guy reads stories because life ends mostly with the shit you expect, but a story, well, you're hoping it's different."

I don't believe what I'm hearing. "Y—y—you're talking about . . . about a goddamn *book!*"

He looks at me real keen. "Cut the cutesy shit. Everybody sees what you're up to."

I hold his eyes a moment longer then I lean back. "I don't know how it ends. You find yourself in the middle and—"

"Whaddaya mean? You're making it all up, aren't you? You're the narrator!"

"Christ, would I make *this* up?" The hot, crackling odors suddenly become unbearable. I fumble for the door handle, lean out, but can you believe it? In this story, not even vomit comes out naturally.

"—dragged me through this hokum pile, year 2000 in 1492, page 632 before 320, and without even the know-how to—"

"Know-how! Know-how! Can't you shut-up about know-how? I know know-how, crammed to fucking spitting up know-how, I just don't know any Goddamn know-how I could ever in thirty lifetimes know-how to believe. Look at Leonardo da Vinci, idiot! Doesn't he know-how? To finish, to start? His whole past's half-baked, plans botched, notes gibberish, crazy scribbles. D'you think Leonardo da Vinci knows-how to die?"

Grendel looks off, sticks his lower lip out. For a minute I think his feelings are hurt. Can it have feelings? I'm baffled. When bodies are burning fifty yards away, ought people still to apologize? I almost squirm, but then the monster speaks and I know, whatever's happening, it's weirder than hurt feelings. "Look, it's okay me and you're not pals. I draw V.A. checks, truck's jacked up. Real different. Americans don't need to like each other. But still I think—now, you don't take this the wrong way—I think I might give you a tip."

"Is there a right way to take it?"

He leans toward me. "When it ends, y'know, it makes everybody crazy."

I look at him a minute. His mouth's a perfectly straight line. "You mean like in a dream?"

"I mean like in a stupid joke."

"We all saw it coming but—"

He nods his head. "I been divorced, I watched my family go whammy, and one thing I know: nobody believes in the end until it's over."

Meanwhile, Leonardo has been down in the courtyard creeping around Salai's yellow engine wondering how it could possibly be his. Just four nights ago the little blackguard insisted the monstrosity was Leonardo's doing, but its carapace is so much more brilliant than any surface Leonardo has ever burnished that, even nose to chrome now, he can see none of himself in it. He has already examined the bulbous haunches fore and aft, the four ebony bladders and six crystalline apertures, has crawled up onto the contrivance, touched his cheek to the tin, and tried hard not to think how much smarter and more corrupt than he ever was some ingegnere must have been to fashion it. But why yellow? he wants to ask. One thing's for certain, Leonardo never invented *that*! Not that he wouldn't have loved to, for the hue is really about the most outlandish thing he's ever drooped his feeble eyes on, almost savage, and he can imagine no home for it. Does the created order conceal such grotesque spectra, elemental tinctures mortal minds have never dreamed? Are there such surprises still waiting? Leonardo has, of course, seen the gaudy sunweeds growing in the hot ditches beside the Arno, has seen date palms flopping their fronds at him, and more than once has been astonished by the earth's indiscreetness—a truth inadmissible if he hadn't observed it himself. Nature's not big on restraint, but in all Leonardo's sixty-seven years he's never known a disorder so resplendent, another perversion half so profuse. It makes him horny.

Take the inner chamber, for example. Peering through the window Leonardo enumerates its salient incongruities. Why would the conceiver of the device—who despite his uncouthness must possess wondrous learning—why would he contrive the design so artlessly? The front-most divan back-turned to the second makes familiar intercourse between the travelers inconvenient. How could the fashioner not see this? Think of the unpleasantness on lengthy journeys, such as from Milan to Pavia, which even for a single, unencumbered rider takes half a day. The gentleman would be forced to sit beside his lackey. Wouldn't there be a lackey? Where else could the driver perch? Or perhaps the master would have to stare his minion in the back of the head. It's uncivil, without regard for station. One can only wonder what erudite pandemonium spawned it. Even at sixty-seven years old and in by no means the best health Leonardo da Vinci can improve on *this* design, and he reaches for the blue tablet he keeps chained to his waistcoat to sketch his conceit so that later, when he returns to work, he will recollect precisely what he sees now, to wit: When drawing the enormous coach-room, remember to turn the furnishings so master and mistress may discourse of domestic affairs . . . etcetera. Unfortunately, Leonardo's hand finds only the thin fabric of his nightshirt, no blue book, not even a waistcoat, and he recalls his decrepitude, the bald fact of dying. This contraption can't be first nature, God's doing, but neither is it second nature to any human Leonardo could know. Perhaps it's nature's mad other, the nature of blind hopes and startling laughter. Anyway, it demands looking into. Leonardo kicks a divot across the yard. Why couldn't he have a little more time?

Meanwhile, a dozen steps to Leonardo's rear, Mathurine wanders the courtyard, scrutinizing designs of water-screws and hydraulic augers—all of which, as Francesco Melzi dove into Battista de Vilanis' arms a few moments earlier, got tossed helter-skelter into the air— scratching her scalp, turning sketches this way and that, in search of the unspeakable wickedness she now suspects is her destiny. Her identity isn't a problem for her, but at times she has wished it were. Anyway, she has passed an undue portion of her years living out the tedious parts of various masters' and mistresses' lives for them and has concluded that the lives of the tormented ones were always the best. Her own life hasn't been exactly bland. She had two sons who died and a daughter who died and a large mother who died and a cottage with a separate room for the livestock and some sisters who died and a striped cat who slept with its paws in the air then died and a brother who died and briefly a husband and goat who were both named Chou- chou before they died, and all this has left her with memories, but approaching the end of her third decade and so no longer young she wants more. Whatever evil is, it looks like an open field. Her dream's to enter it.

MORE

Evil hasn't always meant freedom. In fact, if Mathurine recol- lected herself right now—which she won't do, recollection being the iciest bath for souls hellbent on discovery—she might remember her life's faded allure. How she has gotten boxed, become so confined that transgression is her only daylight, well, it's the puzzle of her past. Didn't her narrow world once seem endless? Not all the kidney beans in hell can quite erase that. And even if Mathurine couldn't say just how every joy got foreshortened, or why, or what put an end to them, or even where these turnabouts have left her, she knows with the certainty of her master's damnation that it all began with Hermione de la Bouche.

Hermione was the daughter of a lord of minor distinction in the

244

environs of Chambord on whose estate Mathurine's grandfather until he died before Mathurine was born and then her uncle before he died after she was born and then the hairy goatherd who passed for her father before he vanished and then her corpulent mother for a time pretending to be the wife of her brother's son—along with miscellaneous cousins and sisters and nephews and a cat and a cow and a goat, briefly, until they all died—all lived as tenants. Exactly how Mathurine before her tenth birthday traveled from this life to that of a menial, mopping her way up the servant's hierarchy in the lord's minor manor, is a tale unimproved by the telling, save the part about the young cavalier who farted so exuberantly during an idyllic tripartite amorous rendezvous that it, the fart, brought the eight-year-old Mathurine out of her mother's cottage to investigate, and so to witness what she was, on the one hand, insufficiently debauched to grasp and, on the other, insufficiently curious to care about, since it differed only in locale, number, permutations, and postures from the humps and grunts she'd observed since infancy beneath the blankets covering various family members not an armslength away from the mat she shared with whoever among her siblings hadn't died yet, and so seemed little more noteworthy than pigs frolicking in the buttercups—well, Mathurine at age eight stumbled onto this naughtiness and thus created the predicament Machiavelli knew so well. Either the libertines would now have to secure the child's loyalty forever or kill her. What these alternatives gained in clarity they sacrificed in appeal, since none of the three rakes—not the pair of youthful, red-faced and alarmingly upright knights or their considerably older, less naked, and far more amused lady of infinite graces—none of these three felt inclined to condescension just then, or much more to murder, although this latter alternative, as the lady jocularly observed, did mean they could enjoy the virgin first. The sophistication of which remark provoked the youngest of the chivalric lads to dispose of his lunch in the shrubbery, having transgressed a lifetime of taboos already that afternoon and so feeling disinclined to more. But the upshot was that the playmates decided they'd have to elevate Mathurine—socially speaking—and from that decision to her life among the youngest children of the lowest menials in the bottom of the de la Bouche minor manor lay a crooked but continuous path.

She slept in a bed, she bathed, she ate sitting upright at a table. Gradually she acquired a new voice and became accustomed to performing tasks that made no sense to her at all. She couldn't make out why anyone would shit into a basin which then had to be dumped out a window, or why people doused themselves with odors when they already had odors of their own. If—as she began to suspect—the minor lord's lady's nieces had bodies much like hers, why did they burden themselves with heavy skirts and cumbersome finery? Why, when the rooms were so cold, did no one cuddle at night with the dogs? There were colors to hide colors, skin to be covered to be shown, and a veritable cornucopia of perfectly obvious facts to be energetically ignored. If it hadn't been for her nights, when she would abandon herself to memories of her mother or to dreams of nestling again between the bellies and butts of her family, Mathurine would've forgotten who she was. Nothing amounted to anything here! But one evening while scouring a butcher's block she overheard a singer's refrain,

For Melancholia's darkness is my soul's true home,

and the words struck her with the force of a revelation. She began to call her sleep her Melancholia, started living for each night's illuminations, and decided that what took place during her waking hours was merely a dream. Over time, this rhythm of light and dark restored order to her life, and she was learning to imitate a sleepwalker well enough to become one, when she finally glimpsed what her pointless tasks had been pointing to all along.

Hermione de la Bouche was a gay young girl but far from happy. Although possessed of disturbing beauty, obscene wealth, and a force of spirits that could hold even aged philosophers in thrall, she was subject to fits of choler so violent they terrified all who knew her. Her curses could be heard throughout the nights and into certain mornings. Her flesh often bore the marks of her own nails. Even her father and mother trembled whenever she was aroused, and more than once she had to be locked in her room, screaming and flailing, by a mob of burly stable hands. Mathurine, who at age eleven had already emptied Hermione's slops for two years and been cursed and kicked at and even struck once on the nose by a shard of flung crockery—an injury for which Hermione thought to compensate her the next afternoon with a flicker of condescension—Mathurine soon realized that here was the object of all her dreams. Hermione's complaints amounted to nothing. Her curses were directed at no one. Ignoring her misery made perfect sense. And so Mathurine devoted her days to making Hermione disappear. She learned to repair the wreckage of Hermione's violence, to cart away broken goblets, mop up spilled food, ignore insults, and generally became so practiced at removing the results of her mistress's tantrums that only in Mathurine's ceaseless effacements could Hermione be sure she was registering her outrage at all.

None of which resembled a life, of course, but which, because its obstacles were clear and penalties unmistakable, resembled a game. Mathurine became good at it. She distinguished the classes of whims and pets and tirades and identified the most effective mitigations for each. She memorized her mistress's hierarchy of aggravations and petty malice, became a past master at cultivating oblivion, and whenever curses or table ornaments were flung at her head, did her best to feel numb. Soon Mathurine was more impressively absent when present than any other servant or maid and began to be rewarded with smaller portions of each day's abuse. She felt confident in her transparency. There was hardly anything she couldn't make nothing of. And for her part Hermione came to depend on Mathurine as completely and unconsciously as on a vital organ. Of course, Mathurine knew it was all a dream, real life being the odor of her mother's skin, the warmth of her sisters' legs, her cat's scratchy tongue, the host of dead relations at home, all of which she preserved in memory and revisited in her Melancholia. However, the dream of Hermione resembled real life in one puzzling particular: it always came back.

Anyway, Mathurine adjusted to Hermione's shrieks and sobs and was well on her way to sleeping right through them when two events combined to disillusion her. First, Hermione discovered she was there. One day while passing her mistress's room, Mathurine heard moans and oaths and crashing and, upon entering, found Hermione in a tangle of bedclothes, writhing and flailing, surrounded by four cousins cringing against the wall. Furniture had been overturned. Shattered crockery covered the hearth. Mathurine immediately began the energetic straightening that would render this disturbance negligible and in the mindless rhythm of bending and stooping was about to return to unconsciousness, when a stray remark, or perhaps something she smelled, awoke her to the cause of her mistress's fit. Hermione was suffering Eve's curse. It was the same affliction that had visited Mathurine's second-oldest-before-the-oldest's-death-then-her-oldest sister, and although Mathurine remained mostly ignorant of the nemesis—knowing only that it metamorphosed the unfortunate vessel into a font of Christ's sacrificial blood, having witnessed in her sleep the stained dressings that stanched her second-oldest-before-the-etcetera sister's gaping wound—Mathurine did know a partial remedy. Her sister walked. This palliative—making the sufferer exercise, thus aerating the tissues of the womb instead of allowing them to seize up like an injured muscle—had been hit on entirely by accident when in her sleep one night Mathurine had thought she sniffed a resemblance between her sister's condition and her mother's calving cow, but nevermind all that. The important thing was, walking helped.

Anyway, all this that had been part of Mathurine's real life for countless nights now invaded the dream of her days. Scurrying around the floor as her mistress continued to shriek at no one and the would-be comforters clung to the curtains and whimpered at the injustice visited on frail them by the heavenly Father who, just because he'd

247

been born with a pizzle, had taken Adam's part—Mathurine began to feel peculiar. Where exactly was she? She knew that the specific causes of Hermione's fits were immaterial, that in reality her mistress's paroxysms were mostly feigned, and yet noticing how much like the moans of her mother's cow Hermione's moans were starting to sound, Mathurine found herself responding as if to pain. Her breath was coming faster. Her palms were sweating. How much like real life everything had suddenly become! And straightening up from the puddle she'd been mopping and looking around, Mathurine was astonished to see herself actually approaching her mistress's bed. Before she'd grasped what she was about to do, she'd grasped Hermione's hand and, with a single heave, had pulled her onto her feet. And Hermione—who, had she been ordered or cajoled or urged or tugged at, would have cut out her servant's tongue—Hermione felt so undone by her cramps and nausea, to say nothing of the unexpectedness of Mathurine's act, that, well, she went along. Down the stairs, into the great hall, out the massive door, along the path, across the little bridge, round and round the pond and gardens, all the while with Hermione's screams unbroken, no talking, never an exchange of looks, just two girls walking hand in hand as Mathurine stared at benches and shrubs and mortified passersby and Hermione bellowed and screeched and swore, until, as the fit finally began to weaken, the two girls started back toward the little mansion where, with the screams turning to sobs then heaves then whimpers, they climbed back up the stairs, traversed the corridor, strode past the awe-struck lord and lady and maids and men, entered the room where the cousins remained trembling against the walls, and still hand in hand, walked right up to Hermione's bed where Mathurine deposited her mistress on her sheets. Nothing was said. Mathurine left. Hermione went to sleep.

From this day forward, Mathurine became a fixture in her mistress's life. Where Hermione went, Mathurine went. What Hermione suffered, Mathurine suffered too. Of course, it still couldn't be said that the two girls knew each other, except in the sense that Mathurine now found herself participating in events she'd previously disregarded and that Hermione now distinguished Mathurine from the domestic backdrop in which she'd formerly made no wrinkle. But the two women were together constantly, and no matter how extravagant the uproar in which Hermione became embroiled, Mathurine always seemed a part. Mathurine didn't find her new position desirable. She attended to the imaginary bodily deformities that exercised Hermione's paranoia, carried the secret missives Hermione traded with her cousins, and helped dispose of the tiny boxes and keepsakes that Hermione, for no obvious reason, from time to time stole, but she found these tasks unsettling. They required too much alacrity to perform without thinking, and yet if she gave her mind to them, they would all but disappear. She tried to listen when Hermione beguiled herself with pointless stratagems, said only what was expected, and behaved exactly as if the chimerical offenses and slights that made up the great events of each day had actually occurred. But it was impossible. She could never take nothing seriously enough. If just once she responded to Hermione's trifles as they deserved, she'd fail to notice the rise of an eyebrow, odd inflection in a voice, or twitch of some lip that in this kingdom of appearances counted for everything. What was the matter? Hermione would demand. Had Mathurine fallen asleep? And Mathurine would stammer that, yes, yes, that was exactly it! Nothing seemed the matter at all!

Which greatly complicated Mathurine's real life but didn't disillusion her. Disillusionment came with the second event, the one that deprived her of home. Mathurine had been born into a dark, wet surrounding where the chill never left the air and life was warm skin and its name was always Mother. Warm skin might attach to any body—to Mathurine's sister, to cousins or cows, to Patrice the dog, even to Chou-chou the goat—but the legs, nipples, backs, sweaty butts and arms of life, no matter where they happened, were Mother. Of course, life wasn't everything. There was more. More was the itch that warm skin couldn't soothe because it entered through your nose. When Mathurine first squirted out of the womb into the surrounding chill, whatever wasn't her mother—not much just then—seemed to be a smell. What these smells told her was that more was on the way. Mathurine sucked them up, filled her sinuses with tangs and stinks and fumes: cow dung, stinging urine, sour hay, brackish hair, sulphur, the ecstasy of meadows, pollen, clover, sister, gas, goat, rotten teeth. Sometimes the itch in her nose was more than she wanted, and she would retreat into her mother's warmth again. But mostly odors were reassuring, made up for whatever she missed, promised that everything she desired had already entered her.

At about the same time that Mathurine was being awakened from the trance in which she'd been passing her days and was being transformed into a collaborator in delusions, her brother Loïc, just before he died, visited the Lord's minor manor to inform her that Mother was no more. Mathurine was overjoyed. Her Melancholia was beginning to seem ephemeral, and sometimes now when she nestled among the affectionate parts and oily hair of her family she'd wake to find herself in a stranger's mansion, abandoned by life, without the first odor. She wondered: Could what you see be all there was? But hearing her brother's news now, Mathurine realized that her mother had grasped her plight. Life had felt Mathurine leaving, had sensed the void closing in, and so had deserted the dark cottage to reside with her in the vivid illuminations of sleep. As soon as Mathurine's brother departed—having held his hat in both hands, shuffled his feet, bowed and repeatedly muttered to the empty space beside her that, if only this great lady would be so good as to deliver his tidings to his departed sister, then he'd hasten home to await her return one fine day in a coach, for wasn't the world just a huge turnip anyway?—as soon as Loïc bid his befuddled farewell and slunk away forever, Mathurine felt overcome with anticipation. For the remainder of the day she was unable to pay attention to what wasn't happening, couldn't see the huge and grotesque follicle growing on Hermione's wrist or care about the love missive an unknown Arcadian hadn't sent, and if Hermione hadn't finally stormed out of the house to flirt off her doldrums with a cousin's affianced, no telling how much abuse Mathurine would have had to ignore, but finding herself negligible at last, Mathurine rushed back to the tiny corner of the tiny room she shared with countless other maidens, snuggled into her stinky coverlets, and abandoned Hermione's dream for the life that was so much more.

Everything was just as she expected. Her sisters were all waiting with a moaning cow and Chou-chou the goat and a string of identical cousins, and they all told Mathurine that Mother was there and would be warm and wet to see her. Everybody smelled like armpits and fur. Mathurine knew just where to look, of course, but worried about the dogs. What if nothing followed her? Chou-chou laughed, said: The important thing about sleep is that it only lacks what you need it to! Mathurine knew this wasn't an answer but strode off anyway down the wide odor of cat shit covering life's expansive horizon. She passed a cottage like the one where her family lived and some hovels similar to her family's hovel and then three little farm houses resembling the hut in which she was born until at last she arrived at home. Patrice her dog who was now a brown rabbit opened the door, but for a long time Mathurine couldn't enter. She struggled forward with Patrice pushing her from behind, the low moans of sisters all around, the squish of mud beneath her feet, but home got no closer. How could the surface have become so slippery? Then without knowing how she entered, she found herself inside. Mathurine threw back her head and guffawed: home was dark, dark! She had recalled it as plum colored with a little button you sucked. A lot of what she saw had evidently just been created here. Above the ceiling sat several dead grandfathers grinning and a bald cousin to whom she and her sisters had each been married once or twice and cats and cups and some warm coals and an oily rug and a variety of small relatives and in every corner all the creatures moved. Mathurine felt so happy that her nose itched. And there was more. High above them all, covering the walls and ceiling, oozing, seeping, splashing, pouring out of every opening, was Mother.

250

Mathurine felt awe. Her mother billowed and gurgled, flapped around like leviathan, spewed all the warm waters of life onto her daughter's face. Her back was gorgeous. Her hair was the zodiac. She was perfectly circular, a shape you could sleep in forever. Mathurine rested her cheek on the blemishless skin. Slowly Mother became aware of her. Where she stood bending over the family's dinner Mother gave a shudder, lifted her chin ever so slightly, held both arms still. The end of the created universe came and went. Mathurine heard the sound of mighty breathing, hiss and heave, the earth beginning to stir after winter. She couldn't keep silent any longer; her rapture broke out. Mother, I'm home! she cried. I'm ho-ome!

Mother lifted her hands up into the air, turned, but her expression was blank. Mathurine sniffed the nipples, gigantic flanks, huge black follicle on one wrist. Where had the odors gone?

Then she heard a voice ask: What was the matter? Had Mathurine fallen sleep? And looking into her mother's face, Mathurine understood at last. Life had turned into Hermione.

From that moment Mathurine lived only in the present. She learned to forget herself, to sniff out nothing but foulness and innuendoes. Seeing became believing; out of sight was out of mind. She still felt displaced and often suspected that her pains and longings were the pains and longings of others, that she'd become, if not insubstantial, then dispersed, but she never tried to return to her family. All her energy was needed now just to keep up appearances. In countless ways, leaving home had turned out to be a huge advantage. She could pass through her days with nothing of herself held back. When she straightened, everything straightened; when she listened, she became sound itself, nothing more. A burden that had previously gotten in the way of her daily tasks seemed to have been removed, and if as a consequence she sometimes felt unreal, if she occasionally experienced vertigo, or if for no apparent reason she itched, she reassured herself that these feelings were only natural.

Among the practical benefits of her change was that Mathurine became much closer to her mistress. Instead of laboring only to escape notice now, Mathurine began to find in her heart unsuspected sympathies. Carrying Hermione's linens or commiserating over Eve's curse or even dodging an insult or saucer, she often felt, not only that no other life existed, but that she wouldn't have cared for it if it had. Her absorption at times seemed total. Listening to Hermione narrate the treacheries practiced on her, all the envies and nefarious plots seeking Hermione's ruin, Mathurine became enthralled. It seemed incredible that so much of this world's energy was devoted to making her remarkable mistress unhappy! But now she saw with her own eyes that Hermione was a victim—like Mathurine herself!—only one far more to

251

be pitied, alas, than a servant girl could ever be. Hermione had been made lovely. She'd been made devious. She'd been made bright and cunning and subtle as the moon. She'd even been made painfully good. The ghastliness of which circumstance being, not that Hermione's fate was shaped by others—that is, that she'd once been a child—but that the subject of her passive constructions remained undetermined. In being so constantly made over, who couldn't Hermione turn into? Now that Mathurine's life was entirely present and nothing more was on the way, she began to sense the depth of this suffering. No matter how devastating life's outcomes, Hermione was always on a verge. Every experience was an omen. Every acquaintance was a chance. As Hermione told Mathurine more than once, Hermione might even turn out to be her own worst enemy.

Mathurine fell in love. Or if love seems too crude, then just say Mathurine found in Hermione satisfaction of the debt life had inadvertently incurred with Mathurine's first breath. Hermione was everything. Carrying her fractured vases and ripped linens and discarded undergarments and shredded bouquets and whatever other fragments of Hermione's daily doings Hermione couldn't bother with and still be Hermione, Mathurine entered into intimacies the world of wealth and sin could only drool over. She prepared Hermione's body to meet her rivals, girded her perfect thighs in fierce satins, armored her bosom with jewels, lace, dizzying scents, and after every sortie, Mathurine restored Hermione's flesh to dazzling purity again. Oh, how hideous that the world misconstrued this frail being! Every recounting of cuts and parries left Mathurine in a swoon. Every tale of slights made her cry out. And the thought that she alone knew the bare truth, saw Hermione as Hermione saw herself, even appreciated splendors Hermione was blind to, well, Mathurine's privilege seemed a sacred trust. And for her part Hermione treasured Mathurine as much as a full-length mirror. In a duplicitous world where nothing was simply itself, where she'd been her own undoing countless times and had heaped more scorn on her own head than any rival would care to, her servant was Hermione's most trusted reflection. Had Hermione lost Mathurine, she couldn't have located herself, and without Hermione, Mathurine would've felt dispossessed. Concealed in Hermione's bedroom each afternoon, the girls began to merge. Hermione absorbed her disappointments by engulfing her servant, and Mathurine became the vessel into which Hermione's emptiness was poured. Only in the other was either fully there.

Over three and a half years the girls lived this strange marriage, Mathurine surviving unreality through faithfulness to appearances, and Hermione descending about as deeply into solipsism as human beings can go. And then one day the mistress alerted her servant to the

252

most nefarious scheme ever contrived to make human existence hell. Her cousin, Ni Ni, was going to make life! The very idea was chaos. Hermione ripped her clothes, scratched her thighs. To think the cool shrew could resort to such lengths! As Mathurine could attest, Ni Ni was a pitifully squat dwarf no fit cavalier could ever admire, and had Ni Ni's family not been without heir—their being plentiful but undecidable candidates at a fourth remove, boasts of bastardy by numerous farmers on behalf of their sons and wives, and an indisputable claim unlikely to be pressed by a putative uncle suspected of cross dressing—if it hadn't been for such fortuitous circumstances, Ni Ni would've been no match for anyone. In truth, Hermione had once welcomed her friendship for just this reason. To think Ni Ni could repay such kindness with betrayal! Now everyone in the minor house had forgotten the beauty around them and was talking of the life to come. How could the artless little gnome have even conceived such a thing? And if all this weren't enough, Ni Ni insisted on limping from room to room, pantomiming fear, whining that she was only thirteen and ooooo, it was going to hurt, while old Scaramouche—her husband and very likely the child's father!—strutted about the minor manor as vulgarly as a cock.

Mathurine, who had never known her mistress to suffer so, struggled to maintain her presence of mind. It seemed as if the blind multitude were warring on visible perfection, and listening to the inventories of Hermione's humiliations, insults, slights, Mathurine trembled at the conspiracy taking shape. Villainy now seemed ubiquitous. How had Mathurine lived amid such transparent viciousness and never recognized it before? Traipsing through the house or peering out of a cupboard, she sometimes felt as though blinders had fallen from her eyes. Every action divulged a plot or concealed one, often both and simultaneously. The lord's minor lady alluded to preparations without making her meaning plain—even to her servants!—and the smiths and stable hands disputed matters Mathurine could only guess at. Had she possessed no key, their intentions might've remained opaque. But if she recalled how everything revolved around Hermione, she could see through any ploy. Unfortunately, her concentration was weak. Sitting at the foot of Hermione's bed, gazing into her mistress's deepset eyes, Mathurine saw the truth clearly, but a few hours alone could stupefy her again. She mistook the cook's scolding for punishment and imagined that the red-haired groom's jibes were commonplace lechery. Why, if it hadn't been for Hermione, Mathurine would've never thought about Ni Ni's pregnancy at all! Her grasp on reality was so easily loosened that she often felt herself teetering on precipice. Why was it so hard to tell what she was in the midst of?

Her confusion vanished, however, when Hermione's suffering

grew worse. Ni Ni's time approached, and as festivities were devised to display her belly and guests invited to celebrate her husband's achievement, Hermione had to endure mounting humiliation. She became an ornament, a bit of porcelain to furnish another's stage, Ni Ni's trinket. The world seemed to have turned topsy turvy. And to think that such degradation could continue for months or that it could actually produce—from nowhere!—a miniature being, well, Hermione said she would never believe it and then, on the morning when the calf was thrown, said she would never accept it and then, when her acceptance ceased to matter, said she'd never indulge in any act that could under any circumstances be misinterpreted by the fondest fool as approval of it. She declined to go on visits to the wetnurse, certainly didn't coo or prattle or enter any room in which the little beast was beshitting itself. She persevered in this long-suffering manner and shrieked to Mathurine in private and broke everything within reach, and as the months passed and frail and sickly Ni Ni finally succumbed to the fate she so richly deserved but her malodorous little pup went right on surviving, Hermione's rage subsided and became what won't be called madness only by those for whom nothing so reasonable can be. Hermione knew that the child was, in a manner of speaking, innocent, that the infant had never intended her supplanting, but she also knew that as soon as he could speak his mind he'd have his own interests at heart and that if he could be considered harmless only while helpless, he could hardly be considered harmless at all. At the same time, he certainly managed to look guileless, even beautiful, which meant either that he was a born dissembler or that he was dividing Hermione against herself, had provoked her own nature to take his part. Either way, she'd never felt so vulnerable in her life. She argued continually, stopped sleeping, acquired a tic.

Meanwhile, the monster grew and developed hideous capacities. It took firm hold of its uncles' extended fingers, made noises widely misconstrued as speaking. Hermione's own father, a parent she'd always admired for being hers and so, by definition, incapable of the pathetic enthusiasms displayed by commonplace patriarchs, even he considered the creature amusing. And vilest of all, the runt was growing an organ! Or Hermione supposed that's what the tubicle was, a lavender spot of pruny skin that never came right out in the open or entirely withdrew. She hadn't herself observed an adult one, nor did she care to, although she grasped obscurely that it and her preeminence bore an unsettling connection, so that she supposed she wasn't absolutely hostile to the tumors though she'd as soon be spared the spectacle of them. Anyway, all this she recited to Mathurine in the quiet of her chamber, sitting bolt upright on the bed, raven hair askew over her face and shoulders, bedclothes strewn like froth, eyes lined, torn skin.

And Mathurine felt afraid. How sinister forces had become so well organized without becoming more straightforward, this remained a mystery, but that life was threatened, Mathurine could no longer mistake. Her Melancholia now returned. Each day began to be buried again in a zombie-like dullness, and while attending to her mistress, she continually found herself longing for sleep. It seemed now that her first impression of the minor manor had been right, that desolation had been its object all along, only that she'd mistaken everything and nothing, confused her mother's absence for what was infinitely more. Now instead of returning to her family each night, Mathurine returned to Hermione. She could no longer find her in the preoccupied face that stared up at the ceiling all day, and the disheveled beauty who rambled on about demons and foulness seemed either beside herself or simply out of her mind. It was as though life were no longer present, survived only in Mathurine's memories and dreams. But now this inversion of darkness and light, waking and sleep, seemed to Mathurine like madness itself, not order, as if she were herself contracting Hermione's distemper. The thought thrilled her. She seemed to be crossing the final frontier, suffering—not merely like her beloved or as violently—but suffering Hermione's own suffering. She was possessed at last! And as if to confirm this hope, one afternoon Mathurine discovered that she too had succumbed to Eve's nemesis, become complicit in the ancient rebellion, bore the scarlet mark of woman's sin.

And then the veil lifted. During an exhausting week Hermione either hallucinated a blemish on her left breast or pinched and worried it into existence there, and now she became convinced that Ni Ni's spirit was responsible. Mathurine's attempts to reason with her mistress, then to conjure Ni Ni, then to daub the pimple, and at last even to locate the damned thing, only made matters worse, and her flat refusal to dig the speck out with a bodkin left Hermione hysterical and Mathurine with a gash. Mathurine wanted to cry. What was happening? She finally fled the manor on pretext of visiting a sorceress her mother had once frequented, a flimsy fabrication that Hermione dismissed with a nod, and when Mathurine reentered the minor gardens and fruit orchards later, having meandered meadows and lanes concocting bogus potions to distract her miserable lady, the sunlight was almost gone. As she approached the entrance Mathurine heard screams, men bellowing orders, footsteps running. Everywhere figures were in motion, women swooned, stewards commanded, faces looked grave. Entering this disorder, Mathurine slipped through the kitchen, past the cupboard, up the stairs, and tiptoed to Hermione's door. She could hear a crooning sound inside, a note like the voice of doves or a mother singing. She slipped her head through the opening, edged inside.

255

Hermione stood beside the open window, a large bundle in her arms, and in her deepset eyes was a gaze Mathurine didn't know.

Nothing prevents me, Hermione uttered, not quite to Mathurine, not quite to herself.

The sorceress feels confident of relief, Mathurine began. But first we must rub a lizard on it.

Nothing at all, Hermione continued. I know I was made to shine, the stars' daughter, but like everything else, destiny's a trap. I don't know, I don't know.

Hermione's hair was tangled, blotched. The gown she wore had been torn and hung from one shoulder. Mathurine noticed that she rocked the bundle steadily.

I...I was halted by brigands, handsome, terrifying rogues, Mathurine said. But when I mentioned your name they released me. The old woman, when I arrived there, said lizards work best, or sleep naked three nights under a blue moon, though the season's wrong, but either way, the sufferer must be patient, calm.

Suddenly in the corridor, the sound of someone running, muffled sobs, a woman's shouts.

Hermione looked directly at Mathurine. Shhhhh!

There's a disturbance, Mathurine said.

I dreamed I was an angel, Hermione began again. But it's not true. I'm a campaign, irresistible, a law like victory to the stronger. No man owns me, but I'm always my virtue's prisoner. That's plain. So I have to be capable of sacrifice, despite these doubts. Nothing, nothing, nothing prevents me.

She giggled.

Mathurine knew the voice wasn't Hermione's, though not exactly not Hermione's, more like a voice that, whenever it spoke, spirited Hermione away. Mathurine knew without knowing how she knew that she couldn't talk to it, though listening in silence was hard. She needed someone older, even one of the conspirators. Surely somebody somewhere knew what was happening. She edged a foot back, reached toward the door.

No! Hermione screeched.

Mathurine froze.

I—I...,Hermione bent forward, beginning to pant. I—I can't contain myself.

And then Mathurine heard it, from the bundle in her mistress's arms: the raspy whimper, snuffles.

Shhhhhh!

Hermione rocked forward, back: No one taught me evil, but it's in my feet. How else could I have come so close? They fashioned me into a universe, but their conceptions fell pathetically short. Do I look like anything's slave? Anyway, it's too simple, insipid. I lean toward the opening, push—haven't I done as much countless times before? If nothing is all that prevents me, then I have a secret: I'm her.

She took a step toward the window.

The hag, Mathurine blurted. I met her in—in her cottage. The roof's falling in, and she told me every scar's not a visitation. Sometimes your eyes mislead you. What does God smell like? I—I think something must be going on.

It's a darkness, Hermione said. Do you think I'm lovely? Do you want to touch my skin?

My mistress today isn't . . . herself. A sob caught in Mathurine's throat.

Hermione began to giggle. It's starting to rise, ice in my fingers, thighs, sex, nostrils, feet—

And as Hermione leaned into the window, Mathurine heard a scream, heard the door crash open behind her, and felt her whole body leave the earth. There were more shouts, a woman shrieked. Someone picked Mathurine up by the arms, not gently, not cruelly—the hands had hair on them. She saw nothing but remembered everything. Hermione's shrill rage cut the air, the sound of wood smashing, oaths, unspeakable words. And then Mathurine was vanishing down a stairway, cold air on her face, the thump of heavy footsteps. An odor filled her head. For a long moment she did nothing, merely allowed herself to be carried by these arms, yielded to whatever force took her over. Then she vomited. She recalled a man's voice moaning far away. Oh no no! it said. Oh no no no no no!

Mathurine never saw her mistress again. She spent three days alone in an unfamiliar room with a chamber pot and meals pushed through the door—a room of her own—but never tried the latch, perhaps she was a prisoner. On the fourth day an old retainer placed her in a coach and drove her away. She spent whatever remained of her childhood climbing up and down rungs on the elaborate hierarchy of menials in huge kitchens the exact location of which she never ascertained. She rarely learned names, was variously a fire-mender, drudge, scullery maid, cook's girl, pot watcher. Her footing seemed uncertain, she lived as a wayfarer. At the appropriate age she hired out, and secure in labors that could be performed half-asleep, she gradually resigned herself to the scrap of life that remained. She laughed at raunchy songs, slaughtered animals, fucked enough to know what love was, drank wine and got pregnant. Her first son died before his first birthday. Her second son died before his first birthday. Her daughter was stillborn. Then she met her husband whom she named Chou-chou because he didn't have another name and because, when he was lighthearted, he cavorted like her mother's goat. He was small and

257

bushy and wandered off one day. Gradually she came to feel that whatever wasn't disappointing just wasn't disappointing yet and started to live her life as if it were somebody else's. She named each voice in her head so she'd know who was trying to confuse her, bribed God, fortune, Lucifer, luck, Nadira the necromancer in the slough beyond the far commons, and diverted herself with the squalid affairs of the rich and powerful.

Only once during these years did Mathurine ever hear Hermione's name. It was in a conversation between a randy octogenarian and her master's eleven-year-old bride at dinner one evening in a house where Mathurine served just long enough to become unconcealably pregnant. Evidently Hermione had become proverbial in the region for any girl disposed to spectacular choler, a usage that spawned—probably through folk etymology—the widespread practice of recounting an embellished and inaccurate version of her history to terrify female children into permanent adolescence. Mathurine, who was serving soup at the moment, became desperate to catch the end of the octogenarian's unsavory fabrication, and so, in her distraction, allowed her customary eavesdropping to become uncustomarily obvious. The old satyr fell silent. Everyone stared. Mathurine blushed, curtsied, left. But not before catching the maddening hint that Hermione was either crippled or shut up somewhere, infirmée or enfermée, possibly both, a prisoner of her own fears or someone else's. The thought appalled Mathurine but reassured her, too. Hermione had been a gateway into madness, the opening through which Mathurine's childhood had strayed, and although in her perpetual Melancholia Mathurine sometimes missed her beloved mistress, she was nevertheless comforted to know that imperiled beauty or goodness or the delicious appearance of them or their odor or memory or, in general, any childish wish for incalculably more could never unexpectedly reappear and blow her life to hell.

From that day until this afternoon, May 2, 1519, in the little court of the Clos-Lucé as her latest in a long succession of masters and mistresses, the Italian dotard, Leonarde de Vinci, hops madly around the wheels of an ordinary wagon and his two assistants, Monsieur Francois des Melzes and le Baptiste, enact not twenty feet away what Mathurine might join if only she knew how— from that day to this, Mathurine has tried never to itch. But having just lost her soul to a kidney bean and been invaded by Satan, she realizes that the gate Hermione opened—despite Nadira's charms and all the Sacristan's candles—has been left ajar. No point in resisting her fate. Evil's what there is to know. In so many ways, this feels like a damned relief.

Now, observing Leonardo's assistants writhing and gesticulating and pretending to poke prissy daggers in their eyes, Mathurine walks over and proclaims that she too is a member of the Devil's Party. But her revelation doesn't have the anticipated effect. Not only does the little Monsieur Francois des Melzes pay her no mind; he bounces to his feet, shoves her aside, grabs le Baptiste by the adam's apple, and, spewing froth and spittle, drags him back up the stairs that Mathurine and Leonardo just bashed their way down. Mathurine's bumfuzzled. Her diabolical master's universe appears to be far less orderly than she imagined. Not that wildness isn't what she wants, but how do they expect her to get inside? Right now the master is bent forward with his shaggy thighs displayed shamelessly out the back of his nightshirt eyeballing what appears to be a clump of dried pig shit on the front left wagon wheel, and aside from muttering occasional gibberish, he shows no sign of being up to devilment. Mathurine isn't considering a return to her vicarious life, can't. But to sell her soul for nothing is a fool's bargain. So, she picks up the crumpled and muddy sketch of what looks to her like toad stools and stomps over to the head Satanist. Since he made it, shouldn't he be able to explain? With appropriate respect she takes Leonardo by the beard and sort of pulls him upright, stuffs the paper under his nose.

But Leonardo just shakes his head, insists, no, no, the monstrosity can't possibly be his.

Not that Mathurine quite grasps this, but she gets enough to know that between herself and His Satanic Lunacy there's an imperfect understanding. Right here—exactement!—she tells Leonardo in might-as-well-be-Japanese but takes her finger and traces a line:

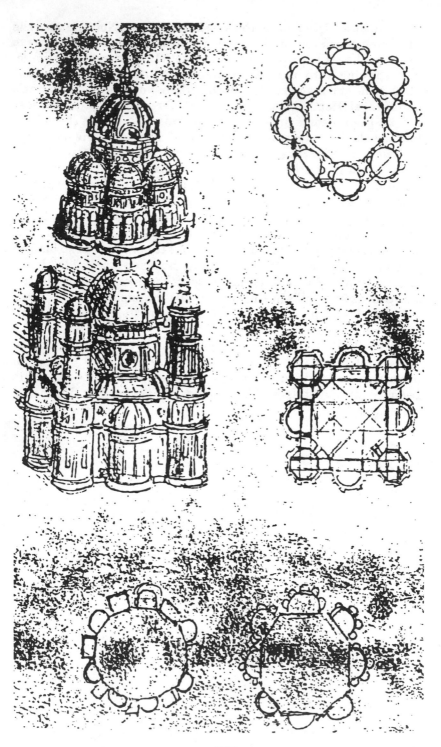

Now, the sketch is for a temple, or several, four floor plans with a couple of perspective drawings, all in the new central dome style, one perspective partially superimposed on and rising out of the other like an afterthought. These are sacred places for beings who dwell on the earth, with just a trace of spires to show that wackiness hasn't vanished altogether, but their principal business is down here. Mathurine's fingernail follows the bubbles, hops four times along what, were these mushrooms, we'd call pilei, then moves to a circular floor-plan, traces around and around.

Leonardo is startled. No denying it, the arcs of these temples and the foremost shoulder of Salai's yellow monstrosity bear a resemblance. He wants to insist it's a mere coincidence.

Mathurine makes her face into a question mark.

All right, he concedes, points to what are supposed to be shade lines, faint slashes shooting from the toadstools' back: It looks like it's moving. So?

Mathurine's pulse quickens. She reaches for another page, this one lying underneath Leonardo's left foot, upends him a little. It's a miscellany of doodles and notes, but in a corner is something like waves or snails: And how about this one?

Leonardo's jaw drops, he edges back: could his foresight have betrayed him? He was certain he'd never dreamed of Salai's behemoth, and now he finds this paradox—the motion of immovables!—deciphered in his own notes, his own hand. The undulations, curves, the massive surge of the beast—why, it's Heraclitus's current! Of course, he'd encountered as much in the colossus, in Milan, nearly thirty years ago: the hardness of bronze, the wildness of Horse. The whole point was to animate matter. And perhaps even then he'd glimpsed—feelingly—the torrent inside the animal. Whirlpools in the Arno, a tumult of hoofs or the perfect roundness at the croup. Why, the neck was plainly a wave! He badly needs his memory to be less crowded, for he suspects that a storm of new knowledge is on the way. How will others accommodate these revelations, the burdens unknown to his countrymen? For it's not just the monster before him that's so unsettling, not even its hatching from the egg of Leonardo's own brain. It's the world it means to inhabit.

Leonardo turns to Mathurine: How has such marvelous learning been withheld? he wants to know. Not that it actually has. He jabs his finger at the diagram: Here's proof!

Here's what? Mathurine wonders. She turns the diagram left right down over, sees a snake, staircase, three shrimp, something's spine, sawteeth, hair, wheat-field. Leonardo could at least tell her which end's up?

Why, it was Salai's whole point! Leonardo exclaims. May the infidel sizzle in witchery's skillet, but didn't he say Leonardo already possessed it? Your own invention! or roughly—Leonardo can't remember verbatim. But Salai stood right there, beside that very window! Leonardo gestures upward.

Mathurine follows his arm past the edge of the diagram toward—what in hell?—Monsieur François and le Baptiste huddled side by side upstairs in Leonardo's chamber. Is that where her new life is beginning? Does her master mean the direction is up?

Leonardo grabs her arm, points frantically at the wagon. Does Mathurine think he's exaggerating? Those were Salai's very words! More or less. Of course, Salai never accused him of inventing the color. Nowhere in heaven or earth is a yellow quite like it, and even if Leonardo would've happily wasted years concocting such a hue, he now suspects—he looks at Mathurine, shrugs—wouldn't the knowledge be damned?

Mathurine follows Leonardo hands, eyes, noises. Her eyes are young in evil; she isn't complaining, matters are so much worse than she perceives. She crooks her neck, tries gazing at everything from both below and above, but she must be blind. Only moments earlier she'd mistaken this wagon for a mere vehicle. Now, staring at it, she's unsure what it could be a vehicle for, what it means to convey. This madman seems excited over the squiggles she's shown him—she tries looking at the drawing edgewise, folded—as if they disclosed secrets, unspeakable deeds. But seeing only so much and no more leaves Mathurine frustrated. She puts her nose to the wheel rim and peers at what, even up close, resembles dried donkey shit. Could evil be concealed by hardened entities? She stares down at the unkempt geezer jabbering away in his nightshirt. She needs a better teacher.

Monsieur le maître le plus sage, intelligent, méchant, etcetera, j'ai aucune idée—aucune! aucune!—ce que vous avez me dit. Si vous pourriez, de temps en temps . . .

Leonardo displays a cow's comprehension.

Mathurine grinds her teeth, grabs another sketch. Now, everybody knows what this is!

Leonardo sees the cataract of the tail, the perfect circle of the hip, the trunk surging up and over like a tide. How could this woman know him better than himself? He falls to the earth, hugs Mathurine's ankles. Yes, yes, he weeps. The monster is his.

AND HORSES

Despite his dividedness, or perhaps because of it, Leonardo continued to make sporadic progress on the horse throughout 1492. He was beginning to get glimpses of it in three dimensions now, had his first dreams of the beast complete. With renewed determination and an orderliness born of fear, he directed his apprentices to construct wooden molds on which a terra cotta-like mixture of Leonardo's own devising could be spread, shaped, smoothed. An entire wooden skeleton was built in three separate sections, each of which was subdivided into threes, and a kiln began to be assembled in the back of the little vineyard where, once molded, the sub-sections could each be heated and baked over a period of several days. Just constructing the oven became a momentous task, for the smallest of the statue's sections was nearly twice the height of a man, and for a time Leonardo despaired of ever finishing it. He spoke with Ludovico about the possibility of modifying one of the huge ovens at a local manufactory, but it became evident that the process of firing would take so long, be so involved and—what Leonardo knew but was careful not to mention to his patron—result in so many failures, that Leonardo withdrew his request rather than place himself on a schedule. Far more than he was prepared to acknowledge, even to himself, the task required experience no human had ever possessed. Until it was finished there was just no telling where to start.

He rarely wondered at his moods now, the devastating invasions of clarity or those exhilarating moments when everything seemed within reach, and if, for no reason, the next step suddenly materialized and the horse strode forward, he merely gave thanks, refused to ask himself why. Even the soft, irregular breathing he took for granted beside his bed each night, even this seemed a phantom presence, part of the massive disorder that surrounded what was really going on, and he reassured himself that, when whatever was happening was over, he'd know what bewildered him now. In truth, only one change in his actions struck the sculptor as inexplicable enough, peculiar enough, plain crazy enough that, in his blind and terrified acquiescence to the statue's whims, it gave him pause. Leonardo talked.

On some evenings after the other youths had wandered off and Salai began to clear away the day's rubbish or shake the dust from the rags or beat his broom against the threshold, the sculptor would look up from what his hands were doing and hear a voice fill the air. It didn't talk to the child exactly, more like talking to itself but aloud, and in another's presence—and Salai would stop and lean on his broom and stand there very still, eyes unblinking, curls dangling over his face, absorbing every word. The voice would talk about anything—the part the sculptor had been fashioning, an oddity of his materials, or problems with a vendor or boy. He'd gaze off, and it would murmur: why did I never notice Baldassare's limp before? Or the voice might guffaw in the midst of a final operation: Why, the wheelwright's daughter is a veritable turnip!

Other times speech would seem to acquire its own force, a current mingling Albano, roots, true-eyed Andreas, chordal harmony, mechanics, anything:

. . . and the rhythm of fours drubbing the earth over the hillock beside the stone wall near the old hut thatched on the south slope without a within where the clucks of pigeons sound and the branches of olive trees rattle their same crabbed noise like bones strung in a row. . .

He'd feel beside himself then, lost in the sound of his own

excitement, and beginning to confound his working tongue with his working hands, he'd imagine his words were deeds. Describing batwings seemed like grasping them. Finding words for water unleashed a torrent. He couldn't parcel out his ecstasies, didn't recognize the man who underwent them, but for the first time since listening to Bellincioni on the Castello stairs, he sensed the capacity of speech to carry him away:

I—I feel like the first to set foot here—an unmapped country! Or perhaps I've been sentenced, marooned. But then I see cultivation— everywhere!—and wonder, what makes the inhabitants so hard to locate? Nothing I already know helps. While my sentence continues, everything comes to me as a present, but no sooner am I free—God's madness!—than the horse seems to be missing. I plunder the book from which my work has been drawn, return to plans. Nothing will stand without support, nothing is simply itself. If this ignorance isn't suffering, then it must be avoidance, fear. Until the horse moves again, I can't tell the difference. As soon as it moves, I don't care.

Beelzebub's boobies! Who did Leonardo think he was? He was like a man striding forward at too sharp an angle. If he'd paused to reflect, he would have toppled onto his nose. He admonished himself to take hold, but if he pushed any further, wondered, take hold of what?—his best answer was that, in spite of conceiving Italy's largest brazen fabrication, or possibly because of it, he was unburdening himself in front of a thirteen-year-old boy. What does a crisis look like? Every day Leonardo rose to work, and at night he slept soundly. The horse didn't make much progress, but then the horse never made *much* progress. Still, the whole situation was unsettling enough that, if other dangers hadn't appeared, if about this time his foothold in Milan hadn't begun to come loose, Leonardo might have tried to revive his friendships with Giacomo Andrea or the Martini brothers or even risked drinking with Bramante again, just to have a conversation that sounded, well, normal. But as it turned out, Leonardo was about to acquire ample and convincing reasons for not thinking about what, when he thought about it, prevented him from thinking about anything else, and so concluded that, really, the entire weirdness consisted in the accident of Leonardo's isolation and the boy's being there. As in the case of most reassuring lies, this one was true.

Intrigues were heating up over at the Castello. There was a three-way scam in progress involving the Holy Roman Emperor, Ludovico Sforza, and the French King, and this had entangled with the plots of Milan's three would-be prima donnas—Isabella, Cecilia, and Beatrice. All three first ladies had sons now, all three of whom were the sole heir to the duchy. Bellincioni connived mightily for Cecilia's bastard against Beatrice's poet, Niccolo da Correggio, ally of Ludovico's legitimate son, hence partisan of the Emperor, while the astrological physician, Ambrogio da Rosate, conspirator of Isabella and Spain, was finagling his way into Ludovico's inner circle. In Florence Lorenzo Il Magnifico had just died. In Rome there was a new pope. And that spring, to everyone's amazement, Cristoforo Colombo returned from Cathay. With threats to everyone's standing and continuous movement on all sides, Leonardo became much more successful at distracting the sculptor from his work. Halfway through the clay model for the horse's head, Leonardo agreed to embellish a pornographic motto Cecilia Gallerani was deadset on displaying over her bedroom door, and before he'd finished, he had to stop and construct a paper-mâché hillside for Gaspare Visconti's absurd masque that fit into somebody's diplomatic strategy with France. Isabella was sending daily requests for allegories on the subject of Fame seducing Vanity while Posterity sharpened its cleaver, and Ludovico—either to insure Leonardo's loyalty or to watch over him—unexpectedly gave him a huge studio in the corte vecchio directly across from Ludovico's own apartment. The space was generous, but moving took forever.

And then one afternoon as he abandoned himself to an interminable series of computations provoked by the possible ratios of the oval of a horse's shoulder to the circle of its hip—a mathematical relation that, if ever determined, would certainly compensate for the day lost to calculating it—Leonardo heard three demure coughs. He flung a scrap of abuse over his shoulder at the annoying lad, something about finding one's dinner underneath the stable, and instead of the expected defiance or footsteps or giggling, he heard nothing. He paused, looked up, and there appearing very sallow and ill-at-ease was the de facto ruler of Milan. A toothy grin split Ludovico's face, sweat trickled down his jaw. Leonardo jumped from his stool, performed acrobatic obeisance, groveled, lay down and whimpered to be kicked, and when Ludovico squeezed his shoulder and laughed off Leonardo's mistake, Leonardo felt the ground giving way beneath his feet. His fears began to be confirmed when Ludovico started strolling about the little workroom, making chitchat about the Pope's vices, repeating the latest Colombo gossip, and generally acting so chummy that even someone as obtuse as Leonardo could tell his intentions must be ghastly. Not only had Ludovico never visited Leonardo's workshop before, but Leonardo was far from certain that he'd ever gotten this much of the ruler's attention.

So Leonardo stood there trying not to wet himself, and when Ludovico's first sentence—after prolonged pleasantries about his new surroundings and were there any materials Leonardo required and did he find his helpers all adept and how often had he, Ludovico, thought of his revered workman and how thoroughly did he admire Leonardo's marvelous fabrications above those of any provincial artisan or the empty word-mongering of scholars and poets and how often he regretted the hurry of his own affairs that denied him, Ludovico Sforza, opportunity to pass more time just like this and how intensely he envied men like Bramante and Bellincioni for their chance to sit at Leonardo's feet and hear the priceless wisdom of etc.—when Ludovico's first real sentence was about the horse, Leonardo knew his time was up. He'd worked a few miracles, but nothing took the shine off a miracle like six months. Three years had passed since his clockwork universe blew Europe's mind, and there'd been plenty to amuse it since. The Holy Roman Emperor was a widower, having for the good of Christian diplomacy been deprived of his first wife so that he could go on another romp of arbitrary mayhem and fornication, and in the process he'd come out second best in a courting competition with Charles of France. This was bad for the Germans but great for Il Moro who promptly arranged to sacrifice his nephew's sister to the barbarian and to sweeten the gift with about four hundred thousand Florins. The strategy was to entice the Emperor as if the Lombards needed him, and upon his arrival, with his string of dignitaries and courtiers and ruffians in tow, make unmistakably plain that the Lombards didn't. There were more carriages in Milan than in all of Switzerland, more people than anywhere this side of Paris, more money than anyplace except Florence, and more treachery than in all non-Italian cities combined, but there was only one twenty-three foot bronze horse in all the world. More accurately, there wasn't even one, and that was the problem. Ludovico's visit was short. Nothing to the point was said. But by the time the simpering residuum of despotic ratshit had slunk off, Leonardo saw his future as never before. He could have a twenty-three-foot-high statue standing in the piazza in front of the Castello by the end of November, 1493, or he could leave Milan. Maybe.

Having already spent a decade planning what anyone reckless enough to try would have completed in a year, Leonardo now set out to complete in a fortnight what no one else would have attempted in a life. He failed. What's more, at the end of his thirteenth consecutive day of virtually non-stop labor, having passed his nights in a continuous state of working insanity, sleeping standing upright against the wall with a broom handle inclined across his thighs and gripped in one hand so that no sooner had he gone fast asleep than it would fall onto his toe, wake him, and start him working all over again, hardly pausing to bathe, to change his clothes, wipe his nose or bum—having so fundamentally strained and tested himself in this frenzy of doing and calculation that at the end of his thirteenth day, as he stood there with his mind as murky and dry as a bog in a drought, recognizing that he'd progressed hardly at all, that his frantic activity had resulted in nothing but a confusion even greater than the one in which he'd been living for the previous three years, Leonardo actually *saw* that he'd failed. He stood up, walked out into the yard. The ground was strewn with pieces of the beast, piles of rubble and mistakes. Some had lain in the same spot almost two years now. A few of the terra cotta figures were badly weathered, crumbling. It was as if Leonardo were surrounded by the pandemonium his life had become: clay and stucco, wooden frames, miniatures in bronze, fragments, bits, chunks, gadgets. In the moonlight they seemed a mockery and a gloom. How had he—by training a painter, haphazardly educated, an amateur mechanic, on paper a builder, a natural philosopher in his dreams, a competent musician, an undisciplined reader, an experimenter, snoop, a child, an impersonator, dilettante, clown—how had he ever imagined surpassing human doing in a medium that, if truth be told, he hardly understood? He shook his head. The fragments of the horse cluttering the little yard parodied something. He'd compiled more lore about the beast, sketched it in more attitudes and contortions, simply knew it better than anyone since God. He'd ridden palfreys, geldings, war stallions, both nags and yearlings, fed them, stood beside the paddock as they frolicked, been charged and kicked at, even tried to get inside their stalls with them. He'd seen them give birth, yanked the colts bewildered into the world of air and light, watched them clamber onto their spindly legs, had smelled their flesh and gasses, watched their dung plop onto the dust, been nearby as they coupled and fought, had cut open every inch of them, knew each bone and muscle by name. So much of him was horses, but even after ten years, so little of him was a bronze-worker.

...already feel them moving.

The voice startled Leonardo. He turned to see. In the dank and shadowy yard he gazed for a second among the phantasmal shapes before making out the boy's thin figure, dark in the doorway, leaning on the shop-broom, listening.

I come to watch. They lie like this in the light, but if—if you're quiet, you smell their fear.

He didn't move, but his stillness wasn't ease. Even in the moonlight Leonardo could see the muscle of his cheek shiver, his fingertips white. There was something fierce about the way he slouched there. He'd probably been dogging Leonardo's steps for hours, perhaps all day, waiting for God-only-knew-what, maybe he'd been lurking here the entire two weeks.

The boy continued: If you imagined them terrifying, so impossible . . . well, they're oafish, aren't they? They don't know any of this, but it's obvious when I'm here. This is the great work, the new earth. I come to—

Go away, Leonardo said with a wave of his hand.

The boy continued: My master's making a horse. The last change. It will be truer than the creatures—

Leave. There's nothing left here.

The boy didn't move. He wanted to witness everything, always at the corner of your eyes, insinuating memory into what should've been a private life—mutterings, calculations, fancies, mistakes, even the blasphemous oaths you lavish on yourself hoping no one else will. In truth, it now seemed to Leonardo in his exhaustion and near collapse that there'd never been a day free of the pest, standing just like he was, insidious. He knew it was a trap, but instead of anger, Leonardo wanted desperately not to see him.

The labor isn't what—, Leonardo almost said *we*. Isn't what I thought. Presumption. Science gets too entangled—money, worldly muck, time. Anyway, it's not a mortal business. So, go away.

The boy didn't move.

Leonardo kept his eyes on an absence over the stone wall: I know I . . . you can't get loose, can't help seeing it. But there are eyes and hands, there's life and there's matter, there's science and there are deeds, there are . . . . The world's halved.

The boy still didn't move.

Leonardo kicked at the ground, spoke sharply: I'm weary. Weeeeeeeeeary!

Don't talk stupid.

Leonardo's head spun round.

The boy hung on his broom, cheek twitching, fingers ghostly white.

Wh-what? Leonardo stammered.

Salai continued: It can't end . . . Weary?! There's no way to see it and walk away. They've eaten us, shat us out in another place. Did you think you made this dream? You're banished, gone. Weary?! Don't be absurd. I've heard you—

You're speaking like this to me?!

I've *heard* you! You can't not know it. You can't wipe it clean. There's a divide, no one . . . . Then all at once the boy dashed past Leonardo into the yard.

Leonardo grabbed at him. Gutter-pissant! Get out of my—

But with his street-urchin's deftness, the lightness that had made him uncatchable in market stalls and had threatened on more than one occasion to turn Leonardo's apprentices into a mob, Salai ducked his master's fingers, wobbled once, lunged, and hardly missing a stride, slipped his hands under a full-size clay model of the horse's cannon. Look! he shouted, and began furiously trying to right the gigantic leg. Here!

The hulk of clay and wood didn't budge.

Obstinate, Leonardo said. Get out. You've no place ...!

The boy flung back gibberish, continued to shove, grunt. Spittle covered his face.

Are you deaf?! Leonardo was shouting at him. Horse is over. I'm not that person, I'm a ...a painter. I made the universe from clock parts. I know Aristotle, they speak my name in Venezia, I—I ...I HATE it! HATE it! There are almond trees on Albano with silver fronds. If the wind blows they make a noise not like vegetation, not part of that sphere, nature's clatter. There are more mysteries than we can—Are you deaf?! Get out of here! I'm weeeeeary!

And Leonardo rushed over to where the fourteen-year-old body whipped itself into a fit, reached out with his powerful left hand to seize the child by the neck and, if necessary, fling him into the alley where he belonged but out of Leonardo's life, suffering, future, heart, was dragging him loose from the clay when Salai exploded.

Look! Look! Look! Look! the youth shrieked and with fists that— though they'd always be smaller than a man's, always resemble a maiden's bones, were nevertheless no longer the unknuckled fat blobs of a ten year old—with his fists Salai began to pummel the holy hell out of Leonardo's eyes.

Whaaaa—?!!!

Here! Here! Here!

Dung-smear! Carrion!

It's ...I've seen ...moving.

Hemorrhoid, freak, rot, hell-blister!

Leonardo tried to strike back but the boy was too close. It was like trying to box your own nose. He didn't know if he was falling, running, struggling or simply trying to get away. Mostly he was amazed. His own hands seemed to be flailing him. The ground went, returned. He tried to protect his eyes, tried to turn aside, but the sharp little bones were legion, pushing into his cheeks, mouth, windpipe, ears. Like a huge bird—either a vulture or a kite—flapping its wings against his face. Then, his shoulder struck something hard, and Leonardo heard the crunch of bones. A voice shrieked inside his head.

—eeeeeeeeeeeee—

Oooph!

...can ...see ...

I'll kill—

Look! Look! Look! Look!

Fuck.

Then it stopped. Leonardo lay on the ground, not moving, his whole face on fire. The earthquake ended. Carefully he opened an eye. Salai lay across Leonardo's chest, his own chest heaving, breath coming in asthmatic gasps, his clothing soaked through with sweat. In the moonlight his wet body glistened like metal after rain. His eyes were as wide as thumbnails, and his black curls lay matted against his skin.

It's here, he choked out. I've seen ...already. I see it, I can't not see it...every night. Horse. And with a jerk of his arm he indicated the yard.

Leonardo felt eerie. Despite his exhaustion, the days without sleep, or somehow superimposed over his exhaustion, inseparable, was a wildness on the surface of his skin. He was boiling. He looked down at the boy who, utterly spent and absorbed in futile grief, half floundered, half lay, like a beached seal, on top of his master's aching body. Slowly Leonardo pushed himself up on his elbows, felt a sharp pain in one arm. He shoved the boy roughly to the ground, tried to look past him. Scattered over the yard were the earthen fragments of Leonardo's creature, somber phantoms, either the nightmare of a life or life itself, he no longer knew which. He understood the boy's anger, of course, felt the rage—the beech and clay piece Salai tried to hoist was a foreleg, half again the height of a man, three braccia or more, probably the weight of four men, so much more than a dream, more than lines on a page, more than replicas, promises, but nothing like horse.

Leonardo looked at the boy, shrugged: Your eyes are misleading you. Between this mud pretense and bronze lies—The boy slammed both fists into the ground, screamed: IDIOT!

Then leaping to his feet, Salai stomped over to a pile of terra cotta fragments, jabbed his finger at each piece as he spoke. It's already here! he said. Clay!

And looking into the youth's black eyes, Leonardo was astonished to find a man there. His mouth fell open, he put his hands on his knees, he sat up. Clay...?

Clay!

Horse...clay?

Assemble the model, Salai said. It's all...they couldn't dream it, the terror's hard...Σ. This is the idea, just build it—

In...clay?

Clay! Clay! Clay! Clay! Yesssss, moron. You want to stay alive, don't you?

How it was done hardly matters, for no sooner had Salai made him see it than Leonardo knew it was done already. So much of the creature already surrounded him in that courtyard that if they'd been strong enough to move the clay and wood hulks themselves and if they'd had a binding solution and clamps and scaffolds and enough lumber and chain and had set to work right then, they could have assembled two-thirds of it before dawn. From past trial and error Leonardo knew that two-thirds of anything was all of it, for to get that far was to see what was missing, to see the absence as something, not as the paralyzing nothing that, so long as it could still be virtually anything,

271

every emptiness threatened to be. As it was, however, assembling the clay model took him three months, and even then, if it hadn't been for fear of blowing even this one last chance or the fact that the fourteen-year-old boy was always hovering over him, snooping, badgering, threatening to destroy his composure with whispered sarcasm or run-on banter, or if it hadn't been for Leonardo's own premonition that, at last, he was concocting the one reply that would leave even Bellincioni dumb, if it hadn't been for these helter skelter senses, he might have dickered with obscurities another year. But regardless of the cause, nearly three weeks before his deadline, in early November of 1493, Leonardo da Vinci found himself hopping around on one foot, shrieking and pleading and threatening as twenty-two stout yeomen and their bedraggled plowhorses yanked and jerked and battered the monstrosity through Milan's streets, up to the Castello where, once miraculously arrived in a single piece, the hulk required seventeen days to move from the ingenious cart Leonardo had devised for it onto the platform that, at the last moment it had finally crossed some ordinary brickmason's mind to build, so that when four days later the entourage of German soldiers rattled through the Piazza del Duomo, swung down the Via Dante, caromed off a barricade, ran over a gaggle of dirty children and, for lack of anything better to kill, began picking off starving dogs and cats with shafts from a wagonload of otherwise entirely useless crossbows, the guffawing Prussians slapped each other on the shoulder, bellowed, guffawed and suddenly toppled right over their horses' heads. For in front of them stood what couldn't be. It was a piece of earth as unmistakable as a valley but as inconceivable as the living dead— or far less conceivable, for ghosts were well-known!—a stone horse more massive than a fortress, something only a mad god would build, a miracle never known, never rumored, never imagined even in the delirium of drunkenness or love. The procession crunched and stumbled and reared and panicked into a huge constipated mob. Every human fell into a jaw-gaping stupor. Each wagonload of soldiers, each cart of provisions, all the weary footsoldiers, and last, riding in one of the only three carriages the Emperor owned, his imperial proxy, a bushy-headed feudal warlord with a bad stammer who before the conclusion of the wedding festivities would have sprayed saliva on the imperturbable faces and bosom of every highborn lady in Lombardy—all of these, in successive waves, piled up, impatiently shouting at those ahead to proceed until they, too, got within sight of it, falling silent, staggering back into the furious rank of travelers behind, creating an impossible knot of astonished humanity, befuddled and frightened, confronting what they could neither dispel nor endure. So this, *this* was Milan!

And Leonardo da Vinci had watched it. In the smock of an ordinary stone-cutter, not disguised, merely negligible, standing on a castaway bucket at the mouth of the stinking alley-of-the-hair-sellers, positioned where he'd see the first wave, the line of German calvary who, rounding the curve from the Piazza del Duomo and coming within sight of the square in front of the castle's façade, would be the first to take it all in—yes, Leonardo had seen everything. He wasn't certain what it proved. After all, the northerners were an uncouth race—except for the Flemish—and their soldiers were as uncouth a specimen of their uncouthness as they could boast, slightly more human than fish or vegetables. What could he learn from lummoxes? Nevertheless, Leonardo had dodged Ludovico's invitation to be among the welcoming dignitaries, had affected modesty and shame, passed up the chance to watch Bramante choke on his liver, resorted to all manner of humiliating balderdash that even to himself at the time had appeared strange, needless, and all because he simply wanted to be alone, standing in this position, now. The soldiers' raucous laughter stopped, the boasting and threats became a hush. Men pushed back against those behind them as if trying to escape. Horses reared, drivers let the reins slide from their hands. A wagonful of imperial gifts overturned and a young soldier was pinned beneath its wheel. No one moved to help, no one took notice of the shiny plate and gewgaws clattering over the ground, shrieks, noise—no one possessed any words or self-importance or presence of mind. Rising above them, almost as tall as the Castello's wall, a stone likeness of the beasts on which the soldiers at this very instant rode, the animals that surrounded them, that had pulled their wagons, dragged them across Switzerland, through mountains and past lakes, swimming, rearing, everywhere—but hardly there, hardly alive, never inscrutable. Until now. As if the creatures on which they sat, these conveniences, these lumps, had usurped the majesty of gods. As if the world had turned upside down. It was monstrous. It was magic. Nobody knew what the hell it was.

Not even Leonardo da Vinci. He was watching a multitude of Prussian warriors fall all over each other at the spectacle of what, now that it was finished, appeared so obvious: fourteen clay horse-sections assembled in a workmanlike fashion, sections he'd planned with the help of calipers and ratios, using the elemental geometry taught him as a teenager in true-eyed Andreas' shop, sections of ordinary river clay and binding agents, relying on painter's perspective and potter's lore, a result of long labor and obsessive planning but, now that it was standing there on its feet, nothing worth all this frenzy. It was plain the Germans were fools. He wanted to step forward and disillusion them, say that, really, all their fuss was over acts that, where calculation and transparent gimmickry weren't involved, were hardly more than natural! This slobbering astonishment wasn't recognition. It was proof of fraud. Even puppet theaters and traveling mimes provoked these reactions, every poet worth his stipend made his listeners weep at nothing. Did the admiration of dupes matter? Did anyone see what was before them? And if not, then why was Leonardo standing here, why did he feel—it was preposterous—almost good? And he had staggered off like a man who has been beaten, wandered into the giardini pubblici, around behind the Castello on the ducal hunting grounds, to the city walls, seeing with his exhausted, delirious eyes all the dreamlikeness of the nocturnal life, naked men dousing lanterns, beggars eating food left for pets, or eating the pets, women loving one another, men prying open windows and doors, all the shameful and delicious crimes of daylight's other side, seeing it all as if a divine manifestation, an opening of life's master volume, until at last he arrived at his little vineyard, stood outside in the yard, among the clutter that he knew but couldn't believe had been the work of his own hands, and there in the moonlight with the chill air and hot blood colliding in his cheeks, setting his skin to prickling, Leonardo all at once felt the enormity of it, felt his back give way, shoulders heave, and with a loud animal cry of victory and pain, he began to shout. He shouted at the threshold, shouted in the foyer where the rough poplar lay against the wall, whooped with his spine against the empty corner beside the huge block of lime, shouted squatting on the floor, almost sprawled out right then and there beneath the workbench and kicked and wrung his hands and shouted, got momentary possession of himself, walked to the little stone stairs leading to his bedroom, felt it well back up inside him, ran outside and shouted his whole repertory all over again. By the time he got back to the bottom of the stone steps he was so exhausted, so spent, that he could imagine himself never waking. At the same instant, however, his thoughts were still frantic. He could see himself at every moment of his future, found all of his previously disappointed fancies rushing back now with the assurance of deeds, he was full, spilling. He couldn't shout anymore, couldn't breathe. He climbed the little stairs, stumbled in the speckled dark toward the bed, fell over the tick, died into the sticky softness, closed his eyes. He had done it. Leonardo da Vinci had made a horse. And that was when he felt the small hand wrap around his ankle.

For a long time he said nothing. They both remained there, motionless in the gloom, tense, monolithic, listening to the air crackling with insects, the shrill silence clattering in their ears. A man, a boy, the dark. Their hush was broken by the sound of smooth fabric gliding over linen.

Have you ever felt happy? Leonardo asked.

No, the boy answered.

It feels like you went on a journey and left yourself behind. Like smoke.

Silence.

The darkness smells of wet straw tonight, the boy whispered. I stood beside the stone wall for many hours, waiting. There were no stars.

If the winters aren't severe, it should last many seasons. That is, if the moisture doesn't swell the seams. Nations should have heard of it before .... Leonardo shook his head, took a breath. Well, something's finally made.

There were two men arguing in the alley, Salai continued. This was very late but before you returned. I heard one of them curse you, said you would bring God's wrath on the city.

Leonardo chuckled.

Salai continued: Black arts, the angry one kept shrieking. The other called you a philosopher, like Brunelleschi, he said. They don't see, ignorant. They gawk but they don't know.

No, they don't know, Leonardo said. He gave a sigh and felt the fingers dig into his foot. It's—

—late. Salai continued: I waited beside the wall, where the yellow cat with no tail prowls for lizards. There was a scent there, as if it had recently rained. I remembered sleeping in the hayloft, rats, lice. The sky was perfectly black, and I waited a long time.

Salai's voice seemed to catch in his throat. Many nights, I've lived with them. They are ...terrifying, vast as starless skies, like this one, and blacker. They make a noise through their noses, a hissing that tells you how nothing you are. Many times they've tried to destroy me. Their hooves are monstrous like—

When you're happy, the soul is here, Leonardo indicated his throat, smiled. There are delicious pleasures, but nothing preferable. Brimming. I saw the Prussians when they entered the city. They were undone. The Moor told me himself that it was magnificent, that it—

...destroy them, defeat their life. I've seen—

Shhhh. It's late—

—late! Late! I know, I waited beside the wall ....

The fingers dug into Leonardo's leg again, took hold below the knee. It was starting to hurt.

You're safe now, Leonardo said. We're ...I'm triumphing. They're not here.

You wanted to flee. You were a coward. I know, because I've been afraid of them. They crush you, they're awful. The sound their mud makes as it slithers from their haunches, the way their tails lift, their straining forward, the eyes as round and empty as thumbs. I—I hate them, I can't .... I used to steal into their stalls at night for it was my only ...I would have frozen, died of the wet. I've eaten the bodies of cats. Rotting, no fire to cook them. Have you tasted a cat? But they aren't

275

like this, they are …no one can eat one of them. I have heard that men do, but I don't believe …or I would, I would eat the stallions, I would chew their flesh, I would taste—

Slowly the sobs took over. Rocking his body, the bed, the small hands clinging to Leonardo's bones. I hate them, I hate them, I hate them, he said, his shoulders convulsing.

Shhhh, Leonardo whispered. Shhhhh. It's made.

The fingers clutched at Leonardo's thighs, arm. He felt the small body climbing up onto the tick, felt the bewildered, fumbling hands.

They're horrid, the boy whimpered. I knew you—

It's all right, Leonardo said as the warmth filled him. It's …we're safe.

…hate them…

Shhhh. The smooth boyflesh on his hair.

I waited beside …the wall a long…

They became one man.

What Arno said to me our last phone conversation was: "You have no sense of history."

"Of humor."

"Nope, moment and milieu, modes of production, kairos, epoché, pleroma. You're a Platonist after the death of God, a secular, angry Platonist. What would it take for you to grasp your situation?"

The attack was so uncharacteristically frank that I had some trouble responding. "Has a Marxist gotten loose in your accounting department?"

He chuckled. "No, I mean it. You're essentially a romantic who has glimpsed modernity. You live as if people read *Ulysses*, like the world's the one Kant knew. You remember the parable about the philosopher's star gazing?"

"Can't you feel safe if I'm not a cliché?"

"When Joyce published *Portrait of the Artist* there were fewer than 6,000 new books published in this country each year, now there are nearly 60,000, and back then there were no TV's. How much time do you think the average American spends reading?"

"Do you have any statistics on people who pay attention to statistics?"

"Nineteen hours a year. That's an hour and thirty-five minutes a month."

I still don't understand why, but over several years as Arno and I gradually stopped talking about anything either of us wanted to talk about we found ourselves talking more and more about time. Or about whatever it is two people are talking about when one talks about the future and the other talks about the past and both are convinced they're talking about the same thing.

"...world doesn't exist," he insisted. "Capital 'A' Art, the transcendent order of world masterpieces, science, patriarchy, humanism—it's just over. Why fight battles that're lost? The West's decentered, meaning's anachronistic—system without origin, vertiginous abyss, endless deferral..."

"This utopia you're describing—"

"Utopia uschmopia, I'm just describing—"

"Things as they are? Thank heavens metaphysics is over or I'd have mistaken you for a disinterested observer."

"All I'm saying—and I'm trying to be gentle; I don't mean to pass judgment—is sometimes a person has to stop resisting and grow. Nostalgia goes nowhere. Maybe it's time you moved forward, opened yourself."

"And all I'm saying is metaphors—even delicious ones like 'growth'—have limits, stark ones. Are you sure this newness is new, even exists?"

Arno sighed. "I don't want to condescend to you, R—, okay? 'Cause I know you really mean what you're saying or something similar, but isn't it just possible your whole life amounts to horse shit?"

"Three futures are competing," I said. "There's the utopia, which is desirable but never anywhere."

"No place isn't nothing."

"What you can't talk about you can't talk about. Then there's the apocalypse which, as I see it, is optimism—"

Arno guffawed. "Holocaust, everything to zilch, then doom ushers in utopia?"

"Nope. That's Nietzsche. I mean more like zilch, ground zero, doom period. No reason to fear it unless justice is real."

Arno yawned. "You said there were three."

"Mucking-on. That's the cynical future."

"You don't call apocalypse cynical?"

"Only a practical utopia leaves you more naked than apocalypse. Mucking-on means there's no end to it. We haven't seen the worst. In fact, I personally find mucking-on unimaginable."

If ever in a long conversation with someone you love you both fall silent and while waiting for him to continue or considering what to say next, you think you hear—far away and so faint and shapeless your impulse will always be to deny it—hear a peculiar whooshy sound you think could be your friend panting, make any excuse, no matter how transparent, but get off the phone. This is a rule like, if you hear footsteps behind you on a deserted street, cross to the other side, or during electrical storms lie down in a ditch. Sitting on my barstool beside the phone, I thought for the briefest instant I heard Arno panting. "How's Ellie? She in middle school now?" I asked.

"How's Dee?"

"What's Ellie reading?"

"I noticed in a *Times* poll last week that forty percent of Americans with college degrees believe the Renaissance occurred a hundred years ago," Arno said. "I just asked because when Dee phoned she seemed, y'know, worried."

"Moliere? Rostand? Balzac? And Ellie reads them in the original too, I bet."

"A taste for antiques isn't gonna warp her." Arno chuckled. "But then I guess Dee told you about the phone call?"

"A true classical education," I said. "Ellie's mom must be proud."

"—*really* worried. She said to me, you're his friend, Arn, and it isn't like this 'novel' is bad, is it? And, R—, trust me, I reassured her it was, y'know, an 'admirable' book, regular tour de force, remarkably similar to what people used to call 'important,' the sort of elitist toy that hardly a century ago—"

"And what's Ellie's mom up to these days?" I asked. "I know she writes. What'd the last postmark say? Can you make out anything when you hold her envelopes up to the light? Does your daughter ever tell you what's in your own wife's letters? Where does Ellie hide them, by the way? Under her mattress? In a jewelry box? When you duplicated the key—"

"That Dee's some kind of woman! A little earnest maybe, martyr-complex, do-gooder, shrill as an air-raid siren, self-righteous, sterile, sexless, obsessed, but blind loyalty like that's nearly extinct! Anyway, Dee asked me, what if admirable books need disguising? Like I said, she's worried about you."

"But then I guess Ellie never talks about her mother," I said. "Or about the books she reads, or about her friends or dreams, certainly not about her future or the jungle she lives in or about anything she loves—"

"So, I explained to Dee how nobody in the business school—and this is graduate faculty—nobody does qualitative research. I mean, these guys can hardly read! Books schmooks. We've even got a philosopher, business ethics, he just published an 'article,' graphs, equations, something about incommensurability dissonance in graduated life-conflict models—"

"In fact, I guess Ellie never talks to you at all since the sound of her own father's voice makes her want to puke!"

I dream my life without end, live it over and over in retrospect, anticipation, as Freud assured me I always would, engine disengaged, perpetual maniacal superfluous motion, rearranging the furniture of possible pasts, the events that might've happened otherwise but didn't, all in search of the new version, a chance to unwound, to unhurt, to revise, heal, mend.

But the situation's so much worse than I feared. My second chance came. I lived as always. I never even knew.

The sound in the receiver was unmistakable. My friend, Arno, was crying.

"Sport?"

I waited for the world to end. When it didn't, a hoarse voice announced, "Leonardo da Vinci is dead." And then Arno hung up forever.

Meanwhile, upstairs inside Leonardo da Vinci's abandoned chamber the young lord Francesco Melzi and the low-born servant Battista de Vilanis stand beside Leonardo's bed like humorless men before a urinal. The bed's empty, its hill of coverlets shoved back in an elephantine rumple. The pillow is covered with smudges and goo. On the floor are paper gewgaws in brilliant colors. They've come to pay their final respects, but neither knows what to make of what's missing here. After all, a lot more than just Leonardo da Vinci isn't in this bed. Salai's not here, the philosopher's stone's not, Atlantis isn't. When you start to think about it, Leonardo seems no more absent than anything else, and this complicates what otherwise might be plain. Looking down at the bed now, Melzi and Battista divide over what its emptiness means. For Battista, it means Leonardo has revived from his deathfit— it wouldn't be the first time—and taken a journey, perhaps to the privy or kitchen but most likely down to the courtyard where, after all, Battista just saw him. His eyes still exert a powerful influence over Battista's unsophisticated mind, despite Melzi's arguments for disregarding them. Of course, Battista isn't prepared to throw himself onto a penknife over it, but privately he's a liberal, finds the obvious explanation as good as any other.

Melzi, on the other hand, is deeply unconfused. Having begun to feel his new powers, he's rapidly becoming a man the exact size of his imagination. For him, the bed is a space for designs. He's trying to recall right now the two ways that Lucca's *Primer of Tropes and Speech Ornaments* recommends commencing a eulogy. Everything depends on striking the right note. As Francesco remembers it, there's the low style:

Well, it's over. (Orator shrugs.) What's to be said?

And then there's the high style:

(Orator looks upward.) Oh thou who dost e'en now gaze down upon bereft mortality from yon heaven's blinding brilliance etcetera!

What Francesco can't remember is the turn in either, the place where unspeakable grief ceases to be an obstacle to speaking. This lacuna might stymie a less resourceful man, but now Melzi sees nature stretching before him like blank paper. There are no laws, only instruments! He thrusts his fist into the air, lets it hang, then opens his fingers one at a time. Both men gaze into his empty palm. Gone, Melzi sighs.

Battista, recognizing that a truer statement could not be made, agrees.

When he lived among us, Melzi says, did we know him for what he was? A source of endless astonishment, a muse, a fountain. I, for one, never grasped it."

Battista shakes his head.

I suppose others more astute than myself may have recognized...?

Nope, nope, Battista admits.

...but I was blind, ignorant. My soul will never aspire so high again.

Battista's nose itches. Yep, yep.

Would you have believed he'd ever seem so...insubstantial? Melzi asks.

Battista says he'd never believe it.

Just this morning his splendid beard lay across these covers, his Roman brow, his mighty hands! He was an imposing figure. Chest like an ox. Once when he was angry with me—this was many years ago, you understand—once years ago he took me here by the neck and shook me. Like so.

Melzi pinches Battista's neck and shakes until Battista's teeth rattle. Melzi chuckles: I thought I was going to be killed.

Battista chuckles too.

Melzi sighs.

Battista sighs.

I can almost see him, Melzi says, snuffles.

Battista snuffles, almost sees him too.

Perhaps, there are final sentiments? Melzi pauses. Words you might wish to utter?

Battista finds himself on mushy ground. Knowing what's obvious appears to be one thing, but talking about it is another. Doubtless the master is gone. Melzi has said as much. Who disagrees? Doubtless an empty bed is an empty bed. No one gainsays it. But then Battista has also watched the sun move and the earth stand perfectly still, has seen sailing vessels fall over the corner of the world, observed men shrink in stature walking away from him, and can tell with a peremptory glance that the water in the center of a lake is higher than at the shore. Last spring he witnessed a traveling sorcerer divide a maiden into two parts, and twice he's observed the sun blotted out, numerous times seen stars fall to the ground, and everyday inhabits a world where everyone rich is bigger, stronger, younger and lovelier than everyone poor. He has seen all of these things with his own eyes and, despite the clever confusions of philosophers, continues to believe in them, but that doesn't mean he's prepared to say so! Right now, it's all he can do not to acquiesce to Melzi's madness, shout, yes! yes! and start talking exactly as if the Maestro were alive. Which, of course, he is. Snot dribbles down Battista's lip. One eye's threatening to tear. His throat's raspy. Gazing directly into Melzi's face, he heaves the heaviest sigh he can muster and says: He looks just like himself.

Melzi nods.

I—I've never known him to appear so...so...

Fantastic.

...never dreamed I could see him like this.

Some seconds pass.

My grief can't be said, Battista concludes.

Melzi nods, rests a hand on Battista's arm. It's all so incredible.

Incredible, yes.

Do you recall the afternoon, was it in Milano? Melzi begins. I sat in the window of the Castello workshop. The Maestro had perfected a contrivance for extracting oil from nuts by forcing their essence through a sieve.

Battista doesn't recall, says he does.

You were learning the science of underlayment, Melzi continues, and having great difficulty. Maestro Leonardo was wondrous patient, for you were slow, slow.

Uh.

It was necessary to scrape the gesso repeatedly for your clumsy fingers were a mighty hindrance. We all pitched in. In fact, it was I myself who corrected your bunglings.

Silence.

How clearly we both see those days. We were comrades! Insepa-rable.

Battista coughs: That must've been another—

Melzi's mouth drops open: Don't remember!

I didn't say—

Don't remember!

I just—

Don't remember Leonardo da Vinci?! Don't remember his infinite condescension, his patience?!

Yes, no, yes, no, yes—

Of course, of course, you remember! How could you behave like the vile and contemptible villain who would forget his munificence, repudiate on death's threshold his miracle of generosity, refuse distinction, the very spirit that lifted you from bestial oblivion, no, no, you couldn't, wouldn't renounce beneficence, wipe clean gratitude's slate, deny memory, wouldn't be such a low-life, stinking, dung-bedaubed, piece of black, mud-smirched....

I remember! I remember! But not *slow*, I was never—

Oh, the Maestro was longsuffering! For hours he taught you, held your clumsy hand. I can still hear his voice. You were a veritable snail! And, of course, we'll never forget—now that we two alone can testify before a disbelieving world, now that we two alone know of his last end, are witnessing his demise with our own eyes, hearing his rapture, seeing this miracle. Oh, I share your pain, my friend. Unburthen your soul to me!

Battista feels Melzi's arm squeeze his shoulder, sees the young lord's eyebrows pinched, lids swollen and red.

Is...is he, then, assumed? Battista croaks.

It was the apex of our pathetic lives that we knew him! Melzi mutters. We'll live on in his shadow, gather fondly in distant kingdoms, be knit together till doom, boon companions, brothers, kin, one fortune.

Promise?

Mmmhmm.

Battista takes a deep breath and bewails Leonardo da Vinci. He sobs, mouths high-toned expostulation, means every word. For a long time the two men outdo each other in exuberant grieving, cloying the air with truisms and covering the furniture in rhetoric and tears. Their laments pour out the window, ascend the stone wall, depart the Clos-Lucé, touch the film of clouds overhead, reaching passers-by along the narrow road past the chateau, all the way down to the Loire. Leonardo da Vinci is dead. The promise has come to nothing. He's dead. Dead.

And down in the courtyard Mathurine hears them. She's astonished by the profuseness of evildoing, all the depths opening around her. For some reason she'd imagined that debauchery would be effortless, a matter of relaxing restraints she'd never been much good at anyway and doing what came naturally, but now she's stymied by sin's intricacy, by obscure designs that complicate everything. For example, she has just noticed a scraggly brown weed growing beside this carriage drive—that is, noticed it as a wound in the otherwise unmarred surface of her day, a plant she's stepped on her entire life, of course, but never once paused over—and is asking herself, in what unfathomable arrangement could it have a place? The question—if long looks can be called questions—has arisen because Leonardo's sketch of burr reed has fallen on the ground beside this plant, strongly implying a connection, and as the moans grow louder overhead, she strains to make out what the connection could be. What if vaster atrocities are possible than she ever imagined?

Leonardo meanwhile is trying to make sense of the miracle confronting—he dreams—them both. He now admits what his companion has already recognized—her perceptiveness astounds him!—that this yellow behemoth is a vast allegory of his failure in Milan. Each part of the contrivance divulges a meaning, but reading it seems to demand the rarest art. He jabs his finger at the near flank. For example, how could these four holes be equine? Not even in Leonardo's search for visible ratios, measurable proportion, did he ever imagine nature so geometrically. Why their brilliance amounts to shiny nothing! Or still more troubling, here beside what Leonardo speculates is the stern, here's a letterish looking filigree that he can almost replicate. He goes through the motions of copying it in the mud at Mathurine's feet, left-handed, struggling to avoid turning it around backwards, mirror-fashioned, getting it almost right,

BUICK

except for the end, which he keeps returning to, seeing there's a problem. He thinks this figure is a mere embellishment, but having uttered —ICCI since childhood and having heard —IQUE for three years now and confusedly sensing that the barbarous morpheme hacked out by Georg back in Rome just might be —ICK, Leonardo's not sure it isn't a cryptogram. Could these recondite syllables be the meaning of his doom?

Anyway, Leonardo's carrying on like this in a self-absorption that's total, and despite Mathurine's efforts to follow him, she's none the wickeder. She needs some direction, and if Leonardo's too far gone in depravity to provide it, she'll have to strike out on her own. So while Leonardo prates and shudders and gesticulates, Mathurine's starting to organize his depraved universe for herself. With the images he's abandoned, she's arranging sequences, diagonals, chiasmata, circles, heaps, parallels or whatever other figure seems delicious to her mind, all around the courtyard, and right now she's trying to decide where to place this sketch of burr reed, when Leonardo notices she's no longer paying him any attention. Why, his companion is idling! And stomping over, Leonardo grabs the drawing—Is she blind?—and flings burr reed all over Mathurine's creation.

That's it. Mathurine picks up the sketch with one hand and her master with the other, slams the muddy page against his nose, and informs him his time is up. He's been fussing over these frightful depictions for three years now, and she's tiiiiiired of it. She knows his worthless disciples have horded his designs—she shakes the sketch in the air—in the back of that paltry vehicle, and despite their refusal to confide in her, their secrecy confirms her worst suspicions. Not that she sees in Leonardo's drawings what's worth selling your soul for, but she can certainly see that her own life contains nothing like them. Before Monsieur François deprives her of these graphic obscenities, she means to find out, once and for all, what's behind everything. Mathurine points Leonardo at the wagon, gives him a shove. Okay, show her what's inside those containers. Now!

Leonardo's astonished old eyes dilate, his jaw flaps. How Destiny torments him! Has Salai turned even this woman against him too? He bites his tongue, gestures inquiringly toward the yellow behemoth.

Mathurine nods.

He sighs, edges beastward. Its yellow gate swings open, displays a green cavity in the ocher surface, a verdant wound. Could the divans actually be *inside* the color, could he be plunging, not through, but *into* its yellow skin? When Leonardo stretches out a hand to steady himself, he's startled by the vehicle's mass. It feels like a chateau on bladders, a fortress that rolls. How many sturdy German draught horses would be required to move this creature? It's too much! He whirls about, tries to flee, but runs bang-up against Mathurine's bosom. There's been a horrid mistake, he wants to shout, but feels himself falling backwards onto the green cushion, into Salai's nightmare. And then WHUMP, if Mathurine hasn't closed the goddamn door!

AND HORSES

(A section is missing here. In it Leonardo tries to abandon the horse—he's sick of this work that has consumed fourteen years of his life—but his bond with Salai won't let him. In bed each night he hears the child panting, "When? When? When? When?" etc., and gradually this rhythm contaminates Leonardo's pulse, footsteps, breathing. He knows the clay model is only a plan. Exposed to the elements it will deteriorate quickly. The real horse must be cast in bronze. He starts building the statue's female shell, has alder and pine timber hauled in, huge windlasses built, and arranges for pewter scrap and pigs of copper to be stockpiled at a workable distance from his furnace. But the political situation in Milan is changing, and the Sforza monument no longer seems to matter as before. Leonardo sends Ludovico a list of materials, even commits himself to a chronology, but the bronze is slow to arrive, and when Leonardo complains, he receives no response. In his frustration, he tries to lose himself in the boy. Nightly pleasure becomes inseparable from daily work, a grinding out of one thing, then another, and absorbed in Salai's body, Leonardo labors to ignore what he's up against. Everything seems to be slowing down. And then late one night as he and the child fall into the ancient motion, Leonardo hears his own breath chanting, "When? When? When?" etc.

Up to this point the missing section seems to me no worse than others. It advances what's gone on before, brings the action to a crisis. And the question I've been trying to answer—Why didn't Leonardo finish?—now hangs in the air. But what's always moved me about Leonardo's horse seems to be engendering a contrary motion, a desire to bring work to a standstill. The story is beginning to repeat itself, move in a circle, etc. I can't tell why.

Stymied in his effort to cast the statue, Leonardo decides to cast a single part, the massive head, hoping its impressiveness will revive his patron's interest. He hires half-a-dozen master-founders from a local armaments manufactory and sets to work training an army of strong-backed rustics to turn the windlasses. But on the day the casting is to begin, Ludovico dispatches a messenger. Without explanation, Leonardo is told to wait.

The rest of the missing section recounts this waiting. Strangely enough, it seems to me the best part. To kill time, Leonardo resumes his study of Latin, takes long rides on Master Galeazzo's roan gelding, and participates in a duello or theatrical disputation. He dismantles the windlasses in the yard of the Castello, and as winter approaches—it's now 1494—street children steal the alder logs from beside the huge kiln to heat their parents' hovels. He begins to be haunted by the feeling that he has overlooked something, that the present impasse results from his blindness. He begins to ransack the pages he has accumulated, determined to uncover the nature of his mistake. He stares into the distance for hours, opens and closes his fist. How has his desire eluded him? Then one morning he wakes to a cold room and realizes Salai has gone.

If omitting all this seems artificial, elaborating it seems forced, as if two forms of unnaturalness were striving. All my work has been directed toward a culmination that, having arrived, seems immaterial. Moving on now feels like an escape. Writing conclusions becomes a mere pastime. There's a lot I still don't know, but in the end, I don't expect to find it. Leonardo's horse is over, no matter where it stops. So much is obvious.

At some point in what's missing, the following conversation occurs:

"Stop it! Stop it! Leonardo shouted. "There's the nature that becomes you, in you, that's under and on top of you and..."

"No! No!"

"...nature alive, growing, breathing, filling every—"

"There's the horse," the boy insisted. "I've felt it stirring, know it's alive, here."

"What moves you isn't my doing."

The boy's expression was becoming inscrutable, as if he meant to grovel at Leonardo's feet then dismember him. His fingers trembled. "But you could make an end of it, s—s—set us free. It would undo everything."

"Don't be childish," Leonardo said. "I've lived in the work like a fish in a flood. We're immersed, swept away—"

Salai shook his head. "I'll never get over it."

"You were infected before me."

"There's no before you. Even if it started without you, even if it was already moving, you can't just abandon—"

"There's nothing to get over," Leonardo said.

"It doesn't go away."

"There's nothing to get over.")

Francesco Melzi and Battista de Vilanis are standing just inside the kitchen door gazing across the courtyard. They've descended into the cellar, gathered their deceased master's last trunk of notes, grunted and whewed back up to this threshold. They've said enough to perfect their concord but not so much they can't deny it later, and now each contemplates what's still to do. The bodily remains of their former lord squats decrepit and maddened on the seat of their wagon, his nose pressed to the loose end of a filthy harness, nightshirt droopy over his shoulders, beard mucky and bespattered, muttering and scoffing and looking for all the world like the dotard no one much wants to think Leonardo da Vinci could've ever been. And both men wonder: Will it be possible to look past him? Thirty furlongs down the road almost any account of what has happened today can pass for true, but right now the fleshly accidents of a human face, two hands, a voice like their own—it all makes for complications. There are still the horses to hitch, plus this Frenchwoman who, for no intelligible reason, has arranged their spilled drawings into curious heaps on the ground and appears to be untying the trunks Battista's spent the last hour hauling out here. And, of course, someone's going to have to remove that corpse. But if the late master's bodily accidents will just refrain from looking them in the eye or calling them by their Christian names, the men figure they can do what's required. They both wish they were out of here. Melzi says: Fortitude! We carry his genius to Milan. And together they start for the wagon.

Leonardo, meanwhile, is exploring this miracle or mockery—what to call it?—this yellow vessel Salai left behind and feels about as close to his heart's desire as he'll ever be. He sits on the green divan, gazes around. Through the concentric rings of this astrolabe-looking device directly in front of him, he can spy all manner of mystic hieroglyphs, calculations like an alchemist's recondite classifications, only here more numerical, deprived of their symbolical colorings. There is one sphere harbored in a crystalline shield with a calculus spanning from one hundred twenty to zero and another with an expanse of articulations from F to E. Leonardo recognizes these last as figures, allegorical types—Fido or Fidere and Experior, to trust and to prove. Elsewhere there are levers and knobs, dials, clocks, gauges, and his feet bump against two unseen protuberances that invite his slippers to rest on them. Running his hand over the nearest devices, Leonardo is astonished by their unblemished, perfectly smooth carapace. Either he is within the profoundest unnaturalness man or demon has ever devised, an annihilation of all he's experienced, or he is sitting upon Zeus' own throne. Righting himself he gives a little bounce and is delighted to feel his hips go up and down, up and down. Matters seem less terrifying by the minute. By virtue of what twisted reasoning Salai connected him to this miracle, determined it was *his*, Leonardo can't say, but its link with horses is obvious. Surely a caravan of them, half the steeds in Giuliano de Medici's stable, would be needed to pull this colossus over the ground, a spine-cracking labor, and yet, something about its squat, low-crouched mass makes you want it to move. Leonardo imagines himself driving a vast span of destriers, more than two-hundred of them, snarling and nipping at each other, hardly containable, as the yellow monstrosity comes alive, races into the unknown.

And standing to his left Mathurine just watches, doesn't smile. This isn't her nightmare. It's becoming clearer by the minute that she's not even along for the ride. François des Melzes and le Baptiste have just tossed another mysterious container in this wagon and are now beginning to hitch up the horse, and she knows they mean to deprive her of everything she's never dreamed. Perhaps the eventualities her master has pictured are nothing she gives a damn about, but she can't help feeling that, if only she could glimpse the mischief she hasn't

287

gotten wind of, all the plots she's failed to sniff out, her perpetual itch might subside. Mathurine's new-born to evil-doing, no ferocious hellion. How can she hope to preserve the fragile order she's begun to fashion? She gazes over at Leonardo descending deeper into a darkness she can't fathom, finger jabbing frantically at a piece of broken harness, eyes popping out, voice frantic. They don't inhabit the same story. What's happening here isn't outlandish, is just her life, nothing more. And yet she's holding in her hand the sketch of a parachute. A parachute! How deeply is she infected with otherworldly dreams? How much violence will be required to own them?

And for his part, Leonardo has no answers. His chest pounds; in the back of his throat he tastes the coppery tang of bile. Not for the first time during these sixty-seven years, he wishes he could live his entire life over, unmake every thought, each word. Only now, at the end of all his labor, is he undergoing the experience he needed from the start. Such a realization might overwhelm him with futility and bitterness if the beating of his blood weren't so wild. As is, despite a wasted life and the nearness of his end, Leonardo feels complete. A silver filigree or tiny chain hangs just behind the astrolabe before him, and as Leonardo fidgets, his knee strikes it. It makes a faint chiming sound. Leonardo would like to stroke this appurtenance, but to do so requires an acrobatic contortion, for the shiny device depends from a metal hemi-circus that itself emerges from a tight slot on the right face of the column of the astrolabe—that is, hangs remote from his good left hand. He tries banging at it with the withered beast attached to his right wrist but can feel nothing. Why can he never know his desire in the flesh? And so with his body twisted and cheek pushing up against the same glass the woman is peering into, Leonardo weaves his left hand around and up and under the column, snakes it toward the tiny hemi-circus and is beginning to tug, when VAROOOOOOOOOM!!!!!!

It's the miracle Leonardo's sixty-seven years have been one long, blighted agonizing for! The coach-room takes life, a monstrous thundering as of avalanches, apocalypse, cataclysms, earth-rending floods. A tumult erupts in Leonardo's stomach. He gazes over at the woman. Esperienza! he exclaims. And he's both amazed and flustered to find that, yep, here on the precipice of doom old Leonardo da Vinci has an erection.

And taking off the parking brake and giving that dinosaur some gas, Leonardo da Vinci steers his brand new Buick Roadmaster down the carriage path, around the little stone mansion, past the stone porch, and through a gate so narrow that, really, how are you going to get this thing out of here? But no matter. Dynaflow Drive, self-starting ignition, room enough for the wife, groceries, dogs, kids, Leonardo's yellow behemoth rumbles along the tiny lane toward a perpetually retreating horizon. The thick air from the road's so greasy on his face it suffocates him, fills his nostrils with summer and the smell of exhaust, odors alien to stables, earth, wood, stone, and as the walls of the Clos-Lucé slip by, become an unbroken gray like the water of flooding streams, gaining speed, becoming tree tops, lawns, garish signs in peculiar scripts, limitless expanses, vast structures like unto the great horse itself but somehow unthinkably, impossibly larger, becoming a vision of horror and wonder and color and grief—

I close up the box. The beach monster has finished reading; the pages are in "order;" Metro leans over the seat and drools on Leonardo da Vinci's universe. Mercifully, the sun has set, and though it's not dark, the temperature has dropped well below 150 degrees. Nothing is happening. A group of volunteer fire fighters and Explorer scouts materialized a couple of hours ago and erected a dark green tarp-like barricade around what, when last glimpsed, was the smoldering carcass of the crashed helicopter. Some disturbingly opaque containers were rolled into the enclosure and, after half an hour, back out, and a lot of mechanical sounding noises began to be heard. Then the smoke mysteriously cleared. Gradually, everybody in the traffic jam lost interest, and life returned to what we call normal. No more fires, gassings, explosions, geysers of water, Darth Vadar costumes. The situation has proven acceptable. You can hear the stereos blasting, A/C's cutting in and out. A canary would asphyxiate. Metropolis pants.

He pants in my ear, all over each window, on every surface but the Beach Monster. Despite a lack of oxygen, Metro's not upset. Such a perfect presence makes me wonder what we mean by "living." Whatever immense public benefit was extracted from him in the inner sanctum of a life-science lab, it seems to have cancelled his doggy nature, for he displays no fidelity, no tail-wagging mischief, not even an interest in cats. He eats, he collapses, he farts—a kind of terrestrial plankton, but larger, hungrier. He is, thank God, unfailingly housebroken, but this constitutes his last concession to humankind. Metropolis settles but he doesn't adapt. He sits in the backseat now as he customarily does, head upright, frontleg like a pivot, surveying with his eye the 180 degree panorama afforded by the Buick's curving glass. I cannot say he likes the Buick, cannot say he likes, but Metropolis is all there. One suspects this names his single virtue.

"Okay, okay, I'll bite. Whaddaya get straight from a horse's mouth?" The Beach Monster has turned toward me, but his shades are back on, face unreadable.

"Five-year-old horse and a ten-year-old look identical," I explain, "except the teeth. Somebody sells you a five-year-old horse, what you get straight from his mouth is the truth."

"So your neighbor—" Monster begins.

A neuron has fired.

"—your neighbor wants to make you a gift of this five-year-old horse, but you peek in its mouth and your neighbor becomes your enemy. And everybody used to know all that?"

I shrug. "D'you know, Leonardo da Vinci's birthplace—you can still see it—it's a stone cottage about sixteen by maybe thirty, just two rooms with a door between, dirt floors. What's still hard to believe, both rooms weren't for people. Animals—cow, goat, horse, pig, chickens— lived in one. Door between them."

"My mother was poor," the Monster turns back to the window. "But the dogs stayed outa the trailer."

When organizing our dual lives, the lawyer, Deirdre, even I, foresaw two dangers. First, there was the danger that life number two would fail to keep up with its adversary's craving for precision. Exactly what a problem looked like—to agencies, commissions, boards, divisions, foundations, associations, legislatures, committees, departments, officials—was always evolving, and so there was the continual threat that one day on some computer monitor somewhere our names might fall into an unforeseen class of exceptions. This required perpetual vigilance, endless ingenuity. What our real life amounted to could remain constant, but our second life had to continuously metamorphose. And this was danger number two. For if our decoy life became too all-consuming, we might find ourselves creating third, fourth or even fifth lives to manage it, might have to defend ourselves from our own defenses, or worse, we might become unsure where subterfuge left off and we began. Our scheming could occupy us as much or even more than our pleasant, but by comparison, fairly humdrum real—that is, first—life. At such a point it would no longer be clear what we were protecting.

Fortunately, despite being susceptible to these confusions, Deirdre and I never wavered in our conviction about who was to blame. Corporations, TV, the defense department, oil cartels, the media, our parents, capitalism, middle-class prigs, commonsense, transistors, the IRS, universities, churches, testosterone, Republicans, Macdonald's, aerosol spray, Democrats, the AMA, agri-business, Independents, and Hollywood. The fact that none of this made any sense didn't matter. Nothing else made any sense. What mattered was that these were threats we could identify. They drew us together, gave us something to swear at, weep over. I suppose real life has ceased to be a given for anyone anymore, or at least this explains why happy persons often look asleep. But I could certainly see that, in defending our real life, we were locating it, that walling us off from the surrounding emptiness was how we took self-possession. Walls work in two directions, of course. Maybe what a former age called living was what we never knew, but our struggle enabled Deirdre and me, despite doubts and division, never to turn our fears against each other. Until Leonardo's box.

"In a crisis, one serious, energetic life can't be negligible," Deirdre insisted. "For *some*body. People who say otherwise, who ...who claim, oh, I can't make any difference and then make a killing ...well, they don't know children from stones. Other people's children, anyway." She took a long breath. "I badly need a reason why you aren't fiddling while Rome burns."

I'd like to say that the problem of Leonardo's box was that Deirdre didn't understand it, but of course, the problem was that I didn't understand it. Something from a past that was and wasn't my past, a past as remote as physics from painting, had perpetuated itself in me. Like a gene I didn't deserve or DNA whose origin wasn't in my family. I'm going to confess something: I've never been much of a reader. In a former life I tried to study history with discipline, to follow its plots as a career, and I found this ambition exciting, but whatever strange hunger announced itself in me wouldn't digest that food. The boundary that made the past a profession was the first it ate away. I once knew a man who at thirty-eight discovered he'd been abused by his mother. It wasn't that he'd "repressed" his pain, he said, or not in the way he'd ever thought of repression. But he'd never dreamed that what happened to him was what the phrase "child abuse" meant. Then on the day of his mother's funeral, he was stopped by an aunt who begged him to forgive her for never turning her sister over to the police. His aunt staggered away never knowing she'd startled him. But that was the first time he asked himself: Do all mothers spank with the buckle end of the belt? It turned out that this wasn't what "disciplining children" meant. But, as he insisted later, he never had the experience he called "trying to forget" or "struggling to ignore" or "denying what happened," only had the commonplace experience called "growing up." At any rate, the laborious recollection of his past was only part of his therapy. The more prolonged work was closer to home. He had to relearn English. It was as if every word he'd ever learned had been learned incorrectly—"love," "pain," "good," "anger," "me"—as if his own thoughts told lies, as if he didn't know what things were called. And listening to him I imagined that I'd glimpsed what coming to know yourself was like: the maddening frustration of being stumped for a word and then the unspeakable relief of suddenly recalling it. Only now the whole language.

The Monster hauls in a deep breath. "It's funny, y'know, how sometimes you know and don't know something. Like so that somebody else has to say, y'know, what you know but what, until they say it, you don't know you know, y'know." He pauses. "So maybe a guy like me—I'm not sayin' I'd read your book, okay? I mean, I'm not like a modern

291

kind of guy. But if say a guy like me *did* read it, well, maybe it'd be because he just wants to know somethin' he probably already knows. Or that's the way a guy like me figures it, 'cause ain't like you're smart."

A news helicopter flies noisily overhead. A youth in a white cap with a blue Igloo cooler strapped around his middle walks by selling cold soft drinks, eight dollars a pop. We pay happily. I want to talk about Pythagoras and Golden Sections, about the number phi that for four millennia has inexplicably turned up in random calculations, but these are miracles we can't share. I wouldn't mind hearing about his first wife. I desperately don't want to hear about Vietnam, but if I felt free to ask absolutely anything, I'd probably ask about that. But right now nothing's more interesting than my car, a dog, the two of us, this ghastly heat, here.

Finally, he opens the door, says this expletive thing ain't expletive ever gonna expletive end, adjusts his sunglasses, and ambles off. That's it. Except for Metro who whoofs as he passes the window.

Port-A-Phone.

"R—?"

A woman's voice. I'm prepared for nightmares and so have to compose myself before asking, "Deirdre?"

"Wh—wh—wh—who'd you think?"

But something's wrong, her voice is trembling. "Are you—"

"Y—y—yeah."

"Are you—"

"Hahahahahahahahahahahahahahahahahahahahahahaha hah—"

"Are you *laughing*?!"

But she's over the edge, yucking uncontrollably, sides splitting, thigh-slapping. I wait and then I wait and then I wait.

"I've seen a miracle!?" She gasps for breath.

"You're safe?"

"Either a miracle or…or the world's so stupid, such a ludicrous, inept, arbitrary, pathetic—"

"But you're safe?"

"—contemptible, mad, grotesque, amazing—"

"ARE YOU SAFE?!"

"Y—y—y—yeah."

"What happened?"

"In fact, I'm terrific! Happiest, dizziest, craziest, I dunno, maybe I'm just awful…B—b—b—but there's not going to be a—a new development."

"What development? Which?"

"I—I can't tell you—could this phone really be bugged?—but there isn't going to be one. At least, I don't think so. The Whole-Globe mega-center northwest of the old perimeter. Who the hell cares! You don't know about any of this, okay?" Deirdre sounds equal parts hysterical and beatific. "But I guess, since nothing happened, nothing 'irregular,' I mean, not that anything could be much less regular, but there's no reason—"

"I'm about to hang up."

"We—whoever 'we' are—got to the site. They call it the 'action.'"

"The 'they' who're 'we.'"

"...but there wasn't any security. All the equipment right out there in the middle of the acreage—it's a gorgeous spot, nearly two-hundred acres, mature trees, high canopy, not much undergrowth—and not even a chain link fence, no lights, nothing."

"And you were going to vandalize that? Christ! Those guys own Tokyo!"

"We're concerned citizens. Supervising municipal policy decisions affecting the metropolitan electorate. No further authorization is required for any local resident's attendance at any project site where easement of county zoning..."

My not-wife, the answering machine.

"Anyway, we got nervous. A bulldozer costs more than a house. There were five. They don't just leave'em parked, or they do, but not without, y'know, babysitters."

"The 'they' who aren't 'we'."

"So one of our guys—let's call him Finch—Finch says wait, maybe it's a trap. Some of our people think we're infiltrated. Then lots of things got said, and we were trying to decide what it made sense to do and not do and keeping meanwhile out of sight when this other one—call her Bunting—sees somebody. It's a single guy, kid really, twenties, in a suit, or what would be a suit but he's got the jacket off, blue button down, tie, and he comes walking out from behind a backhoe, calling to us—I guess, or some cartoon he thinks is us—come out, come out, wherever you etcetera. Well ...uh, Grosbeak—invention fails—she's our oldest, says he's bluffing 'cause he's turning all around, shouting in every direction, doesn't really know if we're here, and so she makes us all stay put. But it was still unnerving, y'know, like they already knew or ... anyway, he keeps calling a minute longer then just shrugs, climbs up on top of an engine housing and begins to—" Deirdre starts giggling. "—to ... to make a statement."

"All this is like beside the highway or—"

"No, no, we're a good quarter mile in. There's like a rough road through the trees and a half-cleared spot. You can see the top of a condo to the south, about a mile away; otherwise it's just squirrels and airplanes. It's a really nice spot. If they leave it intact, I want to take you."

"When you say 'statement,' you mean like a *prepared* statement?"

"He's *reading* it!"

"To the squirrels and airplanes."

"It gets better. He's got a boom-box with him, and same time he starts to read, he punches the box. The *Stars and Stripes Forever*! The statement's timed to hit with...so the high points will hit with the cymbals. It takes us awhile to figure out what he's saying because...because—" Deirdre gasps for breath, "because...because—" explodes laughing, takes a minute to sober up. "—Well, because of the music and be—be—because there's something very odd about him. He's talking about...about JESUS!"

"Oh God."

"...a—a—and we're looking at each other, rolling our eyes, making those little circles with our fingers around our ears, y'know, cuckoos, trying not to just burst out guffawing, and then it dawns on us: what's weird about him is the guy's mortified! He can hardly pronounce the words he's so embarrassed. Well, then another of our guys—"

"Chickadee."

"Thanks. Chickadee just says, Sheeeeit! Out loud, but not contemptuous, more like unbelieving, and just stands up. And then we all stand up. I think the poor kid in the suit's gonna wet himself when he looks up and sees how many we are, hardly can keep reading, but—what was her name? Bunting, she must've noticed his hands trembling or something, because she says real loud, 'We're hippies.' And of course that cracks everybody up, and then he starts to relax, and from there it's pretty much a party. I mean, we all sit down on the equipment and you can tell he wants to look us in the eye and blurt out something like can anybody believe this is happening?"

"What's the statement—?"

"Somebody in the conglomerate had a—a—a—a—a—a—a—a—a—a—a—"

And Deirdre loses it. She takes so long to stop cackling that I hang up. I mean, cellular service is per minute. In a little while she calls back, but all she gets out is, "had a—a—a—a—a—a—a—a—a—a—a—a—a—a—" Then she's off again. This time she's the one hangs up. We go through this process about three more times before she gets out the whole story. Seems someone high up—"CEO of a parent company or mammoth share holder or just somebody repulsively rich; Grosbeak knew his name"—anyway someone who claimed to speak for the big shebango got taken up in a UFO sent from Jesus, and these space apostles, Dr. Spockrates something, told him the Whole-Globe Center was a no-no.

"...unbelievable!" Deirdre says. "The statement's full of bible verses and quotes from Abe Lincoln, and the PR guy—that's who the kid in the suit turned out to be, a copy writer—had pamphlets he was supposed to hand out, and they're covered with happy faces and scrolls and like Hallmark poems. It explains that Jesus came to see Mr. Whatshisname from Rapturous Siderius Belongini or something in the Green World and told him he'd mistaken heaven's bounty. There was a lot I couldn't follow, that someone's son's or daughter's renunciation had been a last warning and that the Red Bear from the East was Cherokee—both the Native Americans and the jeep—and the national debt would only get worse because the Holy Spirit had taught the yellow Anti-Christ to make better cars and if he, Mr. Whazzits, didn't want Jesus to take all America's money away he'd have to donate the land for the Whole-Globe Center to the Quakers or the Audubon society or the Sisters of Perousia, whoever they are. But the key passage was this: Spockrates said that Jesus said the CEO had to become what he was. Those were the words: 'Become what you are.' Then it ended with some kids' prayer that the PR guy had to get down on his knees—in the dirt beside the backhoe!—and sing. He had the look of a Junior Leaguer eating a beetle."

"Do you really believe—"

"Believe! Of course not. Nobody could believe—"

"No, I mean, don't you think maybe it's a ploy? A ludicrous ploy, but would he really give away—?"

"Everything's a ploy; the question is, does the CEO know it's a ploy? God, I don't know what I think."

"Like something *this* stupid could just be for real?"

"D'you know what the kid answered when Finch asked how much he'd make for this?"

"'More than Nicaragua'?" I offer.

"'Almost enough.'" Deirdre started guffawing again, hung up, called back, lost it again, hung up, called back. "Now, whether they'll actually give the land away, well …."

"You back at DeeDee's?"

"Yep, but you're off the air. Last newsbreak the demonstration got second billing. I bet they'll have you moving in, oh, twenty minutes."

"They mention the helicopter crash?"

"Helicopter crash! Christ, are you okay?"

"Yeah, I mean, what's okay anymore, but—"

We each listen to the other listening to the other. For no precise reason I feel good.

At last Deirdre asks: "D'you ever wonder if you're a character in a story told by a redneck?"

"—full of racist jokes and raunchy music signifying anything and everything?"

"Quit it. I mean, things end great—sort of—but not for any

reason. In fact, for the wrong reasons, awful reasons. And nothing you've ever done …well, injustice makes sense. You know where you are with injustice."

"That was Leonardo's problem."

For a nanosecond a nothing isn't said by either of us that's unlike the nothing customarily not said by either of us. Don't ask me how I know, but I know this nothing means I can keep talking.

"…a failure. Not because he was wrong, but because he'd done enough to see that what everyone saw, well, it wouldn't hold up. Perspective, geometry, mechanics—they were amazing, but they weren't the key. He couldn't build on them, saw why. And so he's coming to the end of his life and—"

"But he painted the *Mona Lisa*."

"Don't you see? He didn't believe in it anymore! Besides, Raphael would've painted it in a weekend. But the point's that Leonardo was a painter when painting meant something. But then he goes far enough to realize, well, it doesn't mean that, the base has a crack in it, his art, well … it all starts to seem accidental."

"So what did he do?"

"Nobody knows."

She sighs. I feel like I want to keep talking, but I know that silence this time means I'm through. Finally, she asks: "How's Metro?"

I glance at the mirror, stare into the buttonhole staring back. "How would anybody know?"

She giggles, a sound that makes me happy. I guffaw.

"Come home, R—," my not-wife says. "Hurry."

Twenty minutes is overly optimistic. Turns out more like forty-five. But finally the traffic breaks up enough for me to creep past the demonstration. Nothing's there. Several fresh-looking policewomen with dayglow vests hurry me along. Two cars with that stripped-down, official barrenness are parked on the shoulder, and a man in a green uniform is sweeping debris and water toward a storm grate. Everything's dripping, but no demonstrators, no pestilence, nothing to witness. I guide my yellow dinosaur along, noting even amid this consternation the open-mouthed stares. It's clear that, for the survivors, I'm the most interesting thing around. Fifty yards past the puddles the traffic breaks open, and I feel like a running back in my opponent's secondary. I push my toe down, feel the roar. The giddiness in my solar plexus recalls a time when no one needed to be careful, when power seemed a reason all its own. People on the sidewalk watch me and remember.

I continue two more blocks, forty miles an hour, before I see it. The only trace of what happened here today. Woven into the grillwork of a wrought-iron fence, a stick with a drooping cardboard placard. "I was unlucky."

I cover the five miles to DeeDee's Live-in Kitchen Kleen and Katering in maybe half an hour, pull into a ramshackle gas station a few blocks from my employee's street and am refueling at the self-serve when this black character, an ancient codger with bowlegs and a country grin, hobbles over. He's wearing an antique Texaco cap and has four conspicuous cuspids in his gums. "Now that is something, that is something!"

I don't pay a lot of attention. If you drive a car like mine, everyone's a chatterbox. Like wearing a tag on your lapel, "Ask me about my vehicle."

He sticks his head in the window on the passenger side, pokes around just long enough to get a low, bored rumble out of Metropolis, then squats and puts his nose up to the chrome. "You got a phone!" Backs out, swings around the back, runs his hands over the tail lights. "I reckon I never ...I reckon I don't ...1957?"

"55.

"I reckon I can't .... You do it yourself?"

"Some."

"Looks like it's never been drove."

"293,000 miles."

"I reckon I (etc., etc.)."

He starts circling, licks his finger and runs it over the paint, watches the spittle disappear. Sniffs the grill, eyeballs the finish, seems on the verge of gnawing the hood ornament. "I reckon I don't mind telling you this here's about the finest automobile I ever seen."

"Mmmmhmmm."

"Yellow," he adds.

I finish pumping the gas—one of the two remaining regular pumps in the city. The codger at least has the delicacy not to ask about gas mileage. I pull out my wallet, hold up a twenty.

"I can remember this car," he says. "I remember it new. It's just like Jesus on the waters, a miracle, something old still new. Like the Milwaukee Braves."

He says *MILL*waukee. "1957," I say.

"Whussat?"

"World Champs, 1957. *MILL*waukee Braves." I pronounce it the same way.

"Awhile ago." He cuts his eyes at me, like, I may be old, but I can recognize a smartass. Then turns back to the Buick. "They made a car a man could feel hisself ride in, not these Jap'nese—I don't mean no disrespect, Asians's some fine folks—not them things." He sneers at a passing Corolla. "How long you reckon it is? Twenty feet? Twenty-two?"

I shrug. Metropolis looks out the window. If dogs could roll their eyes, he'd roll it. Not even a cat can be as sarcastic as an old dog.

"I won't take your money," the codger says out of nowhere.

I don't understand what he means at first. "Do I pay inside?"

"You can't pay here."

There's no other attendant in sight.

"It is a priv'lege …." His voice gets smarmy. I suspect he preaches on the weekends.

"Oh come off it," I begin thrusting the bill at him but see he'll get mad. All I wanted was gas! I wonder if there's another regular pump anywhere. "Thanks, generous," I mutter, stuffing the bill back in my pocket. "Tribute to American technology."

But he doesn't hear me. He just stares at the car. "We livin' in peculiar times," he mutters. "Peculiar."

I get in, crank her, feel the rumble through my back and legs. The codger doesn't step back. He leans forward, Texaco cap propped back on his head, concentrates, like listening to Schoenberg. The pink rims under his eyes loll out, bottom lip droops. Snuff-eater. Then he shouts something. I want to nod and pull out but he's too close. "What?" I ask.

"…many horses?"

"'Horses'?"

"How many horses she got?"

"'Horses'?"

He looks at me screwy. "…understand plain talk?"

"*Horses*'?"

He yanks off his cap, jabs at the engine. "How many HORSES?!" He's shouting. "How many! In there! HORSES! HORSES! HORSES…

…for they can't live, we can't live, nothing moves without them. Only in delusions, dreams. Serve us? *Us*? We're born needing them. Frail, impotent-born. Salai paused: Face pressed into their dung, I dreamed of one day setting a splendid table beside the slips, watching them watching me.

He chuckled: Don't think it's absurd. It was a child's revenge. But you can see the fitness.

Leonardo wanted to defend himself, but against what? Who? A long time ago, he muttered.

Salai stared off. For nearly fifteen years, what for the gods' sake were you …? Did you ever once wake up and think, Now! Today!

Leonardo shrugged. I thought …in my excitement I thought we'd come to a crossing. Who would've believed Brunelleschi's dome? It's unclear what the times will allow.

When they first told me, Salai began, when they said, yes, a man making a horse, right here in Milan, I couldn't disbelieve them. Can you understand that? I—I was gripped, held in a fist. I'd never known a mother's love, so I was hardly credulous. You can't rot from the moment you're born and be credulous. I knew they were lying. I told myself, no, they're asses, ignorant, what do they understand? But from that instant until I touched your flesh I never thought of anything else.

Leonardo felt like protesting. Why, he'd hardly been more than a child himself then! All the talk of godlike power, men dreaming of bird-flight. How could he ... how could anyone have known?

This is futile, he said.

Silence.

Leonardo cleared his throat. Perhaps there's something to the philosophers' words. We aren't what we are.

Salai listened.

Where in nature is a home for man? Our great temptation, downfall, is aspiring to what, in obscure ways, we possess as birthright. Earth, air, beast, angel—

Shit, Salai said. You lie in filth, the ticks and lice and vermin crawling in your rags, and you smell it, horse shit, all over you, everything you touch, your eyes. Horse shit. Someone has poured you into it. You can't wipe it off because it covers your skin, hair. So you look up at their bellies—huge boats sloshing, all guts and swill—and you know they're going to crush you. This is all you know. You know how the hoof feels, the ragged edge, almost not-hard, like a cedar log, round and dead, with its power at the back, an absent center where the bone starts up. If it touched your chest—imagine it resting there now, motionless, the slight pressure, dull, soft ache—well, you'd think: I can stand this. This isn't bad. But then from a remote country or the far end of a corridor, you smell burning, so vague that you aren't sure, infinitesimal, and it gets lost in the steady, dull pressure on your breast. Because this pressure scares you, you forget the smell, but there's definitely something burning. Then you hear a snap, or maybe you feel it, and afterwards you notice the pressure has vanished. You try to turn your head, but now you're hot, very hot. And you taste char in your throat. That's when your face blows up. You're on fire, you realize, and in this perfect comprehension—for there's no word for the mind on fire—in this gorgeous maelstrom, every wall vanishes, and the flood from the chasm you've become gushes over. Enter the red world with your eyes wide open! But if you look up, you'll see the behemoth, hoof lifted, seeing you, seeing nothing, eyes empty, it kills nothing, you weren't there, nothing, it thought your death would be curious, but dried peas are more interesting, you sizzle, explode, nothing, it forgets—

You've gone mad, Leonardo whispered. You're mad.

Salai smiled: I know everything that can ever happen.

NO END OF HORSES

When Salai finally told Leonardo—back in Milan in 1495—what, by then, no one else in the Castello could have felt uncertain about, what even Leonardo, years later, would've admitted was as obvious as a wart on his nose, told Leonardo that his last chance was past, Leonardo stood there stiff as an icon, flapped his arms like an earthbound duck, bellowed, No!

Then Salai spat in his face.

Leonardo stopped breathing.

Traitor, the boy said and walked away.

Leonardo didn't recognize the world into which he was born. He stared at the emptiness before him, mouth hung open. His hand touched the film oozing down his forehead, saliva strings hanging from his nose, beard, slippery on his cheek. How could this have ...? And suddenly he was moving. Stumbling over paving stones, past the little stucco wall, through bodies, bouncing off of children and market wares, vendors yelling, shaking their fists at him, mothers shrieking vengeance, not hearing as he fled, their words beating in frail channels just beneath the skin and tufts of thin hair, their words and Salai's words and Leonardo's words, when? when? when? when? when? when? But at the Castello the Duke was sadly indisposed, and when Leonardo insisted there'd been a mistake, made a ruckus, the fat German guard, who smelled of sheep's wool, chuckled, called Leonardo by name, shook his head, No mistake, placed a chubby finger—terrifying in its softness—upon Leonardo's sternum, gave a thump and knocked panting Leonardo right onto the ground. No mistake.

Leonardo felt the cold tiles on his butt, tried not to faint. He was a cyclone in a box, bones pushing out through the skin. He imagined rushing up to Ludovico's throne, throwing himself at Ludovico's feet or throwing Ludovico out a window. Mayhem seemed the last hope, and when Leonardo realized he wasn't going to do anything, he felt dead. He sat on the walk, clerks and barbers and sausage-mongers passing, until a pasty-skinned crone with purple streaks running from her eyes ambled up to him, nudged him twice with her toe, and without uttering a word, held out her palm. Leonardo sighed, took her by the wrist and dragged himself to his feet. She screeched and struck him, but Leonardo paid no mind. He merely strode over to the German guard who was guffawing uncontrollably and, taking his pizzle from beneath his sculptor's smock, began to piss on the man's leg. The German lunged. Leonardo grabbed him. And then with the huge, beautiful hands that even twenty years later could still bend horseshoes and crack walnuts and with the stout back and thick shoulders that in Verocchio's shop had worked all through the torrid Tuscan afternoons fanning the forge, shaving the gesso smooth, forcing the long beech strips into molds, transforming gold and herbs and unguents and stone into the unspeakable loveliness of civilization, Leonardo beat the shit out of him.

Then he went after Bellincioni. Later it wouldn't be clear to Leonardo whether he actually imagined Bellincioni was responsible, suspected the end had to be the poet's doing. Maybe he'd felt that losing everything on the verge of success, catastrophe before a climax, had suspiciously much of poetry in it, poetry or fate, or the former as the latter's instrument, or the latter as the former's guise. Or maybe Leonardo just figured Bellincioni would relish telling him who'd done it, would detail all the slithery foulness of the world's undigested gorge, or perhaps Leonardo had gone after the poet because Leonardo was angry and Bellincioni deserved whatever he got. But finding him proved difficult. Courtiers who in the past had competed to help Leonardo now seemed not to understand his questions. Conversations dissolved at his approach. Throughout the Castello everyone seemed instantaneously inexplicably unavoidably busy. At last a Spanish squire with a sad mustache and nervous eyes gave him—in private—directions to a small chamber in a part of the Castello remote from the Duke's apartments or his lady's wing, a region frequented only by impotent dignitaries being insulted or mendicant friars.

It was a wet, smelly passageway, much traveled in former times but now badly lit, and Leonardo had difficulty making out the slit of candlelight and partially opened door. The room was dungeon-ish, with a smell of old disease and the soundless sound of bodies not moving. When he entered, two nuns sitting in a corner looked up from their cowls. One opened her mouth to speak but merely resumed mumbling whatever nuns mumble, and Leonardo found himself alone in an abandoned room. He cleared his throat, gagged on mildew, incense. Suora, he whispered, got no response, and was leaning forward to shake his fists under their holy Roman noses when he heard the unmistakable voice: I was afraid you wouldn't come.

The poet lay in—of all preposterous things!—a coffin. Ebony sides, lid against the wall, all shoved into a nook behind the door and almost invisible in the shadow. A bib of damp, blood spattered rags had been arranged around his chin, and amid the tangle of bedclothes his face floated like a skiff in foamy water. His skin was pale to the edge of purple, his pinched mouth utterly unrecognizable, a death-infected wad, eyes yellow, voice disembodied.

...needn't be coy, he began, as if responding to some contention: It was I. I've been advising it for months now. Who can say why His Sallowness finally came round, his ways are not our ways, unfathomable, magnificent but, well, the French have entered Rome, you know.

Leonardo said nothing. He suspected a ruse, refused to feel pity. He had an intense urge to catechise the women, ask their order's name, though Bellincioni would've surely used real nuns. He was theatrical, not deceptive. That was what disturbed you most, the effrontery of his art, its brazenness. Leonardo hadn't much idea what Bellincioni was talking about, shifted his feet.

Have you nothing to say? Bellincioni asked.

Mercy on your—

No, idiot. I mean about your god-forsaken horse! I mean about the idiot bronze!

Leonardo stared at him: How did you—?

That's why you're here, isn't it?

They've sold my ...the bronze for the—the great horse. It's all gone. They've given away my bronze—all of it! For cannons, to Ferrarra.

Now we're speaking like sensible Christians! Bellincioni said. And he started to laugh, spray spittle through his teeth, the manic frivolity Leonardo had witnessed often, when suddenly the frayed string of his body was gripped, stretched, popped like a filthy sheet, flung against the coffin's walls, whipped, pounded into the straw, made to recoil, to jerk upward, bounce, crash back again, leap. The choking, spasms, gasps, terrified Leonardo. He wanted to flee. The nuns never stirred. After a forever that left Leonardo's back throbbing, the poet lifted his hand as if to say: Just a little longer. Then he hacked softly for several more minutes, gradually quieted his breathing, began mopping the hideous goo covering his chin and eyes and neck and chest in webs of pink string. Watching this astonishing spectacle, Leonardo remembered the spit Salai had blown into his own face—only a few hours ago—felt his disbelief all over again, and reaching up to his beard was amazed to find a sticky glob still matting his beard. He almost vomited.

I told him, Bellincioni rasped. I said the clay horse would be sufficient. Its size was already notorious. What point to waste good—?

Bellincioni started to laugh, caught himself: Anyway, the cannons were necessary for defense, and better to preserve the Duke's person than his father's memory, no?

Wh—wh—why?

You mean you aren't convinced by my diplomatic reasoning? I assure you, I'm no novice at statecraft. The Duke, after all, seems to have agreed with ...

Leonardo waited.

Perhaps you'd like to hear more arguments. They're all excellent, really. You're informed about the crisis in Florence? Our pontiff will strike a wily bargain, depend on it. Well, consider Milan's position ...

Leonardo listened, but the words signified nothing. Then he felt paper rub his hand, looked down to see Bellincioni's finger touching him.

For you, the voice said.

Leonardo stared at him.

It was your ruin, you see. Oh, you were so earnest! Preposterous to dream ends, consummations. Your life was ...well, statues are stiff gods, idolatrous.

My—

No earth; overhead no vault. A precipice, heights and depths. You would've ended up quite commonplace, I assure you.

My life, Leonardo said.

Bellincioni smiled: I set you free.

My life! Leonardo shrieked. You sold my—!

I've made you interesting!

Leonardo's fists flew up in the air, started down on the poet's shriveled bones, wadded face. But the gesture was empty. Bellincioni knew it was empty. Leonardo knew it was empty. He stood rigid, fists raised, looking down on the soppy pile of sputum, froth, this blemish, a hole.

You're my greatest work, Bellincioni continued. Quit acting the young ass, more of a prig than you really are. Now you can move.

No deed was ever like it, Leonardo said. No mortal ever achieved—

Why, you're spluttering like a gander! Do you believe this tripe? Move!

Never in all Christendom. You saw the creature! You saw—

Bluster, braggadocio, sophistry, vulgar ornament. Bellincioni flicked a finger in dismissal.

I could do it! You knew I could—

But the poet shook his head. For a moment his yellow eyes turned soft, cream-like, his voice started to swirl. And then Leonardo realized for the first time how utterly the poet's voice lived apart from him, itinerant, so that even dying it could still sound as alive as ever, the wild inflections, rise and fall, dizzying leap.

See in yourself the toy God made you. Laugh at water, drink doom. Did you dream your deeds could breathe? Can you fly? It was small, contriver, smaller than the hemisphere of index and thumb, smaller than—I gave you life!!—smaller than fame or the ball of your eye, briefer than the little death, than ...

Suddenly the coughing exploded, took Bellincioni over, set his face ablaze. His body bounced off the wood coffin like a horse-fly off a window, one hand flailing, thin knees hopping in the air. Leonardo didn't move. The man's finger clutched at his hand, dug deep into his flesh. Leonardo watched each wave of coughing spill over into the next, stood there as the frail body battered itself, tried to shake death loose, pummeled its own weakness. Peace! it seemed to shriek. Peace! But the rebellion was total. His hips shot up off the tick, free arm flopped about like a rabbit in a trap. The poet's voice seemed to have turned into a frantic succession of tiny explosions, each misting the air and momentarily infecting everything around it. Who knew where it might end? Leonardo looked down, shrugged, walked out.

For three years nothing happened. Or nothing in this story. Of course, in that other prodigious, awesome, and utterly squalid story once called Western Civilization, the genius Leonardo da Vinci finished his mural in Santa Maria delle Grazie and painted a portrait of Ludovico Sforza's new mistress and decorated a room at the Castello with a blitzkrieg of twigs. But this story is that story only by mistake. For we're plotting a failure, the despair of art, civilization at crosspurposes. There's a pause in our action. From 1496 to 1498 all that happens is Fra Luca Pacioli comes to town.

Now, brother Luca was as flighty a spirit as Leonardo ever knew. Given an hour he'd regale you with every injustice he'd suffered, and given another hour he'd throw in his sexual encounters to boot. He lived for an audience, and though brilliant in disputation and marvelously learned, his great secret was that he'd read almost nothing. His entire education was comprised of talk, at which he was a master, and his principal talent was his ability to pay scrupulous attention to anyone who knew more than he did and memorize every word. Leonardo was never in doubt about the monk's unreliability, but one afternoon while puzzling over a pistol-ball's trajectory, he'd overheard Pacioli explain to a youth why neither falling nor flying nor stopping nor starting was proportional to weight. Now Leonardo had long since observed that river-stones of a certain size, when shot from a sling, traveled farther than river-stones half so large, did so consistently and in patterns, but never travelled *twice* as far, which reason would lead you to expect. Moreover, he was familiar with the fact that sight-lines in painter's perspective escaped this irrationality, or succumbed less baldly. And so now he inquired of the monk whether math and calipers could resolve this enigma. Fra Luca grinned, bobbed his head, and with a flurry of his crayon showed Leonardo, not a solution, but proportions of proportions—that is, revealed an unsuspected universe of relations, analogs, sequences, convolutions. And even if Leonardo didn't know what to make of them, he decided at once that, fraud or not, Fra Luca could put you in a new place.

At the time Leonardo was preparing for the second half of his life, a period during which a principal task would be to make sense of the first half, and he badly needed a new place. Nearly every day he walked past the huge clay horse standing in the piazza in front of the Castello, gazed up at the withers that—exposed continuously to wind and rain and sun—were already beginning to look pitted. He saw the seams he'd concealed so carefully, especially those along the huge chest muscles, where the damp had penetrated all winter and then, just before Christmas, frozen and cracked. Even from the ground Leonardo could make out the bulges that meant the clay was deteriorating. There might be several years left before the model would be a ruin, before work on a bronze horse would have to begin all over, and even then parts might be disassembled and preserved, but he wasn't sure whether this gave him hope or made him crazier. If he could, he would've preferred simply to erase the horse from human memory, his own included. He was sick to death of horses, sick of all things magnificent and mysterious and demanding, sick of sculpture and art, pretty sick of his life. He was forty-five years old.

So Leonardo took up with Pacioli. Why math gave him hope in his sickness is hard to say. Perhaps numerical recurrences and paradox filled him with awe, as if the universe were ordering itself in secret, or maybe watching matter evaporate from its relations, watching the shape of things stand apart, felt like discovering what he'd always been up against. Leonardo certainly had no practical problem Pacioli's math ever solved. But for whatever reason, starting in early 1496 and continuing seven nights a week, every week, until the day in 1499 when the French stomped into Milan and the Castello collapsed and the tense waiting began, Leonardo and brother Luca met in Leonardo's studio over figures and scrawls. Fra Luca was at work on a treatise of his own, and Leonardo provided meticulously drawn polyhedrons to illustrate it, just the sort of confined task he found relaxing now.

All of this during three years, as Ludovico's diplomacy faltered, his old enemies joined forces, and France finally took over. In the mornings, Leonardo poured over Euclid, Archimedes on spheres, or practiced roots, and during his long afternoons he designed a flushable potty for the dowager, Isabella—whose pleasure in Ludovico's fall knew no bounds—and contracted to do a madonna for the French minister, Robertet. The invaders arrested his friend Andrea da Ferrara. Leonardo and Pacioli discussed a trip to Venice but didn't go. Time passed. The whole city seemed bracketed. Each night after Pacioli left, Leonardo would climb the stone stairs to his bed, drowsy but restless, would lie there in the quiet that isn't peace, or he might—after hours of staring up at the speckled darkness—rise, and in his nightshirt stroll out into the little vineyard where in the moonlight he could see weeds covering the wall and outworks. It would be cool then, and the breeze would feel good on his bare calves. He understood something was over, and the pain of this no longer scared him. At the same time, he felt stupid trying to live in an interim. If the end came, what would it even look like? For all Leonardo knew, it had already passed.

And then one night well into the cold months of 1499, with Christmas approaching and the memories of harvest erased, Leonardo climbed the stone stairs to discover—after he'd thrown his nightshirt over his head and stretched his bones on the tick—that the air was changed. Something buzzed, not really a noise he could identify, but a vibration he felt in his ear. He let his arms and legs float on the sheets, watched his mind swirl upwards, and as he passed into sleep, he imagined it was his first night in Milan, that he was dreaming the dreams of his youth. Somewhere a great throng called out, cheering loudly, and although Leonardo was a stranger to these faces, they appeared to him now as his deliverers, friends. And if this night had passed as such nights normally do, he would have gotten up the next morning feeling released, knowing his sojourn in death had passed, that he could begin his life's final part, might have even—for the first time in nearly three and a half years—made plans. But none of this was to occur, for somewhere in the moonless black of morning he woke, opened his eyes knowing he'd heard a horrid noise. Outside in the street, men's voices cursed. Crashing bottles, laughter. Was it a brawl or cheering? And for a second he guessed this disturbance had waked him, but then he heard an old sibilance, felt a hand creeping to his knee, saw the tangle of black hair beside his bed.

W—w—wait. I'll wait—

Leonardo kicked Salai's face. Peace! he screamed. Give me my peace!

And Salai rolled to the floor like a bag of oats, moaned, made no protest, didn't resist or spit oaths or strike him, picked up his child's frame from the rough planks and limping toward the stairs, turned, and in a voice as pathetic and terrifying as an infant's rage, said: It isn't over, it won't end, I'll always come back.

The next morning Leonardo learned that in the darkness of the night, in a ceremony of French joviality and force, Louis Douze had martialled his countrymen, the celebrated archers of Gascon, and with the town's riffraff and a sprinkling of citizenry looking on, had shot by shot, arrow by arrow, chink by chink, in waves of concentrated and orderly and finally chaotic firing, removed from the piazza in front of the Castello the last memorial of the Sforza line. The clay horse of Leonardo da Vinci had been destroyed. Pacioli, who'd witnessed it all and for probably the only time in his life had maintained sufficient gravity not to recount it blow by blow to the first person he met afterwards—Leonardo—Pacioli would later recall how the bonfires and torches blazed, how bottles of Burgundy brought by wagon all the way across southern France and through the Alps just for this celebration, how they were passed from hand to hand by the archers, so that as the statue came down—the fragments of clay and wood falling twenty-three feet from the mane and head, then simply pulverizing as the arrows got to the shoulders where, already, the weather had done its worst, so that once, when a luckily placed arrow struck a wooden splice or nail or wire or something, an entire hip suddenly came free hitting the ground with a huge explosion, showering the onlookers with shards and bits of stoneware and threatening to topple the entire hind section onto the stand where the viceroy himself was sitting—anyway, with the Burgundy flowing freely everyone was pretty well soused by the time the monster teetered. Then things got crazy. Some importuned rustics came on with a battering ram atop a tall cart with a winch in place so you could adjust the angle of striking—more than one person in the crowd noted how much the contraption resembled Leonardo's own inventions—the whole contraption being empowered by eight stout geldings who within moments had laid their likeness upon the ground. From there, the street urchins and vandals set to work, gathering relics and memorabilia that later might be sold for a hot bath, merciful drunkenness or leg of mutton, and the French archers who were so blind now they could damage nothing but themselves, stumbled off to a pleasant evening of fist-fights and buggery, while the Viceroy—who it was rumored had watched the affair with tears in his eyes—had finally lifted his arm in a gesture of conquest, coaxed the mostly insensate crowd into a scuzzy cheer, and gone inside shaking his head. Well, Pacioli didn't tell this to Leonardo—though later in Florence whenever he gathered a goodly audience he'd recount the event in eye-glazing detail, improving it each time, until finally he had the heavenly host and Beelzebub involved—well, Pacioli never told Leonardo, but what he did do was pack.

So that the next morning by the time Leonardo had wandered outside, noticed the hush that fell on everyone as he approached and figured out why Salai had come back, by then Pacioli had arrived with three trunkloads of notes, a fourth with his monk's cowls and earthly possessions, two good horses, and a map of the road to Mantua. It took four hours, but by mid-afternoon they'd finagled their way through the Vercellina gate where snickering French guards made remarks Leonardo luckily couldn't translate, circled the city to the south, and with Pacioli as watchful as a mother and Salai for no comprehensible reason trailing a furlong behind in a flimsy wagon over-laden with cooking pots and fasteners and robes and knives and tomes and papers, Leonardo abandoned art. It was a chilly and dismal night, and they rode all through it, rode past inns that for a pittance would have sheltered them, past groves where they could have built a fire to thaw their hands, continued riding even as their horses slowed to a trudge and dozed. They needed a new place. Fourteen hours, until at last as the sun rose on an almond orchard beside the Adda, Salai overtook the horsemen, stopped his wagon, unhitched his animals, sat down on the grass and fainted.

Pacioli and Leonardo remained mounted. Their beasts had fallen asleep. The moment resembled one in which men sometimes unburden themselves, but neither could stand the oppression of Leonardo's heart. They stared off into the haze of early light, the moisture rising from winter fields. Finally Leonardo asked: Are we headed somewhere?

Pacioli stared at the question a minute. Hardly possible not to. Direction's implicit. Like number, extension.

Leonardo ignored the challenge.

After a moment, the monk continued. It's Aristotle's shortcoming. Movement's not so extraordinary. If life were just successive states, we'd be in the fix of Zeno's hare, always approaching, never getting anyplace. Think of the fretless viola, not twelve stops, but an infinity of increment, but you can never pluck the precise tone. An entire universe extends between one braccio and two. Nope, even ordinary waywardness, blundering—all headed someplace.

Leonardo wasn't sure he could stand this.

Fra Luca giggled. Imagine a pebble rolling nowhere, a projectile descending nowhere, each successive wave—

Have you ever felt the ground move?

Fra Luca looked at him.

In my home region, in the hills, sometimes the ground moves, Leonardo continued. It resembles a current at sea, when land can't be seen, or a storm, or if you could stand on the surface of a river.

There are regularities, Pacioli said.

Afterwards. In the storm, as the ground shimmies, there's nothing, not even experience, not even oneself.

Pacioli shrugged. We visit God's knowledge; we don't live there. Still, the mind can make things plain.

And so Leonardo told him about the man without words. It was an exhausting tale, full of backtracking and circuitous explanations, and Pacioli posed questions at every turn. Why was Leonardo so sure the man possessed wisdom? What exactly captured his attention? Defied it? And a brothel! Again and again the mathematician's brows rose in surprise or frank doubt, and Leonardo had to stop the forward rush of his telling to chase his friend's refusal away. No, on a roof, he— Leonardo da Vinci!—had witnessed nature divide. He had seen with his own eyes—if doubt lurked here, doubt was universal—Leonardo had seen knowledge vanish.

308

But it was a trick? Pacioli countered. Acrobatics. The man ...what do you call him? The little wind didn't actually transubstantiate?

Don't you see?! Leonardo beat the air with his hand. I knew his trajectory. I know myself less well. I knew where his action led, knew that—

That he had to die?

That he had to strike the wall. Exactly. A movement became its contrary. I witnessed with my eyes! The dwarf, mute, fart was headed forward then became upward—no cause!—then downward—no cause! As if force were its own end. As if direction were—

Mere appearance.

No, as if it were everything.

And you won't be gainsaid?

Leonardo shook his head: I'll be taught.

The two men then turned their faces forward to the line of trees where the sunlight was now spreading across the neighboring pastures and remained in complete silence. It wasn't clear whether they were waiting or finished, but it was clear that, if the truth could bear saying, it could bear it only once. Eventually, Pacioli turned to his colleague and asked, Are you still practicing roots?

Leonardo nodded. They're difficult.

Pacioli nodded, took several noisy breaths, then spoke in a trembling voice Leonardo had never heard: These are the words of an enchantress. When you don't know, study, and while you study, look about you, and whatever you see, preserve, and give yourself over to amazement, and what you come to understand—if love blesses you— you'll one day see is what you didn't know. This doesn't appear to be an answer, but for persons like yourself, well, there's no other.

And Leonardo believed Pacioli or acted as if he did, so that seven years later, standing on the Old Bridge in Florence, watching three whirlpools in the Arno, he finally understood what he'd seen on the Malnido's roof sixteen years before and started reconceiving the world on foundations that moved. Jacopo il Poggio had run four times at a brick wall then executed a front flip. His head started down, his feet up, his center of gravity shifted, yanking him over the bricks, nicking his forehead, skinning his nose but depositing him safely on the rooftop behind. The trick was perfectly timed. And Leonardo who had, of course, flinched, had in the blink of his eye skipped the link between up and down—like film footage with a frame blank—so that he'd witnessed what following misses, had seen the dwarf then nothing, seen stillness and willows and a goshawk circling in the air, seen medieval

309

science crack open, and maintained just enough composure not to fling himself down and shout, No! Everything living moved but, like vortices in a current, in more than one direction. Down was also up. Back was forward reversed. Between words and deeds was a little wind, a scent you never dispelled, someone's unspoken mind. Leonardo would try to draw it, motions within motions within motions, but only fatigue and interruptions stopped him from blackening the page, like so:

And gazing into the Arno that day in 1506, Leonardo should've known he'd never finish anything. He'd found the key to all knowledge only to find it wasn't knowledge, or was just knowledge of his own frailty. His past grew unreal. The revisions multiplied. Making would have to uncover its own ends, or perhaps there would be no end of it, but at bottom nature was a turbulence. It sucked you in, spun you around, threw plans out. Its astonishments were neverending, but nothing you created would rest there.

And that was why—nearly five years later, in Pavia in 1510, standing in Marcantonio della Torre's smelly apartment—Leonardo had been so sure he saw doom coming. The knife was going to betray his young friend, already had. Working beside the anatomist in the darkness, he'd felt crammed with the illumination della Torre seemed to be destroying himself for lack of. Leonardo had wanted to shout at him. This is not your life! Run, flee, hide! But what could he say? And so Leonardo had marched out, heard Marcantonio della Torre's parting groan, and before he could put it all behind him and revisit his young friend, Leonardo learned all he ever would about faith. This was in Milan in 1511. He'd been hurrying toward the Castello—or perhaps back from it—with a borrowed agricultural treatise underneath one arm and an irrigation system in mind when he overheard the Marcantonio della Torre's name muttered in wide-eyed, hand waving consternation by a Persian vendor before a flimsy stall outside the duomo. Leonardo had stepped forward: Here! What was—

But the barbarian was a chatterer and ignored him.

Wait! Leonardo had shouted.

There were a handful of dark-faced idlers gathered, presumably the peddler's countrymen, and the language was one Leonardo didn't recognize. Moorish or some Ottoman tongue or a dialect of Africa or Cathay, for though he'd transcribed outlandish idiograms from Avicenna's commentaries, he'd never heard these languages spoken. But he caught his friend's name—Antonio, Torro, Tower, the Informer—no mistaking, and murmured in mysterious tones, with pious glances heavenwards and histrionic gesticulations.

Marcantonio della Torre? Leonardo asked.

The peddlar fell silent. His interlocutors exchanged looks, muttered something Leonardo missed.

The renowned anatomizer! I heard, I thought—

Wares? the merchant asked. Fine copper, amulets, a cheese, devices?

Leonardo who, at nearly sixty years old, was no longer the brazen ingegnere, began to finger a bolt of fabric beside the merchant's elbow. He stroked his chin: Handsome, for an ornament. A scarf perhaps? Even a shawl.

The merchant said nothing. One of the idlers guffawed.

Leonardo opened his wallet, carelessly, allowed the jumble of coins to sound. My brilliant friend, the physician Marcantonio della—

The merchant nodded: Yes! Yes, a wondrous gown, a robe for his lordship's mistress, his daughter also! With a lovely train, unlike any threads west of Harrar, woven by ancient mothers deeply practiced in their art!

A gown!? Leonardo raised his eyebrows; the fabric looked badly made. Perhaps three braccia, but—

The peddlar frowned. Behind Leonardo, someone spat on the ground. Silence.

Leonardo sighed, took three florins and plopped them down one at a time on the tongue of the man's cart, letting each strike the wood with a smart thwack!

Chatter resumed, now in Italian, with laughter, hmmms, ahhhs, everyone eager to hold his listener's attention, to reveal truths revealed to him alone. In seconds the whole story had come out, far too rapidly, for the men could offer only the facts and could tell Leonardo almost nothing he wished to know.

Marcantonio della Torre was dead. In Riva near the lakes he'd yielded his spirit while comforting the afflicted. An inspired physician, a servant of mortal suffering, a healer of great gifts. His name was hallowed, spoken in prayers daily. The peddlar said there was much hope for beatification. Some claimed he'd worked miracles, there was talk of a peasant girl raised from the ....

But how had he come there? What drove him from Pavia? Healer?! And his anatomies, Galen, the brain's ventricles?

The merchant shrugged, knew nothing of this. But he was sure it was the same man. He'd seen him, at the last, shrunken and suffering, with a most holy countenance, distant cast to his eyes. What were *anatomies*?

Leonardo could get no further. Marcantonio della Torre had died of diseases contracted while ministering to the sick. He'd been a savior sent from the most high, an answer to prayer in time of affliction. More cant, more blessings. Why wasn't Leonardo satisfied? The story was wondrous! Couldn't he understand? They repeated details. And in the darkest hour, when hope was lost, from nowhere, a complete stranger, God's prophet, supernatural gifts, etcetera.

Had any of them ever actually spoken to the ...physician?

Oh yes, all of them, repeatedly, many times.

And what had he said?

Said? Why, he'd said his Father's palazzo had ceilings of purest alabaster, said the Virgin's smile shone in each room, said there were infinite mysteries beyond mortal reckoning. The speakers turned away, began to lose interest. What did Leonardo expect? The man had said what saviors say.

And so the lessons of the horse and Fra Luca and perspective and Bellincioni and river currents, when the occasion for wisdom had come, had all misled him. Or they'd been the way he misled himself. A miracle had occurred before his eyes, but he missed it. Now Marcantonio della Torre was dead. Prodigy, demon, madman, savior. The futility seemed frightening. So Leonardo renounced it, fled Milan, made a last raid on fortune in Rome and, when even renunciation failed, left for France where he hoped only to write it all down. But what was there to write? For the vision of a naked boy zipping in and out of perfectly azure clouds on a leaf the size of a nomad's tent, carried, easy, grateful, kept aloft by being kept aloft, by friendly weather, by wind and luck and circumstance, isn't knowledge. It's freedom. It's suffering. It's the thrill of going unprotected. It's a way humans sometimes live just before they die.

Lying here in the dirt now, as the wagonload of trunks and plans and pages rattles noisily away, Leonardo da Vinci can no longer tell what's a nightmare, what's his story. He's pretty sure that only moments ago something underneath him, a metal horse or some vehicle he was inside, began to move. He recalls a rumble in his stomach, as if the earth were cracking, still feels his thrill as the road opened wide. But instead of conveying him, Leonardo's horse seems to have gone on without him, to have rendered its inventor extraneous. Leonardo shakes his head, plucks at a divot. He remembers that the ten-year-old boy he once loved—what was he called? Giacomo?—he knows that Giacomo has abandoned him, that there were words, that Leonardo has only himself to blame, but he's no longer confident that it wasn't the simpleton Francesco Melzi—outrageous!—who just usurped his position, picked up where his master left off, flung Leonardo onto the ground. Such eventualities are beyond the pale, but that's no evidence against them. He feels thankful that he's dying and so can disregard almost everything. Still, this outcome remains bewildering. What possible conclusion could be drawn? He lies in the little courtyard, hands and feet making the points of a compass, horseshit in his mouth, and with what he persistently hopes will be his dying breath, prays that nothing will ever move him again.

And sprawled not an armslength away, Mathurine sees him through a badly swelling eye. In her hand she holds the corner of a parachute, the only remnant of Leonardo's universe, besides Leonardo, that its proprietors have allowed her to keep. Evil is a divided kingdom, but where that leaves her she can't say. The courtyard looks barren of wickedness, is a courtyard, nothing more, and in the middle of it, the man she mistook for the cause of everything squirms like a beetle in the mud. This spectacle has something depressing about it. She would've happily poisoned this man when she was his cook, but now that she's …that she's …well, what exactly is she? Mathurine shakes her head. What's happening can't be her life. But if it's just nothing, how come it smells so bad? She gets to her feet, grabs her nefarious master by the nightshirt. Can't leave him out here in the mud. With Leonardo in tow, Mathurine trudges back up the stairs.

THE ENDS OF FICTION

And dusk will find Francesco Melzi traveling south over roads he can't name. He's utterly exhausted, can't be certain what has happened to him. He vacillates between the euphoria of having finally pulled something off and the terror that victory's just a set up, that at any turn in the road King François will descend from the sky, dump a pile of manure on him. Inventing catastrophes seems so effortless. One hopeful ending is a life's work. Melzii listens to the wheels crunching, sways with the wagon, but refuses to feel good. Anything could still go wrong. If this weren't the case, then ordinary slobs could refashion the cosmos, a prospect that makes his neck hairs prickle. The clouds have begun to thin so that the firmament sparkles. In the road are shapes that, as Melzi approaches, disappear.

In the wagon beside him, Battista de Vilanis has his eyes closed.

Despite all he has witnessed, even Melzi's assurances, he's not thinking ahead. He has just abandoned the damp corner of the *Gioconda* where, for the only time in his life, he'd tried to make a future with his own hands, and he has no confidence now that his best years aren't behind him. Of course, there's still music, laughter, sleep to look forward to, the tang of wine, the joke of love. For all of which Battista feels thankful. If he never imagined any better life, he probably wouldn't desire one. But sitting here in this wagon as the horses' feet splush in the soft earth and the stars begin to peek out overhead and an owl sends its low moan through the poplar boughs, Battista dreams of nothing. He listens to the insects humming around him, savors the emptiness that's all his own.

Something moves up ahead. Battista yawns. Melzi runs his hand over the dirk, stiletto, poignard, pistol, pike and miscellaneous blunt objects he's arranged on all sides, wherever his palm falls. The wind stirs in the skeletal remains of a fruit orchard. A small bat flutters past, darts at the whip thong, disappears. Silence. Melzi tries to imagine what he'll do if the French catch them and wonders that he's worrying about it, that getting caught isn't just the end. There's so much more to imagine now! He wishes he didn't have all this baggage in tow. What he'd really like is a clean slate. What couldn't he accomplish if only he had an empty landscape before him? No French, no duels in sky-blue cloaks, no mountains of shit blocking his way.

Battista wants to pee. Melzi eases up on the reins. If the King's going to catch them, it won't be because they stopped to pee. He watches his companion stumble toward a stand of twisted fruit trees, listens to the urine splash noisily onto the ground. The night's brisk, not too cool, with that late spring sweetness to the air. For the first time the thought strikes Melzi, We're going to make it! We're going to make it!

Battista climbs back up onto the little perch. The board gives a bounce. It's pleasant in Milano this time of year, he says. But too hot. The water drips from your chin. He touches a finger to his bottom lip.

The gesture, utterly pointless, startles Melzi. Who is this fellow? How did he get here? Melzi never wished for a confederate, wants desperately to be free of him. He imagines raising his poinard, aiming for the tiny patch of buckram between the winglike blades of his companion's back, driving forward as he's been taught to do, following with his shoulder, feeling the grind and tear as blade hits bone, forces past, the taut muscle, wrenching loose...Melzi figures it would be like that. He's never killed anyone, doesn't much want to, but it no longer seems possible to do only what he wants, seems necessary to consider an astonishing array of actions and consequences, some pretty grim. And perhaps this is what seems so upsetting, all the possibilities he never wished for. Gazing up at the gods and lesser lights, Melzi dreams that the wagon has taken a wrong road, that they're straying. What if, instead of France, this is an unmapped country? What if he's passing by his true home?

Battista hums. He taps his foot, twists his neck this way and that. Pretty soon he'll be bouncing in his seat, a cheerful idiot. A scream starts to rise up in Melzi's throat. He coughs, gives the reins a flip—the lead nag looks back, says, get serious! If only Melzi were free. How much smoother these roads could be made, how many cottages for tenants could be located here. Pastures might replace this dying orchard, spread over these hillsides—round as a mare's haunch—all the way to the twisting brook over there. Well, there's no brook, but there could be. Melzi hears the sound of running water, birds singing. And in this potentially empty expanse that, merely by accident, presently resembles a woodland, vast highways might stretch. Of course, Melzi's homeland doesn't look like this from the outset, but there are other inhabitants, and they could begin to see Melzi's pasture and brook, to live around these thickets as though they weren't there. It's a new language. Melzi believes he could teach everyone to speak it: Now, that ridge running parallel to the axis of this arc, that's right, just sixty degrees west of perpendicular, with a three percent grade over here and these trees all out of the way, well, imagine a right angle extending.... A visionary could get something accomplished talking like that!

Battista's elbow stabs Melzi in the ribs, startles him awake. Battista wants to sing. Ballad of the Provençal knight deflowering the Tuscan milkmaid who slits the knight's throat while he sleeps thus rousing an army of vindictive kinsmen, lotsa gore, reciprocal ravishings, sundry pillage, slaughter. It's an ancient ditty with circular chorus and variations, interlinear rondelle, canon, descant and harmony, which make it potentially endless. Battista's already well into a sixth or seventh go-round, rollicking back and forth in the seat, pounding his knee in time, bellowing out an encyclopedic account of a nameless squire's heroic castration:

—Oooooh, they pickled it, tickled it, wiggled it rouuund, then jiggled it till little trickles dripped dowwwwn . . . .

Yes, Milano's pleasant this time of year, though hot, crowded, and in the giardini pubblici the odor of the hyacinth coats your face. Melzi feels a lurch as the wagon goes over a rut. If the French catch up to them, he has no idea what he'll do. He shakes his head, for no reason chuckles. Battista stops singing long enough to chuckle too. Can Melzi actually murder him? And as the darkness becomes total and the small wagon edges further south through unfamiliar land, Melzi feels the weight of the pages he's lugging, feels his nearness to the notebooks of Leonardo da Vinci, and can't explain why this makes him giddy. But they're moving, on the road to Italy, and momentarily at home in the only world either man will ever know.

Whether so many episodes make a story is hard to say. Events waylay travelers, circumstances complicate plans. Once the last border is crossed, what remains? Francesco Melzi guides his wagon into history where his descendants let Leonardo's notebooks pass into sundry hands. Today their pages spread over more than a continent, in museums and libraries and private collections, in batches of one leaf or two or several hundred, often unbound, mostly undated, unnumbered, many examples without precepts, miserly of explication, predicates whose subjects can't be found. It's impossible to determine how much has been lost. Leonardo may have actually finished some of the books he mentions. What if our knowledge of him consists merely of discarded drafts, bad copies, marginalia, excised fragments? Imagine: one day the completed works of Leonardo da Vinci turn up, perfectly preserved by the moronic and bigoted ancestor of some deposed monarch. Virtually all of Leonardo's plans were completed! Or his completed works are found in seventy-three handsewn manuscripts hidden away in the dilapidated cellar of a monastery somewhere between Amboise and Rome, but the moisture has rendered them illegible. The figures are indisputably Leonardesque, with title pages announcing the contents he labored over and a few leaves still discernible. Everything appears to be there, everything fits, but the books' poor condition gives rise to controversies. Interpolation and reconstruction begin. Editors compose competing editions, each construing her predecessor's as misconceived, even fraudulent. Instead of a new Leonardo, our story concludes in a chaos of versions, a richness so overwhelming no one can bear it. Civilization retreats, throws up its hands. Soon, dismissing Leonardo da Vinci becomes the mark of our seriousness. His works fall into disrepute, are forgotten. The notebooks sit on the least-used shelves of libraries. Then one day, a high school student researching a classroom exercise happens across these peculiar looking tomes.... Or the schools close. The contents of the libraries are sold. The past disappears. If Marcantonio della Torre were here we'd show him miracles. But Marcantonio della Torre is dead, and Bellincioni and Bramante and Fazio Cardano, too. Salai sequesters himself in his vineyard. Battista de Vilanis disappears. The legacy of Leonardo da Vinci serves Mussolini's 1939 propaganda campaign as embodiment of the Italian genius, Fascism's destiny. Bereft of conclusions, we stop.

May 2, 1519 in Amboise on the Loire, Leonardo da Vinci is dying. A last, long paragraph: Standing before his bedroom window, Leonardo turns a last time toward Salai, toward the wet curls and black eyes that for twenty-seven years made him crazy, and finds a french woman with whiskers on her chin. It's uncanny, as if two plots had been superimposed: He's lived his tragedy to the end and discovered it to be a farce! He grinds his teeth, flails at nothing, and Mathurine—standing right there—recognizes that he's not diabolical, just finished. She takes this in without surprise. It's not the first time her dreams have turned out ordinary. And then, because she's there and he's there, she does what, doing it, seems perfectly natural, but what, if she'd imagine it yesterday, might've seemed the last prodigy or curio or freakishness to madden life under the sun. She slips her arm around Leonardo da Vinci's shoulders. Ça va? She pats his wrist, and Leonardo wakes as from a vision. Who is this? For the first time he's looking directly into Mathurine's eyes and they're pale, for Chrissakes, with long lashes, like a child's eyes or like his own! He can't recall now what made this scene ludicrous. After all, if he were to lean out this window and hurl a last defiance at Salai or nature or goddamn horses, would that be more fitting? This woman's a world. And leaning against her arm, Leonardo turns to speak, to say that, even if ending like this makes absolutely no sense.... But, as his lips part, his eyes stray into the courtyard. Looking up at him are faces of every complexion, bodies in brightly colored scarves and gowns, uniforms and tightfitting breeches, cheeks bearded and unbearded, skin of unimaginable texture and hue, physicians, ingegnere, Dutchmen, philosophers, inhabitants of undiscovered lands—as far as eyes can see! Leonardo doesn't know these beings. What the hell's going on here? But they're gazing up at him, expectant. Their eyes have the milky, wide-open quality Leonardo has noted in the gaze of maidens and pious men, as if staring through you. He tries to shout: It was a mistake! All a mistake! But shrinking from their faces, seeing the mob stretch past the chateau's battlements, the little tower, the bridge crossing the river, the water so still you could count your whiskers in it, down the road south to the Alps, Italy, Albano's slope, even to the edge of the silver sky itself, Leonardo is startled by a clamor as loud as the end of all things:

Leonardo! They shout.
Leonardo!
Leonardo!
Leonardo!
Leonardo!
Leonardo!